"*Curiosity* is a delight. Set with marvels and rueful comedy, it's a warmly intelligent feat of historical sympathy." Greg Hollingshead, author of *Bedlam*

"Right from its powerful opening, the novel buffets readers with the inescapable momentum of waves against the Dorset cliffs. . . . Thomas draws [her] characters with such depth, power, and heart that they remain with the reader long after the novel's covers are closed." *Quill & Quire*

"Beautifully wrought . . . a work of literary art." *Winnipeg Free Press*

"Sensuous and multi-layered. . . . Thomas's eye for detail and her rich use of language make *Curiosity* a compelling portrait of an important life at a turning point in world thought." *Sun Times* (Owen Sound)

"Meticulous and deeply affecting. The traps of poverty and class, calcified notions of women's place in science and society, fall away to reveal the hidden life below: the human mind and heart excavated with delicate and devastating skill." Marina Endicott, author of *Good to a Fault*

"Wonderful, absorbing . . . [Thomas] makes us see the world from the eyes of people who do not know the concept of evolution." Halifax *Chronicle-Herald*

"Thomas handles beautifully the class-afflicted nuances of a doomed love story." *More* magazine

"Gripping. . . . Mary Anning [is] a memorable figure, vulnerable and indomitable at the same time." *National Post*

"Not merely a good book, but a great one. [*Curiosity* has a] richly layered plot, deeply memorable characters, and downright gorgeous writing." *Praire Fire Review of Books*

ALSO BY JOAN THOMAS

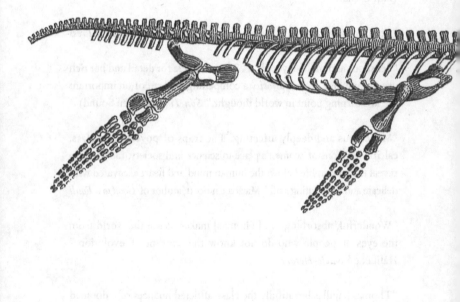

Curiosity

A LOVE STORY

Joan Thomas

McClelland & Stewart

Cloth edition published 2010
This edition published 2011

McClelland & Stewart and colophon are registered trademarks of
Penguin Random House Canada Limited

Library and Archives Canada Cataloguing in Publication

Thomas, Joan (Sandra Joan)
Curiosity : a love story / Joan Thomas

Includes bibliographical references.
Issued also in electronic format.
ISBN 978-0-7710-8418- 8

1. Anning, Mary, 1799-1847—Fiction. 2. De La Beche, Henry T. (Henry
Thomas), 1796-1855—Fiction. I. Title.

PS8639.H575C87 2011 C813'.6 C2010-905373- 7

Typeset in Fournier by M&S, Toronto
Printed and bound in the United States of America

McClelland & Stewart,
a division of Penguin Random House Limited,
a Penguin Random House Company

www.penguinrandomhouse.ca

3 4 5 6 7

Penguin
Random House
McCLELLAND & STEWART

FOR W.C.D.

"Let us now praise nature's folly,
which is the secret of her wisdom."

— Evan Eisenberg,
The Ecology of Eden

The path is wide at first, carpeted with rusty leaves. When it narrows, Mary is the one who hangs back, her heart banging at the downdacious notion of walking into the Undercliff with a gentleman. He tries to usher her before him, but she says, "You go first, sir," and with a little lift to his shoulders, he does. The path begins to rise and he climbs quickly, reaching out to touch the ropes of traveller's joy that hang from the trees. He's wearing the foolish wide pantaloons he calls trousers, their bottoms dark with sea water. Sir Foppling Fossil, Mary heard a porter say behind his back in the square. She keeps pace with him, her eyes on the muddy heels of his boots, and on the burrs that have found him and snagged up the hems of his trousers, and the chert protruding like knucklebones from the clay of the path.

They come to a clearing where a great tree has fallen, wrenching its roots from the forest floor. The tree ripped the canopy, opening the forest to the sun, and anemones push up after their time. The gentleman gives a little laugh and hobbles over to the bench made by the fallen trunk and sits down – he's finally felt the burrs worrying at his legs. "It will be the work of an hour to pick these off," he cries. "I blame Mother. This is absurd attire for digging on the shore. But *a French tailor can do no wrong in my mother's eyes. Did you hear what Buckland said when I came up?* French, indeed! *– he said –* They are Toulon and Toulouse!"

She stands in the clearing and he picks at the burrs and jokes and talks as though they were in a public square and she a lady he encountered there. It's a feint, this conversation. His face is alight with his interest in her, his baffling interest. By his pointedly settling at one end of the log instead of the middle, he conveys his desire that Mary should sit too. And now he is gesturing with his hand and she reads something new in his hazel eyes, something eager and imploring, a desire to plumb her depths.

Mary stands where she is. Her silence is a powerful weapon, and she does not resist, she takes it up. Bees hum in the clearing, and the brown pods of stinking iris overflow with seeds the scarlet of fish roe. His top hat lies on the lush forest floor, a perfect shining cylinder. His hair is neatly clipped and his whiskers are trimmed into a perfect wedge on each cheek. Around his throat, a snowy neckerchief. He's an exotic beast blundered into the Undercliff, this gentleman, and she's a pair of forest eyes, watching. And then it seems her silence is too great, it means to smother her as well.

Something quavers in the order of things. The ash tree falls, and flowers bloom after their times, and she sees a sinister rising of water, black brine leaping the seabed and crashing towards them through the trees. Not the twice-daily filling of the foreshore, but a terrible vengeance of heaving waves, drowning even the mariners and the creatures who swim in the sea, catching them, the two of them here where they never should be. And then one day someone will set to digging and turn up Mary's wedge hammer and the snakestone the gentleman carries in his pocket. Their two chains of vertebrae, and their hips like fluted baskets. Someone will unearth their bones, their long, straight limbs crossed and mingled, their supple bones gone to stone, gone all to stone instead of dust.

Book I

hey were powerful charms, curiosities. The people who came to Lyme Regis to take the waters would pay sixpence for the meanest little snakestone, and carry it for luck. Mary's mother had worked the curiosity table until lately, and if a customer had trouble parting with his coin, she would fix a soft look on him and offer a charm against *wizening*. She was not bold in her manner and the gentleman would startle and wonder at her meaning. But usually he bought, after that.

Now that her mother had the baby to look after, the curiosity table was Mary's job. Mary had come out early to get set up for the coach from Bath. Her wares were all organized on the table, and the square was still empty. There was just the brown hen tethered beside her, and the pauper Dick Mutch lying in stocks a few feet away in front of Cockmoile Prison. Mary sat deep in thought, her eyes on the moon, a useless, daylight moon, floating in a blue sky.

Wizening – it was a complaint particular to men. She needed a more general charm. *Blindness*, she finally decided. She tried it out in a low voice: "They be a powerful charm against blindness."

She watched the moon impale itself on the steeple of the sham-
bles, and then she bent back over her wares: Devil's toenails, sea
lilies, thunderbolts, brittle stars, verteberries, snakestones. Mary
had lined them up in rows by kind. The loveliest were the snakestones, coiled serpents in gold and bronze – missing their heads,
though, in their natural form. Mary's brother Joseph had come
home on his dinner break expressly to rectify this. He used a tiny
stone chisel to make a pointed smile on the outer coil of each
snakestone, unconsciously holding his mouth in the shape he was
aiming for. Then he took up a drill to make the eyes. Six snakes
had been so improved before he'd had to pelt back up Church
Street to work. On second thought, Mary slid these six out, and
made a separate row for them at the front of the table.

Just as the moon freed itself from the steeple, a silver bugle
sounded from the top of the hill. This was the signal for every
peddler in town to pour into the square. Then there was the
coach itself, plunging down Broad Street in heavy pursuit of its
wild-eyed horses, and in a flash it sat, a black and gilt cage,
gleaming in front of the prison. The footman had a stool at the
ready and the door burst open. First out were two small dogs,
touching smartly down on the footstool, and then a collection of
gentlefolk, dazed by their harrowing descent and by the
brouhaha of the men in the prison, who stuck their arms through
the beggars' grate and set up howling at the sight of strangers.
Last off were the poor, struggling down a ladder from their
perch on the roof.

In a trice, the visitors were set upon. Mary got to her feet but
she did not call out. It was not in her nature to hawk, and in any
case, buyers always came to the table on their own. The curiosities drew them – Mary had often experienced this power when
she collected on the shore. And indeed, two ladies strolling over
to look at Annie Bennett's lavender had spied the curiosity table

over Annie's shoulder. And then Annie lost them, they were making their way eagerly towards Mary.

"What curious stones!" said the larger of the two, picking up one of the snakestones with her gloved fingers. "What on earth are they?"

"They were living serpents one day, but Saint Hilda turned them to stone. She were clearing the earth of serpents for the protection of innocents." As she spoke, Mary deftly turned her boot to hide the clot of mud on the hem of her skirt.

The lady wore a red and blue braided jacket, all in vogue with the high-born since the war began. As though these ladies fancied they might be called upon to fight Bony! She held the snakestone up to the light, admiring the way the snake rested its chin on the round coils of itself with a smile.

"King George himself would be proud to wear such a beauty on a sash on his belly," Mary offered. "If he had the wits to know it."

"If he had the wits," cried the large lady to the other, as though a dog had made a jest, and Dick Mutch in the prison stocks (as mad as the poor king himself) set to cackling, so that Mary must smile and say, "Pay the poor lummick no mind." The lady set the snakestone back on the table and made to open the reticule on her arm, but her companion leaned in and said something Mary could not hear, and without another word or even a glance at Mary, the two of them went off across the square with their dogs running behind them. It was foolish to mind the discourtesies of the high-born, but Mary did mind. I should have spoke of blindness, she thought.

The square cleared, and it seemed she would have no luck at all that day, but then a man with a dirty blue bag tied to his saddle rode up on a horse. After he had gone, Mary was burning to go down to the cabinetry shop and tell her father what had transpired, but first she must pack up their wares. Sliding the curiosities onto the tray, she named them all to herself, using the queer words the stranger had used for them: the ordinary snakestones he had called *ammonites*, and the beautiful snakestones worked in gold and bronze, *pyrite ammonites*. But then, before she could go downstairs, Mrs. Stock from Sherborne Lane came bustling up to the house, and Mary must stay in the kitchen with her mother.

Mrs. Stock came inquiring after Percival, who lay like a wax doll in his cot by the cold hearth, hardly bigger than the day he was born. She was a widow with an ardent, reproachful manner that implied she would one day be more than she was, and should be heeded. She sat on the rush chair in the kitchen and darted her hungry eyes around the bare cottage as though their misfortune was secretly to her taste. Percival began to make his mewling cry. Molly picked him up and sat down in the chimney corner, opening her blouse and inching her shift down on the side away from Mrs. Stock. She spread her fingers so a leathery nipple popped out in the crotch between them, and stuffed it between Percival's lips. He gave a tiny cry of helplessness and Molly tipped her head, resting it against his.

Mary sat on the bench and willed Mrs. Stock not to see her mother's breast, which had been full to bursting when Percival was born and hung slack now like an empty bladder. This was down to Percival, who, for all he was an infant, had a part to play in maintaining his own keep and did not seem inclined to play it. At the end, the second Henry had been ill and thin like Percival was now, although Mary remembered him as having a queer smell to him that Percival did not have, a smell of chaff or uncured hay. The doctor came and gave him a medic, and just before he died, he coughed up two worms, both of them dead. It was the medic that killed them all three, Mary's father said.

Mrs. Stock sat talking, talking, puffed up like a rooster with news. She had learned of a lad who had the power to heal, by virtue of being a seventh son. "The seventh son of a seventh son has the power to raise from the dead," she explained, with the air of a teacher instructing the dim-witted. "But this boy is purely a seventh son." The lad was only twelve, not much older than Mary, and already he'd healed boils, dropsy, a child with a withered foot, and a woman vomiting black bile. He lived in Exeter, not so very far away.

Mary's mother hated Mrs. Stock (she had privately said so more than once), but she couldn't help but listen – she was a slave to the hope Mrs. Stock carried into the kitchen. They had no coals, so she sent Mary next door to the Bennetts' to boil the kettle for tea. Mary measured out just two dippers of water so the kettle would boil quickly. When she came back, her mother was still nursing Percival and Mrs. Stock was working her way through a list of questions. She inquired as to the exact date Mary had turned eleven, as though she was hatching a plan for her. Then she turned to Lizzie, who was playing with oyster shells on the floor. "And you're three now, my pretty one?"

Lizzie kept her head down and did not reply. "Four," Mother said.

"And your big lad? Fourteen, I reckon? And he's well? You had good success with the onion?" This last in a clever voice.

So then Mary saw why Mrs. Stock had come, and marvelled that she had waited this long to ask. A few weeks before, word of the pox had spread up the Dorsetshire coast, and Mrs. Stock had advised peeling an onion and hanging it from a string in the doorway to draw the pestilence to it. Mary's mother *had* followed the advice, and she told Mrs. Stock so now. She had peeled the onion and hung it in the middle of the lintel. It was Richard who made her take it down – he had no use for jommetry. "He's a history and a mystery, my Richard," Molly said, laughing in a shamefaced way. "He will always strike his own path."

"So I've heard said," said Mrs. Stock grimly. "Well, give us a look, then." Molly told Mary to roll up her sleeve and show Mrs. Stock the three little circles at the top of her arm. They were healed now, as dry as fairy rings in grass. "God forgive and protect us all," Mrs. Stock cried, closing her eyes and crossing herself. "There were many who told me, but I swore it could not be true."

It had been early morning when they first learned about the pox – Mary's father was going out to the latrine on the bridge when a man came up from the Cobb and told him. Six dead in Bridport, he said. At first, there was excitement in the town, people standing in the square going over who had told them, and what exactly was said. But at noon Mrs. Bennett came running up Marine Parade and announced in a shrill voice that the isolation hut on the Cobb was being turned into a pesthouse, where you could pay to have a bit of pox put into your arm and lie between life and death while the contagion was sweated out of you. Mary saw her mother's face and then she grasped the terror the pox brought with it, although it seemed her mother dreaded the cure more than the disease. "It's one thing to wait till the pox comes to you," Molly said. She was standing in the workshop in the cellar of their house with Percival slung over her shoulder. "It's another thing altogether to go to the pox, and die in a hut with strangers for your trouble." In the light from the high window, her own pox-marks showed on her white cheeks like discs drilled lightly into chalk.

"The beast in the field waits," said Mary's father.

It was an empty argument, thought Mary, sitting on the workshop steps. Where would the Annings find the coin to take themselves off to the pesthouse?

That night, Richard went out to the Three Cups. He was red-cheeked and singing when he came home, lit up by cider and by his bright new idea. He had taken a pint with Farmer Ware and they'd fallen to talking about the pox visited on cows at Ware Manor Farm. He was at the bottom of his third pint, he said, when the idea came to him: he would try his own version of the pesthouse cure, a barnyard version inspired by the fresh cheeks of milkmaids everywhere. Molly kept them awake with her crying, but the next day he took them anyway, just Mary and Joseph, took them out to Ware Manor Farm with its mossy yard the colour of the limes you saw loaded into ships in nets. The farmer led them into the cowshed, where a boy mucking out the stalls was made to put his fork down and pull up his smock. Red sores bloomed across his belly. They used the point of a clasp knife to scrape the boy's cowpox into Mary's and Joseph's arms, three cuts each for good measure. In payment, Richard Anning gave Farmer Ware a thunderstone for the dairy, to keep the milk from souring.

"We be all one in nature," Molly said vaguely. Mary rolled her sleeve back down. She kept her dark eyes fixed on Mrs. Stock. Mary was a healthy, God-fearing girl with a drop of animal humours in her, and if asked, she would assure Mrs. Stock that she felt better for it, although in truth she would have favoured a livelier animal than a cow — a fox with its dashing ways, or maybe a magpie.

Mrs. Stock finally fastened her crimson shawl with a clasp pin and took her leave, and Mary, almost choking by then with impatience, tried to slip down to the workshop. But her mother called her back. She had put Percival on his side in the cradle and she was at the chimney corner, prying the loose brick out to get at her leather pouch. She spilled the coins on the table — it was all half-groats and farthings. "Count it, Mary," she said.

Mary slid the coins into rows by kind. The shillings the strange man had given her were pressed into her waistcoat pocket. "One shilling thruppence," she said, keeping her voice flat.

"What is the fare to Exeter?"

It was sixpence to Axminster and Exeter was ten times as far. "Five shillings, if you ride outside," Mary said.

Molly picked up the baby again and cupped his little head, straightening his cap. Then she carried him down into the workshop and Mary followed. Mary's father was standing at the workbench fitting a dovetail join in a drawer. Molly went over all boris-noris and said, "Pray let me see the cash box." Mary's father laid the two parts of the join side by side on the workbench with a thunk. He reached the cash box from the cupboard shelf and handed it to her. He would suffer her to count the money, but that did not mean he would suffer her to spend it.

With her free hand, Mary's mother slid the top off the cash box and moved her fingers over the coins inside, not really counting. "There be more than enough," she said. Richard did not say what she wanted him to say, he did not ask, *For what?* "That were the Widow Stock upstairs," she said in a heated-up voice. "There be talk of a healer in Exeter. A seventh son." Richard turned back to his drawer and pressed his lips as he wedged the join together. He reached for his felted hammer and tapped at the join, and its two sides squeaked into the perfect little dovetail cells they made for each other. Her mother waited in silence another minute and then she turned and climbed back up to the kitchen.

Mary sat down on the workshop steps, her excitement about the gentleman on the horse suddenly falling away. She took off her bonnet and set it on the step. By what arithmetic did you compute which child was a seventh son? she wondered. They were four just then – Joseph, Mary, Lizzie, and Percival. Mary herself was either the first daughter or the third, depending whether you counted the dead in with the living. Or possibly she was the fourth: between her and the second Henry, there had been a babe that opened its eyes once on the world and shut them again, too early to say whether it was a boy or a girl. The parts were not made yet, Mary's mother said (although, Mary noted, it had eyelids to close). Mary could hear the cradle rocking on the floor above, and her mother's tread. Molly would be making a soft mush to try to get into Percival. Two shillings sixpence weighed still in Mary's pocket. She had not offered the money from the curiosity table and her father had not offered the money from the cash box. There would be no help for Percival in Exeter; it would have to come from another quarter.

Mary sat and watched her father as he took up the second drawer and began to fit it together. He was working from the light of the window, which showed the sky in three rows of its panes, and then the sea. In the soft sawdust on the floorboards, she could see his footprints like the tracks of animals on the shore. This was a collecting cupboard he was making, with shallow drawers for the curiosities. For the rich, who could afford to hoard what the Annings must sell. It was a strange passion with the high-born, filling their drawing rooms with thunderbolts and snakestones, although they could buy all the china figurines they chose. Richard was lining up the dovetails, bracing the drawer on the workbench. He needed a helper. But he'd apprenticed Joseph to Armstrong the upholsterer on Dorcas Lane. *I've enough aggravation in my day*, he said when Molly argued about it. *Armstrong can have the thin-faced nessel-tripe and welcome to him.*

Mary stood up. "I'll brace it," she said.

"No," he said. "Ye've not the meat on your bones to hold it steady."

So then Mary's anger swelled up and sealed her mouth shut, then she could not tell him. About the strangeness of the man, the way he'd sorted the curiosities according to the names he gave them, shoving the carved snakestones to the side as worthless. The way he'd tried to speak to her as though she were a child, and how she'd shown him. "Last time I was at Lyme," he said, "I ran into an antique fellow wandering the shore with a staff in one hand. On the search for the creatures he'd refused onto the ark."

Mary had stood up to her full height and declined to smile. "Noah," she'd said.

"It was, lass," said the man, regarding her with surprise. "I've been burning to know if these cliffs were here before the Flood. But he wouldn't put his mind to the question. *Shun the sea*, he cried. He shook his staff at me. *Water, water, everywhere and not a drop to drink!* He had only two teeth left in his head, the sorry old codger."

"But it were rain that made the Flood," Mary said. "He could have drunk rainwater."

The man had laughed, high colour rising in his cheeks. "Sharp as a blade," he'd cried.

Richard was fixing a handle to the second drawer of the collecting cupboard. He moved to the shelf for his screwdriver. His back was turned fully to the window and his face was erased by its glare. Something stirred in Mary at the sight of his bony form looming large and black against the glass. Then he stepped away from the light and she could see his face again (intent and inward, with no thought of her upon it at all). "Any trade off the coach?" he asked.

"Not off the coach." She paused, and then she finally said it. "A man came on a horse and bought seven curios." She reached into her waistcoat pocket and took out the coins.

Her father's black eyebrows lifted and she caught the gleam of his approval as she opened the lid of the box and dropped the coins in. Then he turned back to the cupboard. "The Philpot dames have spoke for this cabinet," he said. "Pick out a beauty snakestone. We'll put it in the top drawer to start them off."

The Philpot dames! Miss Elizabeth Philpot always smiled kindly at Mary and was a healer in her own way, with a salve she offered anyone who came with a wound to her door. There were three sisters, but it was Miss Elizabeth Philpot who loved the curiosities, although she would not go down to the shore to collect. Mary ran upstairs to the tray she had left in the kitchen and picked out the best pyrite ammonite, one Joseph hadn't yet got his hands on, and slipped it into her pocket.

As Mary carried the curiosity tray down to the workshop, Molly called and reminded her to go for water. Almost no one was out on the street – it was the afternoon lull. Broad Street rose up between proud shops and houses, and Mary climbed quickly towards the spring, wondering where the man with the blue bag was lodging. If he was lodging in Lyme at all. She could not determine where this man fit. He wore a top hat like a gentleman, but also a robe like an apothecary. He spoke like a gentleman, but he carried a dirty cloth bag. The degrees of the poor Mary could tell at a glance, but she was not skilled in the degrees of the rich. The degrees of the poor were the artisan, the servant, the labourer, the working poor fallen on hard times, and the true pauper (who had never been any-thing but). So three full degrees lay between a cabinetmaker's daughter like Mary and the pitiful Dick Mutch lying in the stocks, although the high-born coming off the coach made no distinction between them at all. But Miss Philpot did, and it seemed this gentleman did as well. Mary thought of the familiar yet courteous way he'd spoken to her. As she climbed Broad Street swinging the bucket, she went over their entire exchange.

"Where did you find this gryphaea, lass?" he'd asked, looking at her with pale, protruding eyes.

"The Devil's toenail, sir?" Mary said. "On the Devil's beach." It was Monmouth Beach she meant.

"The Devil's toenail?" he said fiercely. "The Devil's beach? Where did you get such notions? Our Lord made everything that is."

How startled Mary had been at that — startled to her core! As though the man had peered into her head and pounced on what he'd seen there, a question that troubled Mary constantly. Everything you saw was made by man or God or the Devil; even Lizzie would have been able to tell you that. As Mary walked, she noted the handiwork of man on either side: the shops and houses built of brick and thatch, the window in the millinery shop that reflected back her bonneted head, the ordure floating in the sluice lake along the border of the street. But here and there, the hand of God broke through — in the green moss growing along the rim of the sluice lake, and the wisteria drooping purple on the kitchen walls at the backs of the houses. God also made the brambles that climbed up and choked the wisteria, and the stones that sprouted in the farmers' fields, and the weeds growing up around the stones, and the pox. It was here the question grew perplexing. Some of God's works were to serve man and some were to test him and punish him. So how could you be certain where the works of God ended and the works of the Devil began?

Mary veered off Broad Street then, still carrying the bucket. She took a detour to the meadow on Pound Street and, stopping at the edge of it, looked down on the town. All the world she knew lay below her. More than her world — to the east, you could see the Isle of Portland, so far away that Mary had no expectation of ever setting foot upon it in her life. To the west lay Monmouth Beach, exposed now by the outgoing tide. In counting up the handiworks of the Devil, Mary always named Monmouth Beach (over which a mist of wickedness hung even now, from the smugglers working that shore, and from her own sister Martha wailing in terror while the tide washed her around the point to her death). And of course the Devil made the dragons that lived at one time in the cliffs and gave their shape to the cliffs, the shape of their bodies curled up in a lair. So, if the Devil made the dragons, it seemed reasonable that he'd made the cliffs, and certainly Black Ven, glooming over the shore to the east between Lyme Regis and Charmouth.

But with an air of authority as grand as a king's, this gentleman had given it all to God!

Mary stood a minute longer, looking down at the calm sea. The lopsided moon was floating above it. That moon was wizening – the tides would be slack next week. Then she turned back up towards the spring.

She was glad she'd not told her father about the conversation with the stranger. He'd have pinned a sneering name on the man. Her father took pride in scorning what others esteemed. A thought that had flickered in her mind when she saw Richard at the window came to her now: he had never had the pox, her father. But nor had he taken the cure at Ware Manor Farm. *He is a history and a mystery*, she said to herself.

But so was she! She thought of the moment the man had trotted into the square. It was his horse she'd noted first, a big-jointed mare of striking ugliness. The man was not looking in her direction at all – he seemed intent on going down to the shore – but Mary had called as loud as a costermonger, "Curiosities!" With no sign from its rider, the horse had stopped abruptly and dropped its head, moving loose lips over the cobbles in search of an errant stalk of hay, and the gentleman had had no choice but to swing off and come towards the table. Why had Mary (who never cried out) cried out so suddenly at the sight of him?

But what especially chawed at her mind and would not let it go was this: that the man had looked at the curiosities without surprise. Not as curiosities, but as something known, calling each by name, wrapping each one carefully in a separate cloth from his blue bag. All with a bustling and a business-like air, as though he had come into town expecting and prepared to meet Mary Anning.

⋅≪{ T W O }≫⋅

towpath runs along the Thames all the way to London. The officer cadets at Great Marlow always talk about it. When they're homesick, when they've been singled out by the captain and cruelly flogged, they lie in the barracks and talk bitterly about taking the towpath to London. And now Henry De la Beche is taking it. He's been walking the towpath for hours, starving, stinking, limping from the lash, talking out loud from time to time like a lunatic. When barges glide silently past him going in the opposite direction, he squeezes himself into the bushes to let the donkeys plod by, warmed by their salty heat.

The whole day, Henry has felt like an actor who walked off-stage in the middle of a play. The aborted scene began in the guardhouse at Great Marlow, with the entrance of the guard. Instead of picking up the pail of night soil, he scolded the three of them to their feet. It was the little subaltern with iron cleats nailed to his heels. The courtyard was empty when he led them out – all the other cadets would be at matins. Henry stole a glance back at Wyndham and Chorley, but neither would meet his eye.

{ 19 }

They were all moving cautiously, the slashes on their buttocks and thighs from their flogging just starting to stiffen.

At the officers' quarters, the subaltern pounded on the first door, but no one came. Henry knew this to be the door of their victim, Master Truepenny, the history master, who, in spite of being a civilian of dubious social rank, had been offered accommodations among the officers. After a second round of pounding and shouting, the subaltern opened the door a foot and they all looked in at the overly neat sitting room and the cold hearth. Henry had never seen inside before and he was surprised at the humbleness of it, the plain wooden chairs. He had pictured cheap and showy furniture, evidence of Truepenny's low and aspiring character. "Bullocks," said the subaltern. He turned his eyes on them, calculating, and then he asked them to give their word that they would not stir until he came back. Henry was the first to offer it. *On my word of honour*, he said. "On my word of honour," said his two co-conspirators in unison. They all three saluted.

When the footsteps had died out, Henry said, "It's rather touching, under the circumstances. His faith in us."

Something flared in Wyndham's face. "My word still means something," he said. He was bigger than Henry and a little older. He was the second son of the Earl of Egremont, who came to Marlow on parade day and stood by the field and jeered when his son fell out of step. Wyndham had a clumsy way of talking and moving, but he was not as stupid as people thought. As for Chorley, he just stood there with his chin jutted out. Both of them blamed Henry for getting caught. They were never truly my friends, he thought in that moment.

"Well, give my regards to Truepenny, will you?" he said, and he turned towards the archway. He had an instant's impression of their faces, astonishment reshaping them. He walked quickly down the corridor, resisting the temptation to run. A path led down to the river, and with a quick look around him, he darted into it.

Fifteen miles up the towpath, he's still hectically rewriting that scene. Picking his way around donkey dung, he writes in new characters (his mother, Mr. Truepenny, his dead father standing remote and watchful), he tests out various parting lines, adds an ironic salute in the archway. The sun sinks below the line of trees on the far bank and the drama lurches on without any prompting from him. Henry's hunger has taken over, and the pain in his buttocks and back. At Cookham, he climbs up to the town. His pockets are empty. He had close to two pounds left for this quarter, but they took his wallet away when they dragged him to the guardhouse.

A girl stands at a brazier selling roasted potatoes and he leans on a wall across the lane and watches, longing to beg from her. She's gradually overtaken by the shadow of the shop behind her, and then all he can see is an orange nimbus from the invisible charcoal fire. Then it's dark enough to steal, so he drops back to the river where cottages line the towpath. In rooms so dim they might be lit by glow-worms, the poor bend over their suppers. Henry creeps between two cottages and waves a boot experimentally over the earth. Even in daylight, would he recognize food in a kitchen garden? Carrots and swedes – they grow below the ground. He drops to his knees and feels around in the autumn-shrivelled leaves, digging his fingers in, finding nothing but stringy roots. Back down at the river, empty-handed, he crouches as low as he can on his bruised thighs and laps water with his palm.

For the first time, he wonders what Wyndham and Chorley have endured that day. It's possible they were flogged again, for his escape. It would be absurd, but not outside the daily absurdity of Great Marlow. "The subject who is truly loyal will never advise nor submit to arbitrary measures." He copied that once from a book at his uncle's. It would mean nothing to Wyndham and Chorley. *Insubordination* was the charge against all three of them, but really, it was fitting that he alone was singled out to be expelled, because the other two never challenged anything; they were just in the scheme for the profit. Chorley was an atavistic little merchant, about two generations from a barrow-monger, but Wyndham had more complicated sources of misery and need. Lord Egremont kept his son destitute as a matter of principle. The flogging and the guardhouse were nothing compared to what Wyndham would suffer at his father's hands, and Henry felt a stab of guilt because he had known from the beginning that they'd be caught, that the scheme was meaningless unless Mr. Truepenny saw the drawings and knew who had made them. In the place in his chest where he's carried that sweet satisfaction, Henry feels shards of emotion gathering, a stirring that he recalls (from the distant days before Marlow) as tears. Why should I have stayed for more humiliation? he says fiercely to himself. The writ was signed. Marlow had expelled him; it had no more rights over him.

The towpath ends at the foot of Cookham Bridge – it must resume on the other side. A smell of cut hay rises from the fields. A hayfield would be a fragrant bed, but the thought of lying on the ground brings up childhood memories of Jamaica, of serpents slithering through grass. Instead, he climbs over a wall into a yard and eases himself down on a bench. Lying flat on his back with his knees up, he feels the pain less. Something (roses?) climbs the wall opposite him, although by the smell of rust and iron he would say he was in a smithy. A lopsided moon perches on the roof-edge. He wonders sleepily if it's waxing or waning. The phases of the moon will matter to him now, in his new vagabond life. ("On your honour," says the subaltern with the iron cleats. "It's rather touching, his faith in us" – this time he gives that line to Wyndham. "No," Henry answers. "It's just Marlow – they never see what anything really means." His mother bends towards the roses, snipping off faded blossoms. "They never see the meaning of anything," he explains to her. "They're stupid, shrivelled, small-minded old fools." "Oh, my darling boy," she says, straightening up and reaching her gloved fingers out to touch his face.)

When he wakes, the sun is rising over the wall and the sky is the blue of an enamel bowl. The play is over, his mind is scrubbed clean. Dew furs the wool of his breeches. He was right – it's a smithy's yard he's lying in. What he took for climbing roses is a tangle of rusting wire and pig iron tossed against the wall. A hen picks its way through the dirt and flaps to the window above him, settling onto the ledge. He rolls gingerly onto his side. Lying on the bench with his arm bent under his ear, he listens to the carts go by on the road. I'll go into the city, he thinks. I'll go to Clement's, he'll feed me. He reaches down to brush at his breeches and the wool turns wet against his skin.

It's mid-afternoon before he comes up on Hampton. He'd thought to take the towpath all the way to Westminster Bridge, but he'd be days following the wanderings of the river. He turns up the first major thoroughfare he comes to – Talgarth Road, someone tells him – and walks into the clamour of London. Darkness falls and the gaslights glow green in the east. He saw them the year before, when he was on Christmas leave and stayed at his uncle's. Afterwards, it seemed likely he'd embellished them, confused them with the light from a dream. But apparently not. There's the first one on a pole, a fabulous stemmed flower dropping its secretive light on an ordinary patch of pavement, showing the dark up for what it is.

A half-hour later, he emerges from the shadows at his uncle's club. Boodle's squats yellowly under a gas lamp with saddle horses and tilburies crowding the pavement in front. If Henry goes in, there'll be a plate of oysters and a cab ride the rest of the way, Uncle Clement taking him confidingly by the arm, telling about driving drunk through Covent Garden in 1794, being arrested for shouting, "Liberty while you live," from the window of a carriage, oh, the rake he was! Henry's hunger carries him up to the door and then carries him right on past, keeps him on a giddy trajectory up St. James Street. A boy holds out a man's hat to beg. He's in red knee breeches, his feet and legs bare. Henry touches his pocket to say, *empty*.

Then he's on Piccadilly, and then it's another mile or more and he's at his uncle's corner and his uncle is descending a cab. "The young cadet," Clement says, without surprise and with something like pleasure, giving a mocking salute. Henry moves towards him, trying to walk normally. He nods to the doorman, takes in the smell of cigars in the hall, and follows his uncle up the stairs. The false calves sewn into Clement's hose are turned slightly awry.

"Club night," says his uncle at the door of his rooms.

"I thought so," says Henry. "I passed by."

The doorman has given Clement a lamp and now he lights another one. In the blue-papered drawing room, he busies himself with tumblers and a dusty bottle of port from the side-board, moving through the answers to questions he hasn't asked. "Half-holiday, eh. A rum business, officer training. Lucky with this war, bound to be commissioned. Regardless, eh?" He hands Henry a drink. "At the Beach family seat in Bristol, then, your mother?" He's the uncle on the other side – it's his way to affect distaste for the De la Beche family, as though Henry's connection to his father is a youthful folly he'll outgrow.

"No," says Henry. He settles himself on the divan with his legs foppishly scissored to take the pain off his right hip. Clement doesn't ask. "You wouldn't have a bit of bread or cheese about, would you?"

"Never keep victuals in the house," says Clement. "Can't tolerate the vermin. You should have come into the club if you wanted to eat." Two carved chairs flank the bookcase and he settles on one. Columns of squashed laurel wreaths climb the paper behind him. He raises his glass. Victory floats in a halo around his limp fair curls. He's joined the Headstrong Society at Boodle's, he debated that night – what a pity Henry did not stop in! – he built an unassailable case for the affirmative. It was a debate on the poor tax, on parish relief and its folly. "Be it resolved!" he cries. "Be it resolved that the poor tax promotes growth in the underclasses!" He was proud to cite Malthus, starvation being one of nature's checks on rampant breeding. He could see them sitting up straight at the name of Malthus – it was *science* that won the debate. He lifts his glass again, tips it to the light. "To science," he calls. Then, seeming to see something in Henry's silence, he suddenly abandons the debate, agrees to offer it up for ridicule. The comic mask falls over his face. "A riddle for you," he says. "How is a Headstrong debate like a pint of Boodle's ale?"

Henry has heard this before. "Foamy and frothy on top?" he asks heavily, feeling the port rise at that very moment to his head.

"Heavy and muddy within, haha."

On the wall above, Beau Brummel stands in aquatint, a graceful hand on a graceful hip. "I was stood drinks all night by *Forester*," Clement crows. "*Simon Forester?*" He lifts his eyebrows theatrically. London agent for Napoleon Bonaparte? Why, just last week Forester was commissioned by Bony to buy a thousand tickets from London bookmakers. Or so Clement had heard. "It's not right," he cries, finding a segue to the evening's hilarity. "Where does it leave the rest of us? There must be an exclusion for men of destiny."

"Perhaps Bonaparte's betting on his own defeat?" says Henry, feeling a violent longing for the towpath by the Thames.

"Haha," says Clement absently. No contributions accepted, apparently: the hilarity was for members only. He crosses his legs, batting at one of the wandering calves, and then he reaches over to the table for his snuff box, passing it to Henry with a look of suppressed provocation. He knows Henry won't take snuff. He wants to show the box, an enamel of an imploring Negro in chains. And the legend: *Am I not a man and a brother?*

"Thank you, no," says Henry, passing the snuff box back. His head is pulled irresistibly to the arm of the divan. The wall of the drawing room sags towards him, the lamplight swoons. "Where is she?" Henry mumbles. "My mother. Do you know where she is?"

The next morning, Clement takes Henry on a promenade through Soho. Rain overnight left pools of water lying on the streets, and women wearing pattens click along the pavement. Most of the grand houses are apartments let out to members of Parliament come in from the country, or to gentlemen about town and the ladies they consort with. Clement likes to tell about Mrs. Hamilton living on this street when Lord Nelson died, he shows Henry the very house (a different house, Henry notes, than the last time he was taken on this tour). And there's the house where the celebrated actress Mrs. Pope died and from which she was taken to be buried. "In the cloister," says Clement reverently. "In the Abbey."

Clement's friend William Bullock, the famous collector, is building a new exhibition hall on Piccadilly. It's a grand edifice, fronted in a fine granite. An immense statue, extravagantly roped as though caught in a poacher's net, is being hoisted into place on the first floor. William Bullock himself stands on the pavement in a horsehair wig in lieu of a hat, supervising the installation. This is the sort of marvel I can offer up daily, Clement says by his sparkling manner, pulling Henry along. Now that he's had a proper breakfast of kippers and eggs at the Halfmoon Inn, Henry is sullen at having squandered his freedom. Mr. Bullock greets them with professional friendliness, but introductions are interrupted by shouts from the men on the pulleys. The statue rises serenely above them and settles heavily on its marble platform over their heads. Something about the statue's hair is in keeping with the hieroglyphics carved on the granite facing stone. "Is your hall to house Egyptian artifacts?" Henry asks.

"No, no," laughs his uncle, trying to draw Mr. Bullock into amusement at Henry's ignorance.

"There *will* be a mummy in permanent exhibit, lad," says Mr. Bullock kindly. "But the Egyptian is just a style the public's enamoured of at the moment. This hall will house all manner of objects from around the world." The inaugural exhibition, just two weeks away, is to be souvenirs from Captain Cook's voyages, every sort of natural curiosity and artifact of native manufacturing. Spices, shrunken heads, feather cloaks, masks, rattles, helmets, spears, shells – this spiel is word for word from the posters pasted to the hoarding in front of them. "Taking the lad to see the Hottentot, eh?" Bullock asks when he's come to the end of it. "Go ahead, spend your brass at Schmitt's. I'll get it out of you another day."

"Hottentot?" says Clement. "Schmitt?"

"Up at 225. Had a chance to bring her in myself." He's shouting over the din, the story coming rapid-fire from the puckered pouch of his mouth. "I was dealing with Dunlop on a camelopard skin and he offered her to me for thirty pound. The Hottentot Venus, he's calling her. From Cape Town. Says she's a corking example of the type. Grab a chance to lift her loincloth and you'll see the whole business. I was keen. I could have shown her at Bartholomew Fair. But by the time I counter-offered, that dirty Schmitt was in. Oh, well, he can take the fall. The Attorney General's got his nose in, he's taking it to the Chancery. He'll shut it down. You'd best go today."

"He *bought* this woman?" says Henry, trying to understand. "From South Africa? He will be charged under the Wilberforce Bill!"

"Oh, he's the one for niceness," cries Clement, making a little hop. "Allow me to present my nephew, young Henry De la Beche. Officer cadet at Great Marlow. Son of Halse Hall plantation, Clarendon, Jamaica. Commission to be paid in bananas and cotton."

"Cane sugar, actually," Henry says. Clement looks at him sharply. Perhaps only now is he registering Henry's diminished uniform, the crossed white sash from his tunic missing and the plume from his shako gone. His hose filthy, perforated by sharp branches along the towpath, his shoes muddy.

"Pleased to make your acquaintance," says Bullock. "But that's just the thing. Apparently she wasn't bought. She's a full partner. She's on shares of the gate. There's moaning about it all down the street. But think about it. She's got as much right to display herself as your common dwarf, don't she, eh?" He brings his wrinkled lips down to Henry's ear. "But what part is she displaying? That's the question, eh. It'll be a public decency charge they get them on."

The exhibition hall of Mr. Bullock's rival is close to Piccadilly Circus. Henry thought he understood Mr. Bullock's meaning, but still they go. Maybe he got it wrong – there is Clement, strolling blithely along. "I'm not going in," he says, and he sees Clement's eyes light up: here's a story he can trot out for the amusement of his friends. The crowd thickens. They're beset by vendors hawking matches, eels, rat poison, eggs, wooden dolls. Henry tries to put his mind to a pretext for borrowing a couple of quid so he can leave. Clusters of girls in striped gingham stroll the pavement. Clement has clamped an arm around Henry's shoulder. He digs his fingers in as a confiding signal each time they pass a comely one. And then they're at 225 Piccadilly and there's the sign tacked by the door: *Outlandish Beast in a Raree Show*. A permanent all-purpose sign, judging by its patina of grime and tobacco spit. Clement's arm is still around his shoulders, he tries to wheel Henry towards the entrance. Henry stiffens his legs, resisting, and an old affection rises, a habit of play that makes him lean suddenly into the turn. He's as tall as Clement now, he's heavier, and his reversal almost topples them. Then they're at the wicket after all, where Clement parts with four shillings, squeezing them one by one out of the purse at his waist. They're directed to wait in the crowd of chattering sight-seers on the stairs. Spectators exiting the exhibition hall have to use the same stairway, and Clement and Henry are pressed into a conglomerate of bodies at desperate cross-purposes. Finally the deadlock is broken and they're carried bodily up by the crowd and deposited in a lofty hall lit by windows in the ceiling.

Beside a placard reading THE HOTTENTOT VENUS, a boy is hawking two-foot lengths of willow for three pence. "What are the sticks for?" Henry says, but Clement is out of hearing. A keeper, curiously costumed in a beefeater hat and a kilt too short for him, directs the crowd. *Here decorum prevails*, he says by his expression, ushering Henry into a stream of curious Londoners milling around a platform, and through a trick of centripetal action Henry finds himself on the inside of the stream, just a few feet away from the subject of the exhibition, who stands still and erect and bare-breasted.

Two shillings each they paid, he thinks afterwards, as he stands on Piccadilly watching well-dressed Londoners wander out of the hall. The cost of a roast beef dinner in an inn, to ogle an ordinary Negro woman with her breasts bared. Across the Circus, an itinerant clarinet plays. A hawker with a pack on his back calls, "Ole clo," and he perks up – in his blue and scarlet uniform, he's an illicit Union Jack. But he doesn't have a pence about him. Rain begins to mist down. His mother will know of his disgrace by now; they lay three days in the guardhouse waiting for the king's envoy to arrive to sign the writ. He presses against the building, trying to avoid the rain, wondering where he can go. To Mrs. Butterworth, maybe, their old housekeeper in Ottery St. Mary. Or to Uncle Alger in Bristol, his uncle on the other side. Alger will know where Mother is – she keeps in touch with him because of Halse Hall business. But I've got to get out of this uniform, he thinks, before they arrest me. The previous morning, he had lain for a while on the bench listening to the chain of small metallic noises coming from the hen on the window ledge above him. In that moment, he understood that what you do does not necessarily define you. You can choose to say, *Yes, I do this. But I am separate from it.* You can give them the callow gesture, because that's what they're worth, and you can be as you were. *As you were* – it's a military expression.

Clement emerges from the entrance, wiping his brow. "You left too soon," he says. "I swear I caught sight of a tail." He does a little dance of excitement and revulsion on the pavement, flapping his handkerchief. When Henry doesn't respond, he sobers. "That will be nothing new to you," he says. "It's the heat that does it, as you know. You're familiar with pawpaw and breadfruit. Grows in three days, breadfruit does, as big as an archbishop's hat."

They set off for home. Henry is thinking of Marlow, the sunlit study hall. His folio, and the narrow shelves under the windows where they kept their pens, the solid oak tables where they sat copying *Muller's Artillery*. Afternoons hiding in the mouldy barracks attic with Chorley and Wyndham, an earl's son, all of them working on copies of his drawings (tuppence a copy, he paid them), their admiration for his skill and wit and daring evident in their assiduous journeyman efforts. Crossing the Circus with Clement chattering at his side, he thinks of the truest moment there was, in the guardhouse at Marlow after the flogging, when they lay on the packed earth floor without a blanket (Chorley a little apart and silent), he and Wyndham lying side by side in their pain and exaltation, and the torch outside the barred window shone on his friend's head and he saw tiny movements in Wyndham's hair; lice, delicately illuminated.

But he's fallen into a new drama. As they walk up Halfmoon Street, he sees a carriage with his own arms stencilled on the door, and Algernon De la Beche descends in his queued and powdered wig, looking like an advance agent from the Captain Cook exhibit in Bullock's Egyptian Hall, and evidently astonished to encounter Henry here.

Properly indoors, Alger declines a drink. He likewise declines the divan and lowers himself onto a chair, the carved back of which he declines to use for support. His indignation of manner is theatrical, his real indignation having been exhausted, Henry can guess, over the temperature of his tea at breakfast. Ignoring Henry, who stands by the mantel, he addresses himself to Clement. "I was in London town, as it happens, yesterday. Having made my way here to tend to the business affairs of my sister-in-law, as prearranged. My meeting was with a solicitor at Lincoln's Inn."

Henry offers his uncle a sober, attentive countenance. "We had just settled nicely into our affairs," Alger goes on, "when a letter arrived informing us that this young chap's mother had been summoned to Great Marlow on a matter of great consequence and urgency, and asking if I would present myself there on her behalf. Your sister is prostrated, Mr. Mollot, as you can imagine. She is entirely unable to travel. And so I took myself to Great Marlow, anticipating bad news and, upon my arrival, hearing worse. And now, after a day of to-ing and fro-ing and exhausting the horses to no avail on the Great West Road, I find the lad on your premises. Well, Mr. Mollot, whatever your intentions in sheltering him, I must inform you that my sister-in-law has conferred on me the responsibility of paterfamilias. No slight towards you, I'm sure, Mr. Mollot, no slight at all intended." His next observations are broken by throat clearing. Henry hears *my brother, safe from this, God's grace.*

"Sheltering him?" asks Clement. "Safe from this?"

"Ah?" says Alger, sitting back then with satisfaction, casting his eyes about Clement's drawing room, every surface of which, Henry sees now, is felted with dust. What he took for laurel wreaths stencilled on the wallpaper are circles of mould. "He's not told you," says Alger. "He's not had the courtesy to enlighten you as to the true circumstances of his visit." He takes up the vial hanging from a chain on his bosom and painstakingly extracts two peppercorns to chew as a tonic. "Our mutual nephew," he says, looking directly at Clement, his eyes glittering, "has been sent down. From Great Marlow. By royal edict."

"Sent down?" cries Clement. "Royal edict?"

Henry is still standing by the fireplace. "My mother. My mother, where is she?" he asks, chagrined to hear his voice revert to the treble notes of boyhood.

·◄[T H R E E]►·

There was a war on that year, and a naval blockade that left the English with only their own corn to eat, and then the crops failed. But Lyme Regis did a respectable domestic trade. That it was a port town at all and not a squalid fishing village was down to its sturdy, black-haired citizenry, who, hundreds of years in the past, had hauled stones from the beach to build a massive breakwater the shape of an elbow, turning an inhospitable stretch of Lyme Bay into a harbour. For centuries, the weight of those stones and their affinity for each other was all that held that breakwater together. The Cobb, they called it, and by the time Mary was a girl, it was a wide, tilting road capped with massive blocks of dark limestone from the Isle of Portland, with the revenue office and the isolation hut built right onto it.

Mary often followed Marine Parade west along the shore to the Cobb, to buy fish. And often she walked out past it with her father, to collect on Monmouth Beach. There the walking was perilous, the stones a queer shape and neither small enough to be called shingle nor large enough to bear the flat of a boot. It was a common boast of smugglers washed up there in fog that they knew their bearings by the shape of the stones, but that was not such a feat; Mary would have been able to do the same.

The Devil had made Monmouth Beach on a wager, people always said. Mary held such comments loosely in her mind now, thinking of the man with the blue bag. But the curiosities they collected on that beach, they were still a puzzle. They were given to the poor like manna to the Children of Israel, Richard said, although not as regular. And so it would seem God had made the curiosities, although James Wheaton, the pastor at the Independent Chapel, feared and hated them. It was true that some of the curiosities had an unwholesome look to them, especially the curved grey stones the townspeople identified as the Devil's discarded toenails. Even the beautiful ammonites were a mystery. They had the weight of stones, but they were unlike any stone God had made. So intricate and patterned, they had almost the hand of an artisan upon them.

One Sabbath morning, walking out early, Mary and her father met the hedge carpenter Walter Jones and his son, on their way to the Independent Chapel to get the fire started. Walter Jones lifted the cap from his tufted hair and said, "We'll see ye in chapel anon, then," offering them a view of the narrow brown teeth spaced like fence posts in his gums. "Not today, friend," Mary's father said agreeably, and turned to walk on, and Mr. Jones said to his back, "Ye're niver taking that child to the shore on the Sabbath morning." They kept going and then they heard a bellowed, "Oy!" and they stopped and turned. "Or up on the boogerin' cliffs!" Mr. Jones shouted.

When had her father stopped going to chapel? Mary couldn't say exactly. He'd always complained about James Wheaton at the pulpit, for his twitching and his eye fluttering and his knuckle cracking. When money was tight and the foreshore gleamed in the morning sun just at chapel time, Richard would declare a holiday from sermonizing and spend the morning collecting, eager to have first chance at the treasures the waves had brought in overnight and would batter and smash by noon. Eventually, he began to avoid chapel even when the tide was high.

As for Mary, when the tide was low she went collecting with her father, and when it was too high to walk the shore in safety, she went to chapel. She went with her mother or, if Percival was too fretful, she went alone or took Lizzie. She went out of sympathy for James Wheaton, the clever young pastor who had a clockwork spring inside him that pressed him into postures he would not have willed for himself. James Wheaton could not turn his queer white-fringed calf eyes on the congregation but must preach to the side window, and Mary thought she understood why: it was how fiercely he loved them and how mercilessly the Lord's words gripped him.

They were almost at the Cobb, and Mary could sense Walter Jones still watching from behind. No one knew what to do with her father. They looked at him the way she did, with the same bewilderment and longing. He should have been hanged for starting a bread riot in the Year of Our Lord 1800, when Mary was just a baby, a year the crop withered in the fields and the price of a bushel of corn went up to nineteen shillings. But he was not hanged. The army spent a month trying to ferret out the leader of the riot, beating the townspeople and offering them bribes, but there was not a single crimp among them, they were solid against the soldiers. And they did not hate Richard for it – they loved him for the way he taught them their rights and led them up the streets to the mill, with torches burning in the dark, crying, "Bread or blood!" This was ten years ago and they still loved him for it.

It was a book that made a rebel of him. For weeks, Holly said, he'd been reading an unlawful book by Mr. Thomas Paine. After the riot, when the soldiers filled the town, Molly built up a roaring fire and threw the book into it, and she always claimed she'd brought him out of a spell by burning it. The night after the army left, people were at the workshop again, wanting more riot. But standing in his doorway, Richard asked where it was written in Holy Scripture that the price of a bushel of corn was five shillings sixpence. He'd dropped them in it and then he acted as though he had no memory of it ever happening. Everyone retreated confused to the Three Cups and Richard went out and mended the cobblestone in the square, which lay a mudhole since they'd pried up stones to throw at the soldiers. He was the one who'd got their blood up and it was their blood that turned him against rioting. So Molly said. There was more grain strewn along the road those nights, she explained, than was ever carried home for the children.

Mary glanced back and saw that Walter Jones was finally turning up to town. He had cast his head over his shoulder for one last look at Richard. In that look, she felt the pull of the chapel, as though James Wheaton or God himself had sent Walter Jones to summon them. Richard saw where Mary's eyes had gone. "An hour in the chapel, the week with the Devil," he said.

Mary looked closely at her father's thin face. We try to explain him, she thought, but he does not hold to reasons as other men do. His causes were wordless, sealed shiny and hard inside him. No one would ever hold him. He'd been a rebel and he rebelled against the rebels. He'd been a Dissenter and now he was a dissenter of the Dissenters and went to chapel no more. Walter Jones and all of them watched him in wonder – Richard Anning, misfortune's favourite, walking boldly down to the shore on a Sabbath morning.

It was a relief to encounter the plump spectre of Mr. Buckland on the shore, floating a foot or two above the shingle with his popping eyes fixed on the stones – Mr. Buckland, the man with the blue bag who had come to the curiosity table, who disputed the Devil's hand on any living creature and said that what they called dragons were really just crocodiles, made by God and migrated now to warmer climes. He was lodging in town; they would often spy his big hairy-hocked horse munching weeds along the cliff. Mary was always startled at first by the sight of him drifting over the shingle in his gown and top hat. When you worked your way closer, you could see that he *was* attached to the earth; it was just that the bottom of his gown up to his knees was white with dust.

He was a clergyman, she knew that now, and as soon as they were close enough, she called a greeting and asked him, "Be ye not in church this Sabbath morning?"

"Of course I am," he said. "And so are you. We're worshipping in the *Lord's* chapel." And he gestured to the east, where mist veiled Black Ven and Golden Cap shone high above as though it dangled from the sun. He seemed to be addressing her, but really he was directing his cleverness to her father, darting eager smiles in Richard's direction. "Here on this shore is all the bounty of the Lord made manifest," he cried.

"This shore?" Mary said. "But there were grand wickedness done on this shore."

"There's been wickedness done on every shore of the seven seas," said Mr. Buckland. "Man will use the earth for his purposes, for God gave him dominion." Light sparkled silver off the edges of the black cliffs, and the sky was a high dome of blue over them, and it seemed that what Mr. Buckland said was true – Mary could hardly look at the shore for the beauty of it.

The first time Mary and her father talked to Mr. Buckland at the shore, he'd tried to trick them. Richard asked him what he'd found that morning and he reached into his blue bag and showed them a Devil's toenail sticking out of a bit of red shale.

"What do ye take me for?" said Richard, passing it back. "You never found that on this shore." The limestone and shale cliffs rose behind them, all blue-grey. The *blue lias*, people called it.

Buckland laughed and confessed he'd bought it from the curiman who stopped the coach on the Exeter Road. Mr. Buckland asked their names and he told them his, and explained that he was a clergyman and a scholar at Oxford University. "What age is the lass?" he asked.

Mary told him she was eleven and asked with all courtesy, "And you, sir?" and Mr. Buckland and her father both laughed, but he did tell her. He was six-and-twenty. "Sharp as a blade!" he said, and now Mary, who was coming to know his tendency to reuse his words, did not put so much stock in it.

"Ye'd not have said so, mind," said Richard, "if ye'd seen her as a babe." But Mary did not want to hear him tell the story of the lightning again, dwelling on her wondrous dullness, and she rushed in with a question: Could Mr. Buckland explain why the snakes had all curled up in the same attitude to die, so neatly, like the curled horns of a ram? For she'd seen more than one snake dead on the turnpike road and they were not curled tightly up but were laid out like whips.

"Were the ammonites snakes at all?" Mr. Buckland asked. "By their form, you might conclude they were molluscs. You've seen a garden snail with its shell on its back?"

"If they were like garden snails, how did they come to be stone?" she asked.

"Ha!" said Mr. Buckland. "I could ask you the same question, if they were snakes."

"Saint Hilda turned them to stone," Mary said. "When she started the convent at Whitby. She rolled them down a hill and their heads broke off." But even as she said it, she saw the amused look on Mr. Buckland's face and realized how very foolish this story was.

Mr. Buckland asked her father then about the stony jaws often found on the shore. Crocodile jaws, he called them. He wanted a complete example that he could carry away to study.

"You'd best ask at the quarry at Church Cliffs," Richard said. "They're grinding them up for lime morning and night." Her father must have taken hard against Mr. Buckland to refuse such a chance.

"I'd be prepared to pay handsomely," Mr. Buckland said, and Mary studied his face, trying to gauge how many shillings *handsomely* might mean.

"The lass with the anthracite eyes," he called her. She asked him what anthracite was, and he said a kind of coal. Mr. Buckland was from another world; he'd been born in Axminster, six miles away. He did not know the Annings, the ill fortune they were marked out for, although the news of the first Mary's death in a fire had been written up in the paper – not in Lyme (where they thought the tidings too dismal for Christmas) but in Bath. Molly had the newspaper, so old and dry and yellow that it was splitting at the folds. She kept it in the cupboard and, when she was in the mood to look at it, showed Mary, though neither of them could read it. Mary studied it, marvelling that the whole sad story was hidden in those tiny lines of print. Strangers in Bath had moved their eyes over it while their Christmas goose spit and dripped on the fire, and knew about the Annings. But that was long ago.

Asking for salve was just a pretext to knock on the door of Morley Cottage that afternoon, for Mary's arm was healed. All the same, Miss Elizabeth Philpot helped her hang her jacket on the back of a chair and roll up the sleeve of her grey dress.

While Miss Philpot applied the salve, Mary told her a story about Mr. Buckland. Grey snakestones as big as cartwheels were bedded on the western shore, and Mr. Buckland had found a broken one with the centre whorls washed out of it. He hoisted it up and fitted it over his head like a ruff, and then he called to Mary, "How does my lady for this many a day?" The tide was coming in and he walked straight out onto the foreshore and disappeared around a point, wading ankle deep in water with the snakestone round his neck. Mary was worried he'd be caught by the tide, but all her father said was, "He'll swim to France, the thin-faced martel."

Miss Philpot was daubing the salve delicately and without fear on Mary's pox-marks. Her own cheeks were marred with scars (for the pox is not a respecter of persons). She had never asked where the marks had come from; it was not in the way of the highborn to ask. Or perhaps she had heard in the town. At chapel, the pastor had delivered a thundering sermon especially for the Annings, on the practice of mingling animal humours into human blood. A *devilish* cure, he called it. Why the Devil would choose to cure people was something no one explained.

Miss Philpot listened to the story of Mr. Buckland with amusement. "A professor!" she said. "If he has survived, you must ask him what he thinks of the pig-faced lady." And then, with great relish, she told Mary a story about the Philpot brother Charles, riding down a wide highway in the great city of London and seeing, in a carriage beside, a lady famously known in London as the pig-faced lady. There were many who had seen her, but no one knew her name or where she lived. She was thought to possess a fortune, but this was scant comfort to her. The day Charles saw her, she wore a veil, but it had got caught up on her snout. Charles Philpot saw her lift a graceful hand to fix it. A lady's hand in a fine glove, not a pig's trotter.

"Gentlemen have been posting notices in the *Times*," Miss Philpot said, her mouth turned down in the wry twist that passed for a smile, "offering themselves to the lady with the heavy facial affliction, as they delicately put it. For five thousand pounds per annum, they reckon they can stomach a bit of squealing at supper."

If the pig-faced lady did find a husband, Mary wondered, how would he bear to kiss her? If she'd had any thought of saying this aloud, Miss Philpot's poor pox-fretted face stopped her before the words came out.

"Oh, Catherine, Saint Catherine, please come to my aid, and grant that I niver may be a wold maid," Mary said secretly to herself as she went out through the back garden, feeling a bit ashamed as she said it, because of the liking she had for Miss Philpot.

The Philpot sisters had paid Richard a deposit for the cabinet and now, for the moment, there was money to spare and her mother knew it, but Richard took Joseph to the Three Cups for his supper that night and left her no chance to importune him about the seventh son. Long after Mary and Lizzie and their mother had retired, Richard and Joseph came clattering up to the bedchamber and laid themselves down in the dark, Joseph on a pallet on the far side of the bed. Murmuring voices started up from the bed.

Lizzie, who was on a floor pallet beside Mary, was wakened by all the noise. "Mary," she said, putting a hot hand on Mary's cheek, "where did they cut you to put the pox in?" It was the question she asked almost every night.

Mary wanted to hear her parents' conversation. She pulled the cover over both her head and Lizzie's. "Not in one place but in five," she said fiercely. "Like our Lord Jesus Christ. Here –"

She scratched at Lizzie's palm, then she poked at Lizzie's side and grabbed for Lizzie's feet. "– and here, and here." Lizzie began to cry and Mary clamped her hand over her mouth, but pips of sob escaped into the room.

"Hush," their father said, rising up in the bed. "You two hush yer moaning."

Finally it was quiet again, and then Molly asked Richard about taking Percival to Exeter.

"It's a big town, Exeter," Richard said. "Where the devil does the lad dwell? Do ye have any notion?"

Molly was silent.

"Does Mrs. Stock have the name?"

"I hate to ask her." Mary could hear her mother turn over in bed. "She has a gloating way about her, does Mrs. Stock."

"A pullet with its legs tied together could gloat, if it cast for cause as wide as the Widow Stock does," Richard said, turning over also.

They would be lying close, with their legs bent to fit together. Mary heard them both sigh. There was a comfort in their sighs and their silence, and she wished she was small enough to climb into their bed and worm her way into the warm channel between them. She rolled over and tucked an arm under her head as a pillow. The day of the cowpox cure came vividly to her – she had begun to think of that day with a kind of joy. Walking out with her father and Joseph, and crossing a field where black-faced sheep with tattered coats stood to watch them. Seeing Ware Manor Farm, with geese running in a pack in the green yard, and the dead tree that stood with buckets hung upside down to dry on its limbs. It all came to her – Farmer Ware in his smock, walking between the barn and the dairy with stately step because of the yoke over his shoulders, the smell of manure in the cowshed, so strong it made her eyes burn, and her father lifting her up to a railing heedless of the muck that coated it. "Did ye ever see a poxy milkmaid?" he said, and he brought the tip of the sharp clasp knife to her forearm, and she kept her eyes on his and did not let out so much as a whimper.

An hour out on the Great West Road, Henry is frantic with pain from his lacerated buttocks. He braces his boots against the floor of the bouncing coach and shifts his weight from one hip to the other, while Alger, sitting in the opposite corner, watches him suspiciously. His uncle insists on having the curtains pulled across; the light bothers his eyes. So there is not even the distraction of the road. They're locked together in this dim box for three days of torment.

Will I have *scars?* Henry wonders. Tallo, his nurse's husband at Halse Hall, had cross-hatching on his back like woven wicker. Not from floggings at Halse Hall, from before that. In fact, he was sold to Halse Hall because of it, because if the back is thickly enough scarred, the slave becomes indifferent to the lash. So Henry's mother said, in recounting how Henry's father naively bought Tallo the week after arriving in Jamaica and thought he'd got a bargain. Not that Henry's father intended to rely on the lash. It was 1799 when he took over the plantation – before the Wilberforce Bill banned the trade from Africa, but England was all talk of abolition and his father was resolved to be a different sort of planter. A short-lived intention, it would seem, because Henry can remember bare backs in the shed, hands bound to a hook high above. He can remember the sound of the lash, although not the sight of it reaching its mark; just Tomkin the overseer pausing to wipe sweat from his face and neck.

And now *I* have been flogged, he says to himself as they bounce along the Great West Road. The part of his brain that was counting was stunned into silence at about *three*, but Chorley had reported fifteen lashes. Henry stuffs his jacket under him to augment the thin horsehair cushion, and perches gingerly on it, thinking about what lies ahead, living in disgrace in Bristol with this uncle with the skewed wig and a belly that joggles to the rhythm of the coach. They were identical twins, his father and Uncle Alger. His mother always asks, "When you see Algernon, do you remember your father?" and he says, "No, I remember Algernon." Which is to say, between annual visits to Bristol, he forgets entirely what his uncle looks like, and he denies any resemblance at all between them – his father, Lieutenant-Colonel Thomas De la Beche, a distinguished officer with the Norfolk Regiment of Fencible Cavalry, and this tedious, dyspeptic bachelor.

Alger is drifting off to sleep now, his head tipped back against the cushions. Henry watches his mouth slacken and his head fall to the side. Finding himself suddenly in solitude, Henry opens the curtains a crack. He tries to keep his mind off his backside. He needs to focus on the inner meaning of his situation. The meaning no one will see, until he has the chance to share it with his mother. That he acted in truth against a master who *merited* ridicule, by his deficiencies and his vanity and his absurd self-righteous monologues. Mr. Truepenny invited exposure by posturing as something he was not. He was not a military man; he should never have been a master at a military college. And they knew this. All the officers at Marlow knew they were wrong to have engaged him, or they would never have reacted with such wrath to a handful of harmless caricatures and a clever enterprise to circulate them. The guardhouse and the floggings and Henry's expulsion were an effort to deny their error. Henry sits clamped by his pain, keen-eyed, unwavering in his role as a guardian of military standards. But there is still the matter of his leaving the captains' hall after having given his word, still there, pricking when his thoughts brush against it, like a hangnail. He was already expelled, he simply left before Marlow had fully vented its spleen. An act of self-respect, surely? Lying on a bench on the Thames path, he'd seen it clearly, that he must not fall in his own esteem, whatever others said.

But he will not, now, be a military man, either; he will not have a profession, in the military or anywhere else. They take a sharp bend in the road and he's pressed into the corner, and grief washes over him. At the loss of the topography class. And the mensuration class, with its chains and compasses and levels. And fortifications. And his abandoned copybook of perspective landscape drawings. He will not now have that expertise, the dignity of any expertise. All he'll have is his *manners*, his name on a card, and the rumours about him of the failing plantation. A gentleman has his name and his word, and he has given up his word. Wyndham and Chorley will be eager to tell. They'll latch on to it to separate themselves from him. Although what he did in leaving the captains' hall has its inner meaning, too. Keeping one's word was a *fetish* at Marlow. They were always blustering on about it in the middle of something sordid, like the time Harding hung from a tree by his knees and pissed his pants because he'd given his word to do it. His mother will understand his reasoning on this matter: she sees things as no one else in the world sees them.

He's drifting off when the coach gives a tremendous jolt and his pain jabs him awake. Then he finds he's too cold to sleep. He puts his jacket back on and, turning his back on his sleeping uncle, slides to the floor and kneels with his head buried in his arms on the seat, a position that takes him instantly back to prayers by his netted bed in the sudden night of Jamaica, night that fell like an eyelid closing. He thinks of lying in his cot afterwards, listening to the Negroes calling on the road on their way back from the cane fields. In the juddering coach, he sinks into childhood dreams, he floats bodilessly above white sand in water honeycombed with sunlight. Sand-coloured crabs skitter sideways all at once to their holes, like corks on a net being dragged along the shore. A mango sucked to its flat, hairy pit lies salted with sand. Belle carries him up the path, her hands cool and dry. Oh, my stout man, she says. She stands in the hot, dark cookhouse in her white apron, she stirs the soup and raises the spoon to her lips. Her face bends over him, the fine net of moles around her eyes. She holds the iron spoon to his mouth, soup the colour of cut grass.

The loud clopping of the horses' hooves rouses him; the surface of the road must have changed. He turns his head to the side and opens his eyes. Against the curtain of the coach, floating like a moon, he seems to see a little planet earth. The globe with all its tendons exposed, the way he drew it as a boy. Trade routes like veins binding the earth together, ships beaded along the veins ploughing full-sailed to Africa, carrying gunpowder, alcohol, iron. Crossing the Middle Passage with Negroes crying in the hold. Sailing out of the harbour at Kingston, weighted with rum and sugar, bound for Bristol. He drew this as a boy, the world with a web around it, busy ships racing along its veins. He drew it as a boy sitting on the veranda at Halse Hall in Jamaica. Where are all those drawings? Lost. Everything they had was lost on the journey home.

He feels a boot in his ribs, nudging him. His uncle is awake and looking down at him with disgust. "Get up," he says. "You comport yourself like a heathen."

"It's the posture of a Christian, I would have thought," Henry says, but he lifts himself to his seat. And then, to save his pride, he opens the curtain and looks out. They will still be in Buckinghamshire. Mist shrouds the trunks of great trees in a meadow. He thinks of the messages concerning himself recently carried over this road. To his mother, who is somewhere. It's almost a year since he saw her. When her husband died, her new husband, he was summoned to Dawlish to attend the funeral. He closes the curtain. "You haven't said where my mother is."

"Between houses at the moment," says Uncle Alger, taking up his vial of peppercorns. *Between houses.* A good answer, and probably true. Between Jamaica and Great Marlow, Henry lived in Hammersmith, Keynsham, Ottery St. Mary, and Dawlish. Between Keynsham and Ottery St. Mary, there was a prolonged stay at a country house in Berkshire, which they left suddenly one day just before dinner, spinning thrillingly away in a brougham with their host in hot pursuit, bareback and crouched like a jockey. Henry watched with glee, his face pressed against the glass as the man gained on them and his intent, pleading face suddenly loomed in the window. *Close the curtain*, Mother was shrieking. *Take no heed.*

"Where is your sash?" his uncle asks testily.

"I traded it for passage on a ferry," says Henry. "On the Thames."

His uncle scowls and shakes his head.

Just then a horn sounds and there's an exuberant shout from the coachman. Henry opens the curtain again to watch the Bristol post race past, a blur of black and red, London-bound. There was talk of it at the inn this morning – it is said to do the journey in sixteen hours. Alger bends forward and watches in dis-approval. "They cover six miles in an hour," he says. "The human brain can't withstand that sort of speed. A coachman toppled off last week and died, just short of London."

"Were you much affected by the heat in Jamaica, Uncle Alger?" Henry asks, just to torment him.

"Never was in Jamaica," his uncle snaps. "Didn't fancy the voyage."

They stop at the coaching inn at Slough to rest the horses. They're making excellent time themselves, thanks to the lack of luggage. Alger buys him a glass of ale with his dinner and Henry pulls in his horns a little. It's mid-afternoon before they set off again. Henry opens the curtain and Alger does not protest. He watches the countryside crawl by, admiring giant oaks and the decorative curve of hedgerows, and to the north, the Chiltern Hills, lying in a blue ridge like the view of the Mocho Mountains from the Halse Hall veranda.

At first, back in England, his mother liked to recount the early days to him in detail, her own misery as a homesick girl with a tiny baby. She hasn't wanted to talk about it in recent years. But now the abolitionists are all emboldened by the success of the Wilberforce Bill, and she's publicly asked the sort of question that would never have occurred to anyone before. After the funeral last year, one of her callers had the appalling manners to bring it up. A Quaker, she must have been, the sort who insists her cakes be made with honey to avoid plantation sugar. "How could you stomach the horror of it, the whip?" she asked. Henry listened with admiration while his mother deftly recalled the caller to the situation of the moment. "The whip is not a pleas-ant instrument, but the Negroes won't work without it. Certainly they feel pain when flogged, and they let you know it, but when you think of it, physical pain is the pain of a moment. It's *mental* anguish, isn't it, that lingers and leaves the deeper mark?"

It's because of the *flogging* that Jamaica is crowding in on him now. Or because of the show he saw with Clement in Piccadilly. The woman on display was not more than twenty, but her breasts lay heavily to her stomach, their tips turned outwards. Her only novelty was in this sort of proportion; on the question of buttocks, he observed, the lewd caricatures of the red-haired chambermaid he'd drawn at Marlow showed restraint. Yet her keepers led her by a leash and by their manner implied that she was dangerous – it was all the most preposterous charlatanism. On her part too, apparently – she was in it for a share of the gate, Bullock said. What would her percentage be? They were charging two shillings. So it was not the low and ignorant who came out in numbers to gawk at this woman; it was people with means. Had they never seen a Negro woman before? By their ignorance, they made her a spectacle. At one point in the show, she squatted on the platform. She happened to be right in front of Henry, her head just inches away – he was close enough to see the swollen pores around her nipples. When she squatted, a cry of delight went up from the crowd. Clement was plucking at his sleeve, and the woman rose up, looking right at Henry. At the nearness of her curly black cap he felt a childhood ache, felt the dry, familiar springs of African hair under his fingers. Her eyes were puffy and yellowed, tired, full of rage and knowing, and they met his with instant recognition. He could not have been more startled if she had called him by name. He felt his lips part to say something, and then he turned and shook Clement off and pushed his way out through the crowd.

Finally he falls sound asleep, and in the yellow light of his pain, he dreams of leaving Marlow. But not alone – he is running away with Wyndham. They follow the dung-strewn towpath, sensing the rickety fortress of Great Marlow looming behind them, and then the towpath ends and they're on a peninsula that juts out into the Thames, which is become a glowing lake. They pace uneasily on the bank, listening to the dogs pursuing them. Wyndham is taller than in life, luminously handsome, all his secret qualities made evident; the something soft in his nature is like an exposed heart. He has the coins they need for the ferry, he's carrying them in a small leather purse, but he's confused and weeping, and Henry has to wrestle the purse from him and pluck the coins out so they can board the ferry. This they manage to do just as the dogs and soldiers burst furiously out of the woods and onto the bank.

On a morning when Percival took some pips of mush and lifted his head and smiled, Mary had a letter from Mr. Buckland. It did not come directly to her, but was tucked into a letter addressed to Richard. The paper contained a drawing, a snakestone sliced open. There were no verteberries inside such as a snake would have, only a row of empty rooms. The legend was two words, and then there was text. Eventually Joseph lost patience with reading that text over and over to Mary, and began to shout the words to her one by one. *Progressively! Larger! Chambers!* There was an indignity here: Mary, who was of a stature to receive letters from scientific gentlemen, was unlettered, whereas Joseph, who had no interest in scholarship at all, had been sent to the grammar school at six. Mary pointed this out while Molly sat on the bench plaiting Lizzie's hair. "I agree," her mother said, and sat with her lips pressed together to indicate that nothing could be done about it, money being so much scarcer since the war began.

The day the new collecting cupboard was delivered to Morley Cottage, Mary followed the hired donkey cart up Silver Street.

It was a very steep hill; the donkey laboured hard and Richard kept an anxious hand on the cabinet. The wealthy showed a curious lack of judgment living away from the sea, so that they were always having to climb the hill or devise a means to be carried up it, while the poor had the ease of the shore. Even Morley Cottage climbed the hill, the parlour windows being higher than the dining room windows, although (Mary knew, from having been inside) the floors themselves had been built straight, not in accordance with the slant of the hill.

Miss Elizabeth Philpot came to the door in an orange gown. The cabinet was to go in the drawing room, she said, and led them down a hall to the room where pressed flowers hung in frames on the walls and curiosities from the shore and cliffs lay on every surface. Devils' toenails were splayed out in sets of five on the mantelshelf (Miss Elizabeth's little joke) and thunderbolts arranged in patterns on a tray.

"How grateful we will be for a bit of order in this room," said the middle Miss Philpot while Mary's father unwrapped the shallow drawers and slid them into the cabinet. "We can hardly reach for a book without knocking something to the floor," said the eldest. The middle sister Mary had seen before, but not the eldest. In spite of her scars, she was the most handsome, with fine eyes and fine arching eyebrows. They had lived all three in London when they were girls, and were rich enough to pay for the pesthouse, but their father was a pious man and thought it a sin to try to thwart the will of the Almighty. "And so the Almighty had His way with the three of us," said Miss Elizabeth Philpot, the day she told the story of her own pox to Mary.

There were fine curtains in the drawing room and a carpet on the floor, and Mary stood calmly in the midst of it. "Ye have twelve drawers but only five different curiosities," she said to her Miss Philpot (counting on her fingers: *thunderstones, thunderbolts, verteberries, Devil's toenails, snakestones*). They were partners in collecting. Miss Philpot did not go to the shore herself; she bought from the Annings or sent her groom down to the lime quarry to inquire of the quarrymen whether they had turned up anything of interest in their labours. She always asked Mary eagerly what Mr. Buckland had to say. The Ammon Knight, she called him, because of the story Mary told her about the snakestone he put over his head.

Miss Philpot stood in her puckered gown with the sleeves that swelled like pumpkins on her shoulders, frowning over the cabinet. "Twelve drawers," she said. "Yes. How is everything to be arranged?"

"There be ammonites with ridges and ammonites without," said Mary slowly, for she was thinking. "There be the golden ammonite curled up in stones. And the pyrite ammonite that we find clean on the shore. And the grey ammonite, made of stone like the stone it lies in, and brown ones, the ones we find past Charmouth." And then it seemed a lamp had begun to glow in her mind. "But in each of these materials, there be ammonites with ridges or ammonites without."

"Yes!" cried Miss Philpot. "We could sort them by substance or sort them by form. But let us begin by identifying each one as to form. In such a fashion, we will learn." She sprang over to the bookshelf and pulled a large book down and laid it on the table. After she had leafed through it for a moment, she called Mary over and showed her, and Mary saw with a lurch that Miss Philpot was inviting her to read.

On the open page were two illustrations of ammonites. Mary bent her face over the book and stared at the print that filled the bottom half of the page. The two other Miss Philpots, sitting on either end of a divan, turned their faces towards her, and her father looked sharply up from the corner where he was giving a last polish to the cupboard, and she put her finger to the lines, the way Joseph did when he read. *The ammonite shell* (she said in a forceful voice, as from the pulpit) *contains a series of progressively larger chambers. Only the final and largest chamber was occupied by the animal at any given time. As the animal grew, it generated newer and larger chambers, abandoning its previous home.*

When she got to the limit of the words she knew from Mr. Buckland's letter, she halted in confusion. Her father had turned away, he stood with his head down, but the Philpot sisters watched her still, their eyes anxious. Elizabeth Philpot let out a laugh of surprise and looked down at the page and then up at Mary, her mouth caught in a nervous twist, and then she picked up the book and began to read aloud from it herself.

The next week, Miss Philpot stopped by the shop and told Molly that the grammar school was offering free places to apt scholars among the poor – four free places. One day shortly after, Richard was in Charmouth, so Molly and Mary put on their Sunday bonnets and Molly asked Mrs. Bennett to mind the little ones while they went to the school. A senior scholar came to the door of the school and went to call the master. But the master would not allow them into the hall to speak to him; he refused Mary outright as a Dissenter. Her mother heard this with bitterness (months had passed now without any of them darkening the door of the Independent Chapel) and she did not refrain from telling Richard when he came home. If he was angry that they had asked for charity, he did not say so. He said only that the Independent Chapel itself was setting up a Sunday school and if they found a teacher, Mary would go there. "On Sundays, I go to the shore," said Mary, and he said, "Ye'll go to the shore no more if there's the chance of school."

Mary ached with shame that Miss Philpot would think she had set out to trick her. The lie was in the way she put her finger to the print – children who went to school did so, they ran their fingers along the lines in exactly that fashion. But it was not entirely a lie: the meaning of letters was in her brain, just as numbers had always been. If only she were given books and the time to bear down on them, she would certainly produce the sense on her own, and much more nimbly than other children! She thought of their neighbour Annie Bennett's pitiful attempts to read, and the botched writing she'd seen produced by scholars from the grammar school, Joseph among them.

But Mary Anning was not like other children. The whole town knew the story of the lightning bolt, with Mary herself at the centre of it, a little lass of under two years. Everyone told the story to explain Mary's cleverness. They enjoyed dwelling on what a dull child she'd been before, a girl who hardly spoke and whose hair was the colour of mud. They told how a woman named Eliza Hastings had stopped by the workshop with talk of an amusement being held at Rack Field – a lottery, the prizes being a copper tea kettle and a leg of mutton, and horsemen making a display of their riding. Eliza Hastings offered to take Mary, and when Richard and Molly agreed, little dull Mary came happily out and took Eliza's hand. And then, out on the field, a storm blew up. When the rain began, Eliza Hastings snatched Mary up from the ground and sought shelter under a giant oak, where two girls already huddled. And there the lightning bolt found them and the massive oak was split. Mrs. Stock was one who liked to tell it. "Dead in a trice!" she would cry. "Eliza Hastings, Fanny Fowler, Martha Drower! And *you* knocked insensible, stinking of brimstone." Mrs. Stock would turn her eyes up into her head so that only the whites showed, to demonstrate the look of Mary.

Mary listened to this story skeptically. If only she could have been a watcher in the field that day, to see what had really happened to her other, duller self. Thunder must have echoed from the cliffs, although no one ever mentioned thunder. She could see the lightning swing from the sky like a great hairy rope, electric fluid pouring down it. The crowd in the meadow must have taken a breath and thanked Providence that they could still do so. And then someone would have cried out, "Look!" and all eyes would have gone to the oak tree, where the child Mary Anning lay as dead in a dead woman's arms. When Mary turned her mind to the scene that followed, the story grew in fullness, words coming out on its branches the way blossoms come out on an apple tree. Mary would never be able to tell it properly – her tongue was enslaved to Dorsetshire speech. But no matter: the moment its branches were filled in, the story assumed a voice, bypassing Mary's tongue and flowing out of Mary's mind:

Father and Mother were in the workshop when came the news of this heavenly lottery and the unfortunate mortals selected by it. On the heels of the news rode a horseman on a tall chestnut stallion, carrying my senseless body in the crook of one arm. No one could countenance it, so many of the Anning children having been seized already by an ill fate. Doctor Reeves was sent for and said I must be dipped in water. And so they rapidly undressed me, and before the congregation of them all, my naked infant body was immersed. At the touch of the water, I roused myself and then I spoke, although no one can recall my utterance on that occasion, the nineteenth day of August in the Year of Our Lord 1800. My salvation by immersion did not convert my parents to Baptists, as one might suppose. They remained members of the Independent Chapel, and credit my cleverness to the vitalizing effects of fork lightning.

There were the accents of the high-born in that voice. It was the voice of Miss Elizabeth Philpot, Mary realized suddenly.

But the school did not open. Mary grew like a heron that year; she was powerful thin. There was seldom meat on their table, and all the fish from the shore went into salt barrels for the navy or by stage to London, where it fetched a better price. Her mother began to fret about the colour of the bread they were eating, and went to the baker and accused him of putting gypsum in it. Percival still spit back his food and did not grow, and Molly still talked of Exeter. Then a lady's maid from that very town stopped by the curiosity table, and when Mary overheard where she was from, she went to call her mother. Molly eagerly asked the woman what she had heard of the seventh son who worked as a healer, whether she knew the family's name. "Higgins," said the woman. "On Bobbin Lane. They be neighbours of my father. I know them well." But she would not confide in Molly as to the extent of the boy's powers. All she would say was that an older brother, the sixth son, had sickened and died that year.

"What is a seventh son when his brother has died?" Molly cried in bed that night.

They needed something, something to anchor them. As she lay on her pallet and listened to the waves beat against the seawall, Mary had the sense that they were on a narrow platform above it, just an inch away from being washed away, the lot of them. Her father knew it too — he was looking for the crocodile bones after all, tramping the shore every chance he had. Mr. Buckland had put a price on his enthusiasm: twenty pounds, he'd said, for the whole skeleton with all its parts. Twenty pounds! In his best week as a cabinetmaker, Richard made fourteen shillings. So now he walked the shore at low tide and high, clambering up to examine a promising layer, thrusting his shovel in every crumbling ledge. A lunatic, dangerous occupation – Mrs. Stock came by the cottage to impress this on Molly.

Mr. Buckland had left Lyme Regis for a time, but now he was back. They would run into him on the shore and greet him and then drift apart, bent over the rocks with searching eyes. But often when Mary looked up, her father and Buckland had come together again, the wind whipping and snapping at their clothes, their heads bent close in conversation. The wind took up their voices and blew them back in snatches, mixing them with the cries of the gulls and curlews and the crash of the waves. Mary longed to listen, but if she picked up her tools and scrambled over the rocks, they'd have separated before she reached them.

"How could a creature turn to stone?" Mary asked her father while they walked home one day. She was thinking of the mushy bodies of snails rotting in broken shells on the path.

"Drop by drop, the flesh washes out and the stone washes in," said her father. "So the fellow says. He shows me a verteberry and says it's the backbone of a crocodile. Are ye telling me the curiosities be the remains of ordinary martel creatures? I says to him, and he says, I'd never dare tell ye that. A man said it once and they locked him in the Bastille and starved him to death."

"Why would they lock him up?"

"It's alchemy, ain't it. Flesh rots, it don't turn to stone." The sun was high, it shone crimson through her father's nostrils. His thin face was pale, the skin under his eyes was smudged. She thought of Mr. Buckland with his fleshy, high-spirited face. Beside Mr. Buckland, her father was a ragged sparrow.

They angled up the foreshore to where the way was smoother, and Richard began to sing his walking song:

Think'st thou that I have any need
On slaughtered bulls and goats to feed,
To eat their flesh and drink their blood?
The sacrifices I require
Are hearts which love and zeal inspire
And vows with strictest care made good.

It was his only hymn and he never sang it right through, but brought out a verse of it from time to time. Two years before, he'd been up on Church Cliffs when the land fell away under his feet. But he was not like other men – he'd ridden on top of the landslip and landed unhurt on the shore. Now he'd had a taste of death on the cliffs, the way Joseph and Mary'd had a taste of the pox, and he was safe from it.

As Mary lay in the dark, she turned her thoughts to the seventh son in Exeter, dislodged from his place in the family by the death of another. At first, it seemed he had been chosen, as she had been. At a time when she was too young to know what she was, a lightning bolt had killed three others, but Mary Anning it had taken from one sort of child and turned to another. Even her hair was improved, becoming a rich, glistening black. The lightning bolt did not heal – it transformed. But whether its transforming powers had been exhausted in her on that August day ten years ago, she did not know.

I n Uncle Alger's house in Bristol, he's given a bedchamber
that was shut up for years, a perfectly square, whitewashed
room with one wide window. The bed itself is a hulking
affair, two hundred years old and fitted with brocade. The fireplace is still boarded over and a smell of must exudes from the
curtains. Henry keeps the window open when he can. It looks onto
the garden of the house next door, where a tangle of blackberry
vines and the dried spikes of delphiniums rise out of the mist.

This is the house where his father was raised. It's not one of
the great merchant houses of Bristol, but a two-storey thatched
cottage. The heyday of sugar was past by the time the De la
Beches came to the trade. It was as chief justice that Henry's
grandfather went to Jamaica, leaving his twin sons in Bristol with
their mother. He had accepted a four-year term, but he took to
island living and found the money to purchase Halse Hall and
never set foot in England again. When he died, the Bristol house
was left to Alger and the plantation to Henry's father, an uneven
bequest on the face of it, for the plantation comprised four and
a half thousand acres, and its hundred-year-old great house was

the finest in Clarendon County. But not so unfair when you consider that Henry's father had to sell his commission to go to Jamaica, and that when he arrived, he had first to remove a Creole wife and his father's five natural children from the great house and set them up in the nearby town of May Pen, then to arrange a mortgage to settle the generous bequests to these surprising relations, a branch of the family not acknowledged in any way in the house in Bristol. No, not so uneven after all.

There is, in the drawing room, a grand painting of Halse Hall itself, with a grey curtain hung in front to keep the sunlight and flies off. In fact, the drawing room is crammed with paintings, and Henry spends afternoons unveiling them one by one, setting himself the exercise of seeing something new in each one. He always starts with his favourite, a painting signed *Chardin*. A robed monkey looks at coins with a magnifying glass and a discriminating eye. He's an antiquarian by profession, a model of decorum. His hair is white over the temples and brushed neatly back. Curled on the rug lies his tail. For the first time, Henry notices a stove smoking into the room, warming the monkey's naked long-toed feet, the most human part of him, somehow.

Next to the intelligent monkey is a portrait of Uncle Alger and Henry's father as small boys. They're about eight, identical brown-haired boys dressed like miniature men in red jackets and riding boots. One stands with a hand buried in the ruff of a collie, light playing over his eager face. The other, erect with a testament in the crook of his arm, turns a sober and wary eye to the painter, as though he's sulking from a morning scolding. Whenever Alger catches Henry studying the painting, he bustles over to assert his identity as the more appealing child, to claim possession of the dog, recall the sittings, what a trial it was to get the dog to stand still. He'll discourse for hours on the entertaining question of how he differed from his twin brother and how he was the same.

But what an exercise, to paint identical children – to represent, through pigment and brush stroke, two opposite natures in the same form! Henry studies the boy with the dog. How do you paint curiosity? As a glow laid onto the temples, he decides: white flake and lead-tin yellow in equal proportions. He gets the magnifying glass from the map stand and holds it up, gazing into the swirls of Kassel umber that make up the eye itself. The eye (he chooses to believe it is his father's eye) looks warmly back through a dab of zinc white.

At the beginning, there was just twenty minutes between them. Uncle Alger was born while Henry's father lay wailing in a receiving blanket and the doctor was out in the latrine, thinking his day's work done. The women were pouring tea and waiting for the afterbirth when out came a foot! How could you have a second infant in your stomach and not know it? Henry carries this question over to the next painting, a portrait of his grandmother dressed in a handsome gown in the Chinese style that accentuated her homeliness, her hair powdered and her hands folded over her stomach, hands arranged to display her wedding ring (a fretted gold band with some sort of pebble mounted in it).

Alger comes in, wigless, his hair chopped short and unevenly powdered. Sullivan follows with two glasses of port on a tray. From the armchair by the hearth, Alger moves through his preparatory throat clearing. "A lady in London has been left a fortune of 1,800,000 gold sovereigns!" he announces finally. He's labouring over the London *Times*, brought to him courtesy of the daredevils on the Bristol post. "Think of it! Reckoning sixty sovereigns to the troy pound, that's a weight of thirteen tons, seven hundredweight, twelve pounds."

"Indeed, you are quick," says Henry.

"It's all here, they've done the sums for you. The ordinary man needs assistance in comprehending this sort of wealth, and the *Times* has kindly provided it. This is how we must think of it: if porters were hired to carry the coin, and each of them carried 298 pounds, 107 porters would be required."

"Why not give each porter an even three hundred?" asks Henry, pulling the settle closer to the fire. As he sits down, his father stands momentarily on the edge of his vision, on the edge of the veranda at Halse Hall, dark-haired in the sun. He's dressed in white, his face looking questioningly down to Henry, who's on the lawn below. Sums — was his father talking sums? And then his father is swallowed up again, swallowed by Alger's moving mouth.

"Why, it's the weight of a sack of flour, isn't it," the mouth says. "That's all you can ask of a labouring man, however stout. Ten weeks, two days and four hours it would take those porters. It's all here, they've worked it all out here."

"But where are they carrying it from and to?" Henry asks. "And why are they moving it at all?"

"Why, *I* don't know, do I?" cries the mouth, irritated. "To her marriage home, I suppose." The tumbler is raised to mottled lips, the pleated throat pumps warm port downward. "Now there's a match for you, supposing she could be prevented from discovering your recent history!" The corners of the mouth turn down; this is in the nature of a joke. "Although the lady in question is twenty-six. Twice your age, what?"

"No," says Henry, reaching for his own drink. "I'm fifteen in February."

For the first week in Bristol, while Henry's scabs fall off and his bruises bloom privately brighter by the day, it is Alger who presents a wounded aspect to the world. His inaugural duty as paterfamilias hangs over them: the speech castigating Henry and all youthful folly, evoking Henry's honourable, tragically dead father, rendering in dark strokes a life of failure and disgrace. A speech that remains undelivered, although Alger alludes to it from time to time. No doubt he worked it to a perfection of furious rhetoric in his mind and thinks he's delivered it.

In any case, Henry's uniform, which he's still wearing, is a moment-by-moment reminder of what he was and is no longer. In the famous Marlow mutiny five years back, all conspirators were stripped of every vestige of uniform by drummers – jacket, cap, boots, braid, in full public view – and driven out of town in their underwear. No one spoke of drummers in Henry's case. Of course, there was real arson in the 1806 mutiny, not just incendiary drawings. But daily, annoyingly, needlessly, Alger forbids Henry to leave the house, banishes him at the sound of the door. Soon Henry will divest himself of the uniform and then it's just his name that will remind people. For all time. So said the king's envoy when signing the writ.

A trunk of Henry's civilian clothes finally arrives, packed up and sent on by the housekeeper at Dawlish. He can't get into anything. Alger agrees to communicate to Henry's mother the extent of her son's rampant growth. A week later, a bank draft arrives and a list of what his mother deems necessities. A frock coat, a dress coat, an overcoat, *four* morning coats. Alger sends for his tailor. Bolts of wool are carried into the upstairs sitting room and fittings conducted. Gradually, the wardrobe in his bedroom fills. He's being costumed for a drawing-room life. It is a hermetic life he wants.

He could weep with relief at having his own room again. Before Marlow, he never contemplated the fact of a barracks. The bodies packed in rows like stalls, the quarrelling and crying out, the bedbugs, the rats, the foul smells. The insane laughter, the tiresome pranks, your response at every moment scrutinized to decide whether you were more truly a pillock or a ponce. Oh, they were the sultans of minute discrimination! He stands by the window and breathes the vile air of it out of him. *Burn in the flames of hell*, he cries to the barracks at Marlow.

With its heavy brocade curtains, his bed is a Bedouin tent. Henry opens the tent and sits cross-legged inside it. The tent takes him back to the bed nets of his childhood, hung against mosquitoes. He has no memory of anything before Jamaica. When he woke up to himself, he was running on the road with Belle's sons Cuthbert and Ben (it's the road to the boiling-house, they're rolling an iron hoop, passing it back and forth between them with sticks). And then they're in Belle's cabin, and Tallo is there, it's the dinner break, and he's whittling a green coconut open for them with the cutlass he keeps hidden in the floor, and they're drinking thin, sweet milk and scooping the jellied flesh out with their fingers. Then they're stealing through the bush, on wickered paths that wind through dense foliage, Henry and Cuthbert and Ben, tormenting themselves with the terror of duppies, who look human but have their feet put on backwards.

One day, the three of them were brothers, creeping around in the bush, and the next, the grass gang was walking up the road and Cuthbert and Ben were part of it, loads of wet grass for the livestock on their heads, loads like haystacks — they were swaying under the weight of them and Henry knew them only by their skinny black legs. Sophie, a great beautiful girl they all admired, was driving them with a switch. Henry ran towards Cuthbert and Ben on the road, thinking to tease them when they couldn't see him for their loads, and Sophie laughed at him and said, "You go back now, massa Henry, these boys be mine."

Peter, the houseboy, was sweeping the veranda when Henry went back. "Henry vex," he said sympathetically.

Darkness has fallen on the neighbour's garden and in Henry's room. The butler knocks; he's come to light the lamps. Henry kicks a chair against the door by way of response. He pulls the bed curtains closed and curls into the cave of his bed. He's at Halse Hall, he's sitting at a table for his lessons and his father sits beside him. It seems that Father discovered Henry when Cuthbert and Ben were taken into the grass gang.

Mrs. Sutton from Sutton Estates is there (she is always there, she comes on horseback and stays for days) and she and his mother are in rocking chairs drinking glasses of rum punch, although they have only just finished their dinner. The dogs are out – everyone is worked up because a slave is missing. Sophie. Henry's father requests that Mother and Mrs. Sutton sit somewhere else so as not to further distract the boy, but they will not. They sit on the veranda to admire the view of the Mocho Mountains and because the house is too hot – they are likely to suffocate, says his mother, if required to sit inside.

Father went to May Pen that morning to post a notice of the missing slave, but he is back now for Henry's lesson. Father is teaching Henry because it has dawned on him that Henry speaks fluent Creole and precious little English. "You said he should not be one of those mollycoddled plantation sons," his mother says. "And now you find reason to reproach me for what he is." And so Henry must sit on the veranda and listen to the far-off baying of the dogs, and his father teaches him the history of Jamaica under the English. It begins with General Venables, from whose mistakes many lessons can be drawn. General Venables was sent by Oliver Cromwell to take the great Spanish island of Hispaniola. He anchored his ships at a beach he believed to be 10 miles from the Spanish stronghold of Santa

Domingo. In reality, Santa Domingo was 35 miles away. (*How many extra miles was that?* Father asks, and Henry says, *15.* Mrs. Sutton laughs and his father says, *No, 25.*) The men tramped through the jungle for days. They got dysentery and yellow fever and finally were forced to retreat. So Venables took to the sea again and conquered Jamaica instead, as a sop for Cromwell. But Cromwell was not impressed and had Venables thrown into the Tower.

The mournful sound of the conch rings out and Henry stirs. The two-hour midday break is over; the slaves will be returning to the fields. Mrs. Sutton gets up and comes to the edge of the veranda. Her hair is wet to her head with perspiration. She has an over-wide smile. "He was thrown into the Tower for cowardice," she cries. "He pulled up anchor and sailed away in the dead of night, abandoning hundreds of men who had not yet gained the ships. And tell the boy why, Colonel De la Beche!" She does not give him a chance to speak. "Henry, precious, the silly man fled in the night because, in his addled brain, he thought he heard the Spanish army approaching. And the Spanish army was nowhere near. It was *fiddler crabs* migrating – that was the sound he heard in the jungle!" Henry's father gives his chair a hitch in irritation.

Mrs. Sutton peers down the carriage road. The house is on high ground – you can see the whole plantation from the veranda. She points out that the slaves are still down at the cabin-line and out on the road. Henry can hear the dogs baying. Sophie will not be caught, he thinks – she will go to Spanish Town to look for Tom, who was sold last week. The dogs will never find her. They're still on the plantation, following the bush paths where the duppies wander. His father turns to look at Mother, who has tied a turban around her head to hold her hair up off her neck, and he questions how much rum punch she is drinking at this time of day. "My complexion needs replenishing," she says, "from all this perspiration. Anyway, don't bother about me. You should be going down. Go down and send them back to the fields."

"Leave it to Tomkin," Father says. He gives his chair another hitch. This is dangerous, because granny-sugar is pouring out of holes where the termites are eating it. Any minute now, that chair will collapse into a pile of hollow sticks, as others have done. He reaches for a clean sheet of paper and writes numbers on it. They'll leave the history and switch to pure sums, which may be of less interest to their audience. Father sets Henry the sum of 22 and 41, and then leans towards him and says softly, "Consider how many tens are in each of them." Then the houseboy Peter is at the edge of the veranda wanting to speak, an anguished expression on his face. He says in Creole that they have found an armadillo down at the creek. He is an Igbo – his Creole is unique to him. Henry repeats what Peter said for his father and mother. He translates it exactly, although he understands from Peter's face that it is not an armadillo, it's something else they've found, that Peter can't bring himself to say.

"An armadillo!" says his father. "Let's go down and have a look!" He goes eagerly down the steps of the veranda and Henry follows. They cross the sloping lawn and hurry onto the road, and by then, terrified, grieving cries are rising up from the creek, and people are running towards it from all directions. His father begins to run. Peter is running with them; he reaches down for Henry's hand. When they come out into the creek bed, the whole plantation is there, and the slaves part so they can come through. Tomkin is splashing across the creek from the other side, the dogs on leash. Henry glimpses a figure lying at the creek edge (a duppy, the way its feet are splayed) and then his father yanks him up by the armpits and plunks him onto Peter's back and shoves them back towards the road.

Henry rolls over in his bed. He tries to call up Sophie's face, but the face of the woman he saw on display in Piccadilly has overlain it. But then he thinks of being out on the veranda early on a Sunday morning and he sees Sophie coming down from the provision grounds in the hills. She's going to the market in May Pen, walking tall and proud with a stupendous tray of pawpaw on her head, and she flashes him a smile.

Eventually, Alger receives a letter from Henry's mother. She has nothing to say to Henry. "I have nothing to say to Henry," she writes in the only line Alger will show him, isolating it through assiduous folding. After two days, Alger lets fall the news that Henry and his mother are to settle in the coastal town of Lyme Regis when his mother condescends to send for him. *Lyme Regis?* Alger can cast no light; he endeavours to know as little as possible of his sister-in-law's doings. On the subject of watering places, he tells Henry over tea and oatcakes of going to Brighthelmstone to take the cure. It was a nasty business. It involved drinking a gallon of sea water each morning and then surrendering to the will of the hired dippers, who, once contracted, ensured that you were fully submerged, whatever your final thoughts on the matter. "It was anti-septic," he says, tea dribbling down his chin. "Anti-bilious. Anti-spasmodic. It did me a world of good."

After the letter, Henry understands that his mother has abandoned him in Bristol until he shall make something different of himself. For his sins, he is sentenced to a season of whist with Alger, the Widow Rankin (Alger's only constant friend), and Sullivan to make up a fourth. He writes to Clement pleading for money and for intelligence regarding his mother. Instead, a cart stops on the road and a case of books is delivered. Clement's house has been heartlessly sold. After eight years, he's been flung from his rooms and would have perished on the pavement but for the charity of his old friend Marshall Bentley. Henry may have the books on loan for the duration. It's a collection of titles recently talked about in West End drawing rooms. Most of the books have an unread smell and feel; many of them are uncut. Among them, though, is a worn edition of *Muller's Artillery*, the forty octavo pages of which they were assigned to copy at Marlow. He was on *sea-mortars* when he was hauled away to the guardhouse. That's his biggest regret, leaving his copybook behind, and the half-finished drawing of the sea-mortars, with their shaded chambers. He asks his uncle for money to buy a folio and charcoals, and sets to work where he left off.

The gardener comes in to pry the fireplace open. The upstairs maid is with him with a bucket of kindling. Winter is coming; it's time he had a fire in the morning. They'll start by burning the boards that sealed the fireplace. The nails squeak in the boards as the crowbar gains a purchase. And then the maid screams and scrambles back. Henry turns and looks with the gardener into the hearth. A pile of tiny bones, the remains of some terrible destruction. They're intact, miniature skeletons. "Birds," says the maid, crouching on the floor with her face turned away. "They flew down the chimney and couldn't find their way out. This room's been closed up since the war began. It's birds, it's terrible bad luck, Mr. Henry. Walter will clean them out."

Henry has lit a candle by then and he holds it in the hearth. He can count seven or eight skeletons lying in a soft bed of ash and down. They're ancient, intricate, anomalous life forms. It's a desert scene – they perished of thirst.

"No," he said. "Don't. I'll do it."

He picks one out carefully and lays it on his sketching paper. It's like picking up nothing. With its guts gone to dust, this is what a bird weighs. It's intact, its wings a close fan of quills. Its skull and beak curve downward, bent in supplication. At the end of long straight legs, claws clench in spasmodic appeal.

"Find me a box to put them in," he says to the maid. "I want to draw them."

the English ...

... ...

·❧{ S E V E N }❧·

Finally, the Independent Chapel found a teacher, and every Sunday Mary sat on a bench with smaller children and learned her letters and the queer way they were used. She learned why pounds are marked *L* (it is the Latin *libra*) and why pence are marked *d* (for *denarius*), but why the English should choose to use Latin words for their own coin her teacher Mr. Pippen could not explain. He was a kindly man, but he lacked curiosity – the small store of his learning lay drying in his brain like the butterflies pinned into a collecting cupboard at the Philpots'. This was just the ragged school (so it was called in the town); her mother said she should be grateful the man could read and write. But in spite of Mr. Pippen's dullness, in spite of the other students hiding sticks up their sleeves to poke her from behind when she was called on to recite, the ragged school, which had such a feeble effect on ordinary children, was a potent tonic to Mary and within four Sundays she could read.

And then she read every day to her father. She sat up on the stool and held the book to the window to save lighting a candle. With every passing day she improved, until her reading was as quick and accurate as Miss Philpot's. This would never be believed in another scholar, but was believed in her because of the lightning.

It was a bible she read from. They did not own a bible; they owned no books at all since the *Rights of Man* was burned. But then Mr. Buckland came to their door one day, as he had business to conduct with their father. He walked directly into the house and Molly brought the rush chair for him to sit on. He still wore his dusty gown, but he took off his top hat. No longer just a student of Undergroundology, Mr. Buckland was now a fellow at Corpus Christi College in Oxford, where he taught young men to read the Gospel in the text of the earth. For example (he told Mary, pointing with the toe of his boot to the coals glowing in the hearth), they noted the way the Creator laid coal into the ground, with the seams tilted up to the surface at one end. "This is our Father's beneficence writ in the earth," he said, "the coal laid down for man's ready access."

"On behalf of the citizenry of Lyme Regis, let me congratulate ye on yer advancement," said Richard dryly. But Mr. Buckland was eager to deflect the honour from himself. It was to the credit of the dons at the University of Oxford, he said, that they chose men of faith for academic positions, aware of the danger that learning could be perverted against the interests of God's revealed Word. In France, for example, clever men not content with throwing over the political order now insisted on studying natural history with the feeble light of their own intelligence rather than the light of Scripture.

Lizzie stared reproachfully at Buckland from where she sat under the table and Buckland stopped his lecture and made a funny face at her. "You should come to my kitchen," he said. "I keep a monkey tethered to a pole. What do you think my monkey eats?"

"Crumbs?" said Lizzie.

"No, no, no, it's far too clever for that. It guards the crumbs for the black beetles and when the beetles grow fat, it eats the beetles."

Joseph had come to hover in the doorway and Richard sent him to the workshop to bring up the fossils they'd found and kept for Mr. Buckland. There was a jaw Richard had found at Pinhay Bay; Lizzie shrank further under the table at the sight of its sinister teeth. It was as big as a horse's jaw – Richard had had to borrow a sling from the porter to carry it home. He had laid it on the workbench and chipped it out of its matrix with his chisels, and Mary had counted the teeth. There were sixty. It was not a crocodile, Mr. Buckland said to their disappointment. He showed them how the sharp pointed teeth grew in a furrow, like a fish's, not in separate sockets, the way a crocodile's did. But he offered Richard a guinea for it.

They had three verteberries, each as broad across as Joseph's outstretched hand. When he saw them, Mr. Buckland stripped off his black gown and his waistcoat and turned himself around and had Joseph hold up one of the verteberries to compare it in size to his backbones. He stopped just short of pulling up his shirt to show them his bare white back, and while Mary recovered from the shock of seeing a gentleman strip off his waistcoat in their kitchen, Mr. Buckland stood by the hearth in his shirt sleeves and told them about the giants that lived somewhere on the earth, as described in the sixth chapter of Genesis. "I would like to think these vertebrae are human," he said. "We know the cliffs here were made by the Flood, and God sent the Flood to wipe out a generation of evil men, but we have not yet found the remains of man among the fossils."

He was holding one of the vertebrae and he ran his finger around its outside edge. "But no. There is more of the fish about this. You see, it's concave on two sides. I'll make a sketch of it to send to Cuvier in France." He sat back down in his chair and told them then about the scientist Monsieur Cuvier, who had made such a study of the animal kingdom that if you gave him one bone, he could immediately tell you what animal it came from. Georges Cuvier did not base his work on Holy Scripture and so his studies often led him to a false understanding of the world. But there was no one as informed as he about animal anatomy. Once, Cuvier's students dressed up as devils, wearing cow horns tied to their foreheads, and crept into his chamber in the night calling, "Cuvier, Cuvier, we have come to eat you." Monsieur Cuvier opened his eyes and said, "All creatures with hoofs and horns are herbivores," and fell back asleep.

While Buckland slapped his hand on his knee and laughed at his own joke, Mary thought of the pig-faced lady seen from time to time in London. What would Mr. Cuvier make of her?

"I would like to have a scientific book, like Miss Philpot has," she said boldly as Mr. Buckland got up to leave with the stone vertebrae in hand.

In all likelihood, it was a *Sowerby* the Philpots owned, he told her. He went out to where his horse was tied in the street and rooted through one of the many pouches strapped to his saddle and came back with a book. "This is all the science you will ever need," he said, handing it to her. "You want no better teacher than Moses." It was not the Sowerby, but a bible.

She was disappointed, but Molly was very glad. Though Molly could not read it herself, she was glad just to have it lying on her mantel, and this was something Mary understood.

"I wish I had lived in Genesis," people always said, and Mary thought of a land where the earth was new, it was always springtime, and the trees were supple and green. But *Genesis* was not a place; it was a book within the big book of the bible, and it told the story of how God made all that was. The paper was thin and yellowing, and tiny type covered more pages than Mary could ever read in her life. Holding it flat on her knee, Mary sat up on the stool and read in a sermonizing voice:

> *And God said, Let the waters bring forth abundantly the moving creature that hath life, and fowl that may fly above the earth in the open firmament of heaven. And God created great whales, and every living creature that moveth, which the waters brought forth abundantly, after their kind, and every winged fowl after his kind: and God saw that it was good.*

When her father had had enough and set off for the Three Cups, she often slipped down into the workshop with the bible and lit a rushlight there so she could continue to read without interruption. It was the mystery of reading that thrilled her as much as the words did. *Winged fowl.* In those tiny letters and her eyes moving across them was the seagull stroking its way across the harbour on snowy feathers. In words like tiny ants lay the heaving sea and the whale lifting its massive bulk, the varnished waves torn open and all their hidden depths revealed. She sat and read until the huge tableau threatened to drown her and drove her out of the house and along the seawall. There the roaring wind and the waves beating on the rock and the cold spray falling on her face scoured out her mind and gave her relief.

In cold climates, hairy elephants were found in the earth, their flesh frozen. Buckland had told her. *Mammoths*, they were called, a word for the earth mole, for they were always found buried and it was thought they lived underground and died when they came into contact with the light. Elephants living in tunnels under the earth! Georges Cuvier had looked closely at their jawbones and said they were not the same species as the elephants that now lived. He said the mammoths had all died and were no more. He said that the earth and the creatures on it in ages past were very different from today, that over and over again terrible catastrophes had wiped out the life on earth and God had replaced it with a new and different world.

Mr. Buckland told them this — it was an example of Monsieur Cuvier's apostasy. "Everything God makes endures," said Mr. Buckland, quoting Scripture. Richard asked where the hairy mole-elephants were to be found now, and Mr. Buckland said, "America."

They did ciphers at the ragged school, but she had lost her love of numbers. It was words that pressed on her now. The store of numbers was set at nine. There were no new numbers. But there were new words. Mr. Buckland's word *fossil*. It was a word they used in France: things dug out of the ground. There was a need for new texts — the bible explained many things, but not all. If I can read with such ease, I can certainly write, thought Mary. She would broach the question that so interested her father and Mr. Buckland, the nature of the stony curiosities found on the shore and in the cliffs, which question Genesis did not appear to touch. She resolved to ask her father for some pages from his accounts book. If Mr. Buckland will not give me a book about curiosities, Mary said to herself, I will give him one. I will post my text to him. She saw Mr. Buckland standing in a grand doorway, turning the letter over in his hand to see what was written on the front: *To Mr. Buckland at Oxford University from Miss Mary Anning.* She saw him breaking the seal to open it and her brain sketched it out.

Unless it be frozen (she would begin), *a body will rot in the grave. It will not turn to stone. The stone eagles carved in front of the Great House on Broad Street were always stone and never alive. It were not within the powers of the stonemason to breathe life into them. God worked as the stonemason works. The curiosities were the stony matter of all creatures before God breathed life into them. Some were sports of the Creator: for respite on the Sabbath, He fashioned certain forms with never a thought of breathing life into them, and left them scattered in the cliffs. They were not dead. They were less than the creatures that walked the earth and now lay rotting in their graves. They had never lived. And yet they endured.*

She put the bible on the workbench and pinched out the light and went up the steps to the kitchen. Molly sat on the bench rocking Percival. "Put the bread to soak," she said, and Mary realized with astonishment that her mother had no idea of the thoughts that roiled in her mind. All her mother cared about was coals collected on the foreshore and washing hung on the bushes by Church Cliffs. Mary's mind was an invisible world that no one else entered.

Mary wrote her first text at home, sitting for many hours in Richard's empty workshop, where the smell of shavings hung. She left the Undergroundology alone for the moment; her ideas sat within her like a mass of the lias cliff, awaiting excavation, and one day, when she knew which thread to follow into the mass, she would do it. But for now, she wrote another of the stories that came to her when she lay on her pallet in the night. She did not show it to her mother, but stayed back at the school and showed it to Mr. Pippen:

Two Sisters of Mary Anning, Both Departed

The first of my sisters were a girl named Martha my mother tells that as a babe she had a way of crawling up the kwilt of a morning to peel Mother's Eye open and see if Mother be flown away in the night. She lived until a lippen May day when two lads at the shore entise some children to take up a woden Door that washed in from a Shiprek and float on it though the Tide be risin and they were sucked around the point crying when a wave spils them off and they all drown their Bodies never found. The Luptons on our road lost their Jane off that Door as well. It be well known in Lyme the two youts that did this and they be rightly shunned. The one joined Bony's navy and lies in the Sea but the other by name of Digby dwells in the Underclif and sells counterban and folk slip up the Path and buy their Tea from him today though not we.

Then the first Mary were born who they say were like me in every regard the thick black Hair and the way of starring I be scolded for. Then the year after her my brother Joseph who be now fourteen. For three years they held this Mary as their Mary. Until the day before our Saviour's birth in the year of our Lord 1798 when this Mary and my brother Joseph play by the herth and my mother goes down the street to take the rent to Mr. Axworthy because it be Saturday. A pile of shavins lay by the fire. For sport the children do pick up the shavins in their fingers and throw them on the fire and the fire flare and catch Mary's peticoat. Joseph but a little lad of two there be no one to smother the flames and Mary run into the street crying for our mother because the shop be closed up and Father down at the shore and the air fan the flames and she be terrible burned and die as night falls.

My mother had no Respit for she bore me some four month later and they give me the name of Mary and keep shavins in the house no more and warn me of the tides. In the year of our Lord 1799 I was born Mary Anning.

Mr. Pippen read it and water filmed his eyes. "The ending needs a homily," he said at last. "You must think what the homily will be." When she was silent, he suggested in a gentle tone, "Is it the suffering of this life that teaches our hearts to long for the next world?"

But she could not, she could not put a pen again to that paper. There was a homily of a sort in the last sentence, so it felt to her, and she took the story back home as it was.

·⊰[E I G H T]⊱·

O n nights when there was only barley gruel for supper, Mary closed her heart against the ghostly children. How would they ever have fed them all? But her mother seemed to find no comfort in sharing the pot into five bowls rather than ten. And yet, whenever they talked about the dead brothers and sisters, Molly said the same things. The story of little Martha crawling up the quilt to open her mother's eyes, for example. Molly had only one or two thoughts about each baby. How could you be so completely gone from the earth that you no longer lived even in your mother's mind? Not that Molly did not grieve – but it seemed to Mary that she grieved for all the babies as one.

Some days, Mary woke up stony towards her mother. Mary herself was pale and thin no longer. Her eyebrows were bold and straight, her face in the looking glass beginning to show the bones of the woman she would be. Molly did not notice; she thought of nothing but Percival. She would not cut his nails or his hair until he was fully weaned, and it seemed he never would be weaned, because he did not have the strength to swallow porridge. Molly fidgeted over him, she walked the floor with his wizened pixie face over her shoulder. When he slept, she laid him down and looked at him fondly, stroking his cheek with the back of her finger. "Pray keep your voice down," she said to Mary, as though Mary's strong voice were the cause of all their troubles. Mother would have sorrowed as much if all her children had lived and grown away from her (thought Mary on her stony days, hauling water from the spring in a bucket), for she found little pleasure in her big children now.

There was general misfortune and misfortune particular to them. All of Dorsetshire and Devonshire was hungry that year. Other joiners became undertakers. When people will not buy a china cabinet, they will find a way to buy a coffin. But Richard would not make coffins. When he did not have the capital to buy oak for the workshop, he collected on the shore, seizing every opportunity to look for one of the big stony crocodiles Mr. Buckland wanted. Whenever the tide would let him, he went back to Pinhay Bay, where he'd found the big jaw, and often he took Mary.

One day William Lock, the curi-man in Charmouth, sent word that he had something for Mr. Buckland, but Richard was busy with a cabinetry job all day and didn't have time to go. After supper, he went to the Three Cups and the sun was sinking over the Cobb when he came back in. When there was a drop of cider in him, he had a way of appearing in the doorway before you sensed him on the step. Once inside, a line of his song escaped him and he picked Lizzie up and tossed her so she squealed, and then he said he was walking to Charmouth.

"The tide will be in," said Molly.

"I'll take the path." He meant to walk up on the cliffs.

"What, in the dark?"

"It's wonderful bright." Richard went down to the workshop for his collecting bag and his wedge hammer and Mary knew he meant to collect along the shore on his way home; he was going now so he could collect at first light. No one else would do that. No one would climb the cliff path over Black Ven in the dark, not with three pints of cider in him. He's had a taste of death on the cliffs, Mary reminded herself, reaching up to touch her pox-marks, and he's safe from it. "I'll be back before you've had breakfast," he said.

It was Mary and Joseph who found him mid-morning the next day. Searching frantically from the cliff road, Mary spied him halfway down, lying on his side, a smudge of grey on a black ledge. He called up to them not to come down, so Mary stood on the path above him while Joseph went for help. The lip of the cliff was gouged by his boot where he'd skidded, going over. He had managed to hold on to his collecting bag; she could see it on the ledge with him. He did not look up at her again or speak. He lay on his side and seemed to be afraid to move. She watched the gulls circle the cliff until Joseph brought three men back with a rope. Mr. Lupton told Mary to step out of the way, so she stood back on the path and watched them put the rope down to him. He was able to tie it around his waist and then the men drew on it and shouted encouragement to him as he scrambled his way up. He came up over the edge of the cliff like a mackerel being pulled into a boat, and stood grinning on the path. His injuries were not so bad! But he was fainting with pain as he walked towards home.

They stopped at the first cottage on the Charmouth Road and the Widow Bradshaw who lived there said they must take one of the doors off her cowshed to carry him, and they did so, Joseph and Mr. Lupton on one side of the door, the wheelwright and his son on the other. Mary walked beside him into town, carrying his bag and hammer. Coming up Bridge Street, she saw sea shining lustrous in a gap between the prison and the town hall. She looked at her father's still white face with his eyes closed on the door, and for a terrible moment it seemed to her that the men walking on either side of him were the pallbearers carrying him to his grave. A gull hung motionless above them and a shadow crawled at the corner of her eye and she seemed to see a long, snaking line of friends and neighbours following in a procession, crepe tied to their hats and their heads bowed in sorrow. Among them was a lone mummer who had come to the door one winter's night, and she closed her mind to it and ran ahead to open the door.

He fell ill, an apt phrase for it because his illness began with the fall. They made up a pallet on the kitchen floor near the hearth so he would be warm, but when it seemed the convalescence would not be quick, Mr. Lupton brought in a cot. It was a sturdy cot; Richard himself had made it years ago. They did not spend coin on Doctor Reeves because Richard would not agree to be bled and there was nothing else. In all kindness, Farmer Ware brought an ass right to the door and milked it into a jug, and Richard drank it warm, warm ass's milk being a powerful tonic. Molly bought butter, a butter made from the milk of a cow that had grazed on the churchyard. He did not quarrel with her for it, he ate it, winking at Mary when Molly's back was turned. At first, he climbed the stairs to sleep, but then he did not. Molly would settle him for the night and Mary come in to see him lying on his side on the cot, the pot for night soil beside him. Molly herself sat with a rushlight lit on the table before her, not speaking, and Richard lay with his eye open and his cheek against the pillow.

Week by week, he grew whiter and thinner. His eyes burned black in his white face as though urgent thoughts were collecting in his mind, but he talked less and less, because his throat pained him. Instead, he coughed. It was a torture for them to hear him because they knew the pain his ribs were giving him. That winter, Mary polished up their store of fossils for sale at the table, and she wrote a text on the monstrosities. It was a slight, cramped thing in the end, not what she had imagined. Working with pen and paper, she could not capture the ideas that fluttered like moths in her head. She would not send this text to Mr. Buckland. She had written this one for her father.

"Ye must add," he said, handing it back to her with an admiring look, "*The remains of those animals that Noah wrongly judged could swim but could not.*" Which she liked, and did add, and set to work making a fine copy.

After she finished, Mary went upstairs and knelt by her parents' bed. She knelt until the sound of the sea outside the window had washed everything out of her mind. Then, in her prayer, she led her father up a smooth wide path. He walked beside her and leaned against her shoulder because of his weakness. She led him up to where God sat on his throne in a white robe, and said to God, *You must make him well.* She tried to raise her eyes to God's face, but she could not. He won't answer, she thought in despair. He has already answered. Why do I plague God when He has already shown me the end of it?

But was it *God* who had sent her the vision of her father being carried to his grave? Mary bent her head back into the cover. Oh, let it be black mischief sent to trouble me, she prayed. Let it be the Devil who sends me such visions! For only the Devil could wish such a thing, to take their father from them. *If I see it in a vision then*, she thought, laying her cheek against the cover and feeling peace wash through her, *the contrary will befall us. If I see his death, he will be well.*

Her father could not talk a great deal, but others talked. Friends came and sat in the kitchen all through the winter, Walter Jones and Mr. Dobson and Mr. Lupton. They sat and conversed heartily to Richard, even when Richard was too ill to respond. But there was something shamefaced about their manner to Molly – they would never meet her mother's eyes. Mr. Buckland visited when he came down from Oxford on the coach to carry out his studies on the shore. Miss Philpot came, carrying a pot of rich broth. And the baker John Besley in his white coat, carrying in a gallon loaf and the lovely smell of bread baking.

"Himself's back up to nine shillings," Mr. Besley said, pulling the rush chair up to the cot. The price of a bushel of corn, this was, for *Himself* was always the miller, for whom Mr. Besley had an intimate and dignifying hatred. Mr. Besley's hair was orange and his sidewhiskers and eyebrows were white, as though he had dropped his face in a bowl of flour. He leaned his elbows on his knees and looked at Richard with affection. It was clear now why Richard had abandoned them – he'd left them leaderless because he was ill. Soon he'd be well again, and then they'd show the miller! Mr. Besley looked around the room with kindly regard for them all, as though he had no memory of Molly standing in his shop not six months before, accusing him of cutting the flour with plaster.

He wanted to talk. He wanted to go back to the finest hour of his youth. Tenderly, he took them back to the Three Cups the night of the bread riot. He described how Richard had got their blood up, how he had persuaded Morris the bell-ringer to go to the tower and jangle the bells in the night, how they'd lit torches and run up and down the streets to get the dogs barking, to draw the sleeping townspeople out of the houses. *No man should profit from his neighbours in time of dearth*, he said, giving Richard the voice of an orator. "He were a true leader, this fellow," he cried. "He were such a leader, he made rebels of the women!"

Molly, sitting at the table cleaning oysters, said what she always said. "Women! It were faint-hearted men. They took to the streets with their faces whited over and wearing their wives' pinafores. They wanted a disguise to hide behind and it were the only disguise they had."

Mr. Besley looked at Molly fondly for her innocence and went on to tell how, at the mill – men and women together – they smashed windows and threw their torches in and tore the cribbing off the bins.

"But the magistrate did not arrest you," said Mary, to help him to the heart of the story.

"Oh, that cheese-paring old coot," scoffed Mr. Besley. "That cowheart! He sent his boy out to post a notice in the butter market, telling how bad his gout were and the trouble he would drop on us the instant he were well. Then he heard us a-laughing and his pride swoll up and he sent a man on horseback to the barracks at Weymouth. It were William Cooper who went, the weasel. He sold his neighbours for the joy of a bare-ridge ride to Weymouth on a fine horse. He had the grace to die there, not two month later. But he raised up the army, he did, and they rode in with guns to their shoulders, and there we were, not an arm to our names but the two arms God give every man. Nought we could do but prise up cobbles from the square to pitch at the soldiers. And so prise them up we did, and pitch them we did, by Christ!"

Mary looked eagerly at Richard, who sometimes joked about this scene. And her father had lifted his neck up from his pillow, his thin neck clamped rigid by a cough that would not come out of him. The cough was like a chunk of bread in his throat choking him – he sought her with desperate eyes. Molly leapt towards him and Mary ran for the water jug, and suddenly she heard a cry from Mr. Besley. She turned, and the hen was peering in unconcern under its wing, but the rest were seized as her father had been seized, all rigid around the cot, her mother bending towards him and Lizzie crouching with her little dolly, and Mr. Besley with horror on his kindly face, Mr. Besley in a white coat splashed with blood.

A consumption had laid hold of him and from that day on, it consumed him in a pitiless fashion. It seemed that the fall had broken a rib and the rib pierced a hole in his lung and let the consumption creep in. When James Wheaton heard, he came and sat in silence on the chair by the cot, his hand pressed to his brow and looking the whole time through his fingers. His lips were pulled into a grimace against his teeth. At the door, he finally spoke. "Let us pray for the night to come," he said, "for then the day will soon follow."

Mary ran after him out onto the street. She reached out and laid hold of the back of his jacket, unable to speak, and he turned and they stood looking at each other in Cockmoile Square. When her voice finally came, it was harsh, it was an accusation against his prayer. "Our Lord *healed* the sick," she cried. "It's on every page of the Gospels. I have read it." Standing in the square while rain drizzled on their heads, she railed against her mother also, for the charmed butter and the mulberry bush hanging over the cot. She railed against her father. "He does *despise* jommetry," she said, her voice shuddering out of her. "But he says nothing. He suffers her to do it."

"If he chided your mother, it might be that harsh words would be his last," James Wheaton said. "It is a good man's death he longs for."

When he was gone, Mary did not go back into the house. She walked quickly through the rain down Bell Cliff and stood against the seawall. It seemed clear that a curse had been visited on their father, the old witch's curse: *Ye will die by inches*. She was filled with fury at her mother, who opened the door to fear, who sucked them into witchery, who had tried to work a charm so hideous Mary could never tell James Wheaton, a charm too dark for his ears, worked in the darkest hour of a dark night. Mary had woken up and saw her mother gone from her bed, and a gasp came through the darkness. She thought then, This is his death come. She was wearing her cloak in her bed for warmth and she got up and stepped over Lizzie to go down, and from the stairs, she saw Molly on the cot, crouched over Father, rocking, her nightdress pulled up along her thighs. Mary melted back upstairs, but the image of their faces was pressed into her mind. It was not a coupling such as she had seen in dreams from her pallet; it was something different, the way Father lay, the orange light from the hearth on his face, his face and his shining eyes so alive, and Molly with her hair clutched back and her face like a skull, as though she was taking his death into her.

Her father died in a kitchen where a brown hen pecked and the prisoners roared outside the door. Molly wanted him to be carried upstairs to die peacefully in his bed, but he was in too much misery to be moved. In the last month, he was transformed to lizard, heated from without, and they begged what wood and coal they could and piled all the blankets over him. They tried to keep a fire going in the night; they crept back and forth up the stairs, Mary and Joseph and their mother. If his eyes were open, one of them would sit with him. Mary sat one night, and when it seemed he was asleep, she laid her head wearily on the cot beside him. He lifted a hand and rested it on her and she was soothed into sleep by the weight of his hand on her shoulder. When she woke up in the grey light of morning, he had lifted his hand to his eyes. "The poor man's clock," he said faintly when he saw she was awake. "What?" she whispered. "When ye can pick out the veins in your hand, it be time to rise," he said.

That was the last time he spoke to her. He was gone before Michaelmas, his spirit was gone, although it was winter before his breath ceased. It was God's grace to them that Percival died the afternoon of the same day and could be buried in the crook of his father's arm, where he so often lay in that last year.

How Mary's father had provided for his family through the last years of his living and the months of his dying then became clear. He had borrowed from every tradesman on Broad Street, and some in Charmouth and Uplyme.

The first to come to the door was Mr. Dobson. The week after the funeral, he stood on the doorstone and told Molly that he'd been lending Richard money, quite a lot of money, in all eighteen pounds, six shillings, tuppence. Not that he was trying to collect. He simply wanted her to know of his regard for Richard and the lengths he'd been prepared to go to see Richard comfortable, although he had seven children himself and his youngest babe not thriving. *Eighteen pounds*, Mary thought in wonder. But he was just the first. Some had chits of paper with Richard's signature on them. One man came from Axminster riding on an ass with a boy walking behind to whip it. Men *and* women – the laundress at the Monmouth Inn alleged a debt of ten shillings. And they found they believed her. There had always been coin in the tin box, even when their store of curiosities was long gone. A bit of money, like the bit of flour in the widow's flour barrel in the bible, that never got to be more but was never used up. It was always there, and they'd spent it as they had to. Like children, they'd never asked.

The Widow Anning, Molly was now. Every morning, she washed carefully and pinned up her plaits and dressed herself in her Sabbath dress. In the face of their creditors, she was curiously composed. She received them in the workshop and called Mary in to help her, to write the sums down. She thanked them for coming to tell her, as though it were only the lack of this piece of information that had prevented their being paid in full. Mary had never attended to her face before, the oblong face with its long nose and her large, pale mouth. She was a stranger to Mary, an agent sent from the Overseer of the Parish Poor to manage things.

Mary used her father's account book, opened to a new page. She entered a line for Henry Jefferd, joiner, for her father's coffin. And for James Jessup, stationer – the account book itself had apparently never been paid for. She kept two pages, the way her father had, although for a different purpose.

BY WARRANT OF RICHARD ANNING	£/	s/	D
Mr. Axworthy For Rent two quarters	18/	–/	–
Mr. James Marden chemist	4/	8/	3
Mr. Henry Jefferd joiner	8/	–/	–
Mr. James Jessup stationer	–/	4/	2
Mrs. May Williams grocer	6/	4/	–
Mr. James Boone Uplyme clothier	9/	6/	–
Mr. Henry Dobson on loan	18/	6/	2
Mr. Joseph Angel on loan	12/	2/	6
Mr. David Dunn Axminster on loan	14/	–/	–
Mr. George Swain on loan	–/	2/	6

BY WORD OF MOUTH	£/	s/	D
Mrs. Elizabeth Cox on loan	–/	10/	–
Wm. Lock for goods consigned	7/	–/	–
Mr. Wm. Dommet on loan	5/	–/	–
Mr. Walter Jones on loan	9/	–/	–

There were more. Three or four letters were brought to the door but went undelivered because it cost thruppence to receive a letter.

They'd surely have been sent to the workhouse, but by God's grace it had burned down. Instead, they were accorded outdoor relief by the parish, by applying to a table set up on Fridays in the churchyard. Poor relief of three shillings a week. Again Molly seemed to know the proper demeanour. When she went to collect the poor relief, she pulled her shawl up over her head, she kept her eyes cast down and declined to greet her neighbours, who paid the Poor Rate as hard as their own lot was, who lived within their means, who had not called such misfortune down upon themselves. When the poor relief was spent (as it was by Tuesday of each week), Mary went to the Williamses' shop three times a day because one spoonful of tea was all she could bring herself to ask for on credit. She kept her eyes down as well, so that May Williams would not be ashamed if she had to refuse her.

Mary reckoned the debt at 120 pounds, most of it over her father's signature. Mary asked Joseph to verify the sums, but he would not. He said it might as well be 1,000 pounds as 120, because neither sum would ever be paid. Harry Tupper was in the Cockmoile for a debt of 15 pounds. He'd been imprisoned as a prod to his three idle sons. Would it occur to someone that the Annings might benefit by Joseph Anning being moved next door to the Cockmoile?

They would need to become a different sort of family. They stood in the workshop (not Lizzie, she was in bed) and it seemed to Mary that they had met to decide what they would become. They looked first at Richard's tools lying along the workbench.

"If I was a boy, he would have taught me," Mary said, and saw pain blow across Joseph's face, for he had never taught Joseph. She did not repent saying it. For he would have, and why lie?

"When my father died," said Molly, as though she had not heard, "my oldest brother had to go out to tell the bees. He had to knock on each of the hives until a buzzing started up within. Then, after the funeral, we brought cake out to the bees. We sewed a hood of crepe for each hive. Without it, the bees would have swarmed, they'd have gone out to seek him." She stood straight and tall and calm, Percival no longer hanging from her.

"I told Armstrong I'd not be back," said Joseph. "I'm going to sea."

"You will never go to sea while I draw breath," said Molly. "You will go to Armstrong, as you have been."

"I'll go to the shore at first low tide," said Mary. "I'll look for the crocodile Mr. Buckland wants."

"No," said Molly, rounding on her. "You will not go collecting. You will not die on the cliffs as your father did. You will stay and help me at home." What she would do at home Mary did not ask, for there was no answer. When Molly was a girl, all the girls and women sat in their doorways and made lace, but the lace had gone north to the steam mills.

Molly turned back to the workbench and ran her hand over the tool box. "I'll offer the planer to Henry Jefferd," she said. "It's not worth one pound let alone eight, but if he has any sense, he'll settle for it. He's in dire need of a new one. That coffin were a dishonour to the trade."

One hundred and twenty pounds. It was a fortune to have associated with their name. Mary could not comprehend it. She had tried to understand her father, but she had failed. She thought of a day they had walked up to Ware Manor Farm to buy eggs. Richard had lifted Lizzie to his shoulders and she was drooping, she lay over his head. "Sit up," he said. "You make yourself heavy." He was singing as he walked up the path where a huge sycamore leaned, Mary trotting along behind. When they came up on the sycamore, he was still carrying Lizzie a-pisty-poll and he did not slow his pace. He gripped Lizzie by her bare ankles and strode on with springy step. The tree was pruned for passersby, but Lizzie sat high and free on Father's shoulders, she rode inno-cently towards the lowest limb with her hands in Father's hair (he is only playing the fool, thought Mary as Lizzie rode towards the limb), and Mary screamed "Watch!" and he ducked just at the last moment, and the branch skimmed over Lizzie's bonnet. He stag-gered a little getting his footing, and Lizzie's laugh rang out, and he tipped her like a package to the ground, where she recovered herself and ran ahead of him up the path. And Father kept on walking with jaunty step, kept on with his song without missing a single word.

He had imagined himself a man to whom rules did not apply. He had imagined himself a man who could carry the weight of a fortune. He had put off their disgrace until he would not be there to witness it.

onths pass and spring drapes itself over Bristol, and still his mother does not send for him. Mornings he reads for a couple of hours (he's read through Clement's books and started into Alger's) and then he sketches and paints. The birds from the hearth lie in a box on the desk. It's a sturdy casket with fitted joins the maid found, MELTON TEAS stencilled in black on the side. The skeletons are arranged in two rows. They're dressed in aromatic shreds of tea: tea-coloured bones, smelling of tea. Rescued from the hearth, they continue their passage towards dust, drying and loosening, their joints unhinging at the slightest touch. In his palm, Henry holds a weightless, intricate basketry of bones. It's a dunnock. He knows it by its tiny beak, and because it's written up in a folio in Alger's drawing room: *Prunella modularis.* He'll do a line drawing in India ink, and then a sepia wash.

Mornings he reads and draws and afternoons he walks. He walks down to the new floating harbour, and admires the marvel of ships sailing right into the city. Boys his age swing from ropes, intent on their trade. He aches with all he doesn't know. He wanders around the old friary and looks down at the gleaming mud of the Avon at low tide, and then he sets off for Clifton Wood, one lane delivering him to the next. New growth clamours around him, reproaching him with immateriality. He walks with eyes lowered, deflecting the glare of light and the raucous birdsong. Pinks and yellows assault him from gardens on either side – he doesn't know their names. *I'll be away from here soon*, he thinks. *I'll go to the Continent. When this war is over, when I come into Halse Hall.* An image from his reading lifts itself in his mind: *I'll climb Mont Blanc.* He sees himself towering at the peak, substantial against the barren snow. *I'll join the Royal Society*, he resolves, *I'll deliver a paper on glaciation.* He walks until he's hungry and then takes a straight trajectory back to town, blundering through gardens and scrambling over walls. He pictures them sending dogs out after him, savouring the confusion when they corner him, a gentleman caught tramping, heedless of boundaries.

One day, as he returns at dusk, a man and woman stroll towards him. As they pass he turns, and just as they vanish into darkness, he catches a glimpse of the man's hand creeping up to the nape of the girl's neck, sees the *intention* in the hand. Then there's no shutting it off. He falls into it, he's forced into speculation regarding each house he passes, where and how often it is happening behind dark windows. In the attic chamber of a townhouse, or in the loft of the carriage house. A telling nimbus hangs over the carriage house, of smoke and shrouded torchlight. It is the high attic windows that stir him most, the maids' quarters, where you could go straight in, as you can with the low-born, you just say what you want.

St. Nicholas Street is full of ladies crowding into teashops, coming out of the milliner's. In the sunshine, girls wear gowns of a thin, limp fabric cut low over the breasts. Surely a girl donning this sort of dress understands its language? Finding yourself fortuitously alone with her, you could take her at her word, nudge the gown off. It would slip like the dust cloth from a statue, fall to a pool of white at her feet. He can see a cage of narrow ribs, but he can't get the whole picture, the way these small breasts are fixed to the chest, for example. Or the contour of the abdomen. In Jamaica, naked or almost-naked women squatted on flat stones at the stream, scrubbing their laundry, waded into the water with light splintering brilliantly between them. Perhaps they wore aprons like the woman he saw on Piccadilly; he can't remember.

Back in his room, he picks up a charcoal. It's the Hottentot Venus he draws: her torso, the great breasts hanging like gourds. He pins it to the wall behind his desk. It is quite good. In the tent of his bed curtains, he lies in his underwear in a litter of drawings and books. Twined bodies float on the walls of the tent, a frank alphabet of legs and torsos. He'll paint them in India ink, the whole series, and leave his folio in the dining room. His uncle (with his sagging bolster of a belly that has never known love) will pick up the pages and puzzle over what Henry has drawn, as over an oriental script. Or Sullivan, standing baffled at the sideboard on old legs like wooden stilts, or the Scottish housekeeper, Mrs. Witherspoon, frowning, or the thin maid with the cast to her eye, passing indifferently by.

None of them will have an inkling. It's in him, Henry, that the energy of the house hums. He's an unlikely champion of love, with his way of talking that makes young ladies smile with private amusement and dart away to the buffet table, and the hints of Uncle Alger he sometimes sees in the looking glass — the long upper lip, the tufted eyebrows. He stands up, pushes the bed curtains aside, feels his new height and the bulk of his shoulders. Outside, rain has started up. An underground current runs below the houses of Bristol and it's bubbled to the surface in him. This is the purpose of his banishment. It will happen here, he thinks while rain patters on the window. In *Bristol*, he thinks, and the scrolled letters float across the window, glowing with erotic light.

Eventually, the force of his desire produces her. It plants her in the overgrown garden of the Irish captain next door. It's laundry day and unusually windy, and Mrs. Witherspoon's gaunt little helper has hung their washing on a clothesline. Between flapping sheets and linen napkins and the long, writhing legs of his own underwear, he spies a girl. She's standing facing him. She wears a white cap over a haze of apricot-coloured hair. White napkins and their shadows dance over her face. Watching her between the waving towels is like trying to read the meaning of a flag show at Marlow. She's looking straight at him, a square of something held breast-high in front of her. She's signalling, part of the flag show. Then the wind flips a napkin right over and he sees it's an easel she has before her. She's not looking at him at all, she's painting with studious attention some object he can't see. He watches her through the fluttering laundry until noon. Then Captain Whyte's butler comes out and speaks to her and she goes in, leaving her easel for the butler to carry.

The next morning, the laundry's gone and from under the ragged fringe of thatch protruding over the casement, he has an unimpeded view. She has somewhat repositioned herself; she's turned to a three-quarter perspective. She wears a soft gown of pale rose with an orange sash tied under her breasts – a bold combination. Her subject is propped on a ladder-backed chair. A lacquered tray, perhaps, or it may be someone else's painting, a copy exercise set by her painting master. She has a long neck and a fine, pert-featured face. His mind flips through a catalogue of thin, faun-coloured animals. Fauns, of course. But she's livelier: quick, intent, squirrel-like. She never looks up to the tangled garden or the birds jousting in the vines on the wall. Except once, when she glances around, lifts her cap from her head, and smooths her hair before resetting the cap. She smiles constantly: it seems her subject amuses her.

He takes up his folio and turns the pages, past the shaded diagrams of sea mortars, past the drawing of the tendoned earth (a turnip with its roots grown round it), past the frail bones of the birds. He finds a blank page, where he sets about sketching her in pencil. He works quickly. This is an angle he likes; it presents a charming, inescapable line of brow and cheek and chin. He can't see lashes from this distance, but he draws them in. They will be pale but thick. Her eyes will be drawn from the same pale palette as her hair and gown: green, ideally. Who could she be? He doesn't know Captain Whyte's household. He'll persuade Alger to present his card tomorrow. He'll accompany Alger on a morning visit, wearing his green waistcoat. *In London just briefly in the fall*, he'll say to the young lady. *Amusing exhibitions on Piccadilly.* These are tactics – but to what end? To portray himself as a young man with prospects, of course. And if he's successful, then – well, then: he sees himself ensconced in Captain Whyte's drawing room, handing dowagers in to tea, dozing at the whist table. The supporting player in endless rehearsals for a life of tedious domesticity. He falls back onto the bed and lets the folio slide to the floor.

That's the folly of beginning with *tactics* and not with *object*. He sits back up on the bed and watches her bend gracefully over her easel. The object is clear. How to attain it? He'd need to arouse in her a corresponding hunger. Is that so preposterous? Animals mate, the female is persuaded – and without the artifice of billets-doux and flowers. Of course, a young lady is not of the animal kingdom. Although a young *man* is. Man is a beast, made in the image of God though he may be. Curious that the human male and the human female should be so different, when in the majority of species the sexes are almost indistinguishable. Two modest, brown creatures, scurrying together into earthen tunnels, drawn wordlessly into the dark. Cruelly, his mind produces his own mother, one day on a secluded bench in the park at Hammersmith, breaking apart from Mr. Ridd when she saw Henry on the path (her hair come undone under her hat, her breast flushed raspberry, her bright eyes darting in every direction but his).

When next he sees the young lady in the garden, he puts on his hat and walks quickly down Pennyworth Lane in the opposite direction to Captain Whyte's house. This tactic is a feint. Pennyworth Lane curves around a woods, and narrows into a path, and wanders back through the woods until it ends near where it began, behind Alger's and Captain Whyte's gardens. He hurries along the dwindling path, almost running. Sooner than he expects, he sees her framed by greenery, cut off at midthigh by the garden wall. He stops and watches. She has her back to him now and he can see her canvas. A pale bulb rises from the lower margin. It seems she's painting a cabbage.

Henry reaches into his pocket. A sixpence, that's all he has. He throws it in her direction. It's too small, she's not disturbed. He crouches and finds a toadstool, uproots it and tosses it. Then a shell, an oyster shell dropped incongruously by the path. This time his aim is better; the shell lands almost on her foot.

She turns and looks curiously in his direction. She's facing the sun: she can't see him. There is a gate at the back of her uncle's garden that's been left open and can't be closed; it's been stitched to the earth by the brambles growing up it. She passes through the opening, holding her skirts, and comes lightly down the path. In little white slippers, she *trips* along the path – that's what they say for this way of walking, so feminine, so consciously feminine even now, when she thinks herself alone. Then she sees him and she stops. "Oh!" she says, wrinkling up her eyes. "What are you doing in my uncle's garden?"

He's still crouching. "Pardon me," he says. "I've disturbed you. Although I'm not, strictly speaking, in your uncle's garden." He stands up. Her eyes are, as he hoped, unusual: truly green, at least in the green light of the woods. Light and shadow dapple her face and throat and bosom, her bosom nakedly white in patches of light above her flimsy gown. He has her in the woods now and he is without a further tactic.

"I'm watching the birds," he says. "The dunnock. People call them hedge sparrows. But the bill of a dunnock is much finer than a sparrow's. *Prunella modularis*, I believe is the formal nomenclature."

She gives a little laugh. "You paint birds?" she asks. She has seen him through the window after all! She glances to either side. "But there are no birds here."

"Not this morning. But they're often here. They shuffle along the ground, a modest, nervous bird. I watched them as a boy. The male and female are identical. I found a nest close to here, with eggs. Blue, like a robin's. Except for one larger egg, which was grey. They are often host to cuckoos, inadvertent hosts. Rather like my uncle Alger's situation at the moment." He stands among the bracken and watches her, letting a long moment pass. He notes the tendrils of orange hair escaping from braids coiled under her cap. Here is the subject of a grand canvas – their two forms under the trees, painted from above. The green that frames her is made of tissues of light, not material except where each tissue overlaps the other and manifests itself as leaf. "Do you watch birds?" he asks.

Again she gives the little laugh that seems to preface every speech. "Last October, I went out with a party from Bath," she says. "We had opera glasses and we looked at wild geese in the priory garden. There were some who took great interest, but I didn't really see the appeal." Her smile and her tone are pert.

"Well, there is something very interesting about the dunnock," he hears himself saying. "The females are polyandrous. That's very rare in the bird kingdom. It's a term used more for flora than fauna. It's used for flowers that have more than one stamen."

"Stamen?" she says, with the little laugh.

He moves towards her. She stands still. She does not back up, but stands and looks at him with an expression of intense interest and excitement. He understands her stillness: it is a subtle, wordless offering, as large a gesture as the female is allowed.

"I paint birds because I lack any other model," he says. In the moving light, he sees the notch at her collarbone, as though it were moulded by a thumb. He reaches out as though to thumb it himself, but instead pinches a bit of her gown between his fingers. It's just the colour of her skin. "What is this fabric?" he asks.

"Muslin," she says. She smiles up at him.

"But what is that? Is it cotton?"

"I have no idea."

Something black clings to her bosom just above the lace of her gown. A spider, perched on the lip of the shadowed drop between her breasts.

"Don't move," he whispers, leaning over her, still not touching her. He pictures a gallant young gentleman in his place on the path, pinning the gown closed with his finger and gently blowing the spider off.

"What?" She is also whispering.

"A spider. It's landed on you. Careful, it will run down your gown."

He bends over her. To his surprise, she tilts her face up towards his and offers her lips to him. They are soft, as they must be. He presses his mouth experimentally against hers, opens it a little, and then he wants her to tip her chin higher, he wants to plant a kiss under it, on the underpart of the chin that curves so beautifully, like the merrythought of a bird. As he bends, he spies again the dark spot on her breast. It's not a spider. It's a bit of pigment, a mole growing darkly on her white skin. He moves his lips along the pure line of her jaw, and suddenly her breath catches and she leaps away from him.

"Sir," she cries. "You presume!" He reaches a hand tenderly, reassuringly, towards her, but she has turned by then and is scrambling up the path, running in her little white slippers for the garden. He laughs. The excitement in her voice is so at odds with her words that he understands this rebuke as a move in a contest they have just begun.

It appears the maiden is not entirely the creation of Henry's fevered imagination. She has a name and Alger knows it, although he's never thought to mention her before. She's Letitia Whyte, the daughter of an Irish captain from County Down. Her father is dead and the Captain Whyte next door is her uncle and guardian. She is always in Bristol when she is not somewhere else, as she must have been through the winter.

He mentions it now because Captain Whyte requests the honour of an immediate visit from Mr. Algernon De la Beche. "Standoffish," says Alger when the note arrives. "Doesn't mix much. I'd suggest you accompany me, but he wishes to discuss a sensitive matter. Connected to his *niece*." He clips the note into one of the three fat clothes pegs he uses for his papers. "Why ever would he wish to discuss his niece's affairs with me?" he adds jocularly, in case Henry has failed to appreciate the compliment in this.

As soon as he has swallowed the last of his tea, he makes ready to go next door. Henry goes up to his room to wait, trying to ignore the dread gathering in his stomach. He stands by the window a moment and then walks restlessly back down to the parlour and looks at himself in the mirror hanging over the side table. He's back in the woods behind the garden, at the moment when courtesies began to issue from his mouth like a catechism, and he shut them off, he stood silently in the bracken, and something sinister and unschooled, some *cunning* overtook him and he spoke of the wantonness of the female dunnock and moved towards the girl and saw response rise in her eyes. A response to seeing something true, the one true thing. And how he stood over her, bent towards her, parted the veil of decorum hanging over her, and put his lips to her bare skin. He stares into the convex bronze mirror. It reflects back an empty, cavernous room and he sees himself in it, a dwarfed, blunt-featured bronze god, alone in an enormous cave.

The sky outside the windows is darkening and Sullivan comes in to draw the curtains and light the lamps. Lamplight falls on the side table, on Alger's only porcelain, a lady bearing a fan before her ugly, eager face. And a Negro holding the train of her gown, the Negro in blue pantaloons and a yellow jacket and boots. His face is a black-painted mask and his hands are black gloves. Above it hangs the painting of Halse Hall. The painting and the porcelain are the only tokens of what built this house. He'll go to Jamaica, sooner rather than later, and he knows how he will present himself upon landing at the wharf in Kingston harbour: as *Beach*, Mr. Henry Beach.

His uncle finally comes in and goes straight upstairs. Then Sullivan opens the door to the drawing room. Henry is required in his uncle's bedchamber. He finds his uncle sitting in the opening of his own Bedouin tent wearing a dressing gown and nightcap. The window to sleep swings open at ten and closes at ten-thirty, Alger explains genially. If he fails to avail himself of this opening, he will lie sleepless till dawn. He's flushed with society and port; there's not a tinge of accusation in his demeanour. Mrs. Witherspoon is there. She's come in to help him to bed. She's at the table spreading a grey paste on a long strip of linen. The linen will be applied to his feet as a sleep aid, a remedy recommended by the Widow Rankin.

Henry sits on a wooden chair, dazed with relief. And with admiration for the girl, who apparently kept her council after all. While Mrs. Witherspoon binds the cloth to the yellow soles of his feet, Alger is pleased to share the recipe with his nephew: camomile and vinegar boiled together and then stirred into breadcrumbs. He lies back, a lazy predator in his den. There were two Captain Whytes, he tells Henry, brothers, his neighbour being the elder by a decade, and the younger, whose name was Charles, being dead. Perished in the Dardanelles in aught-eight. A nasty engagement in a futile campaign. Vice-Admiral Cuthbert Collingwood's little scheme. He sent in eight ships of the line. He was sure the Turks wouldn't fight – it was October, they were fasting. But that engagement cost England a hundred men, including Captain Charles Whyte. Then Alger veers suddenly to the girl, over whom this elder Captain Whyte is legal guardian. Her mother has remarried, but by the terms of the father's will, the uncle retained wardship. Remarkable foresight on the father's part, for the mother's new marriage was regrettable. However, that has nothing to do with the girl, who has an independent income of *four thousand pounds*! And, like Henry, no brothers or sisters.

"I had to inform Captain Whyte that you have no hopes of this property," Alger says. He cranks his head up on his thick neck to look at Henry. "But that of course at majority, you'll come into Halse Hall." He lies back down. "Her father was highly decorated. Had a better career than his brother here. Shame about the Dardanelles. It was Admiral Duckworth led the engagement. He pled with Collingwood for infantry to seize the batteries onshore. But there were none spared them."

Mrs. Witherspoon goes out carrying her basin of paste and Alger sits up in the bed, his bound feet under the cover. "By blood a most respectable young maiden," he says, apropos of nothing. "A pity I've not been more discreet about Halse Hall in years past. But who would ever have thought?" He's speaking jovially, man to man. "How could I have foreseen such a thing? No one could have! However, with respect to yourself and your recent history, I can assure you I was the soul of discretion. The very soul." He tugs at his nightcap, which seems to have shrunk in the laundry. With respect to Marlow, he hinted only that his nephew might not, after all, be well suited to a military career. It's always possible Captain Whyte may make inquiries, however: haste is called for.

Henry sits motionless on the wooden chair. Inside the tent, his uncle abandons the nightcap and struggles with his pillows. *Engagement*, his uncle has said repeatedly. Referring to Captain Charles Whyte's campaign in the Dardanelles, of course, but with a panicky squeeze of his heart Henry sees that he has mis-understood the terms of this manouevre from the beginning.

·≼| T E N |≽·

From up on Pinhay Meadow, Mary could see the whole gently curving harbour. A row of bathing machines stood in deep water on the ladies' side of the tidal ledge. Two heads emerged from one, like hermit crabs crawling out of a whelk shell – the lady and her dipper. Mary watched fascinated as their two bonnets lowered into the icy water and then rose again. A second machine was being drawn through the waves by a single horse. The driver was trying to turn it, he was broadside to the surf, and then the horse caught a wave in its belly and rose in its limbers, almost capsizing the machine. Mary thought of the lady inside, lurching fearfully like a lobster in a trap. Any sensible man or beast would shun the sea in February, but the high-born streamed to the black water for the greater misery winter bathing offered them. In pursuit of wellness, they sought tonics the poor took for granted: sea air, the only air the poor of Lyme Regis had ever breathed, chills, terror, hardship, suffering.

So many visitors in Lyme Regis that year! Marine Parade was crowded with their parasols. From up on Pound Street, Mary could see their own little cottage, perched in the heart of the town, the first thing visitors clapped eyes on when they alighted from the coach. A useless, taunting advantage: the curiosity table sat in the cellar with driftwood stacked on it. Mary turned her eyes to the eastern shore where a band of morning mist rose like a collar of swan's down from the edge of the sea. Sunlight would be shining through the tip of each wave as it broke on the shore, sunlight would be glinting off the rocks where treasure lay. She folded her arms tightly over her empty stomach and turned her eyes resolutely away.

There was still the bounty of the Lord's creation: oysters in the sea, cresses plucked where mist hung over the mouth of the river, blackthorn leaves that could be brewed for tea. Mushrooms pushed up between the roots of trees, rushes grew in the shallow trout ponds at the Squire's estate. Mary walked out on a quiet morning and collected rushes. Leaving her shoes on the bank to save them and hitching up her skirts, she stood in icy pond water and cut the rushes green. She could see Colway Manor, a stout, featureless house of the sort favoured by the rich, sitting squarely on its own reflection in the pond. Then she spied Squire Henry Henley, stout and featureless himself, standing up to his leather-wrapped thighs in the water, stolidly tossing flies onto the surface of the pond, and she snatched up her shoes and melted into the trees, lest he put his dog after her for picking his rushes.

At home, Mary transformed the rushes into primitive candles, peeling away the hard outer skin until her fingers were raw with small cuts, and then laying the pith along the bottom of a long pan and covering it with warm mutton fat that the cook at the Philpots' kindly gave her. When the pith was well soaked and hardened, she laid the rushlights out on the curiosity table, a row of drowned grey fingers. They smelled foul and poured greasy smoke when they burned, but she asked only a penny for three.

No one bought. Only the poor would burn rushlights, and they made their own.

In another month, there would be wortleberries, but for now, there were just nettles coming up along the turnpike. She collected them and made soup, but after they'd drunk it, Lizzie crawled back into her bed, and lay whimpering with hunger. "Hush," Mary said, her fingers still prickling from the nettles. "Hush your moaning." God made all the fruit of the earth? Surely not nettles! In the kitchen, Molly sat motionless. Her weird composure in the weeks after Richard's death was gone: she was all grief now. "I'm going collecting," Mary said, coming down the steps, and her mother shook her head, but in truth, it was the dread weighing down Mary's own heart that stopped her.

James Wheaton lodged across from the Independent Chapel with Mrs. Buffet, in a cottage with chickens penned in front. Mary stood on the doorstone for a minute and then she sucked in her breath and knocked. It was Mrs. Buffet who answered. She asked Mary to follow her in and wait in the sitting room. Mary heard Mrs. Buffet climb the stairs and heard her say, "Mary Anning wishes to see you," and then there was a long quiet. Mary looked around the room. It was all as it should be, bare and clean.

When James Wheaton appeared in the doorway of the sitting room, he had a bible under his arm. His forehead was picked at and terribly inflamed, but his strange spasmodic movements were stilled as they sometimes were when he was filled with purpose. He crossed the room swiftly and fixed his avid eyes on her. Mary looked steadily back and held to her courage. "I wish to know why my family has been marked out for so much misfortune," she said.

"Oh, my child," said James Wheaton, as though her words had knocked the breath out of him. When he was finally able to speak, he said, "After we buried your father, I approached Our Lord with this very question." In the quiet, the sound of the chickens floated in from the window. "He answered me," said James Wheaton in a heavy voice. "Oh, he answered me." He pressed the heel of a hand to his eyes. "Our Lord has been wrestling with me since, that I must go to you. And now He has sent you to me." A sob broke his voice and Mary thought he was about to fall to his knees in front of her. "Oh, my sister, you heard His voice, you obeyed, you came to me. When I, a weak, unruly minister, struggled against Him."

He touched her arm and she got up from her chair. He led her to the window, as though to study her face in the light. "Have you been recently to the shore?"

"To the shore?" said Mary, the blood thudding down her body.

"Yes, collecting."

"I dug oysters last night," she said faintly.

"But not the fossils?"

Mary did not answer.

"You must not!" he said urgently. "You must shun your father's path. It was the works of Satan he gave himself to studying! He studied Satan's handiwork on the Sabbath."

"But Mr. Buckland studies curiosities," said Mary, "and he be a clergyman. He be always on the shore on the Sabbath. I asked him. He said that God made all that lives in the world, that we must study it."

"But Mary," cried James Wheaton, "the curiosities do not *live*. The sea teems with life, but it gives us no creatures such as the stony forms we find on the shore. Serpents convulsed into flat stones. Dragons with their terrible fangs."

Mary stared at him.

"They are the works of Satan. They are a dark creation that imperfectly mirrors our own. They are a manifestation of the curse. Their purpose is to tempt the weak away from God's true works." He pulled a chair up to the table and gestured to her to sit back down. He opened his bible and from Genesis he read her the story of Cain, who killed his brother Abel, and the mark God placed on Cain, so that people who met him would not kill him.

"Who were these people?" James Wheaton asked intently, his eyes burning in his face. "These people, strangers to Cain, who must be stopped from killing him? For we know that Adam and Eve had but two children, Cain and Abel."

"Yes," said Mary slowly. "I asked Father the same question when I heard this text in chapel."

"I wish you had come to me then," James Wheaton said. "And I trust I would have had the wisdom to answer you. Mary!" He pulled his chair closer to the corner of the table and slid the bible around so that she could see. "Look! They were a satanic tribe, made by Satan after the Fall. God sent the Flood to wipe out the whole perverse race of them. We live among their hideous ruins." He showed her the engraving at the front of his bible, of terrible dragons with their coils all tangled in a paroxysm of fury and pain. Then he turned with trembling fingers to a passage near the end of the bible, and read out: *There was war in the heaven: Michael and the angels fought against the dragon and the dragon fought and his angels, and prevailed not. Neither was there place found any more in heaven. And the great dragon was cast out, that old serpent, called the Devil and Satan, which deceiveth the whole world: he was cast out into the earth, and his angels were cast out with him.* "Oh, Mary," he whispered when he was done. "You must be warned."

She stepped out of James Wheaton's lodgings into the sunlight, where two small boys played with a hoop and the street ran down to a sea full of ships in billowing sail. She walked through the town in the usual way, in her modest skirt and jacket and her mourning bonnet over her plaited hair. A flock of young ladies dressed in pastel gowns chattered outside the Assembly Rooms, and at the edge of the sea, a band of seagulls splashed together in their communal bath. She lingered on the bridge for a moment, watching the ducks floating at the mouth of the river. Then she went into the house, where a note waited for her. It was from Mrs. Stock, who said she had work for a willing girl and asked Mary to report to her house in the morning. So it was clear, then, that she had not dreamed this conversation – it *had* happened, and God, working in partnership with James Wheaton and Mrs. Stock, had contrived a way to help Mary resist the seduction of the shore.

Mrs. Stock had had a sudden rise in fortune. She lived now on Marine Parade, in a house called Tower Cottage. It was a bequest from an uncle that had elevated her, and the passion of the high-born for taking the waters, and her own canny decision to purchase two bathing machines from Mr. England.

Molly sponged the collar and hems of Mary's mourning dress, a dress Mrs. Bennett had kindly lent them because of Mary's great size. Washed and combed and pushed out the door early the next morning, Mary took herself to Tower Cottage. It was Mrs. Stock herself who came to the door. She led Mary down the hall and let her peep into the parlour, where two ladies sat with needlework screens in front of them. Mary could see their lace morning caps and their hair, sculptures of fair coils with braids entwined. "Come all the way from Salisbury," Mrs. Stock said. "Come to take the waters. They have each a maid come as well."

Behind Mrs. Stock hung a silhouette of Mrs. Stock, done on convex glass. It was all new, the bell pull, the tasselled lamp, the bootjack in the hall. Mrs. Stock drew Mary back to the kitchen. "I need a clever girl to assist me," she said. "To run errands." Mary was the same height now as Mrs. Stock. "Occasional work, as the lodgers come and go." They arranged that Mary would present herself every mid-morning to see whether Mrs. Stock needed her that day.

On the days Mrs. Stock wanted her, Mary went to the butter market and the baker's and haggled with fishermen at the Cobb. When she returned with basket laden, Mrs. Stock counted out the change with glittering approval, as though Mary's honesty was born of just this sort of close supervision. Sometimes Mary was sent on errands a small boy could have run, carrying messages from the lodgers to their friends up the hill (usually just a card with a name on it), but Mary did it willingly, for Mrs. Stock paid sixpence a half day. But often it was messages to Doctor Reeves or Doctor Coulson Carpenter that Mary carried. They slept on horsehair mattresses at night, these gentlefolk, and had calfskin boots and gloves to protect their extremities from the cold. Plates of mutton and flaking trout cooked for them daily. Cheese, eggs, sweetbreads, as much as they fancied. But they were not well for all that.

On the Sabbath, Mary went to chapel without fail. At the pulpit, James Wheaton vibrated with the force of his message. Thinner by the week, his cuffs ragged, his fingertips fretted raw, he was a rare pastor. It tore and ripped him to utter God's truth, but he would utter it. He had delivered the Lord's warning to her and he trusted her now, to do what she must. He never fixed his eyes on her these mornings as he preached, but there was a shining bond between them and she felt it. Every Sabbath, she sat on the bench weighed down by her love for James Wheaton, and by his anguished love for her.

After a busy fortnight or two, the work became scarce. When she had no lodgers, Mrs. Stock sat in the parlour and read her books. She tried to lure Mary into staying to hear her discourse on what she was reading, although she declined to pay on such days. It was the science of craniology, the study of the skull. A gentleman who had lodged at Tower Cottage had introduced her to it and left the books in lieu of rent. This gentleman, come all the way from Coventry, would run his fingers over people's skulls and measure their heads with calipers and so predict what would become of them. It was a matter of size and shape and the bumps seldom seen under the hair. Mrs. Stock had no calipers, but she desired to measure Mary's head with string. "It's ill luck to be measured," said Mary, backing away. "My mother says so," although what her mother had said was that it was ill luck to be *weighed*.

"It is a science," said Mrs. Stock. "By science we can predict our fate, and so control it."

The next day, Mrs. Stock again had no errands for Mary. "But I need an upstairs maid," she said. "I'm prepared to train, although I prefer her to live in."

"Ask Miss Philpot about a maid," Mary said. "Her maid has a houseful of sisters." Fury and shame pulsed through her. She could not find the voice to speak further. Without a goodbye, she left through the kitchen door. She walked back through the town, feeling the cool wind against her flaming cheeks.

Instead of going home, she went straight across Cockmoile Square and walked slowly up Church Street. It was not her mother she wanted to see, who might well welcome Mrs. Stock's offer. She went through the gate at St. Michael's. The stained stone church sat above the shore, guarding the entrance between two worlds – the world of the town and the world of the shore, where the remains of Satan's henchmen lay. Mary climbed the stairs cut into the side of the hill to the graveyard, with its stones leaning here and there. It looked almost empty, this graveyard, but it was not: the dead of the plague had been buried in a mass grave here long ago, under a green hill they would not open again for fear of contagion. Towards the back, a patch of brown earth was Richard's grave. None of his children were there, except Percival. They'd been buried in the Friends' Burying Ground, the two Henrys and the other Mary. Not Martha, who was never found.

Mary stood by the broken ground of her father's grave. But he was not here, she knew it. She walked to the edge of the cliff and looked down at the sea, a silver band withdrawing, leaving a bed of gleaming sand. Anyone who walked the path through the graveyard on a sunny afternoon and looked out over the sea dotted with ships in full sail must follow the path down the cliff. It rose and then fell in such a way that no one who came upon it could resist following it. Below Church Cliffs, yellow coltsfoot bloomed among the stones. On a sun-tossed afternoon, it was hard to believe that you lived in a cursed world, the mouth of hell. But Satan was a deceiver and dressed himself in light. James Wheaton, God's tormented angel, could never look at this scene; the light would scorch his eyes.

Along the shore, the cliffs rolled out in their order: Church Cliffs, Black Ven, Stonebarrow, Golden Cap, four more whose names she didn't know, and beyond them, the Isle of Portland. When the wavering cliffs dipped, you could see the fields on top of them, like glimpsing the inside of a ribbon. Green, the winter corn was coming up like grass. Up there, the farmer thought he was ploughing a field he knew, and then he came up on the edge and found the sea had bitten a chunk off it. Daydreaming sheep fell to the sea. Some said the sheep had been possessed of an evil spirit and run off the cliffs, but it was the cliffs that took them by surprise; daily, the landscape changed. She was below Black Ven now, and from the shore she could see the path where she had stood while they pulled her father up. The ledge where he had lain was already gone – the rains had washed it into the sea.

But her father was there, he was still there. On the path above her, he'd walked that wonderful bright night, the path a black seam through the gorse, the sea below shingled with moonlight. She could picture the way he'd slipped, throwing an elbow out for balance, clutching his bag and then skidding down the cliff, falling too fast for thought – until the earth caught him, a soft provisional ledge, just as wide as it needed to be. Not wide enough for him to move. Nothing to do but lie and look, his collecting bag under him.

There he lay on the stony cliffs with the bones of dragons buried below him. Hawks hunted for mice on the field above. A smuggler rowed silently to shore. Digby, maybe, Digby may have prowled below while Richard lay and watched. The moon sank into the sea and white stars washed up in the sky. And he lay, watching from his perch where the land and the sea and the sky met, lay and knew himself alive in the night. He was who he always was, that night. He refused to be fearful. He would not be stooped and shrivelled by fate. Fate had had many victories over him; it would not have that one. It would not make him into the sort of man he had never been before.

Walking home along the shore, Mary did not search for fossils, but she collected every loose curiosity she happened to see. A handful of thunderbolts, grey. A lovely pyrite ammonite glinting in the sun at the base of Church Cliffs. This is not witchery, she thought as she bent to pick it up and felt its weight. We have always found them here, scattered among the rocks. She fingered the tiny, perfect golden coils at its centre. She would never in her life see a jewel so fine.

As Mary came back up the path through the graveyard with the ammonite in her hand, a gentleman and a lady strolled ahead of her along the cliff, looking out to sea. The gentleman was

Mr. Aveline, who had a fine house on Broad Street; she recognized him by his thin, elegant shoulders. They were walking very slowly, arm in arm. Where the path widened, Mary went to hurry past them.

"What do you have there?" called the lady in a friendly fashion. A lady Mary had never seen before, wearing a velvet coat and hat. Mary stopped and showed her. "What a beauty!" the lady said.

"Oh, it's an ammonite," said Mr. Aveline, nodding at Mary. "They're sometimes called cornemonius." He reached out and ran a gloved finger around its coils. "They do so resemble the curled horns of a ram. It is striking, isn't it! The Creator favoured certain patterns, as all artists do. He used the same designs over and over in very different spheres of the natural world." The lady smiled at him – not at what he said, but as if she loved him for being the sort of man who would say it.

"It's an ammonite stellaris," said Mary. They looked at her in surprise, for the science coming off a Dorsetshire tongue. Then the lady offered to buy it. She said it was something her son would fancy.

"They call them snakestones in the town," Mary said. "People carry them for luck." What a soft face the lady had, like a flower blooming under her velvet hat! The word *luck* felt like a black charm on Mary's lips. But she went on, she said, "I can make a head on it if you wish."

"Oh, no, I prefer it in its natural state," said the lady.

"Just let me clean that bit of iron off it."

And so Mr. Aveline and the lady walked down to Bridge Street with Mary, and they waited in the square while Mary washed the ammonite and chipped the iron off. Then the lady gave Mary a half-crown, and when she had gone up Broad Street, Mary held it out to Molly, who was sitting in the kitchen with her head down as if to shut out the sight of what Mary was doing. Mary pressed the half-crown into her hand and she threw it to the floor with an angry gesture, but this was just for show. Finally she raised her face and gave Mary the look she used to give Richard when he came in from the Three Cups or from a Sabbath at the shore: a look that said, *This is the way it will be, then.*

Alone in the workshop, Mary pulled a blank page from the accounts book and sat a long time thinking. Finally, she took up her quill and wrote a letter to Mr. William Buckland at Oxford University, informing him that Richard Anning had gone to his rest and requesting that, if there was any money owing Richard for goods provided, it be paid now. *Oxford, England*, she put by way of address, because it was all she knew. But surely Mr. Buckland would be known by the citizenry of any town he frequented? She melted a bit of the beeswax left from a candle and used it for a seal. On her way home from posting the letter, she stopped at the Bennetts' and asked their boy to carry a message to Mrs. Stock, saying that she would come no more.

·≪[E L E V E N]≫·

Henry's manoeuvre in the woods secures another unanticipated object: it brings his mother to Bristol. She
arrives in a velvet hat and coat in a fetching shade of
lavender; she wears her *nothing can touch me* face. She stands in
the hall while Sullivan helps her with her coat and crinkles her
eyes at Henry. The smile is her *I will solve this* smile. He trembles
with happiness at the sight of it. She was right, right to have left
him here for so long to expiate his sins. Marlow is gone now, and
the eager, silly youth he was then. It's all over, they need not
waste time on it.

Alger has promised Mother to Captain Whyte for tea that
very day, so there is very little time to talk. Again Henry's presence is not required. He clatters up to his room and brings down
the sketch he made of Letitia, offering to send it along. It's both
a true and a flattering portrait, as he knows, having had the
benefit of a close view. The vines on the wall behind her make
a playful motif with her curls. And (he thinks, pleased with this
insight) it will make his sally in the woods seem *premeditated* and
thus less rash.

His mother hands it back. "I rather doubt she'll appreciate having been spied on," she says.

His mother spends the entire evening at Captain Whyte's. He works for an hour on a bird study, based on one of the tiny skeletons. Since the encounter in the woods, birds have been his resolute focus. He did the India ink detail the morning before, and now, carrying a large candelabra to his desk, he does a sepia wash, admiring the professional look the ink imparts to the study. Sepia. It is his favourite medium, pigment offered up by the living cuttlefish. But the instant the wash is applied and dry, his patience evaporates. He stomps back down to the parlour and tries to read. By nine o'clock, he's choked with fury and humiliation. It's incomprehensible that he was not included in these discussions. Perhaps he should go and present himself at the door.

At ten o'clock, he climbs the stairs to his room. Shortly after, she knocks lightly on his door. Happiness still glows on her cheeks. She takes off her hat and sets it on his bureau. "What an endless evening! What a long-winded man! We must examine all his sordid mementoes from Singapore and hear the story connected to each, and all this on the meanest little glass of sherry." She arranges herself in the chair by his desk. "Well, Henry," she says, tilting her head at him. "She seems a nice enough girl, and very pretty. Why did you not find a way to be properly introduced? There may have been an opportunity to ask her for a kiss."

He stood up when she came in and he is still standing, wearing his dressing gown. "I can steal, but I cannot beg," he says. "That's something I learned on the road between Marlow and London." What an awful popinjay he's turned into! – the sort of person she loves to mock. If only he could tell her about his solitary journey on foot by the Thames, about this last long winter. But she doesn't ask.

"Well, it appears she's sensitive about the mole on her bosom. She's never been on the Continent, poor child, or she'd be decorating it with kohl."

"What was it she was painting?" he asks.

"Herself. It's a head-and-shoulders self-portrait, made with the use of a looking glass. I saw it drying in the hall. The mole does not figure in it."

"Did you think it skilful?"

"I thought it rather . . . Oh, never mind. It's not the sort of thing that matters, is it? In the flesh, she has an air of mischief that's quite appealing. As you know – you've spoken to her. I think she may be an interesting woman one day, Henry. I refrained from asking why a maiden of her station would creep into the woods with an unknown man. But it does speak of a lack of supervision, and her uncle's very eager to have this settled." She's up now, she has the wardrobe door open, she begins to go through his new clothes. She takes the three waistcoats out and spreads them side by side on the bed. "Oh, this one's *very* nice. You see so much canary satin on Regent Street this year, and I was afraid they'd still be using ivory in Bristol." She looks for the coat that goes with it and lays it on the bed, comparing the embroidery on the lapels. "The girl's mother is not well connected, it's true." Her voice drops. "It's worse than Alger let on," she says. "The stepfather is an *innkeeper*. The publican of a coaching inn – you will have seen it. The Moonlight Inn or some such thing. It seems to have been a moment of folly on the mother's part. They have done everything in their power to keep Letitia away from all that, to the point that she seldom sees her mother. Captain Whyte is fully empowered with respect to his niece."

She takes out his frock coat and examines the lining. "I suppose we have to be realistic. You could argue detriments on each side. It was rather a delicate conversation, as you can imagine. I gather your uncle Alger was less cautious the other night than he should have been, but he didn't grasp the situation immediately. Captain Whyte is not what I would call *direct*. And Alger can't resist dwelling on the sinking fortunes of Halse Hall. It's a way of gloating, isn't it, for having got this place, while your father was stuck with the plantation. So there was the old captain bringing up the Wilberforce Bill, whether the cane-cutters will be fully emancipated, all that business! It required a deal of deft foot-work on my part, I can tell you. Perhaps there's a post for me in Whitehall!" She laughs merrily and turns back to the jacket, turning a sleeve inside out, running her fingers over the seams. "I dwelt on your scholastic prowess. I portrayed you as a solitary boy, unaccustomed to female society. Overcome by her close-ness and her beauty. In other words, Henry, I was entirely frank!"

Henry picks the candelabra up from the side table and sets it on the desk so he can see her face. She smiles at him fondly. "Short-sighted as well, I said to Captain Whyte. My son is in *desperate* need of spectacles. I said this to explain the business with the spider!"

He steps between her and the wardrobe. He stares until she stops talking and looks at him. "Is marriage always consequent upon one kiss?" he asks. He folds his arms; his hands have begun to shake. Then, in the candlelight, her colour rises. He has done it — he has managed to call them up. Without stooping to speak of them, he has called up Mr. Ridd on the path in Hammersmith. And the ridiculous painting master caught in the upstairs hall. And Captain Outhwaite, always at their house in Dawlish, always there day and night with his stinking hounds, although there was no hunting.

Her throat has bloomed scarlet, but she does not avert her eyes. "When the maiden is innocent," she says steadily, "as this one appears to be, then it is." They stand with eyes locked until finally he moves aside and goes to the window. "On every occasion that your name is spoken in society, Henry, a story of Great Marlow will follow. This would be a second scandal, to abandon this maiden after such a liberty. It would be *fatal* to all your hopes. And all in all, you could do far worse. Four thousand is a wonderful settlement. Given the situation at Halse Hall, it's a godsend. It's a pity, I agree, that young people are not allowed some few years of indiscretion. But no one is talking about your marrying for ages, not until you come into your own."

Now she has his scarlet uniform in her hand. She holds it up to herself and looks in the mirror. "What was this about, Henry?"

He's considered all winter what he will say. He squares his shoulders, regretting his plaid dressing gown with the ribbon around the waist. "I refuse to be subservient to inferior men," he says.

She sighs and drops the scarlet jacket on the floor. "Oh," she says. "You are such a baby."

"We were *locked in* at night," he cries. "There was a terrible danger of fire. The other cadets were always hiding live coals on a shovel under their beds to drop on someone's head in the dark. Once, they stole over and ignited a boy's bedclothes to frighten the hiccups out of him. And Woodbury! Oh, what a fool! He would squat over a candle in the night to entertain us by igniting his farts."

To his fury, she laughs. "Well," she says. "Courage under fire! It *is* a military academy."

He listens, appalled. This was his trump card, the prospect of a hideous death for her only child. "There is something else," he says. He'll tell her, then, about the subaltern leaving them outside Mr. Truepenny's chamber, and how he gave up his honour. She'll see his need to be taken in hand, she'll understand the dimensions of her neglect. He hadn't planned to come at the subject like this, but it seems he will have to.

She moves towards him. She reaches up and kisses him. "Yes," she says. "There is something else, but it's very late. We'll talk in the morning." She opens the door, leaving her hat behind, and lets in a single strike of the hall clock on her way out.

Over breakfast, she tells him that she herself is engaged to be married, to a Mr. William Aveline of Lyme Regis, a man he's never met. "I regret that you haven't made his acquaintance before now, Henry," she says. "I regret it with all my heart. You will be the best of companions. He is a great walker, a great lover of the natural world." She gives Henry a curiosity that washed up on the shore at Lyme Regis, to show him the sort of pursuits that await him in his new home. It's a heavy stone, flat and solid like a huge coin, seemingly made of a snake tightly curled up into itself.

"Is it a shell?" he asks. "How was it made?"

"It's a curiosity," says Alger in rebuke. "Why would they call it a curiosity if they knew?"

"In any case, my love," his mother cries gaily, putting out a cheek to be kissed, "engagements are the order of the day! And a lifetime of joy to us both." Then she ties on her bonnet and goes to town.

She comes back in the afternoon with a pin in a brocade box. It's a dove, pavé-winged in turquoise, and it bears a tiny ring in its golden beak. Letitia will apparently understand this pin as an offer of marriage. Sullivan will deliver it (When? *Directly*) with a note written by Henry, assuring Letitia that the writer of the note and the dove are united in their sentiments. Tomorrow morning, Henry will present himself at Captain Whyte's front door. He will request permission to ask for Miss Whyte's hand, and Captain Whyte will give it. Then Letitia will receive him in the morning room. (What will I say? *You will begin with a contrite apology.*) There's also the matter of the ring, which Alger takes from the safe and presents to Henry with great ceremony, the ring with the pebble in it – an unpolished tourmaline, as it turns out. Hopefully, all will be accomplished without delay, for it's imperative his mother be on the road by noon. Letitia is spending the next few months in Bristol, perhaps the whole year, and so shall Henry. It will be a fine opportunity for them to become better acquainted.

She arranges all this over four o'clock Madeira in the panelled drawing room, Alger wheezing and interrupting. She is handing him over to the girl in the woods. Henry has no way of understanding tactics gone so terribly awry. Most matches are arranged this way, Alger assures him in the self-satisfied tones of one who's escaped. They typically begin with a youthful indiscretion. His mother talks gently and warmly about his new obligations, but he can't listen. He sees what's at the heart of it, how well this suits her purposes. All is changed. He has crossed a river: to adulthood, to where his mother was (he thought, throughout these last months). But she's changed too; she's moved on ahead and vanished into her own private bower of happiness. The poise she carried in Alger's front door under her lavender bonnet was not an affectation. It was utter indifference to Henry and what will become of him.

·❊I T W E L V E ❊·

Squire Henley's desire for a piece of blue silk fabric changed everything for the Annings that fall. He saw the silk in a shop in Charmouth – a bolt of it, enough for a cushioned divan, although it was only when he got home that he realized how much he fancied it, and had to arrange for someone to go back to fetch it. Mary would not have imagined Squire Henley a man to develop a passion for silk upholstery fabric, nor a man to have difficulty making up his mind. But both of these things appeared to be true.

Mary gained this access into the Squire's character while she and Joseph sat cleaning and polishing fossils one evening. In the months since Richard's death, Joseph had become a version of their father, tall and tense and unkempt, his eyebrows growing together over his nose. The way his upper lip rested on the bottom spoke of nervous secrets. But that night, he was congenial, and as they worked, he told her how Squire Henley had visited the uphol-stery shop just before closing and how Mr. Armstrong had offered to send his apprentice to Charmouth to fetch the fabric in the morning. A purse of money had changed hands. Fourteen shillings! For a piece of silk on which to park his beefy thighs!

But an hour after Joseph left in the morning for Charmouth, he was back without the fabric. He had gone by the shore and discovered a landslip under Black Ven. Not that he couldn't pass – but in the black marl and limestone was something he wanted to show Mary. Teeth in the rock!

"A crocodile?" said Mary, standing very still in the kitchen. She'd been getting ready to go to the shore herself, although a storm was brewing.

Joseph's face was scarlet and sweat dripped from under his cap. "Certain-sure," he said. "Or a great boogerin' bird. I stepped on its boogerin' beak before I saw it."

"You were afraid to look at it."

"No! I'm afraid of Armstrong, if I don't get to Charmouth and back betimes." He shook the purse in her face to show her, its drawstring looped around his wrist. "He'll *skin* me if he knows I turned back. Are you coming?"

Molly sat at the table mending Lizzie's stocking. "Pitch a stone before you go near," she said, not looking up. "Be sure it's dead."

Pelting over the sea-combed weed on the foreshore, Mary kept her eyes pinned ahead for the first sight of a dragon lying on the sands. A dragon washed out of its lair. When Black Ven loomed over them, Joseph clambered past her and ran ahead. The debris of the landslip lay at the foot of the cliff – clods of rude mud as though a giant had cleaned his boots there, and broken slate and stone. Up near the base of the cliff, Joseph stopped and stood over something like a pointer. It was a slab of limestone as big as the two of them. Above, Mary could see the broken cliff face it had fallen from. Twenty feet up.

It was not a dragon, it was only figured grey stone, sunk into grey stone. A skeleton fused with its own monument. She could have passed by without seeing it. But there was Joseph panting eagerly over it. "See!" he cried, and she bent and put her hand down and felt exposed teeth. A prickle moved down her legs and she pulled her hand back.

"Go back to town," she said. "Ask Armstrong for a day off."

"He'll never give it. He thinks the collecting is a sin. We'll write to Buckland. He'll hire men to get it out. Twenty pound, he said."

"No!" said Mary. "He said twenty pound for a whole skeleton. If Buckland digs it out, he'll never pay us." Besides, he had never answered her letter.

Grey clouds sat right down on the cliff above them. Terns dipped and spun through the clouds. Joseph stared back at her, but it was her anthracite eyes she'd turned on him, and his eyelids fluttered. He took his cap off and wiped his forehead and then, on his hot face, she saw something astonishing: surrender, relief. "Mary, I must go," he said. "Or he'll sack me, certain-sure. I'll come back this way. I'll see how you're getting on."

"No," said Mary. "The tide will be in, you won't get around the point. Take the cliff path home."

She waited while he dwindled along the foreshore, not wanting to examine the creature until she was alone. She had known they'd find the crocodile, but she'd never pictured it in the rock like this. Months, it would take, to chip it out. The thought did not numb her – it thrilled her. Months of work, and then twenty pounds. We will be *depauperized*. She whispered the word, a favourite expression of the Parish Overseer. We will give half to the Overseer to distribute among the names in our book and we will keep half for ourselves. And I will write a text like the texts in the Sowerby book and sell it to all the scholars.

Joseph had come to a halt. He was standing like a stunpoll on the satiny foreshore to the east. What was he waiting for? "Go on!" she screamed, and threw her fist at him. But it was a distant rock she was scolding — he had turned up the path to Charmouth and she was alone on the shore.

Only one side of the jaw was visible, as long as her arm. It was like a weathered log cemented in the limestone. Top and bottom jaw both there, the teeth clenched. The teeth were pointed, meant for killing, each tooth as big as her thumb. She'd wanted Joseph gone, but now that he was she could hardly force herself to touch it. But she did, and it was cold to her fingers. There would be claws to match the teeth, a lashing tail. Not in this rock, though. The whole head might be here, but the body would lie in the cliff above. She scrambled back, frightened suddenly to be standing between the creature's head and its body.

The storm was brewing up. It was very close, black over the Channel. She watched the breakers slam against the rocks and then the water sink in a low, moaning retreat to meet the next wave. Lightning flickered and there was a smell in the air. *Brimstone*, she thought. Very near here, in a cottage just outside Charmouth, a woman noted for cursing had been killed by lightning. It had burst open the door of her house and torn off her hair and clothing. Please, Mary prayed in a panic, bring Mr. Buckland back! Let him float over the stones in his top hat and gown. Let him raise his face to the sky and cry, *Here is all the bounty of the Lord made manifest!* She braced herself to look again at the dreadful teeth in the rock, and it came over her with a shock how real they were, ridged and graduated, the remains of a real creature. She'd had the notion that God had carved such fossils in stone, just for sport. But this dragon had crawled or swum along this very shore. Frightened fishes had darted before it and it had snatched them up with these teeth. Just here, under this black sky, a dragon had lived its awful life, thoughtless of God. And something in its life or death had turned it to stone.

Black clouds collided over the Channel with a terrible thud. Raindrops fell hard on her face and shoulders and pocked the grey water. If I die here, the angels will be afraid to come for me, Mary thought. She turned to leave, and then scurried back and kicked soft mud over the teeth to hide them, and then she pelted with all her might towards town.

By evening, the storm was over. The sky was clear, although you could hear the sea still fretting over the disturbance. Mary lay down for the night as the sun sank below Ware Cliffs. Molly had asked her to move up to the bed now that Richard was gone, but Mary would not. Every morning now, Molly's sorrow woke with the light, and Mary did not wish to share it. So Mary was on her pallet and Molly sat above, undoing Lizzie's plaits, running her fingers down the kinky strands. "In the morning, we will wash it," she said. Then she laid Lizzie down and said a bed-charm over her: *Four corners to my bed, four angels all a-spread. One at head and one at feet and two to keep my soul asleep.*

When Molly was gone, Lizzie dangled a hand off the bed. "Mary?" she whispered. "Will I have an egg at market today?"

"Tomorrow, you mean," Mary said. "Maybe. Now go to sleep." When Lizzie was quiet, she cautiously approached the idea of the creature, lying outside this very moment as the sun sank redly below the cliffs. Methodically, she outlined the situation: The fossil is above the high-tide line, right up against the base of the cliff. Unless a huge tempest blows up, the sea will not touch it. I will have time to chip it out. I will chip it out and sell it. We will pay down our debt, and we will have ten pounds for ourselves, if I be not a cowheart. God has sent it to save us. But why has he sealed it in rock, and what will I waken if I free it?

She slid away from the thought, she slid towards sleep. Then James Wheaton was at the pallet in the dark attic, leaning over her, saying her name. *Mary. Mary. Mary Anning – do you not hear my voice? Do you not see? It is the Great Dragon Himself, cast into the world. He is a deceiver! He will suck you all down.* We are starving, she murmured, putting her hands over her eyes. *Better to starve.* James Wheaton said. *Better to die in the love of the Lord.*

Mary was awake then. She rolled over onto her stomach and turned her face to the side, against the smell of moulding straw in her pallet. Molly came in and lay down in the bed, and soon after Joseph, dropping heavily down on his pallet on the other side. Molly's breathing turned to a thin snore and Mary lifted herself to her knees and laid her face against the bed. She pressed her face into the blanket and rocked for a minute to comfort herself. She tried Lizzie's prayer: *Four corners to my bed, four angels all a-spread.* But when she got to *two to keep my soul asleep*, she could not say it. She sank back onto her pallet. She did not want her soul asleep.

Sometime in the night, her father came in. Not in a dream; she did not speak to him nor he to her. But in the morning, when Mary was wakened by her mother's low keening, she saw the long shape of him lying in the bed. His form faded away as the light came in around the shutter, but when Mary scrambled out of her bedclothes and sat for a minute on the edge of her mother's bed, she could sense him still in the room. He was there in the way she pulled in her breath, dark and heedless, unafraid.

Downstairs, Mary built a fire and boiled the kettle. She made her mother sit up before she would bring her tea. Then she combed out Molly's hair and wiped her soft white face with a wet flannel. Molly smiled as though Mary's solicitude carried her back to a time before sorrow had chosen her as its favourite. She smelled of her sad bed and her unwashed nightdress, but Mary's kindness would carry her no further – she was desperate to get to the shore. Joseph was up by then, filling the kitchen with Richard's shape. Mary pulled her father's codgloves over her hands and got her tools from the workshop. As they left, they carried the table between them out to the street so Molly could sell later in the day.

"Did you start to open it?" Joseph asked in Cockmoile Square. He meant the fossil.

"I'll start today," said Mary. Molly called to Mary to check the weather vane on the market tower but Mary turned and ran up towards Church Street as though she had not heard.

It was a day of fog and rain. The cliffs had vanished. The town was the whole world, a brave, wet circle of thatch and stone in a sea of dove grey. She left the circle of the world and started down the beach.

THIRTEEN

H enry walks the ten paces to the house next door as if he's facing his execution. But Captain Whyte, who receives him alone in his study, merely puts his newspaper aside with a *let's be quick about it* expression, and Henry is obliged to launch directly into his proposal. Neither does Letitia seem to expect anything more than the mandatory question when he bows over her hand. "Yes," she says with a giggle, and he slips the rustic ring on her finger. She holds her hand up to show how much too big it is. Captain Whyte, standing at the door, says, "There's a goldsmith on the bridge who will size it for you," and Henry promises to see to it.

Then they sit all three in the morning room and the coals in the grate turn silently, flamelessly to ash, sending out the stuffy heat that induces sleep. Captain Whyte does indeed love to talk, and holds strong opinions about what he calls "the Guinea business" — he seems to relish the fact that the young scion of a plantation has fallen under his influence. The mismanagement of the trade disgusts him, how fearfully gutted Bristol commerce was by its collapse. Why was the Royal African Company's monopoly allowed to go on for so long? Why did the Bristol ships insist on trading in beads and textiles from the East Indies when the Liverpool traders were clever enough to stock themselves in domestic goods? Henry raises his eyebrows and smiles on cue. "Black ivory," the Captain calls the slaves, as though to establish himself as an insider. But there is something about the man Henry likes, the hint of Ireland in his speech, and the young adventurer he was still peeping from his narrow eyes. Across the room, Letitia inclines gracefully in a pale blue gown, pleating the skirt between her fingers, looking up from time to time to catch Henry's eyes, her own greenly glittering. At the first chance, she jumps to her feet and asks whether Henry may take her walking. And so they go out, Letitia holding her white parasol in one hand and clinging to his arm with the other. They walk out to Redcliff Way and gaze at the cygnets reflected on the water, and he feels grateful to these birds for their calm beauty, for providing the adornment the day seems to require.

After that, they walk together every morning, and the cygnets are always there. Mute swans, they are: he points out the distinguishing lump at the base of the beak, and the curve of the neck. "People assume all swans are white," he tells his fiancée. "But the swans of the southern hemisphere are black and white, and the swans of Australia are black. In the Americas, there are swans with pink legs and feet. So I have read."

He feels a pleasant heat when she takes his arm. Her physical perfection amazes him – her poreless skin, the curls springing out between her bonnet and cheek, glittering like copper wire, her perfectly oval little face, the pretty curve of her lips, the white teeth revealed when she smiles. I could kiss her with impunity, he thinks (the liberties to which an engaged man is entitled having been the subject of a deal of private speculation). But it seems a preposterous notion – as though by entering into this pledge, he's taken on the role of protector, a proxy for her uncle. In any case, the libidinous tide that had swept him up has somewhat withdrawn. His foray into the woods seems mad to him now. They were all mad. That their guardians should, for so slight a thing, allow the fates of two young strangers to become forever entwined is deeply perplexing. There must be some hidden logic in it, a social precept so profound as to be unknowable, and he will have a lifetime to uncover it.

Her family is originally from Ireland. She was born in Lough-brickland, County Down. She's only fourteen, but she's been out for a year. She came out at the time of her mother's new mar-riage. In the past season, she stayed with families in London, Shrewsbury, and Bath, and has collected many friends in her travels, with whom she corresponds avidly: Miss Francine Mortimer, Miss Mathilda Sheffield, Miss Ann Wakefield, Miss Sarah Morland (the latter two have recently acquired fiancés), and her dear cousin Penrose. The adventures of her correspondents, their flirtations in assembly rooms and country houses all over the kingdom, she breathlessly recounts in confiding tones, as though Henry is intimately acquainted with the individuals in question.

"I spent the early years of my childhood in Jamaica," Henry says. He has volunteered several pieces of information about himself, including the fact that he was briefly at Great Marlow, but she seems incurious. Or perhaps she is extraordinarily tactful.

"*Jamaica!* Did you go to St. Kitts? Miss Fogg grew up in St. Kitts. She is seventeen, do you realize, and not betrothed. She had hopes of a captain with the Staffordshire Regiment, but all the time he was pursuing her own sister!" They've reached the junction with Baldwin Street, and she stops short and looks at him with an expression of high animation. "*Baldwin Street,*" she cries. "When we promenade on Baldwin Street, we must converse in French all the way up and all the way back. It's one of my rules!" She resumes walking, playfully spinning her parasol. "*Et qui connaissez-vous à Bristol?*" she asks. On the evidence, it would appear her French tutor was educated in Belfast.

"*La veuve Rankin,*" he replies. "*Personne d'autre.*" She looks at him with disbelief and wrinkles her nose.

She comes to tea at Alger's and is given a tour of the paintings in the study. Then Henry displays his bird drawings. She falls into silence at the sight of them and he is encouraged to go on, to draw the tea box of tiny bones onto the table. "I never imagined birds to have such a large pelvic bone," he says, using a quill tip as pointer to trace the bone in question. "Actually, there are many features to these skeletons that surprised me. Imagine if you'd stumbled across one and had never seen a bird! Look at the little chain of vertebrae at the base of this spine. If you were unacquainted with *feathers*, wouldn't you assume this creature to have had a short tail, like a terrier?"

But in response, she flings herself away from the table. "Who is there on God's earth that has not seen a bird?" she cries shrilly. "Certainly not Mr. Henry De la Beche, who knows all there is to know about swans and hedge sparrows and their precious feathers and the colour of their legs!"

It is Alger who rescues him, opening up the pianoforte and inviting Miss Whyte to play, which she is happy to do. Henry closes the tea box and takes his place on the settee, where he sits smarting through a surprisingly expert rendition of a Haydn sonata.

She makes a point of telling him that she's never once been to the Hotwell spa, or to the Pump Room, or the Clifton Assembly Rooms: her uncle refuses to take her. Having established himself as a pedant, having failed to proffer a collection of distinguished friends, Henry can at least escort her to the Assembly Rooms, although whom they will converse with there without an introduction is a mystery to him. Uncle Alger offers the closed carriage, and on the agreed-upon Wednesday afternoon, pleased with the prospect of a drive up the Avon gorge to Clifton, Henry goes to collect Letitia and brings her to the house first for a word with his uncle. She is standing in the drawing room in high spirits, handsomely dressed in a new ensemble of rose and tan, when Sullivan announces a caller, a Mr. William Conybeare. "The bishop!" Alger cries. "I thought he had died."

He's still puzzling over the marvellous honour inexplicably bestowed upon him when Sullivan opens the door again to reveal a tall young man with a strikingly handsome and engaging face. The *grandson* of the famous and long-dead bishop, as it turns out, a fellow of Christ Church College, Oxford, and about to take holy orders himself. Mr. Conybeare hastens to explain the call: he's a frequent sojourner in Lyme Regis, where he recently dined at Aveline House, and it is Henry's mother who has sent him. After introductions are performed, Henry confesses that he has not yet met Mr. Aveline and their caller goes on to describe him as a fine fellow, an expert on many subjects in the natural world. "He owns a clockwork model of the heavens. When I was there, he set the spheres revolving for my amusement. He has been a bachelor all his days, and there was much amazement when his engagement was announced. Apparently your mother accomplished in an hour what maiden ladies of the region had spent years attempting! And you will both be in Dorsetshire before long, I understand?" With Alger chiming in on the third syllable of every word, trying to finish his guest's sentences, Conybeare tells them what unrivalled scenery they will find there, what delights await them in the spectacular walks along the cliffs and the shore.

"Henry is going to Dorsetshire, but I am not," says Letitia, perching on the edge of a chair and taking off her gloves. "I am going to London for the season. I am to be the guest of Mrs. Billings of Mayfair. Mrs. Anthony Billings?" And to Henry's chagrin, she arches her fine brows knowingly at their guest. But it appears that Mr. Conybeare *is* acquainted with Mrs. Anthony Billings, and can attest to her amiable manner and the amusing pug that sits by her chair. The very model of a gentleman, Mr. William Conybeare, with his slender aquiline nose and quick, candid eyes, and a flourish to the tying of his cravat to which Henry can only aspire (and also the tiniest pause before each of his graceful utterances, as though his new acquaintances are the subject of some amusement to him. But perhaps not). Deftly setting aside Alger's detailed inquiries into his health and the health of various members of his family (individuals entirely unknown to Uncle Alger), Conybeare turns back to Henry. "Well, sir, if you are to be on your own in Lyme Regis, you must join the ranks of the gentlemen collectors! You will be amazed at the variety of fossils one is able to procure on those shores."

So (at the risk of appearing a child) Henry draws the curiosity his mother brought him out of his waistcoat pocket, where he's taken to carrying it for the pleasure of its weight and the feel of its coils.

"Indeed, that is a beauty!" Conybeare declares.

"I have no idea what it is," says Henry. "I confess to ignorance regarding the very nature of fossils."

"They are an age-old mystery, indeed," says Conybeare, and then he will not unravel it – he makes them guess.

"It was left by fairies!" says Letitia immediately. "They stole a child and left this stone in its place!" Conybeare laughs heartily. Uncle Alger pronounces it to be a stone carved by the Druids. As for Henry, he hesitates, palming the curiosity. There is something so marvellously delicate about its descending coils, each of them minutely ridged in gold, as to make him believe it must be organic. This is the sort of detail that an artisan can only allude to.

Finally he asks, "Can it possibly be the shell of a sea creature?" and Conybeare says, "Well done," and goes on to tell them that science agrees that curiosities of this type are the remains of molluscs unknown now in Britain, presumably migrated to other waters. This one is an *ammonite*, although Conybeare cannot classify it as to type. As to its strange composition, why, perhaps it turned to stone as a consequence of the unique atmospheric conditions at the time of the Great Flood.

"Where at Lyme Regis does one find them?"

"Oh, there are curiosity-mongers in the lower town who sell them for a pittance."

They're seated on either side of the fire, and somehow Alger's sitting room has transformed itself into an inviting salon, and Henry has begun to anticipate the pleasure of discussing his bird skeletons with Mr. Conybeare. But Letitia moves restlessly to stand by the hearth and it is difficult to avoid her eyes. How can he suggest postponing the outing to the Assembly Rooms without driving their guest away? Then, with an agile leap into the conversation, Letitia pre-empts him.

"And will we find Lyme Regis a lively centre for dancing and card playing and such?" she asks. From there, it's just a few neat steps to the Clifton Assembly Rooms, and to the happy discovery that Mr. Conybeare had considered attending that very afternoon and would be pleased to accompany them now. And then Henry is settling himself into the carriage, he is waving goodbye to a disconsolate uncle, thinking all the while, Never must I underestimate Letitia Whyte, where social arrangements are concerned.

Here at last is Letitia's entry to Bristol society, for if William Conybeare is not acquainted with every person in the room, he is certainly acquainted with the most prominent. Cards are abandoned in favour of dancing, and then Henry is abandoned in favour of a partner who knows the steps, and so he finds himself happily standing by the punch bowl with Conybeare. The fiddles strike up and the dancers rise unevenly from honouring their partners, and Conybeare tells Henry that this particular dance sprang up in Devonshire, inspired by a military exercise performed on horseback. *Walk. Trot. Canter. Gallop*, he says softly at intervals as the linked couples swing past. He confesses to a fiancée of his own, who also loves to dance. He confesses as well to the hope of a lectureship at Bristol; it was the need to cultivate old ties that prompted his current visit. And he frankly tells his age: he's ten years older than Henry, yet in his telling, Henry is encouraged to believe that they may become friends.

"How did you begin to collect at Lyme Regis?" Henry asks.

"My friend and colleague William Buckland was born near there. He teaches now at Oxford. The little curiosities found at Lyme Regis are fascinating, but it seems also that many large creatures perished there in the Flood, and these are the focus of his study. There's a great deal of pressure on Buckland to find evidence for his theories, if he wishes to retain a chair in Undergroundology. He's been on an extended research tour for that purpose, although the Lyme Regis area remains the most significant site. Buckland has spent years trying to dissuade the ignorant townsfolk from grinding valuable fossils up for lime, for the stucco trade."

While he talks, his eyes are on Letitia's curls, the brightest patch of colour in the long line of muslin and ribbons. She executes a graceful turn a few feet away from them and Conybeare looks back at Henry, flashing him an approving smile.

She has very little family left in Ireland, just a few cousins. In England, there is only her cousin Penrose and her mother, to whom Henry is soon to be presented. The occasion is several times postponed, although the inn in question, a prosperous establishment called the Full Moon, is not a mile away. Its proprietor is a Mr. Auriol. "On the evidence of his name, your stepfather would appear to be of French extraction," Henry observes.

"I really have no idea," Letitia says coolly.

Finally, on a Sunday afternoon, Mrs. Auriol appears at Captain Whyte's, alone and in ill humour. She's a dark-eyed, unhappy-looking woman – Letitia bears very little resemblance to her – who resided in Bath before her remarriage and makes much of the absence of sedan chairs in Bristol. "It was a moment of folly," Henry's mother said of her marriage, and Henry studies Mrs. Auriol's face and bearing for evidence of a passionate nature. She asks Henry three questions: where his mother lives, what his annual income is likely to be at his majority, and whether the cane-cutters on the plantation live in trees, as she has heard. She receives his answers gloomily. "It would be more commendable to provide employment for the destitute Christian of England," she observes.

"Alas, the English constitution cannot withstand the tropical heat – to work in it, I mean. Indentured servants from Ireland and Scotland were used in the early days of the West Indies colonies, and a year or two of cutting cane generally killed them. When you consider it fully, slavery is in some ways more humane than indentureship. Ownership provides an incentive not to drive your workers to death – when indeed, with indentured servants, the impulse was to do so, to avoid paying them out at the end of their term." He has no idea where this argument is coming from, but he finds himself propounding it with some heat. "When the workers are your greatest capital investment, you must maintain them. Especially now, with the Wilberforce Bill, now that the trade has been abolished and the workforce can no longer be replenished at the next docking of a ship from Guinea, we must subsist the slaves properly so that they will breed."

She looks at him, confounded. The old uncle seems to be biting his tongue. Perhaps he's developing a new respect for Henry.

After Mrs. Auriol leaves, Henry invites Letitia out to the garden. "I sense your mother may have been angry about something."

"She loathes my uncle because he will not receive her husband."

"Your stepfather."

She gives her little laugh. "Hardly that. I was in Bath when they married and I did not trouble myself to come down. I don't speak of him. It is one of my rules." And then, to his surprise, tears well in her eyes. She looks up at him with a transparent expression he's never seen in her before, and goes to speak again, and then puts her hands over her face.

He reaches for a hand, draws it down, and leans forward to plant a kiss on her damp cheek. "When I come into my own," he says, "we shall marry and never trouble with such things. We shall take a Grand Tour. To Paris and Venice and Mont Blanc. The war will be over by then."

"Do you think the war is going to end?"

"Well, of course it will end, one day."

She shakes him off and trips back across the garden, swinging her skirts like a child. "I hope the war is never over!" she cries in a falsely exuberant voice. "Never! I *adore* the uniforms. Oh, Henry, do enlist!"

"How can I enlist?" he shouts, exasperated, as she disappears through the door.

All their courtship was squeezed into five unconscious minutes in the copse behind her uncle's house. He feels the loss of it, of *courtship* itself; the very word has about it a sense of ritual and leisurely pursuit. It also seems a pity to him that she came out at such a young age, in that her lessons were stopped. Her life looks unbearably tedious to him – worse than his. But she is never bored for long. In the vicissitudes of dressmaking and hair curling and calling card and post, she manages to find drama. She comes down the stairs on his arrival, breathless with eagerness, and Henry listens closely to discover the pending event that accounts for her excitement. But it all seems to spring from a source within herself, her own talent for endowing the day with intrigue.

On a sunny morning, he suggests they take their easels to the back garden to paint together, but she professes to detest painting, she adamantly refuses. "But you were painting in the garden the day I made your acquaintance," he says, "and for several days before."

"How ever would we have met, else?" she asks saucily. "My uncle would not be troubled to arrange an introduction."

There is a terrible clatter – the butler is tipping coals into the hearth – and she sits smiling up at him, picturesquely arranged in the divan cushions, and then gives the little laugh that has so begun to annoy him. Henry turns and walks out, snatching up his hat from the hall table. He does not trouble to see that the door is closed properly but turns sharply away from his uncle's house and angles across the road, fury clutching at his stomach.

Pretending to paint – pretending to an interest that was never hers – how much of what she seems to be is pretence? The ridiculous little laugh – it is the laugh of a coquette! He sees himself floundering in the woods, a helpless dupe caught in her snare. A snare laid with absolute indifference to the real qualities of the man she'd chosen as her prey. And he fell into it. He allowed himself to become fodder for prattling letters to her silly friends. He is at Queen Square by then, walking kitty-corner across a park lined with mansions built by the Guinea trade. As would be evident to anyone walking through the square, by the number of Negro servants one sees – here a groom leading a pair of geldings towards a stable, here a gardener bent over the hedge (and he thinks briefly of the fierce and piteous woman he saw in Piccadilly, and wonders what became of her). He feels himself outside it all – Henry Beach, who will live life on his own terms. The day he walked to the neighbouring house to propose marriage to this girl, the thought he held to was this: I shall get the foundation of my gentleman's life in place and then I need not trouble myself. *I shall give them this because it's meaningless, and I shall be as I was.* And it's true, he will need to have a home, and that home will need to have a wife in it. Or I shall become Uncle Alger, he thinks.

He's a little calmer now, and he asks himself whether he loves her to any degree, and whether it matters. He considers how similar they are, their childhoods both spent on green islands far away, the lost fathers they hardly recall. She's not sensible, but from all reports, young ladies are not. She is pleasing to look at and thrilling to touch. She seems to know how to conduct herself in society, if you make allowances for how very young she is. Already she has a facility with dress and charming gesture that surpasses that of other, older girls. His mother felt she would grow into something.

Henry is out of Queen Square now and walking quickly, almost running, along Welsh Back towards the bridge. *She is willing to overlook my disgrace at Marlow. She has an annual income*

of four thousand pounds. I will have nothing, nothing from the plan-
tation. She has a dreadful mother, but one unlikely to meddle.
Any man would be proud to have her on his arm. And then he is
on the bridge, darting nimbly between the strolling couples.
Most engagements begin in this fashion. So fine a gentleman as
Mr. William Conybeare admired her.

He returns to her house the next day. He does not apologize and
she does not reproach him. She asks him whether he will paint a
formal portrait of her and he agrees. He decides to pose her
indoors, as many sittings may be required. Inspired by her gown's
evocation of the classical period, he arranges her standing with
one hand on a chair, which he will afterwards represent as a broken
column. He does a charcoal sketch first to test out the composition. The arms and torso are three poorly stuffed sausages, and
the face, while recognizable as a young lady's, is not recognizable
as hers; it seems he saw her more clearly a month ago, when he
sketched her through the window. Captain Whyte shuffles into the
morning room and looks at his easel, bemused.

When Henry is leaving, the old man follows him into the hall
and slips him a shabby leather-bound book. "We'll keep this
away from the young lady's eyes," he says, winking. It's an
anatomy, which opens to a plate of a dark-haired young man
smiling amiably, lifting a flap of skin in his abdomen to show the
musculature beneath. "He may smile, poor wretch," says
Captain Whyte. "They're all miscreants. Cut open still warm
from the scaffold."

In the privacy of his own bedchamber, inside the Bedouin tent,
Henry pages through the folio. Typically, the corpse is represented
in three panels: a cadaver lying on a slab, its head wrenched to the
left shoulder by the hangman's rope; then the flayed corpse, apparently called the *écorché*, then the skeleton. It's dead, he thought,

staring at the first panel. But there is still deader and deadest. He examines the *écorché*. It's like a mummy, thickly bandaged in muscle. Its penis and testicles are gone, stripped off with its skin. None of the plates in the book represents the female form.

In the end, he arranges her at her desk in the morning room, writing a letter – a most appropriate pose, and thus he has only the head and bosom and shoulders to tackle. And the arms and hands. The hands will be difficult, but he can practise at home, using his own as a model. They work together at the desk to make a pleasing composition of her inkwell and blotting paper and a candelabra.

As he begins, she reads him her morning post, lapsing occasionally into silence, laughing softly, her colour rising. Then she takes up her own pen.

"To whom are you writing?" he asks.

"To Penrose. My cousin."

"And what are you telling him?" He's talking like a ventriloquist to encourage her to be still.

It's futile. She wiggles in her chair, turns her shoulders, dips her pen. "I'm telling him about you," she says dreamily as she writes. "My fiancé . . . is . . . painting me. He is . . . in a foul temper . . . but he is painting me."

This is his opportunity to know her, to spend hours studying her face. She's wearing the delicate muslin gown she wore the day he met her. There is the infamous mole, and the shadow where her breasts divide, and he returns to his recent preoccupation: how incomplete a picture of the creature does a set of bones provide! An inquiring mind unacquainted with the human form would never dream of *breasts* on a skeleton, for example. Suddenly he is that mind: suddenly he is floating in the dusty sunlight of the cluttered morning room, he is a point of view unacquainted with birds or with man, lifted beyond the ivy growing at the window and the artist's palette smeared with pigments, staring, fascinated and aghast, at hairless limbs and a bosom like the flesh of a fetal pig he saw once in a bottle in Piccadilly, staring at an alien creature of the forest or ocean, incongruously clothed, its eye a greenish membrane with life peeping frighteningly out of it.

ary crouched beside the creature for a long time before she set to work. It was the colour and texture of a driftwood log, only the shape of it was animal and the feel of it was rock. The limestone was a frozen sea and the creature was just surfacing in it, coming up for air. Was it a crocodile jaw? How could she know – she'd never seen a picture of a crocodile. Only dragons. The roiling dragons in James Wheaton's bible had smaller mouths, curved fangs like cats.

God had sent this creature to save Mary and her family. Or Lucifer had sent it to destroy them. If she took it out and looked at it, she would know which. Once its beak is free, it will speak, she thought, it will tell me what it is. She would start with the beak because it was partly exposed and also for a secret reason: because there are dragons that can slay you by casting their eyes on you.

On the shore, when your head is bent, it's easy to imagine someone coming up behind you. You have sight, but the surf blocks out sound, the shingle scraping as the sea rakes it, the sea dumping its water on the foreshore, load after load. But she kept her head bent, and in the course of the morning, she exposed a section as big as her hand, working slowly with a quarter-inch chisel and her father's hammer, the chisel discerning stone that was only stone from stone that was bone.

She took off her bonnet and felt the sun warm her hair, brushing shards of shale off the fossil with her fingers. She was not afraid to touch the creature now. She felt the long, hard teeth with admiration. They were not in separate sockets, as Buckland had said they must be – this was likely to reduce the value. But when she was done, she would look for the body, although how she would climb up to the cliff she could not imagine. When she found it, while she chipped it out, she would keep the head in the workshop, safe from storms and landslips. She no longer worried that someone would steal the head, for stealing it was what she was doing, and it would take many a day. All the same, when the tide was halfway in and she had to leave, she shoved marl up close to the beak to cover it.

Back home, wet-shod, Mary hung a blanket over the window of the workshop. They will get used to the workshop closed off, was her thought. Later, when my creature is here, no one will ask.

"To keep the house warm," she explained to Mrs. Bennett, who stood in the kitchen talking to Molly.

"If it's freezing you be," said Mrs. Bennett, "'tis better on your bed than on the window." Complaints about Mary hung in the air. Mrs. Bennett, who had always been so kind, had begun to complain: that Mary took no notice of their Annie, that she chawed high, with her creeping after that maggoty professor and the Philpot sisters.

Molly looked fondly at Mary with her sad, luminous eyes. "Oh, she's a history and a mystery," she said, "our Mary."

———

Joseph would help on the Sabbath, he said, but Mary would not go to the shore on the Sabbath. So she worked alone. She worked along the tapered beak for many days. The second week, she uncovered a nostril as big as her thumb, set into the beak the way a bird's nostril is. In the end, the beak was the length of six hand spans. In one hand span, she counted eighteen teeth. This meant two hundred teeth in its whole jaw. Imagine it opening its maw in appeal to Noah as the rain fell! Noah must have fled in terror. But Noah kept tigers. Of course, tigers have a mighty fear of water, and would mind themselves.

On Sunday she went to chapel. They all went, and sat where they used to sit when their father took them. Did James Wheaton know? He could not know about the creature, but he certainly knew that she was selling again from the curiosity table. Yet he did not preach warnings from her father's example in chapel, did not go from cottage to cottage to get Mrs. Stock and the other chattermags riled up. His text for the day was a mild one, from Timothy. *For the time will come when they will not endure sound doctrine; but after their own lusts shall they heap to themselves teachers, having itching ears; and they shall turn away their ears from the truth, and turn unto fables.* She listened with half a mind, watching a father-long-legs on the wall lift its legs one by one, as though to count them. And then, in a stroke, she saw that the text was for her. A duller pastor might think it was for *coin* she collected, might preach against the love of money. But James Wheaton saw her for the girl she was; he saw the questions and the striving, the hunger gnawing in her brain. She crossed her feet at the ankles, lifted her face to the light of the window. *Itching ears*, she said to herself, and her love for him swelled and caught at her breath.

This was what her life would be without her father. The wild squabbles of gulls on the seawall, waking up to acrimony. The cold fresh air in her lungs, her body beginning to tingle with moving, the line of crimson showing over the tops of the houses on the eastern shore. The smell from Mr. Besley's open door, and the warm bread, for Joseph would go ahead to get a loaf and cut it into four with his pocket knife and run back to give the others a portion. Then he and Mary would stop to drink from Nancy's ladle at Gosling Bridge. But they would not dally. Mary must be early to the shore when the tide allowed, for Joseph's Christmas pay was long gone and they were living on the collecting she did walking out to her dragon and back at the end of the day.

It was the right eye she opened first — it took her most of a week — and she was amazed by the size of it. Its socket was oval, not round like the eye of a bird. Had that eye been compressed by the weight of the rock that lay on the dragon, or did it always have such a shape to it, like no creature she had ever seen in this world? There was a wheel of small bones inside the eye cavity. The left eye was not so easy to study: it was somewhat crushed. When both eyes were exposed, the creature looked out to sea with a comical vacant gaze. Strange to be so acquainted with its face and not to know whether you were talking to a bird or a fish or a lizard.

On the Sabbath after she'd chipped out the last bit of the skull, she walked out for a visit after chapel. Coming up the shore now, she stopped at a distance and stared, struck by this new presence at Black Ven. A long, pointed head lying on the rock like a dog's head on the hearth. It was only a head, but it was strangely complete. For all its teeth, it looked meek. It is the eyes that betray character, thought Mary. Cruel people have small eyes (Mrs. Stock came to mind, and the ostler from the George Inn), whereas babies and roe deer and other innocents have large eyes. James Wheaton was wrong: this creature was never one of Lucifer's dragons.

She sat on a rock beside it and thought about her father, the Sabbath mornings when she lay sleeping and felt something strike her cheek – he would have thrown something to wake her, his comb or whatever was to hand. She would climb over the warm breathing heap that was Lizzie and crawl out of the litter of bedclothes while Mother slumbered on her back with Percival on her breast. She'd put on her heavy petticoat and plaid overskirt and slip downstairs, where her father would be munching on yesterday's crusts, and they would set out to the shore. They'd walked this very shore so often, walked it unknowingly, while the creature slept in the cliff above them. And now her father slept in the cliff, and the creature watched the sea.

The creature's piteous, empty eye contemplated her bleakly. Mr. Buckland had not appeared in Dorsetshire since months before her father died, and he had never responded to her letter. And she felt glad of that now, for he would take the creature over, he would make it his own and have it frolicking in God's garden. Perhaps she could find a different buyer. The waves crashed in and withdrew, and oystercatchers ran back and forth on the sand, and she buried her fingers in her soft, hot neck, shrugging a shoulder high to warm them.

That night, she and Joseph stood by the seawall. "I wish I could leave it there while I dig the body out," she said.

"We'd best bring it in so we don't lose it," said Joseph.

"How will we carry it?" asked Mary.

"Put it on a door," said Joseph, and a thread of pain connected them briefly. "If there be something solid under it, the two of us could carry it."

"I reckon not." Mary thought of her father when he brought the skull (the *little* skull, as she thought of it now) back from Pinhay Bay, borrowing the porter's sling and struggling over the rocks. "We need four porters, two on each side."

"I'll ask Ralph Downing and George, then." This was the wheelwright and his son, who had carried Richard home.

She said the thought that was chawing at her: "Whose property is the shore?" A question her dragon had ignored when she'd asked it. Joseph nodded gravely; she knew he understood. Private ownership rose up around them and hemmed them in. Their house, which they let from Mr. Axworthy. The market, where you had to pay a half-crown to put up a stall. The commons, all divided up now by hedges and gates. The hares and grouse and woodcocks hunted by no one but the Squire. Everything owned, everything in the town fenced and paved over, everything belonging to the gentlemen who tipped their top hats to each other outside the Assembly Rooms. One of them owned Black Ven. She had broken into his cellar and she was plotting to haul away the treasure she'd found there. Who from the town could they recruit into such thievery?

There on the western shore at the start of Monmouth Beach was Avery Cottage, brambles filling its garden and creeping over the door. Above it was the path to Ware Manor Farm, and the sycamore with the leaning limb where she'd cried "Watch!" and her father had ducked at the last minute with Lizzie on his shoulders. There was the fork that led to the Undercliff, a narrow path now with rusty rotten leaves trod into it and broken fallen trees that the vines and bracken tried to cover and scarlet stinking iris seeds spilling from their pods. And then another fork, and she knew which path to follow, she had always known, although she'd never followed it, never seen the hut sitting in smoky light

with a barrow pig rooting beside it. A hen peered with cocked head
from a twig-cage and all the gear of a smuggler's business was
scattered huck-a-muck around the clearing, a porter's sling and a
stoneboat and broken crates and barrels, and a stone oven built
outside, smoke rising from its chimney with heat flowing on either
side of it, performing its trick of making the roiling air visible.

A big lad sat slouched on a stump beside the oven. Not Digby —
this lad was too young. He was not Joseph's age. When he saw her
on the path, a smirk came over his face. *You are a wench!* the smirk
seemed to say, and then it grew to a leer, as if she'd shown herself
in her petticoat. Then someone else moved, a hand moved. A man
sat on a bench with his head tipped back. He wore a brimmed
calfskin hat from which hair straggled down to his shoulders. He
was smoking tobacco, not a pipe but a brown stick like a pork
sausage. The clearing stank of the pig and the stick the man was
smoking. "What do ye want?" he said, breathing a curling vine of
smoke out into the sunlight. His face was big and flat and mottled
under the skin, but she could not see his eyes for his hat. He didn't
ask who she was.

"Two porters," she said. "For a night job." She had brought
a sixpence and she tossed it towards Digby. It fell wide and both
men laughed, and neither one bent to pick it up.

"Six shillings when it's done," she said hotly.

After Molly went to bed, Mary and Joseph sat polishing curiosities in the workshop. "Digby!" said Joseph.

"He works in the dark," said Mary.

In the curse of the night was something they said about that
hour. Afterwards, it seemed something she'd done in a dream,
meeting them at the base of Church Cliffs, sensing him there by
the smell of tobacco and then walking single file along the sandy
foreshore, a bleary quarter moon retreating ahead of them. At

Black Ven, the moon's claw retracted behind the cliff, and when they came up on the skull, it was only a gnarled rooted trunk they were lifting onto Digby's carrying board, although he grunted in surprise at the weight of it. A comfortable grounding weight it was as they began to walk, two on each side, grasping the leather straps he had fixed to the board. All the way up the shore they did not speak, and their footfalls were carried away by the surf. Mary began to breathe hard when they came up the path through the graveyard, and it seemed a fearsome thing to carry the skull up past her father's grave and over the mound where lay the mouldering bodies from the plague and then between the dark, unconscious houses on Bridge Street. As they came up into Cockmoile Square, a horse galloped past, sparks leaping from the cobblestones. There Mary called a halt and they rested the board on the top of the empty wooden stocks in front of the prison while she ran ahead to open the door and light the candles she had left at the ready. It was a trick to angle the board down the workshop steps without the load shifting, and the lad put a hand on the log and then cried, "Bleedin' Jesus," at the sight of its grinning jaw in the candlelight. And then their burden was on the work table and Mary was asking herself how they would safely ease it off the carrying board. But both porters had turned and were pounding up the stairs. Because the creature had caught Digby with an accusing eye? Or because he saw where he was, he knew it suddenly for the house of Richard Anning? Mary (who had not a single shilling towards the six she had promised them) called after his retreating back, "I will write you in the book," but they were past hearing. Mary and Joseph both turned then to see Molly standing on the steps with a shawl clutched over her nightdress, staring at the skull. "He's been in our book these dozen years," said Joseph.

The strange thing was that Molly was pleased down to the ground with the monster in the workshop. She said it resembled the figurehead on the prow of a ship, a particular ship she remembered from girlhood, the *Pisces*. Mary grabbed Lizzie by the arms and dragged her in to show her, enjoying her terror. "It's the fish that swallowed Jonah," she said. "Look at its smile!"

Privately, Mary was shocked every time she approached it. At its size – her heart thudded at the size of it indoors. At how indifferent it was to being moved into the house. The house was just two hundred years old, while thousands of years had passed since this creature had swum in the surf or rowed on vast wings over the waves. *Six thousand years*, Mr. Buckland said. She propped her broom against the fossil and stared. She looked at it from each end, and clambered up on the stool to survey it from above. It was a text she could not read, like the lines of print that had once taunted her.

Mary spent a week chipping away the shreds of limestone that still clung to it. She found a soft brush and washed the skull all over with sea water. Outside, emptying the bucket in the river, she scrutinized their own house, wondering whether it looked as it always had to passersby. Dick Mutch, back in the stocks and calm that day, tried to engage her in conversation. "It's by cheatery I be here," he said.

"I believe you," she said, going back inside.

When she climbed up to Silver Street later to get a bucket of sweet water from the spring, she encountered Miss Elizabeth Philpot with one of her sisters. "You haven't been to see us for months," she said.

"My mother needs me," said Mary. She could hardly look at her Miss Philpot, so sharp was her longing to tell. Hesitantly, she asked whether she could come now and Miss Philpot gladly agreed. The three of them climbed the street together. Mary kept her face down. She'll see me changed, she thought. In my face she'll see my conversations with the dragon.

At the cottage she set her bucket by the door and Elizabeth Philpot took her down the hall to the drawing room, where stood the twelve-drawered cabinet Mary's father had made. On its top was a large luminous egg, held at a tilt in an ivory bracket. "What is that?" Mary asked.

"Oh, it's an ostrich egg," said Miss Philpot. "You haven't seen it before? We bought it in London."

It was the eye, the very size and the very shape. An ostrich egg! She could say this when she wrote her text about the creature. *Its eye be ringed with tiny bones and be the size and shape of the egg of the mighty austrick.*

Meanwhile, Elizabeth was sliding the drawers of the cabinet out one by one and showing Mary the tickets she had made for each specimen. She had filled a whole tray with bezoar stones, those oddly shaped ridged brown stones they often saw on the beach.

"Are you collecting stones now too?" asked Mary.

"Only these," Miss Philpot said. "They're believed to be from the gall of ancient goats. It's said that if you put one in a glass, it will counteract any poison in your drink. I am well equipped, if cook should turn murderous!" She looked at Mary with an expression that was almost shy. "I must display what I have," she said. "You haven't brought anything for my cabinet in ages."

"I have a little sea lily you will like," said Mary. "I'll bring it tomorrow." And then they sat on the divan and Mary asked whether she could look at the big Sowerby book, and Elizabeth brought it. Mary turned the pages from beginning to end. But there was nothing in it of a creature such as hers. Sowerby was all small things, eggs and claws and shells. All small, harmless things.

"Are you looking for something in particular?"

Mary looked at Miss Philpot's gentle, humorous face and did not wish to lie. She put the Sowerby on the table. "Do you have a picture of a crocodile?" she asked.

Elizabeth Philpot took down another large book in a leather cover. A bestiary, she called it. The room had lost its light by then, and she lit a candelabra on a wooden stand and moved it close to Mary. With the heavy book between them, she turned pages until she found an etching labelled *Cocodryllus*. Mary bent over it. It was a dragon, although prettified for the picture, the scales on its back curled like waves on the sea. It was in the process of swallowing a man: two bare human legs and feet protruded from its mouth. The creature's oblong eyes (small eyes) were guilty and distracted, like a dog caught in the act of devouring the joint from the table and unwilling to disengage its jaws. It did not appear to have a ring of bones around the eye. But unlike the dragons in the bible, it did have a long jaw and pointed teeth. Mary studied it, taking careful note of its crooked legs and its long-clawed fingers.

When she went back to the shore two weeks later, she could see from the start of Black Ven that the landscape had changed. The cliff was a different shape: there had been another landslip. She tried to climb up and over it, but mud held her boots. She sank deep, and had to crawl back down. Ill fortune, it was – but not really: if the cliff had collapsed a fortnight earlier, the head would have been covered and crushed. She would collect, elsewhere and other things, until the cliff invited her back in. Daily it changed; soon it would open again in a different way – although she would not know the alignment, where the body was.

Back in the workshop, she interrogated the head about the rest of its remains, but it lay grinning, silent on the matter. All through the spring, rain fell. Mary had a large stock of ammonites and she spent her days cleaning and slicing and polishing them. There was a little burst in sales with this. But Lizzie was unwell, and Mary might need to sell the head to pay a doctor. Lizzie was tired and thirsty and constantly needed to go to the lavatory. It was shocking to see how loose her gown was – she was shrinking when she should have been growing.

Then, on a cloudy spring morning, Mary went out to the shore to find that the mud had sunk and hardened and a new path opened up over the landslip; it was on its way to becoming a different cliff. She had brought a shovel, and she climbed up to her best idea of where that ledge must be. There was footing firm enough for her now, and she began to dig, using the shovel delicately, imagining a fossil just below each thrust. Almost immediately, she struck something hard, stone or bone, a shovel's depth in. She knelt then and worked carefully, removing earth.

It was a chain of vertebrae. She could just encircle each one with her two thumbs and forefingers. She dug outwards from the vertebrae, following the ribs. Ribs like willow wands, bunched together for carrying. She sat back on her heels for a minute to rest, trying to judge how long the tail would be. Gulls circled around, expecting flesh in this grave.

The cliff was giving the creature up to her.

·✦[F I F T E E N]✦·

veline House is a stage just grand enough for his mother and her furniture. There in the modest hall are her girandole sconces and the gilt armchair; there in the drawing room is the console table with its marble top and the blue-striped settee, uneasily mingled with Mr. Aveline's things. His folios of maps are stacked in orderly piles on a narrow table. There's his spectacles case, his pipe and tobacco, his cribbage board, his bachelor chair with its sunken seat. A hassock covered with the stitched-together skins of roe deer. His books alphabetically arranged in forthright categories, with tickets glued to each shelf: *Beasts, Birds, Fishes, The Heavens, The Earth.* On a stand is the famous model of the heavens with its seven clockwork planets. Above hangs a picture of Christ kneeling to pray in Gethsemane, worked in what looks like silk thread. Henry reaches out a finger to touch it. "Hummingbird feathers," says Mr. Aveline from behind him. He crosses to the chair, a whippet of a man, and picks up a book lying open on the table. "My morning devotional," he says. "In the works of William Cowper. Care to join me?"

"I'm just off for a walk around the town."

It was dark when they drove in last night. Henry had smelled the sea, but opening the front door, he feels a shock at how dramatically close it is, glistening at the foot of the street. In this town, there is only up or down. He walks slowly down, giving the right of way to carts and porters moving in both directions, stepping out of the path of four dirty sheep. The street is lined with prosperous houses and shops, and an open sluice runs along the side of it. Then he is at the lower town, where the river empties into the sea, and the stench of sewer rises. He passes under the weather vane, a fish cut in tin, and crosses a little square.

Coming out to the seawall, he has the sense that the lower town is opening its eye to the sea. Here the aqua waters of his childhood lie cast in pewter. He stands and watches the surf throw itself on the rocks and then withdraw for another attempt. Everything is in motion, the waves and the swooping gulls and the sparkling light. He looks in amazement at the cliffs to the east. They're close, but the light renders them delicate, as though they're at a great distance.

The tide going out has left an outcropping of wet rocks, and Henry can't resist swinging over the wall and climbing out on them. From out on the rocks, he looks back at the town. A row of shabby cottages lines the river and the shore. There's a latrine built to empty directly into the river. This is the domain of the poor, this brilliant world, and they turn their backs on it, and drop their waste into it. Over the surf, he hears someone calling, and he turns his head the other way, and slips, and rights himself. A girl wrapped in a dark blue cape is standing at the seawall. "Master Henry!" It's Maggie, the housemaid who lighted him to his room the night before. "You're wanted at the house, Master Henry."

He picks his way back. "What can I be wanted for?"

"I'm not one for listening at doors, Master Henry," she says, putting up her chin. She has a pretty mouth that can't resist smiling. "But I warrant it's about the dragon."

"The *dragon*?"

Mr. Aveline is standing by the window in the drawing room, and Henry feels fresh surprise at the sight of him, at how painfully thin the standard allotment of human clay can be stretched. Henry's mother is lounging on the settee in a wrapper of the most miraculous aquamarine. The Squire called in, Mr. Aveline says. Not a minute after Henry went out. "A crocodile," his mother laughs. "I thought the fellow meant he'd *shot* it! For a minute, I was back in the West Indies!"

"Indeed, he shoots at everything that breathes, does Squire Henley," says her new husband. But it's a curiosity the Squire was talking about, one of the strange stony creatures they've told Henry about, found not far from town. "He stayed only a moment. He's on his way out to the cliffs. His men are crating it this morning. How would you like to walk out and see?"

Mr. Aveline fears rocks, dreads twisting an ankle. Rightly so, Henry thinks, eyeing the lathy legs scissoring along the shore beside him, a shore littered with rocks in umber and rust and grey, and with beautifully uniform slabs of limestone with limpet shells cemented to them. The going is smoother on the foreshore, so they angle towards the sea. In places, the waves have scoured away all pebble down to the bare Channel bottom, a wide tilted road of uncracked limestone, sand washed into its shallows in streaks of gold and black. Not a bed of shifting sand, as he'd always thought, but bedrock, like bone scraped bare. Mr. Aveline's thin shoulders convulse. He lets out a sneeze like a door slamming. "I shall die in the pursuit of science," he says. Henry can hardly contain his excitement. A new curiosity! I will write to Conybeare, he thinks. *I* will be the one who tells him about it first.

Half a mile or so on, they spy a clutch of men twenty feet up, working on a black ledge where the cliff has slumped. The cliffs that looked like delicate aquatints from the town are heaps of marl when seen close up, water oozing out of them here and there. There is a path of sorts and they climb it. Henry slips and puts a hand down, and brings it up black. "Bid farewell to my new boots," Mr. Aveline says gamely. In the mud sit three crates like rude coffins, their lids propped beside them. The whole cliff is an open grave. A dozen men hover over the excavation. Under the direction of a large gentleman in a top hat, a workman is mixing in a bucket with a great iron spoon. When they crest the top, Henry almost slides back down in his astonishment.

Splayed before them is the skeleton of an enormous finned animal. Twenty feet long, at the least. It lies in a debris of chipped shale, headless and defeated and somewhat flattened. The ribs on the left side are intact, those on the right are crushed – from the weight of the creature's own body, it would seem: it was not lying entirely flat when it expired. The fine ribs are all agley, crowded and interwoven, as though the Maker had thought initially to make a basket of it. The spine is the spine of a huge fish – it must have sixty vertebrae. "It *is* a crocodile!" breathes Mr. Aveline beside him. "It's enormous!"

"But it doesn't have a crocodile's feet," says Henry. In the place of feet, it has paddles, made of tiny bones pressed together like miniature paving stones, like the Roman mosaics in the British Museum. Bones in rows that could almost have been fingers. The front paddle is much larger than the back one. It did not walk on land, this creature, not easily. He surveys it eagerly, committing details to memory for his letter to Conybeare.

Beside Henry, a shepherd boy stands leaning on his crook, his blue smock the only patch of colour in the crowd. "Where is the creature's head?" Henry asks him.

"She's a-taken en hwome, zir," he says. "Buried under 'er bed, it were."

He does not know the Dorsetshire tongue and struggles to understand. "She?"

"The maid that found en." He gestures over the open grave. There a girl stands. Henry has not noticed her, for her dress is dark, like the men's coats, although she wears a white bonnet. The shepherd thrusts his crook in her direction with a rude sticking out of his lips, as though to hook her over and present her to Henry. "She were all the winter long a-choppin en out, Meary Hanning."

This girl dug it out! She stands among the men, looking across the excavation, a brown face in a white bonnet. He tips his head in greeting. Her expression doesn't change — it's the creature, not him, that is the object of her severe scrutiny. He glances around to see whether anyone has caught his gesture, and then looks back at her. She's almost as tall as he is. Her face has the bones of a grown woman, but this is the unconscious absorption of a child. Twelve or thirteen, she would be. Mud cakes her rough skirts. She's gloveless, and he can see mud on her hands.

"What an undertaking!" says Mr. Aveline.

The man in the top hat has made his way around the excavation to be introduced to Henry. "It took a good deal of arranging, I confess," says the Squire. He's a stout man with a small, mild face surprised to find itself at the top of such an imposing body. "Nothing is easy in science! We were out here for over an hour yesterday, taking measurements, rain leaking under our collars. It was Sir Everard Home who showed us how we must collect it. He's a surgeon — he knows everything there is to know about handling bones. Unfortunately, he's been called back to his post."

"Did he say what the creature is?" Henry asks.

The workmen are calling. The Squire clamps his hand over Henry's sleeve by way of excuse. "You must sup with us at Colway Manor tonight!" he says to Mr. Aveline as he hurries away. "We shall have a scientific dinner."

Under the Squire's direction, the contents of the bucket are poured onto the skeleton. It's plaster; they're encasing the skeleton in a matrix again. The stream of plaster falls from the lip of the bucket in slow motion, breaking into globs. Across the excavation, the girl leans forward anxiously. It's the tail they're covering first. The tail – he's not taken sufficient note of it. It's long and thin, and bent at the end like a scorpion's. It must have been folded to fit it into the grave. By whom? Not folded – it must have kinked in the paroxysm of death. If only they'd arrived sooner. If only he could have drawn it! He watches the bones disappear under lumps of grey plaster with the excruciating sense that the shape of the tail would explain everything.

"What a pity Letitia must be in London," says his mother on the way to Colway Manor. "There will be no young people at the table, I'm afraid." Henry gives a little grunt.

Colway Manor is the dull revelation at the end of a long lane of ash. There are the panes of crown glass on either side of the door, there are the greyhounds panting and pushing at their legs as they climb from the coach. There in the hall is the Squire, his periwig gleaming in the light from a high window. But in the library, a surprise awaits them. They are to see the *head*, the Squire says, taking Henry's hand in his meaty palm. His men carried it up from the maiden's house and they have postponed crating it to please a family friend who dropped in unexpectedly.

The head lies on a table in the library, on a wide board with leather straps fixed to the sides. At the sight of it, a current runs up Henry's spine. It is a bird! It's one of the bird skulls he's carried from Bristol in a tea box, grown to monster size and (he discovers when he touches it) turned to stone. It is all eye, the skull created as a case for a huge oval orb. It won't be fused to the fish he saw lying in the cliff – his mind refuses to do it. But then, at second look, it is all jaw, a long ledge of teeth, and he decides it is a crocodile.

A man crouches at the jaw end, the recently arrived family friend. He gets to his feet with obvious reluctance as Squire Henley introduces him. Mr. Buckland, a professor of natural history at Oxford University, with a lively face and popping blue eyes and his hairline creeping back from his forehead. He's dressed in a dusty academic gown. The smudges on his cheeks can only have been made by wiping tears off with dusty hands. "Imagine my astonishment," he cries, "coming by chance to call on the good Squire, bearing in my saddlebag a gift – which, incidentally, you shall all sample at supper – and seeing carried before me up the lane, as on a gigantic platter, the splendid specimen I had sought for a decade! Imagine my grief upon learning that the creature is *sold*. That the cart I'd encountered an hour before, bouncing along the turnpike towards London, contained the key to the entire geology of the lias cliffs."

"I had a close look at the spine and fins this morning," Henry says. "If you would like me to, sir, I dare say I could make a reasonably accurate sketch from memory."

"Oh, you are most kind," says Buckland, distracted. "Most generous indeed. I do have a fair idea of the creature's anatomy. I'm able to extrapolate from the head."

It appears that when the French revolutionary army occupied Maastricht in 1794, they found a similar gigantic skeleton enshrined there, and shipped it off home as a trophy of war. It ended up at the Jardin des Plantes in Paris, where the great Georges Cuvier examined it. Cuvier knew it for a saurian. Not, contrary to appearances, a fish. The professor paces and points. He will salvage what he can from this occasion, Henry thinks, by knowing more about the creature than the people who actually saw it. He talks at length about the bones around the eye, a structure found only in certain turtles and lizards and in birds. These bones are used to increase or diminish the curvature of the cornea, he explains, thus increasing or diminishing its magnifying power, performing the office of a telescope. Henry's mother listens for a while and then sinks down on a blue upholstered divan, lifting a serene, vacant face towards the professor. "Thus could it pursue its prey into the blackness of the sea," cries the professor. "Thus was it marvellously equipped by its Maker to bear, on an eye so large, the vast weight of the deep."

On the table, the great eye stares blankly and the great beak grins.

Squire Henley and his wife bring an awkward exactitude to their hospitality, avid hosts unaccustomed to entertaining. The table would nicely seat twelve and they're confronted with a party of six. Mr. Aveline and his wife sit opposite each other towards the Squire's end of the table, and Henry and Mr. Buckland are stranded at the dimmer end of the dining room with Mrs. Henley, who has come to the table armed with a list of suitable conversational topics, resolute in her effort to calm Mr. Buckland. "And what is your opinion of Lyme Regis?" she inquires of Henry. "There are many who remark that it has the air of a Turkish town!"

"I've never been to Turkey," Henry says, beginning to shake with laughter. His mother darts a cautioning hand across the gulf between them.

"But I am not surprised at this opinion," Mr. Aveline calls down to the Squire's wife. "I have always thought the Lyme Regis climate more like Italy than like England."

"We have had great success with hibiscus from the Bahamas. You may demur at Turkey, Mr. De la Beche, but there are those enthusiastic visitors who compare our climate to the tropics. Mrs. Aveline may wish to comment on that."

Mrs. Aveline touches her hair and gives her hostess an elaborate smile. "It's a decade since we were in the West Indies. But no, I don't find Lyme Regis quite tropical."

The Squire frowns uncertainly and turns his efforts to the suckling pig lying on a board before them. As he carves, he offers the news that a certain Mr. England is building warm-water baths near the Assembly Rooms. Lyme Regis is destined to be the next Brighton, he tells them, deftly running the point of his knife around the piglet's neck. The carving proceeds, a wicket of ghostly ribs is laid bare. The skeleton of the suckling pig lies exposed for their examination. The tourism prospects of Lyme Regis falter; they are recalled by bones to the irresistible topic of the day.

Buckland is the one who finds a graceful segue. "To Lyme Regis!" he cries, lifting his wine. "To the blue lias of Lyme Regis, where lie treasures richer than the pyramids of Egypt." They raise their goblets to the blue lias and then, prompted by Mr. Aveline, jump to their feet to toast the creature listening from the library.

"What a shame the creature's body was carried away before you had the opportunity to view it." Henry's mother says charmingly to Buckland, lowering herself back to her chair. "But from reports, I can tell you that its mother was certainly a fish and its father a crocodile."

"Perhaps fishes took a different form in ages past," Henry ventures. "Perhaps fishes have changed."

Buckland leans forward in his chair, galvanized into professorial mode, and the Squire's wife lunges towards him to snatch goblets and pitchers out of the way. A scientific gentleman in

France has proposed just such a notion, that species have changed over time. Consider the camelopard, a long-necked creature reaching to eat leaves from high trees. As the lower leaves are consumed, it must needs stretch its neck. Perhaps its offspring were obligingly born with a longer neck. "So goes the theory of the Continental gentleman," Mr. Buckland intones.

"The great Georges Cuvier," explains the Squire helpfully.

No, no, nothing of the sort! Mr. Buckland is seized with hysteria at the notion, he's in danger of choking. Mrs. Henley passes him the goblet she's taken under her protection. It is the theory of one Jean Baptiste Lamarck, Buckland says when he's able to speak, a professor of insects and worms at the great Paris Museum. A mischievous fellow – he endeavoured to interest Napoleon in his ideas, but Cuvier advised Napoleon to refuse a copy of his scientific paper. And rightly so, for Cuvier had explicitly *refuted* the suggestion that species can change; he refuted it absolutely and forever. Monsieur Cuvier had the opportunity to study animals found by Napoleon in the Egyptian tombs and carried back to Paris. Cats. Dogs. Crocodiles. He made his usual immaculate measurements. He compared them to creatures living today. These animals had not changed one iota. Not in four thousand years! The notion of transmutation is discredited, *fully* discredited! Mr. Buckland takes another drink of wine. He digresses into a story about Georges Cuvier, the clever master foiling a student prank. It is not, Henry thinks, quite to the point, but Mr. Buckland has lost his point, he is struggling to batter back a hurricane of emotions. Finally the rising water floods the banks and spills from his eyes. It's the mention of Monsieur Cuvier that has done it. In a broken voice, he confesses his distress that he will not be able to present a scientific description of today's discovery to the great anatomist.

"I summoned Sir Everard Home," says the Squire into the

silence that Mr. Buckland's tears provoke. "He's a surgeon from the naval hospital at Plymouth. He was on the cliffs with me last week and spent an hour looking at the specimen and noting down his observations. He can be trusted absolutely to write a faithful description."

"Sir Everard Home," groans Buckland into his handkerchief.

"But my dear Buckland, we had no idea where you were. In any case, you are free now to study the skeleton in London. I shall provide you with a letter of introduction to the proprietor."

"Tell me again the name of the carnival where it is to be displayed."

Even from this distance, Henry can see that the Squire is regretting he so kindly accommodated Professor Buckland today. "It is the London Museum, popularly known as the Egyptian Hall. The proprietor is a Mr. Bullock. Not a carnival at all, a very scientific endeavour."

"Mr. Bullock," Henry says eagerly. "He is a friend of my uncle's. I was in London last year when he was opening his hall. He had acquired artifacts from the voyages of Captain Cook — they were to be the first exhibit." Henry's mother's smile encompasses the whole long table. *My clever son!*

"There, you see," says the Squire gratefully.

"My son will accompany you," Mrs. Aveline offers brightly. "Henry is a highly skilled artist."

Buckland inclines his flushed face towards her. "I would be much obliged," he says mournfully.

"But we are neglecting your gift, sir," trills their hostess. It has been roasted and lies on a platter beside the principal dish, like the suckling pig's unnatural offspring. A guinea pig, it is called. It is found in South America. Big-headed like a pig, but with the bleared face of a baked cat. "It is not quite a pig, I believe?" asks the Squire's wife delicately.

"*Cavia porcellus*," says the professor. "*Porcellus* you will know, having been Latin scholars. But *cavia?*" He shoves his handkerchief away and rallies himself to the parody of a schoolmaster. "Come, come. You there, with the spectacles!" Mr. Aveline, he means. They gaze at the professor, dull students all. The word is Portuguese, he tells them finally. For *rat*. The creature is in fact a rodent, and very high in protein. It's a scientific experiment! Mr. Buckland is eating his way through the animal kingdom. He has tasted shark. Rat. Ostrich! *Hyena!* A nasty flavour, as you might imagine. Why would he choose to eat his way through the animal kingdom, will no one pose the question?

Mr. Aveline declines to pose the question. He likewise declines a slice of guinea pig. "I have had rather more of the *Porcellus domesticus* than is good for me," he says. He leans in Henry's direction. "Henry, do you realize that the ammonite your mother gave you was found by the very maiden who came across the specimen we saw today? You remember, darling, when we met her in the churchyard."

Indeed she remembers. She raises a hand to her bosom. In honour of the occasion, she wears a brooch purchased in the maiden's shop. An impression of a sea lily, polished in its matrix. The Squire is telling how the maiden came to his door, to his front door, all drabble-tailed in the rain and her boots caked in black marl. They sent her around back to the kitchen, but still she insisted on speaking to the Squire himself. He was away for the morning and she refused to leave. *I wish to sell a dragon* were her words when he finally came down.

"You can thank me for that," says Mr. Aveline through their laughter. Earlier, Mary Anning had approached *him* in the butter market. "Please, sir, can you tell me who owns Black Ven?" she'd asked.

But having lost possession of the dragon, Professor Buckland will not be denied possession of Mary Anning. In full command of his emotions now, he outlines their intimate acquaintance. The morning excursions under his tutelage, her fearless and perspicacious questions. The letters he wrote to her, the visits to their humble kitchen, his charge to her and her father to contact him with just such a find. He has been away, on a geological tour in Scotland; that explains everything. He would have called at her workshop this very afternoon, but he chanced to call on the Squire first, just as they carried the saurian head up the drive. The girl on the cliffs comes into Henry's mind: black hair and eyes and ruddy, healthy cheeks – a Celtic face, the face of the region (it would seem from the people he's encountered on the streets), a very distinct physiognomy.

"She dresses so plainly," he says to his mother.

"Why, she's a Dissenter. They see colour as vanity, poor thing. Remember Susan St. Ives, when she married that dreadful Congregationalist, all those grey gowns done up at the neck." Standing by the coach in the afternoon sun, he'd remarked his mother's own gown, the rich purple of a plum. Now, in the candlelight, it's the crimson-purple of the plum's flesh when you bite into it. "Or the girl may be in mourning," she says. "Perhaps she's both: a Dissenter in mourning." Her cheeks and bosom are flushed from the wine. She laughs, the stones in her earrings catching the candlelight.

"Come, tell us," Buckland is calling up the table to his host. "How much did you pay the maiden?"

"Twenty-three pounds," says the Squire after a pause, and his wife's head flies up.

"*Twenty* pounds I promised the father!" cries Mr. Buckland. "That explains it, the shrewd little dealer. That explains why she didn't wait for me. And what did you manage to extract from this Bullock fellow?" The Squire declines to say. "You turned a tidy profit, I have no doubt," says Buckland.

"Twenty-three pounds!" says the Squire's wife, dabbing at her chin with her napkin. "It's more than they'll know what to do with."

It is beeswax the Henleys are burning in three small iron chandeliers hanging over the table, wooden dripping-dishes overflowing under each candle. The smell floats over the long table, the incense of a country home. An amber drop falls beside Henry's fork and he picks it from the table and presses it between his thumb and finger, feeling its warmth, fingering the hardening impression of his thumbprint in the wax. In his reverie, he slides a chair into the gap between Mr. Aveline and Professor Buckland. It's for Mary Anning, who materializes sitting up very straight in a plain black dress with a white collar. Her dark hair is caught loosely up at the nape of her neck. She turns her head from one party to the other, listening gravely to both conversations. Then she catches sight of the mutilated carcass of the guinea pig and leans forward, touching it with her fingertips, seeming to count its frail ribs.

The next afternoon, Henry finds the girl in the flesh standing behind a round table in front of one of the cottages clinging to the seawall. The weekly coach from Bath has just arrived and the square is full of hawkers and travellers and townspeople idling about. Eight or ten customers crowd around her table, most of them men. A boy tries to crawl between his legs and Henry delivers a sharp kick. He waits till everyone's gone but him. He's clutching the casket of bird bones, having brought it with him on impulse.

On the table are stones in the shape of vertebrae, long pointed grey rods, curled mollusc shells. But her best trade seems to be in ammonites. He looks with interest at the range of matter in which they are formed: some made of ochre sandstone, others of grey limestone, some like gooseberry jelly embedded in grey rock. The finest, like his, are iron infused with fool's gold. He's carrying his in his pocket, a better specimen than anything she has just now on the table.

"What is your shop called?" he asks her bent head.

"The Fossil Depot, sir," she says without looking up. The last customer paid her with a handful of brass and she's counting coins.

"You need to hang a sign out," he says. "I came by this morning, and it was not apparent to me which house was yours, and so I went away again."

Then she does look at him with her black eyes. "This were my father's shop, sir," she says. She has the vowels of the shepherd he spoke with at the excavation. "He scorned a sign. His trade came from his good name in the district."

"My name is De la Beche," he says. "I have something I wish to show you."

"I saw you at the cliffs, sir, with Mr. Aveline," she says. "You were collecting?"

"No," he says. "It's something else. I'm afraid to show you out here. It's so windy, and what I have here is very fragile."

She frowns, and then says, "I must needs pack up." He waits while she transfers her wares to a tray. Then she leads him down six rough steps to what she calls the workshop. As he descends, he catches a glimpse of the one room that must serve as both kitchen and sitting room. A woman in a black widow's cap sits motionless on a chair. A slab of bacon hangs smoking over the fire. It looks to him like a very poor kitchen enjoying an unaccustomed prosperity.

The workshop itself is a damp, cluttered cellar – not large (though it must be the size of this whole humble house), reasonably lit by a high, shallow window at each end, and smelling of mud and the rancid-mutton stink of tallow candles. The end near the door appears to serve as a shop, with shells in shallow boxes laid along a shelf. A table runs almost the length of the room.

"You kept the head here?" he asks. She nods. "I saw it," he says. "At the Squire's. Professor Buckland was examining it."

Surprise or anxiety moves over her face. "Mr. Buckland," she says. "I were a-keeping it for Mr. Buckland. But then I learned it were rightly the Squire's. It were buried in his cliffs. He were kind enough to pay me all the same, for my labour."

"How long did it take you to dig that skeleton out?" Henry asks.

"Four month I worked."

"Every day? All the winter long?"

She nods. "Anywhen the tide favoured. It were banging cold."

Then her eyes are on the box of bird skeletons, so he opens it and begins to lay the birds in a row on the work table. "Where did ye find such clean skeletons, sir?" she asks, bending eagerly over them.

"In a hearth that had been boarded up for several years. They strayed down the chimney and perished. The dumb beast blunders into the world of man at its peril!"

She touches one with a grotesque aspect to its claws. "This en fought 'is death."

"That's exactly what I thought when I saw it! I've been making a series of paintings. It was a deal of work to identify them. You can begin to classify them by their bills, whether they eat seeds or insects. I believe those are the two principal classes of land birds."

He can see her considering this. She slides the robin skeleton to one end, and the dunnock, and then she stops and looks up at him. "They have a powerful kinship to the crocodile head."

"It's true. They're very like. If I had seen only that head, I would have thought your creature was a gigantic bird."

She looks at him levelly, as if trying to decide what he is about. "Would ye wish to see my notations?" She picks a dog-eared accounts book up off the table and shows him a page, and he moves closer to the window for the light. In pencil, in a neat script, she has written:

Cocodrille
Number of teeth — 184
Length of skull — 9 foot
Length of body — 17 foot
Number of verteberrys — 60
Bredth of verteberry — 3 inch
Number of ribs — 47–60 (some be mashed)
Shape of eye — austrick egg
Found by Joseph and Mary Anning at Black Ven Cliff,
Lyme Regis, Dorsetshire
In the year of our Lord 1812.

He looks at her with surprise. Was this an attempt at some sort of scientific description of the creature? "How did you do the measurements?" he asks.

She shows him the willow rod she cut to twelve inches and took to the shore. "I were chary of spoiling my father's tape in the mud," she says.

Eventually, they're sitting on rush chairs at the corner of the long table. Behind her, the window is a perfectly halved rectangle of sea and sky. The light fades, and she gets up and fetches a tallow candle.

"Be there classes of dragons?" she asks abruptly as she sets the candle on the table.

"Of dragons!" She is a child after all. "Well, there was the Worm at Durham, that was killed by being hacked into pieces. And the dragon at Knucker Hole, with its delicate underbelly." He's thinking aloud of stories he heard as a boy. "And one that was killed by having a sword thrust into its tongue. So you might classify them by their vulnerability to attack. Although it often took generations of carnage to learn it. Did you ever imagine it was a dragon?"

"I confess I were sometimes afraid at first. Death be not to dragons what it be to common beasts. Especially when weather brewed up, the crims would come over me. I feared it might rise up out of the rock. Until I saw how mild its eye were."

"Mild!" says Henry, thinking of the massive empty socket. "Miss Anning, as you excavated the skeleton, did you form an opinion as to whether the creature breathed air as mammals and reptiles breathe, or took in water through gills?" He knows as he asks that this is the salient question, and he can tell that she does too, by the way she quickens. "Did you see any indication of gills? They would need to be a grand size for so large a creature." He estimates with his hands, an aperture of twelve or fifteen inches.

"It had a nostril, sir," she says simply, and his face warms. "It had a nostril in its beak, the way a bird do. As big as my thumb." How did he overlook that – he who boasted he could make a scientific illustration from memory?

Suddenly he thinks of a wonderful day in Jamaica, standing with his friends and his father on the shore and watching a phalanx of silver forms lift out of the green water. "I think what you've found is related to the *dolphin*," he says. "They are lovely sea creatures, graceful and playful, and they breathe as mammals do, and have much the same form as the skeleton you found, although only one paddle on each side."

"If it did swim, how came it to be buried five-and-twenty foot up the cliff?"

"The creature must have died in the sea, and silt covered it, and then what was the seabed became the shore." And now red surfaces in *her* cheeks; perhaps she's never considered this before, that the earth changes.

"The tail had a bend in it," he says. "Like a scorpion. Why was it bent like that, do you think?"

Afterwards, he will realize that he had ceased to notice her accent. Afterwards, he will ask himself if she is comely in the range of working-class maidens, and he won't know. He won't be able to recall her features at all, only her self-possession, her gaze: as steady and open as a babe's.

Five gentlemen, a lady, and a girl made their way in halting conversation along the eastern shore at low tide, navigating the lower edge of a landscape that would have required, on that spring day of sun and cloud, three separate mediums to render it: smears of vegetable dye for the purple seaweed and the shocking green of maidenhair; dabs of sombre earth pigment for the near cliffs; and the pastel air – it must be done in fine chalks, as must the far cliffs that gave themselves over to the air.

The tendency of all was to let Professor Buckland lead. But then, of course, he was ignorant of the exact location of the excavation site, so Mr. Aveline and Mr. De la Beche must show him. And the Reverend William Conybeare was there, having hurried to Lyme Regis at news of the find, and a gigantically moustached half-pay lieutenant colonel named Birch, a ginger-haired fellow gone white and coral, eager as a boy and sporting a sheepskin jacket and great boots gaping on either side of his skinny flanks. And Miss Elizabeth Philpot and Mary Anning, all of them assembled at the jetty.

A bit ashamed that he had overlooked the girl (who was it who knocked on the door of the narrow house on Bridge Street and invited Mary Anning?), Professor Buckland made a great show of setting off with her, and he appeared the image of sparkling goodwill. Mary returned his blue gaze with a steady brown one and was relieved to see that he bore not a whit of resentment towards her. But their walking together was of short duration. "I encountered an antique fellow on the shore this morning," he said as they descended at Church Cliffs. "You will never guess whom!" And when she said with a twitch to her shoulders, "I reckon it were Noah," he made some pretext to fall back, leaving her alone, letting Mr. De la Beche and Reverend Conybeare pass him, and walked then with Miss Philpot, whose poor marred cheeks were flushed with exercise and fresh air and the excitement of walking out in company on the shore. As often as Mary had suggested such an outing, Miss Philpot had demurred. It had taken Mr. Buckland. And now she lifted her face to the breeze with something approaching rapture. Sitting in the back garden at Morley Cottage, she and her two sisters always remarked on how fortunate they were to live by the sea and to feel the sea breeze and smell the salt in the air, what a tonic it was, but (as she saw now) to sit in a garden up on the hill was no more being at the sea than reading a book about it was.

In his blue bag, Mr. Buckland carried, along with his usual collecting tools, a measuring tape and a compass. These he had packed with the thought that the depth of burial of the creature, the angle at which it lay, and its general coordinates would yield information about the prevailing currents in the Great Deluge. But of course, it was a tedious undertaking, and he need not have involved the others, except to demonstrate how grievous a loss this was to one whose passion for science rendered even the examination of a robbed grave an urgent enterprise. And then, who knew what else they might find? Always at the edge of his vision was the ghostly image of the ark, its timbers rotting into the lias, and the bearded patriarch lying with hands folded on his sunken belly. Why here? Why not, if it must be somewhere? And England swelled behind him like a hymn, its dappled meadows graced with solitary oak, its fields so green, so filled with light, its shores defended by the elect as Christian lands around sank into papism. *England,* his heart sang, as he turned his eyes to the dark cliffs that outlined the beauteous isle, and then to the scallops of gleaming surf that decorated the borders of the map, and the emotion rising within him seemed to presage it (what? *Something.* Some apotheosis, some divine proclamation of the sacredness of everything that fell within his gaze), seemed to declare, "It will be soon."

Mary Anning was leading on her own now, and behind her walked Henry with his intimate friend William Conybeare. Walked in the glitter of Conybeare's regard, under the protection of Conybeare's decorum as under an umbrella, observing Conybeare's fine kid gloves and the precisely calibrated attention that Conybeare turned to everything, stooping now to pick up a shell and knowing it to merit a keen three-second glance and no more. And (Henry saw with satisfaction) he understood his friend perfectly, rightly perceived Conybeare's discomfort in following the lead of this girl in the fustian skirts and rough boots, a discomfort that was perhaps felt by the whole party and was eased only when Conybeare looked around him with his handsome eyes and called ruefully, "A little child shall lead them."

It was a phrase that Mary knew to be from Scripture, and walking at the head of the party with her basket over her arm, she felt a tremor of disgust and pride (disgust at being called a child, and pride because the little Child was Our Lord Himself). But then, as they crossed the shingle that marked the end of Church

Cliffs and the beginning of Black Ven, both feelings were overtaken and swept away by a painful recall to James Wheaton's
plight, by an up-swelling of terror for him. After last Sabbath's
sermon, he had fallen to the ground and been carried insensible
from the chapel. He lay rigid in his bed now, one corner of his
mouth pulled down. Others of the congregation had been to
pray at his bedside, but not Mary. She tramped along, glimpsing
again, as in the corner of her eye, the evil that had seized him
(glimpsed it in the light sparkling off the shoals at the creeping
tide line, a malevolent vapour from the bowels of the earth, from
rocky chambers broken open by a wilful girl with a hammer and
chisel). But why now, weeks after the deed? *Unless it was the
reassembling of the creature's parts* – and she considered whether
the head and body would have arrived in London just on the
Sabbath to be put together in one piece, and pressed her trembling fingers into the palm of her codgloved hand, trying to
compute the hours of its journey. But this was a going-
backwards, to think of the creature in this way, and she shook her
hand, shook the numbers off her fingers, resisted going backwards. By what authority did she resist it? By the authority of
Richard Anning, whose path down the shore she followed,
whose firm, confident gait she recalled with every step.

Mary Anning's progress down the shore taxed Colonel Birch
to the end of his strength, but the blood in his eardrums roared
his delight with this outing. He'd expected to spend *days* closely
questioning individuals in the region before he discovered the
local savants and ingratiated himself with them. And then he had
got off the coach and the curiosity table was right in front of his
eyes. Gasping for breath, he clambered now after the damsel,
keeping his eyes on her sturdy back (and found himself judging
the width of her pelvis, saw this black-eyed maiden in a cottage
with a babe at her breast and another at her feet – but surely she

had three or four years before that?). His eyes went to the
ground and, desperate to rest, he stooped to pick up a rock and
called, "Miss! Miss!" Mary Anning turned and angled back
across the foreshore towards him. He thrust it at her. "It is surely
a petrified bone! Look at the grain of it."

"It is beef rock," she said. "It may look like bone, but it is
not. Bones are dark brown or black."

And then some of the others drifted back to her and Mary
must instruct them all. Mr. Beach had picked up a rock with
the rim of an ammonite peeping through its surface, and Mary
opened it with a deft blow of her hammer and handed it back to
him, the fossil revealed and intact. She thought of the townspeople who'd watched from the jetty as they set off, herself
the only low-born girl in this party of gentlefolk, and wished the
townspeople had spyglasses and could see how she was listened
to. By Mr. Aveline, and Mr. Beach, and the gentleman in the
beaver hat whom no one had presented to her. Daily, strangers
descended the coach and addressed her as *Miss Anning*. This was
what it meant to be famous. Colonel Birch was in a hunting party
in Sussex when he heard about the dragon and that it was a
maiden who'd found it. He'd come directly to Lyme Regis and
to her table to present himself, this stout man who was both
round and square in the way of the rich (round as to belly and
square as to the form of his jacket above his thin legs in their great
buckled boots). And Mr. Beach, examining his new ammonite,
smiled at her in a friendly fashion, although it was a different
friendliness from what he had shown the day before, when he
called on her in the workshop. The tall gentleman with the beaver
hat had cast a spell over him. They were all as changeable as the
wind. However, she, Mary Anning, and her brother Joseph
Anning had done something everyone in this company would
be proud to have done, would have worn as a feather in their

caps. She could not adorn herself with it, putting on airs as they would have, but she could walk out with them now. And this was a great deal.

She turned and resumed walking, and Henry De la Beche pocketed his new calcite fossil and swung along behind her with his friend.

"Mr. Conybeare —"

"William, please."

"William. The other night at dinner, Mr. Buckland talked of a pair of fossil jaws found in the Netherlands and examined by Cuvier. Are you familiar with this find?"

"I am indeed. It is several decades ago that they were first unearthed, but their significance was immediately grasped. They were enshrined in a glass case in the town square, like a relic of the Holy Cross. The European peasantry is much superior to the English, I regret to say."

"And what did Cuvier have to say about them?"

"The find posed a great challenge to Cuvier, for it seemed to combine so many anatomical systems, as our creature does. Finally he pronounced the jaws the remains of an animal related to the monitor of the tropics. But not a monitor — different in several significant ways."

"And not a dolphin?"

"He believes it to be a reptile."

"And what did he say had happened to such huge creatures and their kind?"

"Ah. Well, in that regard, Cuvier is an unrepentant apostate. He argues that such creatures no longer exist, eradicated by some catastrophe, perhaps. Cuvier would have us believe that this," and he waved his hand to take in the cliffs and the sea, "this is all a recent and transformed version of what might in another age have been a very different world."

"I suppose it's possible that creatures such as Squire Henley's were wiped out in Noah's Flood. What do you think?"

Conybeare looked at Henry kindly. "*I know that, whatsoever God doeth, it shall be forever. Nothing can be put to it, nor anything taken from it.* From the Book of Ecclesiastes, by the great King Solomon."

"The king who built the temple in Jerusalem? And does that temple still stand?"

Conybeare simply laughed. As a clergyman, Henry saw, he would be a model of moderation. Not sanctimonious, slow to take offence, deftly balancing faith and worldly erudition.

Close behind them walked Mr. Aveline, his eyes on his stepson, whom he'd been sent along to supervise. It was Mrs. Doctor Carpenter who last night had made a point of telling them she'd seen Mr. De la Beche go into the carpenter's daughter's house sometime around noon and come out again some long time after. Henry had laughed when they took him to task about it, as though the idea was preposterous, but the laugh was a lie. "I will send him to Jamaica," Beth vowed afterwards. But she would not, and they both knew it. Mr. Aveline watched Henry striding along beside William Conybeare, still laughing, walking straight through tidal pools, heedless of the water staining his boots and splashing the pantaloons he'd donned that morning. He'd laughed openly at the Squire's wife while a guest at her table. He had an ungovernable energy; he did not respect the proprieties. Those absurd pantaloons! He'd have worn them to the Assembly Rooms the other night if his mother had not sent him back to change.

Behind him, Miss Philpot walked alone. How neat her gloves, how strong and shapely her hands and her long feet in their tan calfskin shoes: how well put-together for this world she persisted in being, though the world never remarked on it. She looked over at William Conybeare, noting the neat nape of his hair below his top hat, his body formed in every aspect to house a fine intelligence. Oh, yes, Mr. Buckland's friend satisfied all requirements as to handsomeness and civility and fortune, indeed so far exceeded requirements that you could not fault him for thinking well of himself. She turned her head and looked at the sea, and there stirred within her the moment in the night when she'd wakened and seen through the window (for she never drew her curtains across) the sinewy boughs of the sycamore tree in the garden lit up, and she'd thought to see the moon dangling from an upper branch, the full moon with its pox-marked face, but it was not there, just the tree and the counterpane lit up by the light of a moon she could not see.

At the excavation site, it was Mary Anning who led them to the spot where the path she had made herself turned upwards. They scrambled up through the mud and she could see them standing talking at the lip of the shallow pit so familiar to her from weeks of solitary work. Some learned gentleman somewhere, the great Cuvier across the ocean, perhaps, would have a name for the creature – that was what Mary had assumed as she worked. But it seemed that no one did. She'd thought it was her ignorance alone, but it was all of their ignorance. They would be months studying those bones and writing about them. Her name would be written in their books and Mr. Buckland's students at the great university in Oxford would learn of her. Although Mr. Buckland had not once come to the workshop to ask about the discovery. She turned away from the thought, away from the path up the cliff, and set to work scavenging in the rocks recently fallen to the shore.

The group stood and gazed down into the grave. It was the most unpleasant mud, like the castings of gargantuan earthworms. Rain had erased the marks made by the shovels. Except for the pebbles of plaster scattered around the edges of the site, you might have the sense that the dragon had shrugged massive shoulders and wrenched itself up in a hasty resurrection. Colonel Birch was struck dumb at the size of the impression it had left. The great gathering of the quick and the dead has begun here, he thought, and Buckland thought it as well, and found he could hardly breathe. He could not bring himself to ask at which end the head had lain, but someone asked, and someone answered, and Buckland stood at the foot of the grave resisting the impulse to lay himself down and use the length of his body as a measure.

That child did this and told no one, thought Miss Philpot. She looked down at Mary, picking through rocks at the base of the cliff. She came out here alone, day after day, and performed this work alone.

Professor Buckland was down in the hole attempting to secure his measuring tape with a chunk of plaster. "Let me do that for you," Miss Philpot said, sliding down with just a fleeting thought for her shoes. He straightened and lifted his hat and wiped his forehead with his bare hand, and she saw how his forehead was creeping up already, she saw his brow lifting into a corrugated V below the unmoving cap of his balding skull.

"You will ruin your skirts," he said charmingly, in spite of his evident distress. How palpably he hungered to be liked! *Let me do that for you*, she said silently to his back as he bent again over his measures.

At the edge of the excavation, Henry squatted and examined the layers of shale and limestone the dig had revealed. From the corner of his eye, he monitored Conybeare's attention. He'd talked too much all the way out, he knew it. He'd described in every detail what he'd seen the day of the dig, and his proprietary air had begun to irritate Conybeare, but he was helpless to stop himself. "In the composition of this cliff," he said now, "it is hard to avoid the sense of growth through time. The strata are so like the growth rings in a tree."

Conybeare smiled, and Henry saw that he was about to fully articulate Henry's striking and novel idea, and to wedge it back into its narrow niche in the orderly cupboard of Christ Church College scholarship. "Ah, you've been reading Mr. Smith," Conybeare said. "Strata Smith, the blacksmith's son from Oxfordshire? I heard him speak in Bath. It is an intriguing idea, that geological formations could be attributed to natural agents. The quandary it poses, of course, is with respect to time. Consider the abandoned Roman road that runs through Lyme. Almost two millennia since that road was laid down, and its marks on the earth are scarcely effaced." He touched Henry's arm in a friendly gesture. "I confess the notion appeals to me — that the strata could be read as a narrative of past conditions on the earth. But the time is the problem. The six thousand years that Scripture allows since Creation." They picked their way down to the foreshore. "Speaking of time," Conybeare said, "has the tide turned? I wonder if we're in any danger of being cut off."

Henry went gladly across the shore to where Mary Anning stooped with her basket. She stood up and pointed to the town. "As long as you can walk out far enough to see the Cobb, sir, you will be safe," she said. And they *could* see it, and the town, which at this distance looked as though its houses had been thrown together from the stony slope by a colony of alpine marmots. They stood together in silence. He wanted her to speak again but could not think what else to ask. In contrast to the white of her bonnet, her cheeks were remarkably tanned, and colour bloomed below the skin. She had the sort of colouring that would be white or brown or crimson, but never pink. She wore too-large gloves from which the fingers had been cut off.

How useful, he thought, and how cold the tips of her fingers must be.

"I wish we had thought to bring refreshments," said a voice at his elbow. It was his stepfather. "I am perishing of thirst."

"I have water, sir," Mary Anning said, reaching a corked bottle out of her basket. As though he had been struck deaf, Mr. Aveline walked past her and turned up the shore towards town. Mary felt the sharp sting of tears in the corners of her eyes. She had been all of a flummox in the last few days. Last night, when she came up from the workshop, her mother saw how wrought-up she was, and reached out a hand and pulled her into a bony embrace. She did not rebuke Mary with chawing high, but kissed her and said, "When your cup is full, Mary, you must walk steady."

And so Mary blinked her eyes clear and uncorked the bottle to have a drink herself.

The tide had turned, and a storm was brewing up in the south. Walking home is always quicker but often more vexing, for the weight you might be carrying and the danger of the tide. They were hopeless at choosing a path through the rocks, these people. Without a by-your-leave, Mary wove nimbly past them all and illustrated a clear path up against the cliff edge.

Mr. Aveline was limping. His new boots, so beautifully cobbled, were, by the narrowness of their cut at the ankle, restricting the flow of pedal blood. Why did I agree to come? he thought bitterly. After a lifetime of serious pursuits, to be assigned the duty of proctor to a wayward youth! *And he will be penniless.* The plantation will have entirely failed by the time he reaches majority. Mr. Aveline's old friend Miss Philpot was behind him, and he fell back then and said to her, with a nod at his stepson, "Have you noted the pantaloons?"

"Oh, it's a fashion," she said vaguely, and he said, "It's a fashion that reeks of republicanism! It blew across the Channel from France." He tried by his tone to make light of it. And then he presented as fact the prospect he and his wife had discussed that morning. "Young De la Beche will soon have others to account to. Have you heard of the geological excursion Doctor Carpenter is planning? It seems that Henry will be joining it. They will be many months in Scotland."

"Indeed?" said Miss Philpot. "I spoke with your wife this morning, and she —"

But she could not finish. Mr. Buckland was at her side, reaching across with a gift. A devil's toenail. *Gryphaea arcuata*.

"The way you can identify a species with a glance — it is marvellous!" said Miss Philpot, smiling at him.

"Long days of walking on the shore with my father. He was a wonderful naturalist, until God took from him his most precious tool, his eyes. And so, as a lad, I must needs describe every spiny protrusion in detail for his benefit."

"God took his eyes but gave him a bright-eyed son," said Miss Philpot, "and I dare say your father regarded it a fair exchange."

"Indeed, it made of me a man of science." With a wave, he was off over the rocks and she was left with the tinny aftertaste in her mouth of her last ridiculous remark, her preposterous, overreaching effort to flatter him.

The encroaching tide was forcing them to the big rocks at the foot of the cliffs. Mary Anning climbed steadily ahead, seemingly unperturbed. The genial young De la Beche paused and offered Miss Philpot a hand. The solicitude they showed Miss Philpot might impress an observer, but (she thought) it had an absence of genuine interest in it. Except in the case of Colonel Birch, who, when they stopped to catch their breath, and were all drawn by the drama in the clouds to look back at the Isle of Portland, could not resist telling her about the mermaid found on the shore at Church Ope Cove of a Sabbath morning, and carried up past the pirates' graveyard and into the church, where, forthwith, it died. "Did you often see mermaids from the deck of your ship?" Elizabeth asked.

He turned his eyes back to the mirage of Portland. "I was never a sailor," he said. "I was lieutenant colonel in the First Regiment of the Life Guards," he said. "A senior cavalry troop, as you know. I had the honour of serving under Charles Stanhope, Earl of Harrington, until my retirement. I have travelled this twelvemonth throughout the Southwest, awaiting the Lord's direction regarding a new vocation. The day I disembarked from the coach and set eyes on that young miss's curiosity table, I knew that my Lord had spoken." With an apologetic smile, Miss Philpot hurried ahead to join Mary Anning, and Colonel Birch, left walking alone, knew that she despised him and returned to that story which was taking on the quality of a legend (the old soldier's quest) but had within it the moment he could not convey – the ammonites coiled in enduring beauty on the table, a sight that went to the marrow of his aching bones. *This will be my life*, he'd vowed to himself (as he had been waiting to vow, about something, ever since he'd been pensioned, and even before).

"Mr. De la Beche is shortly going away," Miss Philpot found herself saying abruptly to Mary Anning. He was engaged to be married, she went on. Such a well-favoured, well-spoken young gentleman – how could he not be engaged? The tide was closing in, the waves were splashing at their feet, but still she talked as she scrambled breathlessly over the rocks. "Mr. Aveline was telling me. And I had a conversation earlier today with Mrs. Aveline outside the bank. I understand Mr. De la Beche will be spending time with his fiancée in London, and then going to Scotland. Or perhaps it's the other way around. Or he may go to Oxford to study with Professor Buckland."

They were at the place where Mary's father had lain one lonely night – Mary did not so much think this as feel a habitual squeeze to her heart. Mr. Dilabeach, she thought hopelessly. She had not even had his name right. She looked back at him and the other tall gentleman, tramping through new-fallen mud at a dangerous proximity to the cliffs, where they might provoke another landslip.

A wave broke on the rock beside her and she felt the weight of the water hitting her skirt. Out of nowhere, the text of James Wheaton's Sunday sermon came to her, his last sermon before he was stricken and carried from the chapel. *If thine eye be single, thy whole body shall be full of light.* The text resounded in her mind in his voice, and with such force that she knew it would lodge there until she discovered its meaning.

Then they were scant yards from the path that would take them up Church Cliffs and into town. Rain fell in a narrow sheet across the Channel and a rain-washed patch of sky opened to heavenish light before them. At the sight of it, a rainbow occurred to all among them who knew their Scripture, to all of them. In spite of their haste, each wet-shod member of the party balanced on a slippery rock for a moment to look at the sky, the breathing world colliding for a moment with its diminished image in each mind.

But it was only a trick of the light; there would not be a rainbow this time. A double closing off – the encroaching water coinciding with the dying light of day. Across the Channel, the golden light greyed. A breaker slammed on the rocks at their side, leaping at the cliff: they had less time than they thought. But there was the path, and one by one, they scrambled up it. The last to go panting up was Colonel Birch, and then the light was fully gone and the last narrow ribbon of shore was taken over by the sea.

Book II

Under the eaves in Aveline House, Henry hangs suspended in darkness. Like the Ichthyosaurus: no eyelids to close. He's face down on the horsehair mattress, a watcher, intact, self-nourished. Larger than the margins of his body, his bones thinned by age: he's a shape he's tending towards. Then he's awake, Henry is seeping back, recalled by grey light at the window. Kicking a foot to untangle the bedclothes pinned under his thigh, rolling over, hitching the quilt back. Too early to rise, and too cold.

He reaches down, flicks his jaunty morning erection. Oh, the joys of the morning, when the world is made new! Flicks it, cradles it. The girl he posits has Letitia's slender waist, she has that merrythought jaw and lovely throat. He puts her in a coach, the two of them alone in a public stage while the fields reel by. When he buries his face in her bosom, she's the girl who served him the other night at the Monmouth Inn, her breasts tumbling out of her bodice, bringing all the joy of existence gratuitously into his dim bedchamber. Then she's Maggie, his mother's maid, Maggie with her laughing mouth, and a passage opens swiftly in the dark to the marrow of Creation.

He floats gasping on the mattress. Jesus, Mary, and Joseph! His rapture radiates outwards, waves of it dispersing in the dim air. Too soon it subsides, too soon he's back in the dusty smell of cotton ticking. His roughly woven Hebrides blanket, and the bedstead with acanthus leaves ineptly carved on its low posts. He dabs at himself with the quilt and rolls to his side, the horse-hair mattress hard and saggy under him. There's a murky taste in his mouth from last night's wine. He punches at his pillow and rolls over again. All that ecstasy surging up unprovoked within a single mortal – what a matter for scientific investigation, if you could get a man to talk about it! He sees George Holland's amused eyes, the mobile black brows. A fine, frank fellow. On the trip to Scotland, they enjoyed several wine-fuelled conversations about the mysteries of carnal love. One night, they sat and watched a middle-aged baronet making open efforts to lure a serving maid up to his rooms. All the gentry lusted for common women, Holland insisted. "It's the lewdness of low females. Sexual instinct is stifled in the upper classes – in high-born females, I mean. And why is that so? By nature or by moral tutelage – what do you say?" But it seemed to Henry that George Holland's premise was wrong. Gentlemen are drawn to serving girls because they are *girls*, as pretty as any other, popping up in your private quarters every hour of the night and day. Regarding the sexual appetites of high-born women, he really has very little to draw on.

He rolls out of bed and walks over to the corner to pull the chamber pot out of its cabinet. On that whole trip, he drank too much and talked too much, it was a fact. He told Holland about Maggie, about the smear of blood left on his sheets and the mischief-making sow of a laundress who went to his mother in a grotesque parody of concern ("I hope Master Henry's having his wound seen to?"). Pain rises at the thought of Maggie, the way his bed would shake with their stifled laughter, the tender little sound she made then in her throat when he entered her, clamping his head to her breast as though she were comforting a grieving boy. She was from Evershot. Likely that's where she went when his mother dismissed her. Why did he have to make a sordid story of her? And then there was Holland asking slyly every chance he got: *I hope Master Henry's having his wound seen to?*

He crawls back into bed and pulls the covers over himself. He had passed the signpost to Evershot last year, driving through the Frome Valley in a closed carriage. He was with Letitia and three or four others, on their way to a country house. The week comes to him as one protracted and acrimonious faro game, throughout which he toyed with the thought of borrowing a horse and riding to Evershot, although he never did. There was a many-fingered lake on the grounds and he slipped out one day and rowed, glided alone in a still green pool surrounded by cedars. He was in the middle of the lake when Letitia appeared on the shore. She slipped her shoes off and sank onto the landing, dangling one white-stockinged foot towards the water. He sat still in the skiff and watched a slender, inverted figure materialize in the green mirror of the lake, one raised toe just kissing the dangling toe of the girl on the landing, so that it seemed the two white forms had been cut from a single sheet of paper by an oriental prestidigitator. After a minute, he reached out and touched an oar, he sent waves undulating across the lake. They overtook the water nymph, foreshortening her, carrying her off in pieces to either side, while the forest nymph inclined unconscious in a white muslin gown.

She's not talkative, as she once was. Her charming face invites you in and then presents an impenetrable curtain. Once when he saw her in London after a long absence, the little laugh that used to bubble out before every remark was gone, replaced by a poised smile. Her clear green eyes, the graduated hairs that make the fine arch of her eyebrows – she cannot be unintelligent. She unfailingly says the right thing, as though she has a store of graceful comments at the ready in her breastbone. *If she is vapid, it's because she wills it so,* he says to himself, getting up again and striking a light. She avoids any thought that might leave traces on her face, as part of a beauty regimen, perhaps.

It's only half four, but he won't drift off again. This comes from napping on the drawing room settee through rainy afternoons. He pulls his dressing gown on and goes to his desk, where a letter from the attorney in Kingston lies open. The birth rate on the plantation is up – that is the good news – but the attorney is sorry to report that the overseer has found a hidden cache of cutlasses. *To the extent the Negro thrives,* muses the attorney, *he becomes a threat to his masters.* Henry buries this sheet in a pile of letters, pulls out fresh paper, and settles himself to write.

Lyme Regis, Dorset. May 29th

My Dear Conybeare,

Forgive me – I am an unreliable correspondent indeed. Since my return from the North, I've been occupied in writing up a formal record of our travels and the science that resulted. We were just a humble trio of gentlemen scholars from Dorsetshire, amanuenses to the real gentlemen of science, but we dare to hope that our efforts will have lasting value, will even (in the case of one particular find in the north of Scotland) play a role in dismantling the theories of the Wernerians. When you next come down to Lyme (as I hope you do soon), we will share a glass or two and you shall hear a full account.

Thank you for your recent letter and for your congratulations regarding my appointment to the Royal Society. Of course I express at every opportunity my sense of honour in being named a fellow at my age – but I will confess (for your eyes only) how chary I am of the honour since reading certain recent publications of that venerable society. You will know of which papers I speak – Sir Everard Home's various attempts to classify the Lyme Regis reptile. How adroitly the good surgeon skipped from one order of animal to the next – a bird! a fish! an amphibian! We (the British, I mean) are rightly the laughing-stock of the French for such anatonomical nonsense. I fervently hope that your own exemplary work on the subject will go some distance towards restoring our reputation. Your paper to the Geological Society on the Ichthyosaurus has been my constant reference since returning to Lyme Regis. Being based as it is on the examination of numerous specimens, it is a model of thoroughness, precision, and scientific acumen, and my admiration grows with every reading.

Henry stops to sharpen his pen. Perhaps he's over-egging the pudding? But Conybeare himself is most generous in his compliments. Even Mary Anning was recognized in the Ichthyosaurus paper, if obliquely. What was it Conybeare said? Something about being grateful *for the specimens that had found their way into the collection of Colonel Birch*. Henry carried the paper down to the square and read the passage aloud to Miss Anning. "It is *you* he speaks of," he said when she did not respond. "Colonel Birch's collection is entirely composed of specimens that you found and sold him. You are credited in this important paper!" But still she didn't reply – she turned to a customer in her brusque way, seemingly indifferent to the compliment.

What a funny creature she is, he thinks, burrowing a hand into his armpit to warm it. He keeps a pair of gloves on the desk with the finger ends cut off, and he puts them on and lights another candle. Conybeare's paper sits on the shelf, a little dog-eared, for Henry lent it to Mary, surprised to learn that day in the square that she had not seen it and was indeed unaware of its having been published. Three days later, when he stopped in at her workshop, he discovered that she'd made a full copy of its thirty pages of text, the illustrations rendered in such fair duplication that it was difficult to tell them from the originals. He ruffled admiringly through her copy and his eye caught a note she'd written on the bottom of one of the pages: *When I write a paper, there shall not be but one preface.* When she saw him reading it, her colour rose and she reached out a hand to take her copy back.

He resumes:

You wonder that I returned to Lyme Regis and suggest that Bristol would be a livelier situation for a man of my age and tastes. I offer a rejoinder in the words of Mary Anning: "A cheese full of maggots is livelier than a sound cheese." But in fact, Lyme is advancing apace in its efforts to re-create itself as a gentrified watering place. In this season, Marine Parade is crowded with victims of Hydromania, most of them maidens sporting parasols. One may discern furlong-measuring and parcel-tying in the pedigree of some of them – we have not yet the status of grand old Bath or even Weymouth – but the retired sea captains secreted behind parlour curtains, watching through spyglasses as shivering bathers are lowered from machines into the bay, are oblivious to the subtle differences of class! In summer we savour the pleasures of the flesh and in winter the pleasures of the spirit – for then Lyme reverts to its old self and is as silent as a Tuscan monastery. When I returned in March and roamed the quiet streets where seafoam daubs the sides of the houses, I felt myself truly at home.

And in any case, I frequently have amusing and stimulating company in the form of Buckland, who is resident in lodgings on Marine Parade at the moment. In all of his work, Miss Anning is an indispensable resource. Buckland and I visit the cliffs in fair weather and as often as time allows between other pursuits, but she is there at every tide – material want draws her out in storms that would freeze the soul. She is a model of industry and upon her slender form a little family depends for its precarious survival. In spite of the celebrity she attracted six or seven years ago through her first remarkable find, she continues to make a living largely by selling curios to tourists. I credit the fashion of using large ammonites as doorstops to her entrepreneurial initiative. She carries these staggeringly heavy fossils home from Monmouth Beach on her back, employing the sort of brace a porter wears, with leather straps buckled over her shoulders. In fashioning this device, she was assisted by her brother, whom I have met on occasion at the Fossil Depot. Framed in their humble doorway, the pair of them bring to mind the window of a church, both from the innocence of their expressions and from his name (Joseph) comically paired with hers.

But as I set out to say, her daily labours on the shore, month after month, year after year, have equipped her magnificently for her work as a collector. Where Buckland and I must open five rocks to locate one meagre ammonite, she can *smell* fossils and leads us unerringly to the exact strata of the cliffs that will yield treasure. Were we at liberty to work together on a daily basis, we would make an odd but (if I may immodestly observe) formidable trio, with Miss Anning to locate the specimen, myself to render it in charcoal, and Buckland to unravel the mystery of its place in Creation. Although in that regard, his theories are to date less than satisfactory. On the question of why these monsters have vanished, Buckland's recent notion is that other worlds existed before the Garden of Eden (God practising, as it were, in an effort to fashion a realm fit for creatures made in His image). "How could the fish-lizard have died out," I dare to ask, "if death came into the world through Adam?" Perhaps, my dear Conybeare, as a man of the cloth, you would like to posit an answer to that question, as Buckland has so far failed to do.

A last item of news, somewhat removed from the above: the lady habitually referred to as "Henry's fiancée" hopes to relocate soon to Lyme Regis, with an eye to making marriage preparations. In truth, our nuptials have been long delayed. Upon my return to Lyme, Miss Whyte sent me from London the gift of a golden cravat pin in the shape of a harp. My stepfather asserts the meaning to be, "Je réponds à qui me touche," but my dear mother, interpreting it as, "By neglect thou ruinest me," insists that I set a date for the wedding without further delay. As I have now come into my property (such as it is with the sinking price of sugar), I am resolved to do just that. Letitia's arrival will no doubt entail a major adjustment to my daily routine. I find I have little need of companionship beyond my scientific friends and my mother and stepfather (whose health, thank you, is somewhat improved), but, as the shore and cliffs teach us, all of life is change.

I must bring this to a close. When can I expect another pleasant day of geologizing and philosophizing with an old friend on the lias cliffs?

Your affectionate servant,
T. H. De la Beche, Esq.

He picks his pocket watch off the desk. It's now half five. He sets the letter aside and crawls back into bed for warmth. Sometimes, looking out his window at first light, he sees Mary Anning climbing up to Morley Cottage, and then, half an hour later, sees her walk back down with the sardonic spinster of Silver Street hobbling on pattens and clinging to her arm. Off for an outing to the shore, the two of them. But four or five days ago, when he rose early and went out, he was lucky enough to catch Mary leaving for the shore on her own. She was standing on Gosling Bridge drinking from a ladle, and he walked smartly up and handed two coins to the milkmaid and then had his own dripping ladle, milk still warm from the cow. Oh, the joys of the morning!

In fact, Mary had seemed disinclined to let him join her that day – the tide was not convenient, she said, she would have to return by the Charmouth Road – but he'd charmed her into relenting. Then she set a pace up the rock-littered shore that he could not hope to match. Passing the quarry, he felt the amused eyes of the quarrymen on them, a gentleman in cape and top hat tacking clumsily along the beach after the fossil girl. She never troubled herself to glance behind. By the time they got to Black Ven, she was fifty yards ahead, sitting on a rock eating an egg. He was breathless and perspiring, formulating a mild lecture on manners, and then she offered him an egg. "I carry 'em in my hands for the heat. Once they're cold, I eat 'em."

"Your dewbit?" he said, and she smiled in surprise. *Dewbit, breakfast, nuncheon, cruncheon, nammit, crammit, supper.* It was Maggie who had taught him the seven meals humble folk eat in Dorsetshire. The egg was not as fresh as it ought to have been, but it was boiled to perfection and still a little warm.

Mary was waiting for the light to be full on the cliff face, she said. So then he had a chance to talk to her – never possible when Buckland was around. He asked her whether she had ever travelled from Lyme Regis, and she answered in her forthright way, "I have walked as far as Seatown to the east and Seaton to the west – which names befuddle many visitors, but there is some ten miles between them. And I've ridden to Axminster in the Bennetts' dogcart."

She did not hesitate then to question him about his own comings and goings. It was the sort of boldness that enraged his friends, especially Conybeare, but really, how else was she to learn? He gave her a quick account of his journeys to the North. "The world is abuzz with the notion that the strata of the earth were formed gradually over vast periods of time," he explained, "and we were seeking to refute this theory." She was especially curious as to whether he had ever been to Oxford University, so he told her about his decision not to enrol, in spite of the cajolery of his mother and stepfather. "The entire institution is *consumed* with the Articles of Faith. How can a university be a place of inquiry when dogma is its chief concern? There is, furthermore, an unbecoming preoccupation with rank. In all the dining halls, you find separate tables and even separate entrances for noblemen, gentlemen commoners, and commoners. Such distinctions are made in the very chapels! I have been several times to visit Mr. Buckland, and I tell you, Miss Anning, each visit deepened my resolve to eschew the academy and make the fields and the shores my University. Although it would be a relief to be resident somewhere else at the moment. I find myself dwelling like a ghost in Aveline House, so as not to remind my mother and Mr. Aveline that I'm still here."

A vertical frown formed between her brows.

"They wish me in London. My fiancée is there, Miss Letitia

Whyte." She stared at him sternly, surprised no doubt by such a personal disclosure, but he went on. "We've been betrothed for some years, but I've been busy making a geologist of myself and have not seen a great deal of Miss Whyte in that time. How capriciously a lifelong union can be arranged! But perhaps it makes no difference. The institution of marriage was conceived to answer to all manner of material and social and physical needs, and must inevitably answer poorly to some, no matter who your mate or how she was chosen." It was proof of your reasoning, he decided in that moment, if you could explain yourself to this girl and know your logic to be sound, if you could endure the scrutiny of her black eyes without flinching. Henry observed himself failing the test, and so he asked the question that would surely turn her eyes away. "How will *you* choose a husband, Miss Anning, when the time comes?"

"When the time comes?" she asked intently, and she did not look away. "I am past twenty." She kept staring with an expression he couldn't interpret, and finally he was the one who looked back to the sea. Neither of them spoke. A woman of breeding would have found a way to remedy such a silence, but Mary did not. Eventually, he broke it by inquiring about her family, and she said that her sister was ill. So then he offered to send Mr. Aveline's surgeon over to see whether he could be of help. She accepted the offer, but she did not seem well pleased. Possibly she held to goose grease and dried moss and such as cures, like most of Lyme.

The sun had lifted itself over the edge of Stonebarrow by then, and they had an hour or two of collecting before the tide forced them off the shore. He watched her move methodically along the dark layers, using any convenient rock as a stepping stool, pressing her fingers to the cliff face as though to read it by touch. With a twinge of envy, he observed her absolute focus; this mist-veiled shore was her entire world! He found nothing but a couple of belemnites, but low in the cliff, she found a lovely crinoid on a waving stem. He watched while she deftly separated the layers with a chisel and touched her fingertips to its delicate calyx. "When I was a girl," she said, still crouching, "I thought the sea lilies *were* flowers, and I could not see how they could have turned to stone. It takes an animal to be petrified. But then I learned they were animals, and could feel fear like any other."

He was standing over her, noting how tanned the back of her neck was, noting the fine hairs escaping from her bonnet. "*Petra*," he said. "Miss Anning – the root betrays the meaning. It's just Latin for *rock*." She lifted her head and looked at him with amusement.

Oh, only a fool would underestimate Mary Anning! At one point in the walk, he told her about the narrow vertebrae he and Conybeare had found the year before in a tidal outcropping. A serpent perhaps, from the length of that chain. The waves had had sport with the bones all night and they fell into nothing before they could be collected. But Mary knew immediately. "Were they almost flat, sir? Like a shark's spine, but thicker? My father found some in Pinhay Bay years ago. He sold them to the curi-man at Charmouth." But they were not from a serpent, she said – flat vertebrae like that would not allow the mobility a serpent needed. This was the spine or neck of a creature with fins.

"Well, perhaps there is another species of giant reptile along this shore," Henry mused. "Mr. Buckland will not credit it – he'll charge me with inventing the whole story. In any case, nothing matters to Buckland but finding the old patriarch!"

"Buckland!" Mary said with a snort. She was still scanning the cliff face as they walked, her eyes never ceasing from their work. "What confounds me, sir, is this: why do we not find the stony forms of foxes and mice and seagulls in the layers, when they live in such abundance all along the shore?"

Why, indeed?

Then they were at Charmouth, and two boys were digging for oysters. The eager morning light encroached on their silhouettes, thinning them to nothing. Silver was laid down in a sparkling band on the horizon, and the black edges of the cliffs were outlined in silver light, water dripping silver from them. Piles of bracken lay washed up at the foot of the cliff: frilled sashes the rosy mauve of elderberry, and flags of glistening black, and brilliant, torn sea lettuce, all tangled like an extravagant bed of ribbons. Henry stopped walking. Mary looked inquiringly over her shoulder at him. Her bonnet had slipped down, it dangled at her back, and her black hair was twined at the nape of her neck – it picked up the light the way the cliffs did. Her face was flushed from their walk. There was a bloom to her, the bloom that work and sunshine and clear water and simple bread will produce. He could see the fine down on her cheeks and sun shining through the lobes of her ears, showing up the blood in them. He found himself returning with some confusion to their earlier conversation.

"I do wonder if there's something . . . something in the human form that makes man immune to petrification. That spark of the divine that animals do not share – or perhaps it's our capacity for spiritual corruption."

Mary shook her head. "We be flesh and bone," she said simply. "Animal humours will happily commingle with man's humours. My father proved this when I were a girl. You will have heard, Mr. De la Beche, that there is a bit of the cow in me." She touched her fingers to her arm.

"I have heard," he said.

He throws off the covers and swings his feet to the floor, picking up his watch. Half six. The tide will be out, and so will those who work the shore.

izzie lay on the cot in the kitchen with her eyes closed. A copy of the *Theological Review* was open and face down on her chest, as though she was trying to draw its mournful voices straight into her heart. "Mary," she cried the instant Mary stepped in the door. "Read to me! Read the story of Martha Locke at the heavenly gates."

"No," Mary said. "If that's what you want you must read it yourself. Look what I've got." She opened her bag and showed Lizzie. "A dogfish. It must have come up in the herring nets. A fisherman tossed it onto the shore. It's fresh as hay – I had to wait for it to die before I could pick it up. We'll have it for our supper."

Lizzie sat up and peered into the bag, and her hand flew to her mouth. "It stinks of piss," she moaned.

Mary slid the fish onto the table, careful to avoid the dorsal fins that could wound even after death. Its eyes had turned white just in the time she walked from the shore. She bent over it and looked at its fearful, down-turned mouth.

Lizzie lay back and opened her book, holding it as a barrier between herself and the fish. In a voice full of practised pathos, she read out:

Ah, lovely appearance of death!
No sight upon earth is so fair.
Not all the gay pageants that breathe
Can with a dead body compare.

Mary rinsed her hands quickly in the basin and dried them on the rag hanging by a nail from the wall. She took a wedge of cheese from the crock on the table. It was Mr. Gleed, the new pastor at the Independent Chapel, who'd brought Lizzie this book. "Why do these fine pastors despise the only world they know?" she asked Lizzie. "Why is that?" Lizzie puckered her mouth and made her eyes big and round in a comic sign that she did not know, she did not know what Mary meant. Mary took the knife to the cheese, trimming off the mould in thin curls. "Where is Mother?"

"At Bennetts'. I wished to go too, but when I put my foot down, the floor was rolling like the sea." She dropped the book and turned her face to the wall. On the windowsill above her was a tray of beans drying – she'd been sorting them, sliding them into rows with her fretful fingers. Poor Lizzie, never well since her baby teeth fell out.

Mary reached for her and rolled her over, examining her white face and the mauve mottling under her eyes. "I'd be peevish too, never going out. Look, I've brought milk. We'll soak the fish to take away the smell. But you can have a cup first." Lizzie pressed her lips together. She pinched them between her thumb and fore-finger and shook her head elaborately. There was energy in the shaking: Lizzie was rallying.

Mary perched on the edge of the cot and she and Lizzie shared a plate of bread and cheese, watching each other eat in silence.

It was near noon. Mary had until two o'clock, till the next low tide. Then Mr. De la Beche would cross the square and go down the steps to Marine Parade. He'd be carrying his satchel of tools. He'd call at Mr. Buckland's lodgings near Cobb Hamlet and they'd follow the west shore to the bones on Monmouth Beach. Mary had said emphatically that she would meet them there. She did not want to walk with either of them. When she walked with Mr. Buckland, they talked of science the whole way. There was no harm in that, except that he snatched her words out of the air as though he were a frog catching mayflies, never looking at her, never asking himself about the woman who uttered the words. Whereas Mr. De la Beche – with Mr. De la Beche, the vexation was exactly the opposite: it seemed he could not get enough of watching her.

Back when I was a girl, she thought, noting with satisfaction how hungry Lizzie seemed, back when he came to the workshop to talk of birds and dragons, I had no fear of him at all.

It was six feet long, this specimen: they knelt around a grave. Examining the teeth, Mr. De la Beche had pronounced it an *Ichthyosaurus communis*. There were three kinds of Ichthyosaurus, and this gentleman, who counted among his friends the Keeper of Natural History at the great museum in London, had had the honour of naming all three. The new specimen was neckless and hunched, pinned helplessly by a slab of limestone, as though it had been killed by a building collapsing on it. A difficult excavation. Mary'd told them they should hire workmen to chip it out before the tide damaged it. But Mr. De la Beche liked the work, and well he might – for him, work was play. She was proven right, though: the tide had stolen a fin. But when Mary pointed it out, Mr. Buckland shrugged. The sternum and pelvis were what he cared about; he had seen plenty of fins. "Oh, my brave, stony fish-lizard," he crooned, "we'll get your secrets out of you!

What do you say, Miss Anning? Was water its only element, or did it heave itself up to shore? Did it suffer the pangs of childbirth, or did it lay eggs?" The second question would answer the first, for if it laid eggs, it would need to drag itself up to shore like a turtle.

Mary, chipping away at the ribs beside Mr. De la Beche, could feel that gentleman's glad eyes on her, could feel his eagerness to speak. The ribs Mary was excavating were splayed and there was something of great interest between them. She bent over it, wielding a small pick. There was no chance to speak – how could Buckland talk so without pausing to catch a breath? She turned her head then to look at Mr. De la Beche. Hazel, his impudent eyes were, with a band of brown like a chaffinch around their centres. He was laughing, holding her eyes, trying to make a secret fraternity with her against Buckland. "All those animals," he murmured, while Buckland kept talking. "Taken into one ship. There are a hundred thousand animal species on earth, Miss Anning, do you realize? And two of each! And food for all of them. How was such a thing possible?" He laughed in the way he had, trying to draw her into laughing too. "Buckland," he called then, flinging his pick down, not scrupling to interrupt. "There's something you should know. It's about Miss Anning. She disputes your science. Miss Mary Anning is harbouring her own private heresy. She disputes the likelihood of finding Noah on these shores."

Mr. Buckland's cheeks turned scarlet. "I am sick beyond endurance of being tweaked about Noah!" he cried, blinking rapidly. "You insist on an infantile representation of my ideas, purposely to provoke. We all aspire to find the remains of the race of Adam – you as well as I."

"Not so," said Mr. De la Beche. "I question whether man inhabited this part of the globe at the time of the Flood."

"Well, I warrant he did."

"What is your reasoning?"

"What is the point of all this, without man? It was man's sin that caused the Flood. It was to caution man that God turned the drowned remains to stone. Man's old bones are somewhere, and we shall find them, though he fled to the highest mountain peak." He was trying to joke but he still had the stiff face and flat voice of an angry man.

The tie of Mary's bonnet had come loose and she set her pick down and reached up both hands to retie it. "Mayhap the men all took to their ships when the waters rose," she said. "The English be grand mariners."

"No doubt they tried, those that had them," said Mr. Buckland. "But no English craft could endure as Noah's ark endured. It was a whole different order of craft. The master of the Flood Himself was the master shipbuilder."

"Mr. Buckland," Mary said then, seeing the chance to ask, "will you look at what I've found here between these ribs?"

Buckland leaned in Mary's direction. "Oh – my lads and lassies –" he exclaimed, forgetting his anger. There beneath the ribs lay a stone. Buckland took up his brush, his lovely boar-bristle brush that Mary so envied, and delicately daubed. Lined up beside the first stone was a second. Brown and spiralled, like the stones Miss Philpot was collecting. Bezoars, they were called. "This fellow's been swallowing stones!" said Buckland. "It's the chap's gizzard. He's been swallowing stones to grind his food."

"No, sir," Mary said, after a pause. "No, sir. They be turds, sir. Turds turned to stone."

Turds! Coprolites, Buckland called them, and he was as thrilled as if they were diamonds. They must open them, and Mary was the one to do it. A couple of years before his fall, Richard Anning had lit on the idea of slicing ammonites open so that the chambers inside were visible. With the stonemason's help, he'd set up a saw, and Mary had struggled for years to master it. And now they could use her technique in their new practice of studying coprolites. Buckland had a bezoar stone at his lodgings, and on their way back to town, Mary found two more on Monmouth Beach.

Down in the workshop, she showed them the saw. It was a fine iron band held in a wooden frame. They took off their top hats and set them on the work table. Mr. De la Beche fingered the narrow band. "You cut stone with this?" he asked. He was standing close to her. She could not move without pressing against him, and a queer sort of heat passed between them when she did.

"It's not the iron that cuts the stone. You keep sand in its path, like this." She showed him. "It's the sand that does the cutting. But it must stay wet. See this barrel? You must pull the peg out if the stone becomes too dry. Look, a trickle of water will fall in just the right place."

"Oh, my geological maiden," Buckland cried, pushing his way in between them. "You are too clever by half."

They worked, taking turns, until they had cut open all the stones they had. Lizzie put on her plaid frock and pinafore and came to sit on the steps to watch. Each bezoar stone they cut into the narrowest slices possible, to see everything inside. *Sectioning*, Buckland called it, and their fingers hurt from holding such narrow stones under the saw. Inside, they found tiny spines and fins and scales, tiny big-eyed skulls – it seemed the Ichthyosaurus, for all its soft and gentle eye, had no qualms about eating its young. Mr. Buckland was transported with delight, thrown back six thousand years, to the moment of the creature's gobbling its dinner. But Mr. De la Beche became more subdued, speaking in a low voice to her, as if it were just the two of them there in the workshop.

———

When they had gone, Mary rested for a minute in the kitchen. Her mother was down in the workshop sweeping up the mess they'd made. Dust blossomed up from the stairs and pricked Mary's nostrils. She was almost sweemy with hunger. She would cook the dogfish for their supper, but first she must meet the coach. Noise rose in the square and she picked up the stool to drag it outside.

It was not the coach; it was boys scuffling on the street. Mr. Gleed came down Broad Street towards the boys, and they fell apart with a last defiant shove to each other's shoulders. Mr. Gleed had his collecting bag full of curiosities on his arm. Miles away in Plymouth, Mary thought, James Wheaton's body is turning in its grave. Mr. Gleed stood for a minute at the end of the square, a small figure in shabby black. Would he dare to sell right under her nose? She could see him trying to decide whether he had sufficient gall. She stared unblinkingly at him. Finally, he walked nimbly away from the square and turned up Church Street. He was on his way up to the Monmouth Inn. He'd sell in the public house, something she had never done. He will see us starve, she thought. I shall start selling at the chapel door while he preaches.

A knot of young ladies waited for the coach, tossing merry cries into the air. Delicate tendrils framed their faces – the sort of curls you must have a lady's maid to produce. Their gowns and slippers were white, the snowy white you must have a lady's maid to maintain. Miss Whyte, in fact, was the name of Mr. De la Beche's betrothed. Mary looked at the three young ladies across the square until they began to cast glances in her direction. I am a woman of science, Mary thought. I may stare. In her mind's eye, she saw Miss Whyte with hair so fair as to be white, and a high, serene brow. She saw her sitting by a casement with a book in her hand, her chin aloof, wearing a gown of palest yellow, her two white breasts lying open to appraisal like goose eggs in a bowl in the market. Wearing tiny slippers and a lacy shawl, and diamonds dangling where wires were made to go through her ears.

Colonel Birch came hobbling across the square, a fat, amiable ram, and Mary stood up off her stool. "Miss Anning!" he bleated. "What relic does Miss Anning have for me today?"

"Nothing new, I'm afraid," Mary said. He owned scores of the small invertebrates spread out on the table, the ammonites and devil's toenails and belemnites. "Nothing new – oh! – except this." It was leaning against the house – another large hip bone she'd found near Charmouth.

"Capital, capital!" he cried, scarcely glancing at it. "I shall send Charles to carry it home. What do you say to a pound?"

"Colonel Birch," she said, "last month I sold you the very piece." She was always counselling him against buying, afraid he would turn against collecting entirely when he came to his senses.

"Oh, spare no thought for that, miss," he said. "I shall not rest until I have another. If one is good, then two are better. Two by two into the ark!" He lifted his moustache to her, displaying his teeth. They were white and straight and set into a wooden plate. They came from a thief hanged at Bridport – so Will Darby from Sherborne Lane said. He bent over to examine the hip bone, leaning heavily on his stick in deference to his own hip. His rented rooms in Lyme had been full to the rafters and the landlord had complained. Recently he'd moved to a house in Charmouth. If Mary were rich and could keep a collection, she would keep only the best example of each type. It would be the *science* she thought of, not just a greedy piling into cabinets.

And then Colonel Birch was gone, hobbling back to the Assembly Rooms where his mount waited, and Annie Bennett wandered into the square with her basket of lavender. She came from Cobb Hamlet, not from her mother's house, for she was Mrs. George Downing now. Mary looked narrowly at her stomach. Molly swore Annie was childing, but it was hard to tell for the basket. Annie leaned against the prison wall and turned her head in Mary's direction. Some days they spoke to each other and some days they said the same thing with a look: *I am tired and you must be too.* The coach was late. Everyone was hungry and tired, leaning on the prison wall or slouching outside the Assembly Rooms, propping their weary gaze on her. They would stare: she had been written up in the papers, she was a poor woman visited by gentlemen. It was a truth in life that others could look at you and see what you could not see.

Now Mr. De la Beche was crossing Bridge Street towards her. While she'd been waiting there hungry and tired, he had bathed and dressed. He wore now his knee breeches and boots and a beautiful jacket of dark blue wool. "Yes, it's me back," he said. "Try not to look so stricken! I won't keep you. I'm taking tea with Mr. Buckland. It shall be rock cakes at table, I warrant you. But why are you still here, Miss Anning? Is the coach late?" She nodded. "Just as well for me," he said. "You never know what the coach will bring me, by way of passenger or post. And in any case, I hate to miss the excitement. In other towns with a steep decline, footmen will throw a drag out. But not in Lyme. In Lyme, they thrive on danger to life and limb." He eyed her table. "And how is trade?"

She had never seen him wear this splendid coat before, scarlet flowers stitched on its cuffs and down both sides of the front. Everything Mr. De la Beche owned was bought with money earned by blackamoors, who worked for him in the heat of the West Indies. If I were rich, she thought, it would not be lacy frippery I would buy, it would be this blue embroidered jacket. I would have his calfskin boots, and the red waistcoat, and the wonderful cape. If I were rich, I would have his leather kit.

He smiled at Mary now and examined the ammonites, sliding four or five very similar asteroceras into two rows to show the difference between them, winking at her to show he meant no offence, and that *something* passed between them again, although their hands were inches apart.

"Poor to middling," Mary said. "I must pack up now. I have supper to cook."

"But the coach has yet to come," he said.

Oh, this day was all a jumble, all the recent days were a jumble! It was her hunger hanging like a fog between her and the square, her hunger that gave her the sense that she'd been on a long journey and had come back bewildered, somehow she'd lost her bearings in front of her own house. She couldn't take her eyes off Mr. De la Beche's jacket. On each button was stitched a single blossom, the work of many hours by the hands of an unknown woman.

"The flowers on your coat," she asked. "What species be they?"

He turned up a button and peered at it. "I don't know, actually," he said.

Watchers in the square moved imperceptibly, angled their ears towards the questions she was putting to this gentleman. Took in the shine on his boots and the delicate neckerchief tied at his neck, and the clean, healthy glow on his cheek. Took her in as well, saw Mary Anning standing by the table in her rough-woven skirt talking to a gentleman. And then suddenly, so did she: she saw what they saw, a thin woman with unruly dark hair pulled back under a cotton bonnet, a white bonnet gone grey, her hands callused and bare and brown, and the cotton lining of her jacket sticking from her cuffs like crude lace. And then the bugle sounded and everyone turned to watch the headlong plunge of the coach down the hill.

◄〔 N I N E T E E N 〕►

Lyme Regis, Dorset. July 30th

My dearest Letitia,

I am in receipt of your letter this very hour. The question it
poses demands a swift reply. With respect to the embarrassment
you endured in your conversation with Colonel Henry Wyndham
at Ascot, I thank you for your loyal attempts to defend my name,
but must, with full awareness of the pain this confession will cause
you, inform you that in this situation the truth lay with my accuser.
My removal from Great Marlow was not, in fact, voluntary. I was
expelled on the grounds of insubordination. I deeply regret that
you were obliged to learn this from another (and in such public
circumstances) and I beg your pardon for the humiliation this
scene caused you. It was always my intention to reveal the whole
truth to you prior to our marriage, but we have not had a great
deal of leisure together in recent years due to my scientific travels.
In the early days of our acquaintance in Bristol, the episode was
too raw to be broached (or I too raw a youth to find a way to

broach it), and in recent years, it has rather shrunk in significance in my mind. Perhaps my hesitation to set a date for our nuptials sprang in part from a sense that many fundamental things remain unsaid between us.

The incident in its entirety is this: I was the instigator of a scheme to produce and circulate a chapbook of satiric cartoons. They featured one Mr. Truepenny, a risible Marlow tyrant, a pathetic pettifogger whose self-importance superseded all other traits, whose partiality to certain favoured boys was unconcealed, and who was the cause of a great deal of suffering to the poor wretches who met his disfavour. It was from my imagination and pen that the drawings issued (the salacious details forbid their description to a lady), and Henry Wyndham and one Richard Chorley acted as copiers and purveyors, having collected a lengthy subscription list. I was expelled and my two lieutenants were not. My final vacating of the officers' hall was, as Colonel Wyndham has recounted to you, in defiance of the trust placed upon me and of my own publicly sworn vow.

Given that you were ignorant of this episode at the time of our engagement, honour compels me to ask whether you wish to be released from the promise you made to me while still a girl. Perhaps "honour" is something to which I can no longer lay claim. Having been prompted by your letter to reflect on this ancient incident, let me be frank in telling you how I regard its "stain" on my character: I do not minimize my past behaviour, I do not dismiss this as the rash act of a callow and unformed youth. I see in it, rather, a spontaneous and individualistic gesture, the import of which I have not fully sounded – a fidelity to an inner light (as it were). I have taken from it a guiding truth, that the conventions of society do not form an entire and unfailing code for our behaviour. Integrity may, on occasion, lie in deeds that are perceived by others as offensive and even immoral.

We must be grateful to Colonel Wyndham that he has afforded us this opportunity to know each other better. I ask you to consider whether this confession renders your fiancé repugnant in your eyes or rather endears him to you further. Your decision to persevere in this engagement will be tantamount to a fresh vow. As compelling as our families' desire is for us to honour our longstanding promise to each other, it would be folly to enter into a lifelong union you have come to regret. Consider soberly, knowing there is more of your fiancé in this letter than in any other you have received from his hand. I eagerly await your reply, upon which rests the happiness of others beyond yourself.

Your humble servant,
T. H. De la Beche, Esq.

Postscript: If you have occasion to speak further with my old companion, please remind him that through this incident he was spared having me as comrade-at-arms; I should have made a wretched soldier.

———

It's a most tumultuous terrain the Charmouth Road traverses, a landscape caught in the act of moving. And yet the clifftops were cleared in centuries past, and lie cultivated in barley and corn. Some smell of fish from the mackerel worked into the soil, some of sheep shit from the beasts paddocked there. When Henry walks the road with Mary Anning after a morning's fossiling, she tells the fields by name: *Pinch-gut. Labour in Vain. Kettle of Gruel.* Why the farmers bother to plant them at all, he can't imagine – fields torn ragged by landslips, or sinking and being taken over by gorse.

West of Lyme Regis, where Dorsetshire becomes Devonshire, there's no coastal road at all. There the high terrain was never cleared and a forest flourishes whose very trees may have been saplings when Shakespeare was a boy. This riotous forest is called the Undercliff, although it is really the colonized *top* and broken *side* of a cliff, where crevasses and almost-vertical upthrusts attest to the impulse of the cliffs to move, and wild clematis, ivy, bracken, holly, hazel, and brambles conspire to disguise the resulting chaos. How like the tropical bush around the plantation in Jamaica, Henry always thinks when he wanders into it from the top of the town.

In the shadow of the Undercliff, down on the western shore, Henry helps Buckland remove the *Ichthyosaurus communis* for crating. Mary Anning is there, and Buckland has hired four men for a day. They're working to slide a carrying board under the fossil. Buckland's irritation is like a cloud hanging over the site — he's preparing for a trip to the Continent and he's been in a bustling, officious mood all week. In reaction, Henry moves slower and slower, stopping often to rest and look up at the Undercliff. "Could I climb up there from here?" he asks Mary.

"No," she says. He looks at her sharply. There may have been the hint of a dare in her tone.

With a rhythmic series of grunts, the men have the carrying board up and are off down the shore. Buckland hurries after them. No doubt, he assumes Henry and Mary will follow. But they don't move. They stand side by side and watch his robed figure dwindle down the shore, and Henry feels his spirits lift when it falls out of sight altogether.

"Where is he off to?" Mary asks.

"He's touring the Continent. With Reverend Conybeare. They're conducting a study of correspondences in the rock strata."

Still she makes no move to go. She stands and turns her sun-burned face to look at the sea. He picks up his kit and looks at her questioningly.

"Would you like to see where my father found the narrow vertebrae I told you about?" she asks then, with a little smile.

He follows her out around Seven Rock Point. The lapping water has left them a scant few feet. Mr. Aveline has warned him over and over that, should he be caught by the tides at the base of the western cliffs, his only choice will pertain to the manner of his death.

"It was here," Mary says, gesturing towards the cliff.

There's nothing to see, only the layers of shale and limestone put sloppily together. They scuffle around at the base of the cliff, speculating as to what sort of creature might have such an extremely long neck, and whether the size of the braincase is generally a measure of the intellect. They're of necessity standing very close. They have to shout into each other's ears over the roar of the surf. "There is a townswoman with a passion for measuring skulls," Mary says, and Henry makes to measure her head with his hands. She ducks away, well out of his reach, and stands retying her bonnet.

"I want to make a map of this shore, and use it to mark down my finds," she says evenly.

"That's a fine idea. But let me make it for you — it would be my pleasure. I'll chart the shore in either direction, as far as your work takes you." He glances down. Now they're standing in water. "Well, Mary," and he uses her Christian name before he can stop himself, "it appears we may need to fashion ourselves an ark."

She hitches her basket higher on her arm and splashes nimbly around the debris on the shore. He follows her and finds that a landslip has made a ramp that mounts the cliff. She presses herself into a fold in the lias and then they're climbing a steep face where he discovers footholds so regular they must have been chopped out by an axe. He climbs after her, catching glimpses of her tattered petticoat and the long calf sticking bare from the top of her boot.

Finally they reach a narrow plateau and she stops. "I thought you said we couldn't climb the cliff," he says, breathing hard.

"*You* couldn't, I said. And nor could you, without me."

"No one in town believes it can be done."

"How do folk suppose the smugglers reach their dens?" They're flattened against the cliff face with her clumsy basket between them, and she points him to an upward trail. It's barely discernible, but she insists he go first. He scrambles up through gorse and then steps into the cool and quiet forest and onto a surprisingly wide path worn by solitary feet, brown clay with chert embedded in it here and there.

They follow the path east and once he glimpses the sea lying silver below. He's never walked this far into the Undercliff. Here it's a wonderful stand of immense ash, festooned with the creepers of wild clematis, a verdant garden with nets of ivy thrown over it. And burrs – presently he discovers that burrs have caught up his trousers, to the point that he can hardly walk. They're in a clearing then, a fern-filled clearing dotted with snowy anemone, where a falling tree has pulled its roots out of the earth, such a mass of roots that they make a den where you might shelter from the rain. The forest is filled with birdsong. Henry sinks onto the trunk of the fallen tree. He takes off his hat and drops it among the bracken.

Mary follows him into the clearing and puts her basket down. They're alone, more alone than they ever are on the shore. He smiles and gestures for her to join him on the log. But she will not – she continues to stand. So he sets to work cleaning his trousers, careful to avoid pulling threads out of the soft wool, and (in an effort to put her at ease) begins to discourse on *burrs*, which, carrying each the seed of its progeny, have made him their unwitting means of propagation. Why did she lead him here? Surely it's an invitation! But still she's silent. He points out the anemones, blooming so late. It's because of the tree falling, he explains when she doesn't respond: they've been tricked into springtime behaviour by unaccustomed sunlight (light that shines into the clearing now, falling full on Mary's face, brightening the white of her bonnet). She stands still, her embarrassment gone, her intent black eyes meeting his gaze unabashed. He knows the next step, he has been here before, but now he's the one who looks away, who continues to talk. He falls back to Buckland – God knows there are stories enough on that topic. And he finds himself talking again about the tour to the Continent, confessing to these thoughtful eyes how badly he wished to accompany Buckland and Conybeare, but for the fact that his own affairs were in such disarray, the plantation in trouble, and the matter of his marriage, which was to have taken place this summer. He falters and falls silent. Then he hears himself telling her. *There has been a breach in my relations with my fiancée. I have written a conciliatory letter, but she has not responded.*

The light in the clearing changes – if this were a drawing room, the butler would slip in now to light the candles. She's leaning against a tree, her basket at her feet. She is the perfect person to confide in: she listens with a grave face, she does not feel an obligation to respond.

They walk back out on the Pound Street path, and as they cross the meadow at the edge of town, Mary begins to sing in the forceful, natural fashion of chapel singing that he often hears from the street on his way to church:

The Lord hath spoke, the mighty God
Hath sent his summons all abroad
From dawning light till day declines

The listening earth his voice has heard
And he from Sion hath appeared
Where beauty in perfection shines.

Her bonnet has slipped off again, and her black braid has fallen by its own weight out of the knot she had it tied in. On the slope below is the thatched roof of a cowshed, and then they can see the Cobb, miniature ships being unloaded, donkeys labouring along the stones, and side by side they walk towards their separate suppers.

He spends a week making the map he promised Mary and takes a great deal of pleasure in the work. For the eastern portion, he saddles up his mare and rides the cliff road as far as Charmouth, stopping every fifty yards to peer over the cliff and sketch. He was aiming for a scale of two inches to a quarter mile – but finally it's a topological map he makes, rendering the most fruitful fossil areas (Black Ven, for one) in high detail and compressing the others. Monmouth Beach and Pinhay Bay he cannot sketch from above on account of the Undercliff, so he paces them at low tide, savouring the beauty of the shore, exhilarated at being freed from the future, and employed, and outdoors, out of Aveline House, where he aggravates his mother and Mr. Aveline merely by walking into the room.

In the end, he has a simple (and, to his eye, elegant) ink drawing from Charmouth to Pinhay Bay, with a wash to indicate the littoral zone and a few landmarks labelled. He marks in the quarry beds *(Gumption, Specketty, Lower Skulls, Mongrel)* because Mary taught him those names, but he leaves the major excavation sites to her to fill in. His first impulse is to take the map to the workshop so Mary can examine it with him, but he's chary, suddenly, of entering her cottage without Buckland.

Instead, he stops by the curiosity table and suggests an outing to the western shore. Then out at Pinhay Bay, he suggests climbing into the Undercliff to examine the map out of the wind. She assents, and they follow the path to the same clearing, where this time she sits beside him on the log as he unscrolls the map.

She seems pleased. They work out where the Ichthyosaurus finds will be marked, and she pinpoints the site of a huge shipwreck from her childhood, the *Alexander*. It foundered in a terrible tempest, and the body of a lady washed to shore afterwards. "She'd sailed all the way from Bombay," Mary says, "and then she died on the English coast. She'd been three month at sea."

"Well, Mary," he says, "I don't believe I've ever told you about my own shipwreck." He makes a dramatic story of the typhoon that caught them on their journey home from Jamaica, after his father's death, and she listens, entranced. "Oh, we had a merry time. We were being *toyed* with. That wave did not finish you? Well, this one shall! It was a betrayal, a grievous betrayal, the sea so warm and green, turned into a roaring monster. But the Fates were with us. There are small islands everywhere in that sea – they were made by volcanoes – and the waves dashed us onto one. I shall never forget the solid sensation of those black rocks under my cheek! I can still hear my mother's terrified cries. It was a dreadful time for her."

He breaks off a leaf of hart's tongue fern, folding it carefully down the middle, and finds himself wanting to go on. "My father had just died. That's why we'd taken to the sea, to return to England. He was gone from the plantation. He was at Bath St. Thomas on business, many miles away, when he contracted an infection – not the sort of illness you see in England that a soul will linger with for weeks, but a tropical fever that felled him in a day. A messenger came on a donkey to tell us he'd been taken ill."

Mary moves closer, as though she's having trouble hearing him.

"When the messenger rode into the yard," he says, "the field slaves left their work and gathered round the house. How did they know what was in that message? – we never understood it. They sat all around the yard and waited. The overseer couldn't budge them and after a while he stopped trying. As the afternoon went on they began to wail. My mother made me stay in the house. She was frantic with distress to hear them. She didn't know the tropics, she still believed he could recover. And then as the darkness fell – and it falls very quickly in the islands – a second messenger came up the road on a donkey."

Understanding moves across Mary's open face. Across the clearing, sunlight salutes the fronds of fern standing green among last year's black.

They collect together regularly, always on the western shore, and even as the days grow colder and golden leaves fall to the paths, they always come home through the Undercliff; that way, they can steal an hour's collecting time from the tide. They tend to linger in the Garden (how could one not think of Eden, walking the paths of that voluptuous forest?), pausing in the clearing for quiet conversation away from the roar of the surf and the spying eyes of fishers and oyster diggers and coal collectors crouching on the shore. The clearing is nature's drawing room, he sometimes thinks, and we have the chance to get better acquainted here, as people do in drawing rooms. Although the modestly costumed damsel at his side is a most curious companion – almost unlettered, absent an aptitude for flirtation, shockingly bereft of ordinary conversation, completely untravelled (having never once stepped foot on a ship, nor indeed in a coach), and prone to wiping her nose on her sleeve as the need arises. Also (he notes every time he follows her down a path) possessing a grace of motion that comes entirely from a lack of self-consciousness, from the very framework of her bones. Not that she is angular – but he is always aware of her bones, her strong shoulders and the long, striding legs. And he wonders at the candour and intelligence that light up her face, and the breasts that lie unrestrained under her blouse (lifting just perceptibly as she bends to put down her basket).

She would never truly be appreciated in a drawing room, Mary Anning, where reaction to her rough boots and her brown face and quaint speech would eclipse any other consideration. Buckland must recognize her worth, although in him it provokes only resentment. As for Conybeare – for all his gifts, the Reverend William Conybeare views the underclasses through a veil of undisguised contempt. One night, walking home with his friend after a visit to the Assembly Rooms, Henry commented on the darkness in the poor cottages they passed, although it was not yet eight o'clock. Conybeare laughed. "Busy seeing to their duties of procreation," he said. "It's the squalor they live in – they're obliged to produce eight or ten infants in the hope of replacing themselves in the next generation. An onerous task, but one they excel at, the poor of England."

And indeed, the Anning brood numbered ten! With only three children surviving – it is unimaginable. It's a sad, sad story she tells him, of deaths by fire and drowning and illness and deprivation. His own childhood in Jamaica is so far outside her narrow experience that it baffles and amazes her. "Picture me, Mary," he says. "My feet as tough as shoe leather from running barefoot. Two toes swollen where chigoe fleas had burrowed into them. My legs cobbled over with mosquito bites. And as brown as a berry from the sun – brown almost all over, I might add, for I lived in a pair of short pants Belle sewed me from the bolt of fabric intended for her own sons. Osnaburg, that fabric was called, and it was as itchy as sin."

"Do the blackamoors and their masters not live apart?" she asks.

"Oh, to be sure, strictly apart. But I was a child, and caring for me was part of the work of the plantation. The slaves had their own cabin-line, and the field slaves did not come to the house. But certain of them had sly ways of flouting the rules." He tells her about the beautiful, impudent Sophie, how she infuriated his mother beyond any of the other slaves, for her boldness. "The jalousies at the latrine had so many slats missing that anyone who chose could see right in, and one day Mother was sitting in the latrine and Sophie came up the path – where she should never have been, so close to the great house – and stood there as bold as brass and called out, *How-do, missus?*" Mary stares at him, aghast, although no doubt it's his frank talk of his mother in a latrine that accounts for her expression. "Oh, my mother was vexed! She insisted Sophie be flogged. But my father ignored her. In fact, he and the overseer made Sophie the driver of the grass gang shortly after. And then, when he was selling some slaves and could have solved the problem by selling Sophie, he sold a different slave by accident, and this enraged my mother even more."

"He sold her by *accident?*"

Henry considers for a minute how he can explain it. "My father strove to conduct his affairs in a Christian fashion," he says at last. "He tried to keep families together, and so when he sold a slave named Tom, he sold Beryl with him, because the overseer's book said they were man and wife. But really, it was Sophie who lay with Tom in the night, and everyone outside the great house knew it. But my mother was rid of Sophie after all, for after that sale, she vanished. I knew she was gone as soon as I woke up one morning – I heard the dogs out in the bush."

"What would they do if they caught her?"

"There was a bamboo cage down by the boiling-house. Runaways were held there for a period of time."

"Like the stocks in Cockmoile Square."

"I suppose."

"Was she found and put in the bamboo cage?"

"No," Henry says. "In her own fashion, she escaped them."

A noise starts up like a mason chipping stone with a silver spike. It's a stonechat, somewhere in the trees above them. There is no way to make someone understand the reality of such matters. Individuals of his own class can't grasp it, unless they have lived the planter's life. With Mary, explanation is impossible. But her curious mind will not let it go.

"Did your brothers and sisters live in this way on the plantation, with the blackamoors?"

"I have no brothers or sisters. Well, none my father was prepared to acknowledge. Indeed, I regarded my nurse's children as my brothers. One wonderful day, my father took me to the sea, and he kindly took Cuthbert and Ben as well. We dove for urchins and conch. They had never been in the sea before, and yet they dove like seals. They were expert at everything. You should have seen them climb the coconut palms beside the house! It's a good trick, Mary – there are no branches to use for foothold." He tells her about scaling the tree himself, using his bare feet to grip the trunk and reaching as high as the veranda roof before gravity hooked him and he came sliding down, rough bark nipping at his thighs, and landed in a nest of sticks and coconut husks. He doesn't tell her about Cuthbert and Ben shrieking with laughter, and the way he ran wailing through the house in search of his mother. She was lying in her bedroom with the shutters closed, sleeping inside her bed net. So then he started up the path to find Belle, and Cuthbert and Ben met him and drove him back to the great house.

No wonder I thought we were brothers, he thinks ruefully as they walk home. We fought like brothers.

·≺[T W E N T Y]≻·

W hen Mary was worn down by hunger, it was John Gleed her mind seized on, a nasty bit of prey, to be sure. Two years he'd been preaching hard work and industry to his weary flock at the Independent Chapel, urging them to be fruitful and multiply, to subdue the earth, to have dominion over every living thing. Two years he'd been collecting on the shore and stealing her trade. Mary listened every Sabbath to Adam and Eve digging and delving in the Garden and she waited in vain for the Serpent to slither in. But it had vanished, taking with it the dragons roaring and roiling at Black Ven. All that dark world gone, all fear of it drained away the bleak day James Wheaton was carried off in a wagon to be buried with his ancestors in Plymouth.

I shall have to open this hedge-parson's eyes to the true meaning of dragons, Mary thought, and one day after the service, she waited until everyone had gone and slipped back into the chapel. She'd never said more than "Good morning" to Mr. Gleed – around single women, he was properly reserved. She found him hunched over a shelf behind the pulpit. He had a small looking glass and was worrying his back teeth with a wooden pick. He jumped when she came up behind him, and dropped the pick. "Mr. Gleed," she said. "I have a question. About the days when the earth was young. In Genesis, we are told of Cain who slew his brother Abel —"

"Oh, Miss Anning!" he said eagerly, wiping his mouth surreptitiously with his sleeve and snatching his bible up off the pulpit. "The perennial question of the seeking heart: Where did Cain get his wife?" He smiled as though she were a fish he had caught in his net. His black coat was crimped at the elbows into the stiff folds of a bellows, from neglect of sponging and pressing. People said his pig ate from a baptism font seized by his own hand from a papist church.

"Scholars of Scripture explain that Cain married one of his sisters," she said, stepping closer to him. They were the same height, and Mary straightened her backbone and made herself taller by an inch. "My question is something other. It is this: God marked Cain's brow to warn strangers not to kill him. If Cain were the son of Adam and Eve, and Adam and Eve were the first parents, then who were these strangers?"

"Ah, Miss Anning," Mr. Gleed said again. He flipped to the front of his bible and read out: "*And the days of Adam* . . . let me see . . . oh, here we are, it is here: *And he begat sons and daughters. And all the days that Adam lived were nine hundred and thirty years: and he died.*" Mr. Gleed peered at Mary. "Well?" he cried. "Mrs. Brody on the Axminster Road? Seventeen children, and still in her prime. Consider if she lived to be nine hundred. Would she still know all her kin by name — eh? Eh? Of course not. Ye can be strangers to your own kin."

Of course, she could have told him about the satanic race spawned by the Fall, she could have snatched the bible from his hands and read him the text about the dragons being Satan's henchmen. But why would she choose to belabour the wickedness of her own vocation? She'd failed, and was sorry that she'd tried, for now John Gleed was never shy to approach her on the shore, to ask her to identify something he'd found. He would keep on poaching off her custom and sucking on her brains, and she was powerless to stop him. Her custom was already meagre. Buckland was long gone now, having crated up the Ichthyosaurus with the bezoar stones in it and carried it off to Oxford. Not for money – he was not greedy in that way – but for science. Mary had helped him for many a day, but it did not occur to him to pay her. And Colonel Birch was suddenly not to be seen – he was poorly, so she learned from Will Darby. The pound he'd given her for the hip bone would have lasted longer, but she'd paid Doctor Huddlestone. Although that fancy doctor had had nothing to offer them – all he said was that they should not give Lizzie water, however thirsty she was, it would lead to dropsy. Molly did not understand why Mr. De la Beche should not pay the fee, as he was the one who had sent the man. "He can well afford this charity to a poor family with a sick child," she said, and Mary would not explain, she would not put her reasons even to herself. She walked past her mother down to the workshop, her sense of that gentleman stirring, the sense she carried of him even when she was not thinking, a sense of something menacing and bright.

It was a dangerous pastime, stealing into the forest with this man. She was inviting scandal. He seemed entirely oblivious to such a worry. There he would sit, leaning back against the log in the Undercliff with his boots crossed, and talk of things no other high-born person would dream of confessing to such as her. His rear end planted on the damp ground, heedless of his fine wool coat, this gentleman who made his living from black people he owned like mules.

No, not like mules, exactly. When he was an infant, a blackamoor woman put him to her breast and fed him on her milk. There was a dirt floor to the house where she lived and he played there with her children. He was a planter's son who knew about a hole in an earthen floor where a slave's secret cutlass was buried: he took great pride in telling her this. Mary reached for her old categories of the rich and the poor and found she could not sort it out at all.

Every day she would resolve to come home by the shore directly after collecting, and every day they would climb the cliffs. Not that whiling away the afternoons in the Undercliff with Mr. De la Beche took away from her income. Vertebrae were piled up along the wall of the workshop, belemnites and ammonites lined up on the table. No one was buying. All through the years of her growing up, people had said fervently, "When the war is over . . ." Now the war was over and the price of a loaf had risen to eighteen pence. The rich had taken to ships; they'd abandoned Lyme Regis and carried their guineas over to France – the sails of their ships when you stood on the Cobb were a flock of sheep in the Channel. But all to the good, thought Mary fiercely, eyeing the lovely bones on her table. It is not curios I collect now. It is scientific specimens. But how could she parlay specimens into more money?

"Did Mr. Conybeare sell his paper on the Ichthyosaurus?" she found a chance to ask Mr. De la Beche one day.

"He sent out a notice about it," he said. "And everyone at the Royal Society and the Geological Society signed up for a subscription in advance."

The sun sank over the cliffs and the square filled with ladies and gentlemen going to dance in the Assembly Rooms. Mary stood in the shadow of the shop across the street and watched the door in the stone portico of the Assembly Rooms open to a glimpse of bright gowns. She looked through the dusk to see which of the gentlemen crossing the square she could recognize by height and stride and gesture.

In Mary's house, they had no fire. Beside their hearth, Molly sat wrapped in her shawl and a blanket, leaning against the stone as if to draw out a vestigial warmth. Joseph was not there. He was sitting with the stonemason's daughter, Amelia Elliot, who had large blue eyes full of sentiment and a terrified, lying admiration for Mary's work (her startled cries asking in their highest notes, *What strange sort of girl be ye?*). Their wedding was a week away. Joseph could not really love her, but no doubt he adored sitting by the stonemason's crackling fire, drinking hot brandy and beer from a tumbler.

When Mary had wiped the table and swept the floor, she carried the second blanket down from the upstairs bed and settled on the cot beside Lizzie. She lay staring at the charcoal streaked on the ceiling like the trails of flittermice.

"Mary," Lizzie asked. "Who be your friends and who be your enemies?" Excitement crackled off Lizzie like heat – her joy at having Mary lie down with her.

"My friends be three," Mary said, rolling over to her side to face Lizzie. "They start with *B*."

"Mr. Buckland," Lizzie said. Saliva had dried like lime in the corners of her mouth. "*B* for Buckland. And *B* for Birch. I don't know who the third could be, unless it be Mr. De la Beche. But that is *D*." It was a puckish, knowing face Lizzie was turning towards her.

"Of course it's him," Mary said. "The *De la* is just for show. They are gentle friends to the poor, all three." *Mary*, he had taken to calling her, this Henry De la Beche. *Henry*, she said to herself. She folded the scratchy edge of the blanket away from her chin.

Lizzie eyed Mary craftily. "And who be your enemies?"

"My enemies be two. They start with *C*." Lizzie's face was absorbed in thought, her lips moved silently. "I'll give it to you," Mary said, "because you are so dull. *Conybeare*. De la Beche and Buckland's friend from Bristol. He comes to the shore with Mr. De la Beche but he's too fine to speak to me. He wrote about my Ichthyosaurus as if it was his own, with nary a thought for my labours. I could show you, Lizzie. It's down in the workshop. Nary a mention of Mary Anning in the whole entire paper."

"And the other *C*?"

"Cuvier, crouched like a toad across the water."

"How can he be your enemy?"

"He has the disease of all men who are never wrong. That makes him my enemy." Mary eased herself up and arranged the bolster behind her head. She turned her face away from the rotting-fruit smell of Lizzie's breath. "Listen," she said. "I'll tell you a story."

"The wreck of the *Alexander*," said Lizzie.

"No. This is about London. It's a dream, about a meeting at the Geological Society, where the high folk go to talk about science. Only certain men are allowed – they have chosen each other. Every month, as though a bell has rung that only they can hear, they put their stovepipe hats on their heads and ride in from all directions. To one of those grand buildings with columns in front holding up the roof. They walk in through the wide doors and take their place in a great hall." Mary was momentarily distracted by Lizzie's intent face, almost luminous in the dim light. Lizzie nudged her on.

"Well, it's a very particular night that this story takes place. A *monster's* been found on the shore at Lyme Regis. They are to decide its name. Just before they begin, a lad appears – someone they've never seen before. He's dressed in a black wool coat. Everyone falls silent as he walks down the aisle and takes his place among them. Who let him in? The gentlemen tried to catch each other's eyes."

"Why don't they drive him out?"

"They're curious. He knows things they don't know – they can see it on his face. They want to suck his brains."

Lizzie was watching her knowingly. "What manner of hair does the young man have?"

"His hair is black and plaited into a queue down his back."

"Was it a coat like that he was wearing?" They both looked towards the door where Joseph's coat hung when he was in the house.

"Yes," said Mary. "It's a mite long for this lad. But no matter. The meeting begins. The gentlemen fall to debating and arguing. Not the stranger. If he speaks, he will betray more than he wants to betray. So he sits in silence. He takes in everything they have to say, and then he stands up and walks out." She turned on her side away from Lizzie. Rogue tears stung behind her eyes. "That's all I know," she said. "You tell the rest."

Lizzie wove her fingers into Mary's hair. "It were you, Mary," she said sweetly.

There was a long quiet, while Lizzie lay plucking at Mary's hair, methodically picking up one strand after another. In the Assembly Rooms across the square, the scrape of fiddles started up. Mary sighed. "Yes, it's me. It's me sitting there among my friends and enemies. Sitting with my mouth shut. Dressed like a man."

"But your bosom would pout out."

"No, look," said Mary, rolling back towards Lizzie. "I wrap a towel tight around like this and Mother sews it closed. It could be done."

He told her long stories about the blackamoor boys he played with, and how he learned to see that he was not like them and fixed his heart on becoming so. About the slimy green soup he drank, because his nurse Belle said it would turn him black. A great wonder, thought Mary, this gentleman's passion to be something he is not.

And then he was to have been a soldier. He was in officer's training in a great college on the River Thames, but he was sent down. "Just a bit of mischief, and my whole life turned on it," he said with a little laugh, leading her up the path in the Undercliff, talking all the while. There was a master that everyone loathed, and the cadets found a means to take revenge upon him. Mr. De la Beche drew a series of pictures of this master in a lewd embrace with a chambermaid – the redhaired chambermaid who worked in the masters' quarters. Everyone recognized them immediately when they saw the caricatures. "She was – how shall I put it? – rather spectacularly endowed," he said, "both as to bosom and as to buttocks. And the clever thing was that each drawing was franker and bolder than the one that came before – fewer clothes, you know, and the embrace, er, more compromising. I released the pictures one at a time, over several weeks. It was a beauty of a scheme, because the price went up each time, unless you had paid a subscription for the whole series, as many did. Oh, it was boyhood folly – but you have to admire the genius behind it."

Mary stopped walking. "And in truth they consorted together, this master and this chambermaid?" she asked.

"Oh, no, I doubt it. I never saw a more prudish man. No doubt he was entirely oblivious to the wench – and *incapable*, I'd wager, even if he had been tempted. So you see, for boys, we were fiendishly clever – we pounced on his very weakness!"

Mary's anger was a dark cap pressing down over her head. "What of the chambermaid? What became of her? Did she know of the lewd and lying pictures being passed around?"

"Well, I suppose that's something we should have considered

at the time," he said genially. "Lads of a certain age are beasts, aren't they? I don't know what became of her, because I left, you see, before they could drum me out." He moved up the path again, and after a minute, so did Mary. He walked along, swinging his leather satchel, and told her with great relish about running away, walking across the Home Counties like a vagabond, limping into London, and the restless sea of people one sees there, the gaslights and coal smoke, and the fairs that draw spectators of every rank. He himself entered an exhibition hall with his uncle, and there on display was a naked woman, naked except for a small apron, almost the brown of her skin. "They chose that fabric, I warrant you, to give the impression of complete nakedness. She was a Hottentot, from the south of Africa. She had on a collar of shells and claws. They were treating the poor creature in a beastly fashion. A leash was tied around her neck, and the keeper was leading her like a dog."

Mary let out a bark of horror, but he paid it no heed. He lowered his voice, it was himself he wanted to discuss. "You know, I had the strangest experience when I saw this exhibition. I was right at the front, not three feet from the woman, and she raised her head and looked at me, and I was filled with the most vivid conviction that she knew me! It was uncanny – such was my confusion that I could not abide being part of that crowd, and I left the exhibition hall before my uncle. It was all a delusion, of course. She had come directly to London from Africa, I believe, and she was only about twenty – I could not have encountered her in the West Indies so many years ago."

Mary could not make sense of any part of this story. "These gawkers – they came to see how black she were?"

"No, I would say not." They'd come up to the open chalk boulders and he put his kit down and leaned against one. "There are many Negroes in London. Perhaps it was scientific curiosity that drew some of the spectators. There is a deal of interest at the moment in the development of the various races. I have read several papers on it. But of course, the spectators were not all learned, and even among those who were, I reckon it was rather a curiosity of a baser sort. People paid thruppence to buy sticks from a boy, and used them to prod her backside. To satisfy themselves that her rather large haunches were real. A man reached out his stick to try to lift her apron and see what was beneath, but she stepped out of the way. So I suppose it was the novelty of the Hottentot woman's body." He scuffled his feet in the mat of leaves rotting on the forest floor. "An enlarged property . . . of the female parts." She would not look at him. "It suggests to scientists a . . . a heightened sexual proclivity. An appetite untrammelled in the savage of the species."

And then she did look, and she saw the gleam in his eye, a falseness to his manner that she loathed. What did he see when he looked at her — what did he think she was? It was a downdacious act, walking into the woods with a gentleman. She'd always known she was courting danger. But better he should grab at her like a drunken tranter on the Gosling Bridge, better he should know his own heart.

"Did you tell Miss Whyte about this display?" she asked.

"Of course not," he said in surprise. "Oh, Mary! I tell you, Mary, because of its scientific interest." He was laughing, but there was shame in his laugh.

·✦[T W E N T Y - O N E]✦·

S atyrs inhabit a forest, and he becomes one. A sly satyr, who cloaks his intentions in sanctimony, reaching for her hand to say, "When they talk in church about man being in the image of God, it's always the hands I think of. In Rome, there's a wonderful image painted on a ceiling by an artist named Michelangelo – I have an etching of it – God animating Adam through a touch of their fingers." He demonstrates with their two hands. Then he turns her hand over and, before she withdraws it, feels the calluses from her wedge hammer on her palm.

The hand, the satyr whispers, *again,* and in his mind, he pulls Mary towards him, easing her down in the bracken, feels his way through those rough skirts to the long, strong, bare leg within. But still he refrains. Instead, he talks, slides to subjects where the forbidden glitters, his voice coming from some seat deep inside him. Someone, his better self perhaps, is listening behind the trees, cautioning him, but still he goes on, drops his voice and carries on, telling her of boyhood follies, allowing himself a boyhood frankness, and feels a heady sense of liberty in the telling. Mary looks sternly beyond him, her strong dark brows drawn together. It's perverse, this talk, he'd be thrown out of decent company for it, but it's only talk, and as he follows her out of the clearing and through the stands of bracken lining the path, he congratulates himself for resisting when no other man of vigour would have done.

Then it's so cold and stormy that no sane person would venture onto the shore. The bathing machines are carried to high ground, the very fishing boats are beached. Henley's pond freezes over. His mother and Mr. Aveline wait for a fair day for driving – they've accepted an invitation to the Devonshire home of their friends the Talbots. Henry has declined, raising his mother's hopes that he'll be going to London. The morning they leave, he finally mentions the letter from Letitia. "And you have not gone to her in spite of this?" his mother cries. Then she's speechless with fury. She climbs into the coach without a goodbye.

Aveline House is drafty and dark, and he misses the outings to the shore. Free of Mrs. Aveline's influence, the cook serves stewed salt fish every night. Henry commits to a Christmas meal with the Henleys. He toys with excuses to invite Mary to call; they could sit by the fire and talk in a civilized fashion. But he busies himself sorting through his papers, and as one day goes by and then another, his perspective on the past few months alters. Finally, he finds himself outside the thing altogether – he's an onlooker, watching with a frown as a gentleman creeps into the forest with a comely girl of a station far beneath him. There is a name for this, and any onlooker would be quick to provide it. Although (Henry asserts in his own defence) those who would condemn him have no notion of the *inside* of the thing – his respect for the girl, the restraint he's shown, and his kindness to her.

But it will not do, he is forced to admit that night as he takes his solitary supper by candlelight. As to the intentions of the gentleman, the disapproving onlooker would be entirely correct. A pulse beats in the gentleman's veins, a pulse in the nature of an imperative, and in its fulfillment lie infamy and heartache. He must distance himself from her. He will, he vows. He breaks off a piece of bread, dips it into the fish stew, eats it. He takes a swallow of wine. Gazing into the candle, noting the lazulite blue where the flame springs from the wick, he tests out the weight of the resolution. I will avoid the square when the coach is due, he's able to say. He empties his glass. I will end our outings to the shore, unless we are in company. He pushes back his chair. Will she feel this as a loss? It's hard to know what she feels. But an absence in his chest, the absence of a certain goading restless-ness, tells him he's made the right decision. In the peaceful company of his better self, he goes to the library after supper and reads until the early hours.

He has callers. The next afternoon, Edmund and Mrs. Sutton are announced. Edmund Sutton, the son of his mother's old plan-tation friend, and now, like Henry, an absentee planter. Sutton was in school in England when Henry was a boy in Jamaica, they hardly know each other, but Henry greets him with enthusiasm. They're travelling from Weymouth to Bristol, and he insists they stay a day or two. It's clear they're taken aback by the invitation, but the weather is bad and after a moment's hesitation, they accept. Henry has never met Sutton's wife. Her manner is all kindness, a pantomime of kindness, tenderness and sympathy represented by tilted head and melting glances. "A finer wife than any man deserves," Sutton says stoutly on each occasion that the lady crosses his line of vision.

The second night, Mrs. Sutton admires a piece of needlework hanging in the drawing room and asks Henry to relay a compli-ment to Mrs. Aveline. "That piece was not done by my mother," he says. "It was a gift from my fiancée, Miss Whyte."

"Oh, I have never known Miss Whyte to work in petit point," says Mrs. Sutton.

"You and Letitia are friends? I had no idea!"

Something unspoken passes between Mrs. Sutton and her husband, and she inclines her head in assent. It is enormously puzzling, that she did not reveal this acquaintance before now. Nor does she ask why Letitia and Henry are apart over Christmas. Her expression in that moment is anything but solicitous – it is canny, and *righteous*, as though she is privy to the truth of the thing, knows that Letitia has thrown Henry over, and knows why.

Henry refuses to pursue it. He turns in his chair, resumes the subject he and Sutton spent the afternoon on: the future of geology. He describes the amazement he feels riding over the English countryside, at the thought of the unknown layers beneath every roadway and meadow. Looked at in this light, England is as unstudied as America. "What is lacking," he announces, "is a comprehensive textbook for the practitioners of this new science, and I have in mind to write one."

Sutton turns his moon face back to the fire. "A capital project for the gentleman who likes to ride out on an autumn day, especially for one who detests shooting."

"You misunderstand me," Henry says. "I do not intend this as a leisure pursuit." A manual will require a staggering amount of study and research, but it will establish him as an expert in the field. And there are many practical applications to geology. Once his name is known, he'll be sought after by mining companies, by roadworks, asked to locate wells, that sort of thing. What he does not say is that, to date, his living has paid for his geologizing; very shortly, his geologizing will need to pay his living. But no doubt they grasp this.

"You would work as a sort of engineer?" Mrs. Sutton says

uncertainly, and Henry thinks of the chagrin his mother would feel overhearing this conversation.

He sees them off in the morning and climbs straight up to the library. Their discomfort on the subject cemented his intentions. It's a vocation that suits him splendidly – a science in its infancy, where he will not be burdened by orthodoxy, can carve out his own niche. The possibilities are endless and lucrative. He's deferred numerous financial obligations with the expectation of his marriage settlement. If Letitia has indeed broken with him, he has no choice but to find paid employment. All to the good – he feels a rising excitement about a life prescribed by worthwhile work. What a pity he can't talk this through with Mary! Not that she would grasp the entire import of it. He just longs to hear her response, which would be a true expression of her thoughts and feelings. How grateful he is for their conversations through the autumn. They recalled him to the days when he was a barefoot boy in osnaburg shorts, unhampered by codes of social conduct: a precious, essential past.

On a calm day, he walks out and down to the lower town. The sea moves beyond the wall like a forgotten obligation, picking up light from the eastern sky, striations of foam gleaming white on each wave. He passes through the square, glancing once at her closed door. He will not knock, he is firm (but it's a stingy fate that begrudges them even a chance encounter). He meets Miss Philpot near the bridge and refrains from inquiring about Miss Anning. As he climbs back up Broad Street, he stops to admire the mist lying between Stonebarrow and Golden Cap, and wonders if Mary is at that moment on the shore.

At Aveline House, he pauses, reluctant to go back in. What made him think his parting from her had to be absolute? he wonders as he hangs his cloak behind the door. Far too cruel! He can be her gentle friend and protector. He is already her protector – he allowed her to escape him. But escape him to what? Mary Anning will never marry. She is doomed a spinster because of her work, as his mother frequently remarks. It's a sad fact that no man of her own class will take her on. But others would, with alacrity, other men of other classes, and on terms that would leave her vulnerable to disgrace. She is chaste now, he feels no doubt, but she is manifestly a creature of flesh and blood (oh, the way she has of turning her head towards him, as though she is turning on a pillow), such a creature of nature – it is almost heartbreaking to imagine the joy she would take in it! It's only a matter of time before someone snatches up what he has been scrupulous enough to resist. And this future, inevitable rival – will he have Henry's regard for Mary? Henry sees them stealing into the forest together, his rival foppishly attired in blue velvet, leering like an imbecile and reaching his paddling fingers towards her bodice, and Henry swings his walking stick and clips the man in the back of his knees, watches him fall to the path, howling in anguish.

And then, as he sits over his letters in the drawing room, he begins to muse on how an affair could be conducted so as to minimize its risks, both to Mary and to the theoretical gentleman. Resolutely he sets the subject aside, only to find himself teasing at it five minutes later. For the next few days, he is powerless to resist. Mary makes things worse, raising her black eyes to him every hour of the day and night. Then she begins to slide into his room after dark, after the house is quiet and the room lit only by the orange light of the dying coals in his hearth, she takes to pulling her hair out of its knot, her heavy dark hair, and laying the long, lovely length of her body down on him. *Warm me*, she says, and he cannot fail to oblige.

The week after his mother returns to Lyme, Henry encounters Mary in the square and feels a lurch of emotion at the sight of

her. She's the one who issues an invitation to the shore, and he
cannot refuse. He's taken aback and rebuked by her composure.
She is grave, distracted; she seems scarcely to take in his conversation. He's horrified to see *straw* sticking out of the holes in her
boots. Packed in for warmth, presumably. The tips of her fingers
are terribly inflamed and when he offers her a hand on a steep
bank, she winces and pulls back from his touch. It is *blains*, she
says, from the cold. She is uncharacteristically pale. There is
fatigue in the way she moves – he wonders what she has eaten
that day. She was out early, she tells him, she walked to Black Ven
with Miss Philpot at the first low tide, which means that she
climbed the hill first to collect Miss Philpot, who could not
decently walk alone.

Spring is very early. Yellow primroses emerge, taking advantage of the light before the canopy fills in. She ventures down a
different path than they normally follow, and then she stops suddenly and points out a fork in it. A smuggler lives there, she tells
him, a man by name of Digby, who many years ago enticed her
sister Martha onto a makeshift raft so that she drowned. "She
was on a wooden door from a ship. She was playing at being a
sailor. It was a sport of a group of children, and the sea took her.
She was four."

"I warrant he was just a lad himself at the time," Henry ventures. "No doubt he intended no harm," and she flies into a rage.

"Lad or no lad," she cries. "Intended or not. It was heedless
folly!" Tears glisten on her lashes. She will retreat from such a
painful memory, he thinks, she'll fall into silence. But her face
continues to work. She drops her voice then and tells him about
an ominous man who came to her father's funeral, a man in a
torn black coat. Not entirely a stranger – she recognized him as
a mummer who'd come to their door the Christmas before the
pox, on a night when they were starved with cold. A lone

mummer, a very ill sign. Seeing him pacing behind the coffin, she felt the terror she'd felt when her father opened the door to him, she seemed to hear again the song he sang. "My father let that evil body in, though he'd heard the song – he slipped the man a coin."

"What was the song, Mary?"

She breathes painfully for a minute, and then she raises her head and sings with mournful emphasis.

> *Out of nine I got but five,*
> *Half of they be starved alive*
> *I want some money or else some bread*
> *Or all the others will soon be dead.*

At the end, she puts her face down and cries bitterly. She has her own handkerchief and will not use his. "Oh, it was not the mummer I feared – that was just a child's fancy. It was my father." Her words come out choked with emotion, she lapses into dialect. "My mother be full of fearful notions, death all the time clawing at her shoulder, but it were not my mother who let death in. No, it were my father. He would never bow his spine to bear the weight of trouble. He did not know proper caution."

It's an image that pierces his heart – the vulnerable child, seeing accident and illness and starvation threaten to carry off the last of them, her yearning love for her foolhardy father. One must look for fecklessness and superstition at the root of it, he tells himself. It is ignorance and low breeding that compound the problems of such families. But he cannot hold back the truth that she feels as deeply as any woman of his own class would feel, that she has marshalled every ounce of will and intelligence to ameliorate her fate. Then, at the sight of her sobbing figure, a different feeling rises – anger, that he should have let this knowing in, because it will not be so easy to force it back out. She is a dangerous companion, Mary Anning, with her mud-edged petticoat and her sore fingers. There is a contagion here – this comes all from improper fraternization, from closing a gap where a gap must be maintained!

He strides up the path ahead of her. When he comes to the clearing, he has the impulse to keep walking, but then he thinks of her weeping alone in the forest and his anger collapses. He sits on the log. He's losing his footing; everything seems to unmoor him these days. He's *sweemy*, as Mary would say, in danger of floating away. The very globe, untethered from the ropes that moored it, is floating away with him on it. It could be that he's hungry himself – he has neglected lunch. Mary comes into the clearing and sits down on the ground by the log, leaning back against it. She does not seem piqued that he walked away from her. She asks so little of him! He reaches over and briefly clasps her shoulder. "Alas, the young are at the mercy of the old," he says.

Mary wraps her arms around her knees and lays her cheek to rest on her skirt, and they sit in silence. Above them, the stonechat makes its distinctive sound. The ash trees are coming out in bud, dressing themselves in the softest green. It's a very great gift, her opening her heart to him in this way. He longs to be worthy of it. And so he does not speak. He and Mary sit by the fallen trunk and gradually, in their silence, all his chattering words that hung in the clearing these many weeks dissolve, gradually they are scattered and taken away by the forest air. They sit on the damp, mossy ground where fronds of fern slowly uncurl their bent heads – not in a drawing room, as he pretended, not even a cathedral, as many might say. This is a work of nature, husbanded only by its dyings and rottings and seedings, misted by the Channel breezes even when there is no rain. This is a forest, and perhaps, after all, they are just two of its creatures.

O n a cloudy day, when Molly pulled her shawl over her head and went to the churchyard to see the Overseer of the Parish Poor, Will Darby with his rick of red hair came to the table with a note from Colonel Birch.

My Dear Miss Anning,

It is the Gout that felled me, I am Lame as a Hen-haggler's Horse. What news on the shore? Would Miss Anning were itinerant like the good Pastor Gleed! In the meantime I have given Charles a Purse, I have charged the Youth as my Agent.

Colonel T. Birch, S. S.

Mary looked over the note at Will Darby. *Charles*, Colonel Birch called him. Because it saved learning a new name – he'd always had a Charles. Will Darby had picked a sea lily up from the table. She'd cut the shale into a tile around it, and it swayed gracefully across its matrix on a long stalk. Will Darby tilted it to the light, eyeing it with the air of a man intent on exercising some meagre authority. "It is a *crinoid*," she said to him. "They are animals, but they grow on stems like flowers." He scowled, offended at being instructed by such as her. She did not know for certain what *itinerant* meant, but she saw what she must do. "Tell Colonel Birch I refuse to deal with a thin-faced nesseltripe," she cried in a sudden temper. "Tell him I'll be in Charmouth myself in the morning."

The next morning, she picked out as many pieces as she could carry and wrapped each one in a paper. As she opened the door, she saw Mr. De la Beche ride into the square and swing down from his horse in a fluid motion, standing with one hand on the bridle, cupping the soft muzzle of the horse. Henry, she thought. She pulled the door almost closed and waited until he was gone, leading the horse up Broad Street, before she set out on the walk to Charmouth with her heavy load.

At Charmouth, she walked up the single street to the house she knew to be Colonel Birch's, ignoring the townspeople who always stared when she walked through the town with one gentleman or another. Will Darby answered the door, wearing a string tied around his head to keep the hair out of his eyes. With a terse nod, he left her standing in the hall. The light from a high window fell on a carving on the hall table, the bust of a man with a garland of leaves around his head. It was carved in white marble, so amazingly like flesh that she longed to touch it. Then Will Darby was back and led her sullenly down the corridor, to a room filled with tables and shelves of fossils (it was just as she had pictured it), and she breathed in the familiar smell of dust and the shore. Two chairs were arranged at a grand window, with a small table between them. Colonel Birch sat in one with his sore foot wrapped in sheepskin and propped on a stool. "Sit yourself down, maid," he said, gesturing to the second chair. "If ye dare." It was indeed a most curious chair:

a lion, with its head snarling over her head, and its legs become chair legs. On each side a muscular tail curved up to form an armrest. "What do you think of that workmanship, eh?" Colonel Birch said.

Mary peered down at the tassels of the tails, where the carver in his exuberance had carved lions' heads. "There be more heads and tails than nature would allow to one beast," she said.

"I bought it from an Arab in Bath," Colonel Birch said, "when the Egyptomania was upon me. Very well, then! Help the maiden with her bundle, Charles, and we'll see what she has found."

Mary sat on the edge of the chair in this room where all her industry lay around her and watched him go through the fossils. In the end, he bought everything she had carried in – as she'd known he would. For a strange little shrimp-like creature alone, he paid eighteen shillings. And then he sat back and lit his clay pipe, pulling the whole candle flame into the bowl of the pipe by his sucking. With her money pouch like a stone at her waist, Mary sat while Will Darby served wine and oatcakes, she sat back in the lion's lap and looked at her collection laid out on shelves on three sides of the room, narrow, unvarnished shelves that reached from the floor to the height of her head. If they were mine, she thought, I would arrange them in the order they were found, from lowest in the cliffs to highest, and she remembered asking Buckland one of the questions that had troubled her since a girl: if the earth was formed on the third day and the creatures on the fifth, how came the creatures to be buried so deep within the earth? And he said again what he always said, that the rock was all the sediment of the Flood, and so contained the bodies of creatures who had died in it, turned to stone as a caution to man. And she asked him then why the Ichthyosaurus for all its size did not sink to the bottom of the rock as the sediment settled, and he turned away from her without answering.

The wine, called Madeira, was in a china flagon with a duck on the spout so that when you tipped the flagon to pour, the duck seemed to be swimming on a river of Madeira. "What a piece of workmanship, eh?" Colonel Birch cried, and Mary thought how Lizzie would like it. "More Madeira, my dear?" the Colonel asked, leaning over to refill her cup. She drank the lovely Madeira and looked around her in the dusty, light-filled room. This was her collection. She could put a name to every specimen; she could tell where each was found and how it was dug out. If she were not poor, this would be her collection. Colonel Birch sank into a doze and when her cup was empty, she poured herself another to watch the duck swim.

Walking back into Lyme Regis, she felt sweemy being so high above the town. The town, she saw, was a hive: it had been built up in layers and was penetrated by the street, and she was descending down into it. At the top of the hive were the rich, snoring in their castles full of booty from the shore. What a treasure it was to have everything together! Colonel Birch was right, after all, not to be choosy but to save everything. And he did not ticket them, he did not tell the fossils their names, but waited for them to tell him. Better he should have them. He was not clever, but he had the heart of a collector. Whereas she was out under the sky where she belonged, out on the muddy street, going down into the town empty-handed, walking past the house where the pig-faced lady lived with her sisters, down onto Broad Street, where Aveline House sat squarely against the street, where the comely Henry De la Beche in his trousers lived, who knew all the names of the layers in the town and on the shore, and dared to think beyond his teachers. Her own understanding was imperfect — for a practitioner of Undergroundology, she lacked instruction, and so she knocked on the door. "Is Henry in?" she asked when a maid came to the door.

"Mind your tongue, Miss," said the maid sharply, but asked her to wait in the hall all the same, and then Henry himself came out in his shirt sleeves, wearing a waistcoat in dove grey, this fair young gentleman whose betrothed was gone, gone, wiped out in the stroke of a pen.

"The map you made me is wrong," she said to his smiling face.

"Possibly it is," he said. "Well, then we should correct it." He said he would go to the shore with her, but they were just eating their noon meal. He took her into a small room and said he would have something brought in for her. "I shall ask the maid to bring you a refreshment while you wait," was what he said, and left alone Mary repeated this sentence to herself in the tongue of the high-born. Then the maid came back with a large tumbler of drink and a soft bread roll on a tray. "It's *sherry*," she said when Mary asked. It was sweeter than the Madeira, and softer.

When he came back into the little room, he had his coat on. He asked her what was wrong with the map and she told him. "It offers the view of a kestrel hawk," she explained. "I need the view of a mole."

As they walked along Bridge Street and passed the square, she gave a small wave in case Lizzie was watching from the window. They did not turn towards the western shore and the Undercliff. No, they went up through the graveyard and down towards Black Ven. It was Mary who set their course, walking in a demure way she had never walked before. She had changed in the course of the morning, she'd become soft through and through, without a centre. Like an invertebrate – with the same sort of thin shell between herself and the world. They were on the shore then. They stood shoulder to shoulder by the cliff and watched the waves fold over themselves, watched the fingers of water that chased up the shore after each wave retreated. The foreshore was a brilliant blue, the blue of the sky reflected in its pools. She turned and watched him watching the sea, looked at his straight nose and his hazel eyes, and thought with wonder that he did not see the happenings that lingered here on the shore, that left their smudge in the sand and their colour in the air. He came innocent to the shore, a visitor. Although deep in the Undercliff she'd told him about the sinking of the *Alexander*, the way the whole town stood on the Cobb in the howling wind and clutched each other while its great mast tipped. She'd told him about going out early the next morning, among all the other scavengers combing the shore for booty, and how she'd found the body. Why did she tell him? There was never such a gentleman for drawing things out of her, he was unique to his species. And then she had the sudden sensation that he could read her thoughts, and she said in confusion, "It were just here. The body of Lady Jackson. I came walking up and I saw something white on the foreshore, and I knew in a wink what it were."

"What did you do, Mary?" he asked.

She felt heat gather round her eyes. "I went back to the cliffs," she whispered. "I picked the coltsfoot blooming there, armfuls of it, and scattered the blossoms over her body." And that was the truth.

"Did you not tell them in the town?"

"No. I left her to the sea." Mary frowned and looked beyond him. If he carried on watching her in this fashion, he would see through her. "But later that morning, some folk found her. They took her up and laid her in St. Michael's church. And then I carried flowers to the church to keep the body sweet. After a week, we learned who she was. Then her two brothers came from London and carried her away."

She ran across the sand now and stood still on the very spot.

"It was just here I found her. She wore a white gown with lace at the bosom and trailing skirts. Her hair was spread out behind her. It was so fair it was almost silver. It lay on the sand like the wings of an angel. Even in death she was graceful, she had the grace of a lady." And suddenly she had dropped on her side to the sand and she was showing him the way the arms lay.

He crouched beside her, shaking his head. "No, Mary," he said. "That's not the grace of the lady – it's just the action of the tide. A corpse washed up by the sea will always lie parallel to the shore. The trunk will lodge first on the sand because it is heaviest, and then the waves will pick up the clothing and hair."

All this time in her brain, a tide was going out, and then in that moment, it was out. As he bent over her on the sand, she was Mary again, Mary with her strong limbs and her shame contained inside her, her shame humming along the spine that ran along her centre. She was an invertebrate no longer; she was herself. And still she let him untie her bonnet and loosen her hair, showing her the graceful way the tide would lay her out if ever she were caught by the sea. Still she let him bend his face down and run his tongue and lips over hers, as if to taste the salt the sea had left behind.

At the table in the square that afternoon, Will Darby looked boldly into her face. "Well, Mary," he said. "Ye've left the birch grove, ye've taken to the beach." His tongue stumbled on *beach* and his thin face turned scarlet.

"My, the devil's fired up your wit," she said as he turned and walked away. Poor fool, she thought. He's been all day whittling a point onto that jibe.

A wagon loaded with bales of wool creaked across the square bound for the Cobb. The load had shifted and two drivers leaned into its side with all their force, struggling to hold the wagon upright until they made the Cobb. So, she thought. So, this is how it is. If it were Will Darby I were seen with in the Undercliff or on the shore, people would say we were walking out together and ask when the banns will be read. But *banns* and the name of *De la Beche* would never be said in the same breath with *Mary Anning*. Courtesies from Miss Philpot raised her in society. Courtesies from Mr. De la Beche dragged her into the mud. And him as well, perhaps. Or perhaps not. Could anything ever dampen his air of health and well-being and fortune in the world?

Whereas her – they needed to hate her for something. If it was not creeping after dragons, it was creeping after gentlemen. Madness to walk alone in the Undercliff with a gentleman, and madness to tell him your secrets, and greater madness to go to the shore, and slide down to the sand, to have a gentleman bend over you and loosen your hair in a scientific demonstration. She knew the rules of her class and he knew the rules of his. But it seemed that science made its own rules, although these rules would mean nothing to the townspeople, who had a fearsome private knowing. Last winter, they'd said the reeve's widow was consorting with a common tranter. They did not say this in words, but mounted a skimmington on a moonlit night. When Mary heard the rough music and saw the parade come down the street, saw the mannequin with its yellow hair that could only be the reeve's widow, she was bewildered; she'd had no notion. But sure enough, in a few months, the reeve's widow was swollen with child. They were wizards in sniffing out indecency, the townspeople – Mrs. Stock and many others. They would smell the bracken of the Undercliff on her and sense the talk that took place there. They would see it on her, his attention to her and the knowing his words brought out, the glittering residue of his kiss.

A coach had arrived without her attending – the sweet, intoxicating drinks of her wealthy friends had left her brain in distemper – not the Bath coach, but the shabby cab the inn sent to Axminster to fetch passengers from London and Salisbury. Just a sole passenger, it seemed, a young lady in green with fine orange curls tumbling from the front of her velvet bonnet. She had disembarked and was standing uncertainly in the square, looking up the hill, seeming to consider first Broad Street and then Church Street. The prisoner lying in the stocks set up hissing between his teeth at the sight of her. Then, leaving her bag unattended, she walked gracefully across to the curiosity table, holding the stem of her furled parasol in two hands, and spoke to Mary. "Do you know Aveline House? I wonder if you would direct me."

He hears a step and springs to his feet, but it's his mother. "Sherry," she says to Brownley, who is standing in the hall. She comes in and closes the drawing room door behind her, waving Henry back onto the settee, and sits down close for a tête-à-tête. "She's bathing and changing. Daisy is attending her. You can go and see her in a moment." She cradles her round arms in their indigo silk. "What impropriety! What reckless impropriety," she cries, her eyes bright with excitement. "Thank *heaven* she had a companion when she left London, at least. A Miss Francine Mortimer. I recall years ago a person by that name served as companion to Lady Finch. A tall, vehement creature. Do you recall, Henry, when we spent a fortnight with the Beckets in Derbyshire, that business with a thrush flying through a window into the upstairs hall?"

"No."

"Well, in any case, that was Miss Francine Mortimer who created such a fuss." She shakes her head, musing over the memory. "And so Letitia was going down to Exeter?" Her tone is excessively casual, as though she thinks to catch him out.

"I have no idea."

"You don't know these friends she speaks of there?"

He raises his shoulders.

"She did not let you know she was leaving London?"

"Mother, do you suspect us of a clandestine correspondence?"

"Well, Henry. This is all a consequence of your failing to go to her weeks ago, as I implored you to do." She sighs. "At any rate, she had resolved on Exeter, and Miss Mortimer was to accompany her on the public coach. Before they were through Sussex, Miss Mortimer was wretchedly indisposed. Letitia tried to persuade her that they must find a means back to London, but Miss Mortimer insisted it was a passing thing. When they stopped for fresh horses in Salisbury, she was ill on the street in front of the inn."

The door opens and Brownley comes in with a tray. The apparition of a tall, vehement woman convulsed over the paving stones lingers while he sets two glasses of sherry on the side table and goes out. "Fortunately, Miss Mortimer has friends in Salisbury, just down the road from the inn," Henry's mother says as the door closes.

"Why did Letitia not stay with them?" The side table is nearest him and he studies his glass of amber sherry, which seems to have a flower floating in it (a dab of red, cadmium red, blooming up from the red cloth on the table).

"Apparently, she felt unwelcome. As a bedchamber, she was offered a contemptible closet in what she insists was the servants' quarters. She sat alone in the morning room for two hours with no fire in the grate. She says the servants had been instructed to ignore her. And so she came here. She can't account for why she didn't go to Exeter as planned. She says she thought the impropriety would be less if she came directly to her fiancé's home."

"There would have been no impropriety at all if she had simply written and asked someone to come for her."

"Well, yes. She says she couldn't bear to wait. And so, in the morning, she walked back to the inn and boarded the coach. She left without a proper goodbye, poor thing. Just a note on the bureau. And carrying her own bag, if you can imagine."

He hands her a glass and touches his own to the rim of hers. As she leans forward, the tendons of her aging throat clench above her high-necked wrapper. He settles back into the cushions, conscious of his future waiting for him in the upstairs sitting room. "I've sent the boy up to Morley Cottage with a letter to ask if she may stay with the Philpots," his mother says. "It would be better, I think, to avoid further occasion for gossip. You can walk up with her after you've had a quiet word. I'll send Burnley with her cases."

Letitia is reclining on a lounge before the fire in the upstairs sitting room, holding a goblet of wine at a dangerous angle, her legs crossed at the ankles. Her hair is unpinned and tumbles wonderfully over her shoulders. It's as bright as when he first spied her in the garden in Bristol – in the firelight, it gleams like polished brass. She looks up as he comes in. Through these last months, by her lack of response to his open-hearted letter, he had the impression that he had gained the upper hand. When he sees her face, he realizes he's been wrong.

She puts out a white hand and he takes it and presses it to his lips. She's wearing the simple ring with the tourmaline that he gave her at their engagement, on her pinky finger now: once too large, it is now too small. "You've endured a difficult journey. You were not subjected to rude attentions on the coach, I hope?"

"No," she says, shaking her head. Her gown is cut very low

at the bosom: she's abandoned efforts to hide the mole. He lets her hand go and takes a chair beside the lounge.

"Well, I must confess I am very surprised. I had begun to wonder if we should ever meet again. How was I to understand your silence?"

She rocks her wine gently in the goblet and looks at him as if unsure how he fits into the stream of thought that has caught her up. She takes a sip, and her throat is of such a translucence that he seems to see the red wine move down it. Her face in the fire-light is a woman's face, self-regarding, speculative, inward. She has successfully navigated a passage. Due to him, due to the suffering he caused her. She draws him in with her look. *What are the two of us to do?* she seems to be asking, and he feels a huge relief that this question is finally to be asked.

Then tears well up and overflow her eyes. Her head falls forward and her shoulders shake. He drops to a knee beside the lounge to catch the wine before it spills, and their hands meet on the goblet. She reaches for him with her free arm and then she is clutching him to her, pressing her face into his hair while she cries.

The next day she rests, under the solicitous attention of the Philpot sisters. He sends a note up to Morley Cottage to say that he will collect her in the evening for the dancing in the Assembly Rooms. They take the coach; his mother insists upon it. She and Mr. Aveline come as well, and stop in for a brief word with the Philpots. Letitia glides down the stairs of Morley Cottage in a charming white gown with lace at the bosom and cherries embroidered on the skirt. Her hair is pinned up and all her pretty ways are in place.

"What a delicate lace," says Miss Margaret Philpot.

"And in Lyme one can, indeed, wear the sort of light gown that cannot be worn elsewhere in the kingdom at this time of year," says Miss Elizabeth. "What wonderful sunshine we enjoy all the year round! It was in November that the lady novelist stayed here, and she had nothing but praise."

"The lady novelist?" asks Letitia, wrapping herself in a flimsy shawl.

"Oh, Miss Whyte," cries the eldest Miss Philpot. "What delights await you! I shall lend you *Persuasion*. Miss Austen made us all famous."

"But my dear, you do not want to wear those beautiful slippers," says his mother. "There is a dreadful buildup of wax on the floor and they will be black by the end of the first dance. They will be impossible to clean, as Daisy can tell you." The eldest Miss Philpot sends a maid upstairs to fetch Miss Whyte's third-best slippers.

They disembark in Cockmoile Square. While Mr. Aveline and Henry's mother hurry to the entrance, Letitia lingers before the dark windows on Bridge Street. Henry tries to steer her across the square and she leans against him and turns her face up to his, crying gaily, "Pray tell me, what is the impression in Lyme Regis society of Henry's fiancée?"

"No impression at all," he says. "Inasmuch as there is no society in Lyme."

She gives a little slap to his gloved hand. "You've never spoken of me to your friends?"

"Of course, your name is known. But I prefer to leave the pleasure of discovery to others. What does a bachelor have, but his air of mystery?" There is the sea in front of them, night birds hanging motionless over the persistent waves. She says something else, but the moving darkness takes it away, and he pulls at her arm and then they're at the narrow rectangle of light in the stone portico and through it. Looming just inside the door, waiting to greet them, is the Squire and, hidden behind him, his earnest little wife.

In the custom of country dances, they're served hot beef broth in a cup. The fiddles start up and they part and face each other in the wavering lines of dancers. Letitia sinks to honour her partner. When her glowing head comes up, she's applied a mask of gaiety, which stays on through the dance. But the minute the music lapses, she lifts her skirt with a brave little pout to show him her ankle. She's been wounded – why do the cavalry officers insist on wearing spurs? Miraculously, her stocking's not torn, although a mark can be seen darkly through it. There is blood on her gown, though, three red drops like blighted cherries just above the glossy embroidered fruit – his blood, he suddenly realizes: somehow he's scratched the fleshy base of his thumb. They find a spot on the side and he picks up her wrist, feeling along the woven gold of her bracelet until he locates a sharp wire sticking out of it. While he's bending the wire back with his fingernail, the second dance begins.

She holds her skirt out of the way of tramping feet. She looks up at him with an expression of appeal – she wants to say something and the violins are very loud. He bends over. "It was by royal edict?" she says into his ear. So. This will be her method of intimacy: the startling, whispered non sequitur.

They inch further back against the wall. "The king was the sponsor of Great Marlow," he says. "Everything was by royal edict, every trifle. The hay for the stables was ordered by royal edict."

"Will it prevent our being presented at court?"

"Yes," he says. "Yes, I believe it will." Laughter begins to shake his diaphragm.

"Why did you never tell me?"

He watches the swirl of colour on the dance floor and does not reply.

"What was it the edict said, as to cause?"

"It said *insubordination*," he says. "Only that. And I did tell you. Five minutes after we'd met, I'd pressed a kiss upon you. How did you understand that?" He's had nothing to drink, only the broth. Possibly it was spiked with negus.

A solicitor sets out his papers in piles on the dining room table. A sober conversation, long overdue. The house in Bristol has been sold to pay loans drawn against Uncle Alger's estate: nothing there. Numerous reports from the attorney regarding Halse Hall: three hundred and fifty of Jamaica's sugar plantations now closed, over half. How is it that the French colonies can produce sugar at so little cost? A short discussion follows on this subject. It's clear that there will be no income at all without Letitia's. This is understood by everyone at the table, and there is no need for his mother to spell it out. He looks at her with deep resentment. *Madame Trois-Mari*, they call her in town. This is all her fault, he thinks, unreasonably. And yet, what else is to be done? And Letitia (who is not at the table) may be a more suitable wife than most. She's shown remarkable independence, remarkable tolerance of his inattention to her. She is, after all, the stepdaughter of an innkeeper, although this is never mentioned. To demonstrate his good intentions on all fronts, professional and personal, Henry settles two hundred pounds on her for her private use, in addition to a dress allowance. His mother offers up Daisy, salary paid for the year, and tractable enough to serve as both lady's maid and housemaid.

While the documents are being completed, Letitia's gown arrives from London. His mother contrives to have a jacket with square tails made for him, swallowtails having fallen out of favour for weddings. He writes letters postponing the summer's fieldwork indefinitely. He and Letitia will go away immediately after the wedding: society will soon exhaust the topic of the bride's irregular behaviour. They'll tour the Continent while Henry can still raise money against the plantation. He rides to Axminster alone on a drizzly afternoon. The agent can offer nothing for three months, such is the pent-up demand for Paris since the war ended. Finally, he books passage on the *Lady Jane James* packet for July.

"We will have a bit of time to catch our breath before the wedding," he says to his mother at breakfast the next morning.

"No," she says. All the disgust she feels at his lacklustre self is in the *No*. "You will marry now and stay here until your passage. Or you can tour Sussex and Kent on your way to Dover." She has settled on a Thursday morning two weeks away, and he goes to the magistrate and arranges a special licence.

He collects Letitia from Morley Cottage in mid-morning and she spends the days at Aveline House. She's attentive to his mother and kind to the servants, determined to be charmed by the simplicity of everything, eager to take the cure in a bathing machine. She shows an interest in Mr. Aveline's ailments and pursuits, watching entranced when he winds up his model of the heavens and its planets turn sedately around the sun. Colonel Birch comes to call and she listens to his entire life story, taking care to keep the drawing room door propped open throughout his visit; it is her settled impression that military men cannot tolerate enclosed spaces.

He has the sense of a compelling conversation interrupted. No time for fossiling, no chance even for a private word with his mother: she's given herself over to the cultivation of her new daughter-in-law. Whatever do they talk about? he wonders, intruding on a poignant tête-à-tête in the drawing room, the tracks of unwiped tears on Letitia's cheeks. His mother makes a gift to Letitia of her own beloved copy of *Persuasion*. Letitia reads it in two days, and then she must be taken down to the

Cobb to see where the fictional Louisa fell on the steps. The tide is fully out; the fishing boats stranded inside the Cobb sink into the mud. Henry and Letitia walk out on the tilting dark stones and the wind buffets them. He's pleased by how game Letitia is, laughing and turning her face to the wind, her pretty form in a rose-coloured coat a picturesque anomaly against the threatening sky. As she comes down the steps and tumbles into his arms, he presses her against the wall, nuzzling his face in her cheek and slipping a hand into the opening of her coat. But she pushes him away. "You'll spoil your appetite with sweets before supper," she says, and he follows her up to Marine Parade, vexed, not at being thwarted, but at the primness and worldly knowing so casually intermingled in her expression.

In the afternoon, she sits by the window, informing her friends of the impending nuptials and grand tour. She writes on fine, lavender-tinted paper. She never blots her letters for fear of smudges, but looks them over fondly as she waits for the ink to dry. *France!* she reads out to Henry. *How the senses crave what the heart fears! Will there truly be houses and chimneys and sheep in the fields? Are the stones of Rue de Rivoli stained yet with blood or have they been washed clean?* He listens perplexed. How ironic, how perverse, that she puts on this persona for his benefit. Possibly, in a moment of rare authenticity, she frightened herself. Like the subject of a portrait stepping out of its ornate frame, standing disoriented on the hall tiles. He looks at her with a new sympathy. He's changed as well (he sees, to his surprise and satisfaction): forebearance has grown within him without his notice. Marriage will require it, and in the season of all things, it has appeared.

But then she announces her desire to live in Bristol, and an unbearable clamour of distress starts up in him. "It's out of the question!" he shouts. Tears, never far from the surface, rise in her eyes. He turns furiously away from them. Why has he been sitting around in the stuffy drawing room all day? It's essential that he maintain his routine of solitude and work. He slams out into the hall, filled with resolve to allow no small change that will open the door to larger ones. Buckland is back from Europe, but not in town. Very well, he will invite Mary Anning to the shore.

He snatches up his satchel of tools and starts down Broad Street. Mary's mother is sweeping in the square and he hurries towards her, but she opens the door of the house as he approaches, and as she steps inside, she turns her face towards him, her cheeks hollow where teeth have been lost, her eyes exhausted. A face that brings up the regrettable image of a Middle Ages *sage femme*. She has virtually closed the door in his face; he can't bring himself to knock. He walks by and turns up Church Street. But as he descends the path from the cemetery, there is Mary herself on the eastern shore below, walking quickly with her basket over her arm. He calls out to her, but the wind is high and carries his voice out to sea. By the time he's down on the shore, she is nowhere to be found. He can see a mile in either direction. He can't imagine where she could have gone, unless she climbed back up the cliffs by one of the paths that only she seems to know.

No matter, he'll work by himself. He'll make Mary the chart she asked for, one that shows the vertical elevation of the cliffs. The view of a mole, she said. She can have it to work with while he is gone, to chart her finds on it. The territory of her explorations is three miles, from Pinhay Bay in the west to Charmouth in the east. He'll start close to town to develop his method and work outwards from there. He'll use his plumb line to measure along the lip of the cliff where they walked the last time they were out together, when the sun shone so that the shore seemed all to be blue from the tidal pools reflecting back the sky. When she was tipsy. On a single glass of sherry. Perhaps she'd never had liquor before – was it possible?

And he'll colour it. He'll choose pigments for each layer that match the colours in the cliffs: blue for the carboniferous limestone, vermilion for the sandstone, and so on.

Back in the drawing room after an afternoon lying on his belly and watching his plumb line snag itself on the cliff face, he crosses to warm his hands at the fire and a dark, overdressed woman sits up on the settee. His new mother-in-law, who apparently outpaced the letter announcing her arrival. "Penrose," she cries, putting out a row of knuckles to be kissed.

Henry's mother and Letitia hurry in. "Mamma! That's not Penrose," Letitia says. "You were dreaming. You remember Henry." He bends over Mrs. Auriol's hand. And Uncle Clement, whittled down to the fundamentals of sinew and skin, is there too, so there will be gaiety and an extra course at supper.

After he's bathed, they sit down to a game of whist in the drawing room. Letitia has apparently recovered from her distress about Bristol. She's struck up a gleeful camaraderie with Clement, who undertakes to teach her to shuffle and deal in the Continental style. It has always been a question of some import in Henry's mind, how Letitia endured his long absences, how she employed her talent for flirtation. He questioned her the other night about various gentlemen they knew in common. Henry Wyndham was a lieutenant colonel with the Coldstream Guards and was terribly wounded at Waterloo, she told him. Phillip Marchand, who so distinguished himself at faro the weekend near Evershot, has fallen out with his family and gone to America. She was entirely composed in the telling, seemingly uninterested. But now she's set out to charm Clement because she so easily can, or because her mother, posing and purring in purple velvet, has the same purpose.

Lucky Uncle Clement, the thin, nervous rake – the object of attention of two such energetic women!

Letitia watches Clement's demonstration with her chin cupped in her hand. With idle fingers, she pulls at the sausage curls bunched at each cheek, admiring their spring. Perhaps it's this gesture that prompts Clement to a story about a lady of his acquaintance who sadly endured the ending of a love affair not long ago. "She wrote to the gentleman in question," says Clement, organizing the cards in his hand with a flourish, "demanding the return of the lock of hair she had given him as a token. Shortly after, the gentleman's servant appeared at her door with an enamel casket. The lady opened it eagerly, only to find within a tangled mass of hair, locks of blond, raven, and auburn, each tied with its own ribbon. *My lord requests that you kindly retrieve your property*, the servant said."

Letitia's laugh is a tinkle, her mother's a bleat. Outside the triangle of their mutual charm, the smell of the shore clings to Henry.

Letitia recounts to Clement how, when they were scarcely out of childhood, Henry lured her into the woods to see a dunning on its nest.

"*Dunnock*," Henry says.

"In any case, Mr. Mollot, there was none," Letitia says, dropping a trump on Henry's knave.

·⊰[T W E N T Y - F O U R]⊱·

S he'd been ignorant of her own true self when she walked
Miss Whyte up the hill to Aveline House, carrying the
lady's satchel. She understood fully only the day
she saw them coming up Marine Parade from the Cobb, Miss
Whyte in a rose-coloured wrap and pale orange gloves. Then
she realized, not merely that he was lost to her, but that she was
a feeble-brained stunpoll. She'd nurtured a hope so secret it
had been secret to her own self. It was out in the open now, like
debris dropped on the foreshore when the tide withdraws. How
monstrous it was – it had no place in this world. And then rage
seized her, and in her mind she went over all the things *he* had
done – his hanging around the curiosity table and using speech
laden with compliments, as though he could elevate her by
his very manner of addressing her; his curious questions; his
parading himself, a barefoot boy who lived with blackamoors;
his talk about subjects decent common folk shut their ears
to; his following her down alone to the shore, spreading her
hair on the sand with tender hands. She put all these things
on a scale and weighed them up against her lunatic hope. And

then it was clear to her that she was not mad, but that he certainly was.

Far, far better that he followed her no longer. It brought her the relief you feel when you finally vomit up the bit of rank fish that is tormenting your belly. It cleared her head, the way a killing frost will clear away fog. He would soon be gone away entirely, and she would be left, the person she had always been: sturdy, resolute, wholehearted, tramping down the shore, clambering over rocks with her collecting basket. Her strong legs treading a well-remembered path over the stones, her boot unerringly seizing the only passage wide enough for a foothold. *If thine eye be single, thy whole body shall be full of light.* She understood it now, James Wheaton's text. But while she tramped her mind went slack, and then mischievously Henry came strolling in again in his charcoal jacket with tails and his fawn breeches and high black boots, Miss Whyte mimping along beside him, tipping her face up to his to whisper secrets. Wearing her rose-coloured gown and pale orange gloves, her colours all ajar, as if to say how pert she was, how wilful and daring, as if to proclaim why Henry loved her.

Ravens flock into town, they never come singly: Mary knew this from the year of her father's death. They had been told for many months that parish support would cease, and the very week that Miss Letitia Whyte rode into town in the London coach, the Overseer of the Parish Poor carried his table out of the churchyard, never to return. He became once again plain George Davis, a sign painter. It was not his fault, people said. It was decided by the gentlemen in Whitehall, that the poor would never repent of their poverty if they were indulged with parish relief.

There are degrees of everything, thought Mary, standing at the back window watching rain fall on the sea. There were degrees of the high-born and degrees of the poor. Since

Richard's death, they had fallen from the top of the poverty ladder to the rung next to the bottom. How easy it was to topple down, how impossible to haul yourself up! Joseph would never see them starve. But two rents were beyond Joseph – it was the rent that would be their undoing. On the table was a notice from the landlord. They had a week, and then he would be obliged to seize their furniture.

"We must sell what we can ourselves, before it comes to that," Mary said to her mother, turning back and sitting at the table, where she was making rushlights. Molly agreed. The cupboard could go – there was not much to keep in it in any case. And the two rush chairs: they still had a bench to sit on, and the stool. But they would not sell the round table from the workshop – without the table, they could not hope for income at all.

Lizzie lay face down with her braids hanging over the edge of the cot and dreamed of picking mushrooms. At Axminster, a girl went to pick a mushroom and found a golden ring around the stem. "Our Lord put it there," Lizzie said. "And He led the girl to find it."

"Nature put it there," said Mary. "A lady walked in the field and she dropped it and by hap a tiny mushroom grew up within the circle." At the table, Mary stripped the tough skin from a reed and dreamed of her own windfall: a new intact fossil. She would not try to picture it, for it must be another such creature as no one had ever seen. Something to bring the scholars running down from Oxford with their purses at their waists. Something that had not been described, so that she herself could write a text describing it. She had been distracted, but she would focus now and find it. But day after day, she wandered the shore and returned with nothing but threepenny curios.

It was Colonel Birch who came to their rescue, hobbling into the square just as the Moffat boys carried the rush chairs down the steps. He paid the boys a half-crown for their trouble and sent them on their way. "This will never do," he said. "You must have a few sticks to rest your bones on."

He said he would think what was to be done. They heard nothing for days – neither from the landlord nor from Colonel Birch. Then Will Darby came to the door and with ill grace handed Mary a note. Miss Anning was invited to tea with Colonel Birch. Mary read the note at the door and said to her mother, "Colonel Birch has invited us for tea tonight."

"I will not drag a sick child to Charmouth," said Molly. But Mary would not go without her mother: she feared Will Darby's tongue. So in the end, they left Lizzie and the two of them followed the cliff path to Charmouth and presented themselves at the door. Will Darby led them down the hall past the fossil room and into a drawing room, where they sat side by side on a settle. The settle was pulled up to the fire and served as a powerful barrier against the cold. Colonel Birch was in full uniform in a large armchair. At his elbow was a clay bust that Mary knew to be of John Wesley, lips painted in a thin red bow. This room was a museum in its own way – not of fossils, but of ornaments made from china and plaster and clay and marble. "Man's handiwork," Birch said proudly. "And down the hall, our Lord's." A girl served them tea, as well as bread and butter on china plates. Pure butter, without a trace of candle grease added to it.

When they had finished eating, Colonel Birch stood by the mantel and made a speech. He talked of his own straitened circumstances, the fact that he was on half pay and had not succeeded in selling his commission. He dwelt a few minutes on the God-fearing and temperate king, whose gout had flown to his brain, not yet dead, but for these many years dead to himself and his world. He told them of his father, who for all of the years of his adult life had generously fed and clothed a neighbour woman and her six children as they came one by one fatherless into the world. He told them the story of coming up the street in Lyme Regis to observe a brace of stout youths carrying away a widow woman's furniture, her two gentle daughters weeping at her bosom, and then he paused and lifted his moustache in the customary display of his dentures. Behind his long and rambling speech lay the question, Who had made them his responsibility? He did not address it and they (sitting by a warm fire licking butter from their fingers) were not inclined to ask. "And so I put it to myself," he resumed, "*What do I possess of value?* and my brain lit on my collection of bones and shells, assembled through the industry of this young maiden we see before us. And so I sat myself down at this writing desk and composed a letter to a person of my acquaintance in London, one Mr. Bullock of the Egyptian Hall in Piccadilly, and he has done me the courtesy of an immediate reply. He agrees to reserve his hall on May fifteenth for an auction, and to send notices to all interested persons. With no expectation of gain for himself. It will be an alms for you and your family, Mrs. Anning, on the part of both Mr. Bullock and myself, although the auctioneer is a hard-headed fellow who insists on his commission. In the meantime, I have sent Mr. Axworthy a quarter's rent in anticipation of these proceeds. I may never again have what I am about to part with, but I am resolved."

Molly had lifted her apron to her eyes at mention of the king, and at the mention of Mr. Axworthy, she had begun rocking. "Now, now, madam, none of that," Colonel Birch said. "It's time

these bones made their way into the world. I have had my pleasure of them. We will pack them up and send them off."

Molly used the apron to wipe her eyes. "Our Lord will bless
you for this," she said, "and Mary will help you. She will be
at your door at sun-up tomorrow."

Mary listened closely to this conversation, but she was
unsure as to the thrust of it. Did he certainly intend to give
them all the money from the auction sale? "Yes," her mother
said firmly on the way home. And so it seemed, for he had
accepted Molly's thanks.

"But why?" Mary asked. "He has already paid me for everything." They were out on the cliff path, with the sea crawling
below them, walking very quickly.

"It is the way the world works sometimes," her mother said.

Preparing the collection was the very work Mary longed for.
Walking the mile to Charmouth every morning, she left
thoughts of Henry behind in Lyme; she climbed up and out
of them. In the collecting room she was all thought, pure
zeal, shut off from her worry. They chose a hundred specimens
and she made up tickets for each. Miss Philpot had let her
carry her Sowerby books to Charmouth, and she made
careful distinctions between the *Asteroceras stellare* and the
Asteroceras confusum.

"A pity we don't have the whole skeleton of that one," Mary
said, admiring a grinning Ichthyosaurus skull, the centrepiece
of the collection. "It was all there at first, the quarryman told
me, but his mates ground the rest of it up for lime. He managed
to rescue the head – he had it guarding the quarry. But he gave
it to me because I was a girl and needed the money. You know,
I was only twelve when I collected my first Ichthyosaurus. The
first complete Ichthyosaurus ever collected."

"Twelve," Colonel Birch bleated. "You have nothing on Miss Isobel Cutler. A miss of *nine years* when she dug up a silver platter at Hadrian's Wall. Dropped there by a Roman centurion in the year of Our Lord 400. Think of it!"

"But Colonel Birch," Mary said, "Noah's flood was three thousand years before our Lord was born." She turned the centuries over in her mind like the leaves of a book, as she often did. "Think how old the Ichthyosaurus bones be!"

"Oh, they're older, to be sure," Colonel Birch said. "You have that over Miss Cutler." He was such a sheep, Colonel Birch. *Ovis aries.* As she worked, Mary counted up all the ways he was a sheep: his nose like a steep hill, his stretched nostrils, his pale eyes that looked at you abashed with no light of cleverness in them. The white wool before and behind his ears, wool that seemed, in this proximity, to have bits of turf caught in it.

They wrapped the specimens in paper or cotton and packed them in crates. They packed the large Ichthyosaurus parts first, because the smaller specimens could nestle between. For packing the delicate tiles of sea lilies, with their segmented stems, Colonel Birch had a bale of wool brought in. They were three long days working on the Ichthyosaurus parts and the sea lilies. After the first day, Will Darby was nowhere to be seen – it was a maid who brought them their meals. Sometimes they took their dinner in the drawing room, where on the mantel lay a small white card with a name printed on it: *T. H. De la Beche Esq.* Below the name, the letters *PPC*, in ink in Henry's hand. Those letters stood for words in French, *Pour Prendre Congé.* A new husband is assumed to have severed all previous ties, Colonel Birch told her, unless such a card be delivered to the door before the wedding. "He delivered it, but did not have time to take tea," he said. "Hastening back to the fair Letitia. Taken a prisoner of love!" Also on the mantel, as though to illustrate this story, was a pair of lovers. The girl sat on the boy's knee and stroked the boy's temple with her white hand. Her gown was open at the top; her bosom was just at the level of his dreaming face. "From the Chelsea factory in Condon," Colonel Birch called from his armchair. "Soft-paste porcelain."

And so she preferred the collecting room, where there was nothing to intrude upon the clear domain of science. In the end, they had just the molluscs left, the belemnites like long metallic rods, as smooth as though they'd been poured and polished by a silversmith. Colonel Birch told her that when Napoleon's emissaries went into the ancient pyramids where the Egyptians wrapped and stored their dead, they found huge belemnites strapped to the groins of male mummies. He was flushed and stammering in the telling. A good thing the work was almost done, for he grew more distracted by the hour.

After their noon meal, he invited her to the barn, where he kept his milk cow and mare. He wanted to show her syllabub, for she said she'd never tasted it. In the house, he made up two tankards of wine, sugar, and spices, and he had her carry them to the barn. There, he sat himself down on a stool with his belly on his thighs and his little stockinged legs tucked alertly under him. It was a joke, that such as he could milk a cow! He shared the joke with her, putting his hand on the teat and turning his head to wink at her. She had to lean close, holding the tankard under the cow so he could direct the stream of milk into it. Then they sat on a bench in the sun behind the house and drank the lovely syllabub, warm and sweet like mother's milk. All the time, he blinked and leaned towards her, as though he was on the point of confiding a secret. But he never quite managed to say what he had in mind, and then they were back in the collecting room, packing up the belemnite specimens. Truly, he was a *sheep*, with his knack of being heavily in doorways and corridors, obstructing the way with his bulk, blind to her need to pass. And (while they bent together over the belemnites on the table) in the shy and trusting way he pulled his member, proud and purple, out of his breeches – to show how superior it was, was her first thought, how superior in vivid colour to these stony rods. She let out a scream and then vexation raked her, to be so rudely distracted from her work by this stout ram panting and pushing up against her. "Pray put that away," she cried furiously, dodging out of his reach. She ran across the room and snatched up her shawl and bonnet. "I'll have none of such stuff! I am finished with this work!"

When the sky is green with dawn, Henry packs bread, cheese, and two boiled eggs into his kit: dewbit and nuncheon. He can't bring himself to return to Church Cliffs. He'll make a fresh start at the west end of Mary's territory, a rock face untouched by man and one that reveals a higher elevation of blue lias.

He walks all the way to Seven Rock Point at the far end of Monmouth Beach, admiring the calcite circles that giant ammonites made in the limestone shore. Before he sets to work, he peels the eggs, sitting facing the cliff and dropping the frail brown shells to lie on the shore among pebbles and whelk shells. Before him is a slice of the earth's crust torn open by the ocean for his study. Layers of shale and limestone alternate regularly. But even within the shale, there are different strata. Subtly different – as though a painting master set his students an exercise in moving by degrees from one earth tone to the next. Shading his eyes with his hand, he endeavours to count the layers. It is a feat of concentration: there are fifty-three. He'll never make the sort of detailed chart of the whole area that would allow Mary to record the vertical elevation of each find. Has he ever, seriously, thought it was possible? No – it was a project contrived to ingratiate himself with her.

Terns wheel over the cliffs. The limestone layers are dotted with small fossils. These layers will have been made by clear, shallow water, teeming with life. But the slate layers are mud, compressed into stone. Water must have risen and withdrawn, over and over, during periods of radically different conditions. His mind reels at the eons this would take. But he has always known, deep down, that this is not the sediment of a single flood. When he was first in Lyme Regis, when he was only sixteen, he noted that the pattern of layers here matched the pattern on the other side of the River Lyme. And Buckland and Conybeare are travelling on the Continent expressly to look for a similar sequence there. Yet Buckland is prepared to argue that God created the trees in the Garden of Eden fully grown, with growth rings in place. If the rock strata are merely *trompe l'oeil*, why does Buckland spend so much time studying them?

The jovial nights in country inns hundreds of miles from home, the meetings and pontificating! How earnest they were, how complacent, how certain that they'd defeated the heresies of secular scholars. He thinks of a particular night in Scotland years before, of walking the shore at sunset – at Arbroath, a village on the east coast. Carpenter and Holland were enraptured by the sun deepening the red of the cliffs, God painting His creation with glorious light for their benefit. Henry once told Mary about that night, and she was amused by his description of that red shore where the very sheep were stained vermilion, and the smocks of the shepherds red. He told her how he'd stayed back on the shore when the others went to the inn, and watched the light fade and the cliffs loom up before him, how he'd seen the rocks broken and worn by the sea, basins filling up with sand to be turned to sandstone, and the sandstone being worn down again to sand. "It was not God I saw," he said, "but the earth itself, terribly old, constantly changing by its own processes. It seemed the deeper truth."

She listened to him with utter absorption and then sat in silence for a moment. "When I was a girl," she said finally, "the first time you came to the workshop, I asked you how the creature came to be buried in the cliff. You told me that what is now the shore was once the seabed. So you knew this once, and you have forgotten. All your science has driven it out." She was sitting on the ground by the log and she crossed her legs and smoothed her skirt. Then she turned her calm eyes back on him. "The world is every day creating itself," she said, and all around them the buds of early spring bore witness to her words, to a truth indifferent to all his philosophy.

A gull floats motionless above the cliff. There is a moment of stasis – the noise of the surf suspended, the wind still. He has been carrying an unwieldy weight on his head, the weight of a primitive theology, and he will put it down. He will not indulge in the contortions Buckland indulges in; he will say what he sees. This is not a leap into uncertainty and darkness. The earth will be his scripture.

Back at Aveline House, he manages to mount to his room undetected. He drops his cloak and gloves on the floor and sits down at his desk to write.

My dear Miss Anning,

I write to express my fervent wish that we remain colleagues in spite of my marriage. They say that the sailors with Christopher Columbus, first coming up on America, could sense the weight

of a massive new continent before land hove into sight on the
horizon. I have had exactly this sensation these past weeks.

You and I are on a journey to the unknown and we are very close
to our destination. If we find the courage to continue, it will be a
rare and brave adventure. Please, Mary, do not abandon me.

T. H. De la Beche, Esq.

He blots the letter and carries it over to the window to read it
in a different light. "*In spite of* my marriage." He should have
said, "*After* my marriage." How can a preposition hold such illicit
energy? He should re-copy it, but he will not: he would lose his
resolve. He goes back to his desk and reaches into the drawer for
a stick of sealing wax.

Brownley is in the upstairs passage. Henry asks him to see that
Miss Anning receives the note without delay. When he descends to
the drawing room, Letitia is waiting for him. She lures him outside
and plays a little geologizing joke on him – pretending to find one
of her mother's whalebone stays in the garden, pretending to think
it's a fossil. Then Mr. Aveline appears. He invites Henry to the
drawing room to present a special gift: a beautiful leather-bound
journal. He wants to talk about Montpellier and Mont Blanc, the
highlights of his own grand tour; he wants to express his regret
that Henry cannot afford to engage a tutor. At that point, George
Holland is received (with a winking allusion to Henry's wound).
He too has a wedding gift, a handsome kit with a barometric
pressure device and a thermometer. Then Mrs. Auriol ambushes
Henry. She wants to suggest a lovely little hotel in Paris where
she stayed before the war. When he engages the rooms, could
he be certain to ask for *chambre vingt-sept* for her? *Vingt-sept* has
such a charming balcony overlooking the courtyard! Letitia is
standing frozen in the hall, watching this exchange with round
eyes. She runs after him into the breakfast room. She has indeed

invited her mother, but she's contrite and full of pleading apology. "There has never been such sympathy between us as this last week," she says. He stands looking down on the street and thinks, I must see her. Letitia touches his hand. "You will share a maid, at least?" he asks. But the thought of being attended by her mother's dreadful Tilly dislodges the tears she's holding at the ready. "Very well. I'll see whether I can book two more passages," he says. She takes a step back, evidently unsure how to interpret his tractability.

He finds a moment to steal away to his room and writes again: *Would you do me the great kindness of meeting me at the fallen tree in the Undercliff? An hour before sunset tonight? If you are delayed, I shall wait until you come.*

They encounter each other before they reach the Undercliff. There is a path across the meadow at the edge of town, and as he walks out the Pound Street path, he sees her on it, walking parallel to him but a little behind. He walks up to the cliff edge and waits, trying to contain his gladness, looking down at the questioning line the Cobb makes in the surf below and the birds wheeling in a frenzied evening feed.

She bows her head when he greets her. It occurs to him to thank her for assisting Letitia when she first arrived, but he does not want to evoke his fiancée. And so he simply says, "I'm going away, Mary. I wanted to tell you. I will be gone for at least a year."

"You are getting married," she says.

"Yes," he says. "I am indeed." She turns and looks at the sea. He laughs, and hears how nervous he sounds. "I am as surprised as anybody. As I believe I told you, there had been a rupture in our relations. I had reason to assume that the engagement was dissolved." He's struck by how changed her demeanour is. She'd seemed so worn down all winter, but she's standing straight now, exuding vigour. "There's a great deal I need to tell you," he says eagerly. "I've been waiting for an occasion to talk at length. Let's walk out of the wind."

But she will not go, she stands still with an adamant set to her shoulders. Always a woman of the direct gaze, she will not face him now, she's looking out to sea. So they must stand on the cliff edge with the wind buffeting them while he tells her of his resolve to make a serious professional of himself. Still she won't look at him, and it occurs to him for the first time that she might esteem him *less* as a workingman. Very well, he thinks. In for a penny, in for a pound. He moves to the heart of it. "Be assured, I shall not work in the way we have been working to date. By *we*, I mean Buckland and the rest. All their so-called science is grounded in doctrine. It paralyzes the intellect. We are purblind, if you will. Our efforts are more and more contorted, to make the evidence of nature fit with a few cryptic lines of Scripture. I can't countenance it. I am committed to a purer science."

From her expression he thinks she's listening, but suddenly she thrusts something at him. A small paper packet tied with string. "A handsel," she says. "For Miss Whyte."

Confused, he takes the token and drops it into his pocket. "How very kind," he says. They stand in silence. He wants to take her by the shoulders and make her look at him. "Mary," he says finally. "We will not see each other again for months. And I must tell you – I have had such a vision! You know, as in Scripture, when an apostle sees an angel, or a bush that burns and is not consumed – something not of this world? Except what I saw *was* the world. I was out on the shore this morning. I went out to work on the chart I promised you. And I saw the cliffs for the first time. The layers, all those separate layers! It was as though scales had fallen from my eyes. The scales of orthodoxy." He senses she wants to say something, but his words are tumbling out. "*You* know this, Mary! You saw all this before I did. Oh, Mary, no one thinks as you do. I see your mind at work as you speak. There is no cant, no effort to please. And so I must ask whether you will work with me . . . upon my return." He's momentarily distracted by the fierceness of her expression. "Think how valuable we can be to each other! You have an *instinctual* understanding of the fossils. And all my acquaintances in the Geological Society – I can cultivate them for your benefit. And the Royal Society, for all it is –"

Then she is looking at him. "Science!" she cries. "You talk of *science*. You have no idea what you think. You are a child."

He can't speak – the breath is knocked out of him.

"Your letter," she says. She has a paper crumpled in her hand, and she thrusts it towards him, and then in a fury raises her fist and tries to throw it out into the sea. But the wind blows it back and drops it into the gorse. She scrambles down and plucks it out and pitches it again with such a passion that this time it flutters down the cliff. Henry tries to follow it with his eyes, fearing it will lie on the beach where someone may find it. "I have never read such tripe." Mary shouts after it. She turns on him. "A new adventure. It is *not* new, sir. It is a foul tale that has been often told."

He feels his own anger flare up at the injustice of this. "Have I ever been less than respectful of your person? Have I ever laid a hand on you?"

But of course there's the kiss, and it seems a fresh provocation to have brought it back. She looks at him in quick surprise and takes a step backwards. Her nostrils flare. "You have sneaking ways, sir. You used your sneaking ways on me!"

"Oh, Mary, my dear," he says. He reaches for her hand, her rough brown hand, but she snatches it away. He reaches for it again, and this time she hits out at him with it, and then she turns and begins to walk quickly back towards town. He hurries along by her side. "You have been learning the ways of the gentry, Mary," he says, striving to keep his voice gentle. "And you have been an apt student indeed. But you may not have remarked that in sexual matters, the proprieties are universally breached. Indeed, social rank brings with it greater licence, rather than less." The path is narrow just then and he is forced by gorse on either side to fall behind. He is making himself ridiculous, trotting after her, but he must explain. He turns to the irrefutable example of the Talbots, the prominent Devonshire family his stepfather and mother recently visited. "The children in that family are known in whispers as the Talbot Miscellany," he says, "so many lovers has the lady taken and so different the physiognomy of each of her children. And far from *shaming* Lady Talbot in society, these adventures add to her attractions. My mother and Mr. Aveline had no hesitation whatsoever in being her guests. Perhaps it was not always thus, but we observed a Regency court, and we have profited from example." He's trying to joke, but she stops and rounds on him.

"The Prince Regent were *never* our teacher here in Lyme."

He sees in a flash that this tactic was a ghastly mistake. "Very well. Very well, Mary. But may I observe that the chambermaid at the Monmouth Inn has more personal freedom than you allow yourself?"

Then her colour deepens and it seems she can hardly speak. "You compare me to the chambermaid at the Monmouth Inn?"

"No, I don't compare you," he cries in despair. "Oh, Mary – you so badly misconstrue my intent." But she's gone, a black form striding down the path in the falling light, vanishing through the high stands of gorse, and he is left alone with the preposterous preamble to what he'd wrongly assumed would be a lengthy conversation.

It's only much later that he thinks of the argument he should have used with Mary, glimpses the vows that could be sworn to the eternal, shifting verities of rocks and tide.

For Miss Whyte From Mary Anning. Penned directly on the paper packet in a bold script. *Miss White*, she had written first, and then made a crude correction. Whatever could she be giving his fiancée? He cannot imagine and, standing in the hall, he cuts the string with his penknife and opens the packet. Wrapped inside is a pair of earrings. Two slices of Ichthyosaurus coprolite, polished like sections of agate and fixed to dangle from the earlobe. The hooks of the earrings are iron fish hooks. He's breathless with amazement. He holds them close to the lamp to examine each slice of fossil excrement, fish scales running through them like a delicate inlay. The drawing room door opens. It's Letitia, coming into the hall to see what's keeping him. She moves smiling towards him, carrying a candle in a globe. There's still time for him to slip the packet back into his pocket, but he holds it in his hand and she approaches.

"Forgive me," he says. "It was with my letters and I opened it in error. It's a wedding gift for you." Letitia sets the candle on the hall table. She touches the stones in his hand and looks up at him in confusion. "From Miss Anning," he says, showing her the paper.

"Miss Anning? The brown-faced girl selling seashells in the square?"

"Yes."

Letitia fingers the polished stones. "Are they meant to be earrings?"

"I suppose they are. She must have fashioned them with her own hand."

"They really are very beautiful stones," she says. She picks one out of his palm and holds it up to an ear, turning her head to the hall looking glass to admire the coprolite dangling against her cheek. "I could have them fitted properly onto gold. That's what I will do. But what a queer creature, to want to give me a wedding gift! Perhaps it's because I spoke to her on my arrival." She gazes at her reflection. "Does one send a formal note to such a person?" she asks. It's not the earrings she's admiring; it's her own face, the pretty curve of her lips. She's watching herself talk.

"No," he says heavily. "Don't trouble yourself."

Mary stood on Black Ven with her basket on her arm. She frowned at the rock-strewn foreshore. Just here was where she'd found the body of Lady Jackson. And here she'd walked out with Sir Foppling Fossil, and dropped herself down to the sands. She'd been seized by madness, and she'd given him such a story. She'd given him Lady Jackson as everyone imagined a gentlewoman should be – *Oh, lovely appearance of death, no sight upon earth is so fair!* As Mary herself imagined the lady would be, when she first crept across the sand and saw the white hand flung out, palm up, the lady's fair hair laid out by the water, and her slender foot. A fine lady and taken by death all the same.

And now Mary saw her as clear as she had that day. She'd been undressed by the sea, there was no ivory silk gown on her at all, but bladderwort and black marl mashed under her. She was lying on her back, not as Mary had fallen to show Henry. Her eyes half open, unseeing, as though Mary creeping up to her did not exist. The lady was marble on the sand and Mary was the ghost, squatting beside her on the shore, scarcely breathing.

Staring at the white of her flesh mottled with pooled blood, and her nipples pointing darkly up at the sky. Her vacant face with the thick, unlovely mouth. The fine lines at her eyes and the pouches beneath, the faint expression of disgust. Mary was the ghost reaching a hand out, touching the cold skin of her thigh. And noting everything: her woman's legs splayed open (fat legs with blue veins wandering over them), the hair on her woman's mound left to curl like bracken in the sea water, the lips between mauve as an oyster.

The De la Beche carriage rolled out of town laden with cases. Was Mrs. De la Beche wearing her reptile turds? Mary wondered. Then Colonel Birch rode into town on his mare and presented himself at the curiosity table with a chastened face. "Not this week," Mary said, lifting her chin, looking coldly across the square. "Our Lizzie is poorly."

Then they did not hear from him, and it looked as though it would all come to naught on account of her pride. *The work is finished*, was all she told her mother, but in bed at night, she raged still against Colonel Birch, saw him reaching his hand for the heavy-veined udder of the cow, winking at her with his pale-fringed eye. Recalled the syllabub, the taste of childhood with a potent, seductive aftertaste, and thought of how cheese was made, how a calf was allowed to suck its fill before it was killed and the curdled milk from its stomach used to curdle cheese. Her fury grew: she felled the old ram with the flat side of an axe, she saw him falling heavily to the floor. Her rage was like sticky mud; she was sucked down into it. These gentlemen and their lusts – there was Henry, grabbing at her when they clambered over a rock, the heat burning in his hand, his thirst for her shining in his eyes. And there was she, just as bad – *Do not look at me so*, she'd think, and when he turned obediently away, she'd stir beside him or make some little sound in her throat so he'd look again.

She rolled over in her bed. Oh, Catherine, Saint Catherine, please come to my aid, she breathed. The *money* – better to think of the money. All of those wonderful treasures from the shore offered up for sale. Two hundred and twenty pounds – that's what was at stake here. She'd kept her own tally of fair market values all the time she was fitting the collection into crates. Two hundred and twenty pounds! But an auction sale was different from transactions conducted in the sober light of day. It was buyers vying with each other. Sometimes in the heat of the moment, prices went sky-high – a man might pay a fortune to keep a rival from getting what he desired. She told herself stories of such feuds, she peopled the hall with petulant rich men who loathed each other, and in her mind, the total grew and grew. It would be enough to pay off the last of their creditors and keep them for a year. She would be independent, above the insults of sordid men. She turned over again and slid one icy foot up into the hot angle of the other knee. These imaginings were Hope come to taunt her, her new enemy, Hope – for really, in giving her anything at all, Colonel Birch would be paying twice. And what must she expect to part with in the end for such a windfall?

Finally, a note came to say that he was back in Charmouth with the proceeds of the sale and awaited her attendance. It was not Will Darby who brought the note but a new and friendlier Charles, a boy from Cobb Hamlet wearing a tremendous pair of hobnailed boots. "*You* must go," Mary said to her mother. Her mother, who was scrubbing out the kitchen, set to humming and did not reply. Mary began to suspect that what she dreaded was what her mother desired. But she could not mount an argument – she could not further jeopardize this windfall. And so she put it to herself that she was a woman who could outwit a sheep, and she fetched her bonnet. Her mother walked a ways with her. At the edge of town, she stopped and put her hand on Mary's arm. "Better a little fire to warm thee than a great fire to burn thee," she said.

Colonel Birch was in his big chair in the drawing room. Mary was struck by the streaks of colour running down his massive moustaches, as though the iron hull of his cheeks were rusting. She could tell at a glance that he was in a fine, dignified humour, and her fear drained out of her – it would be like the day when she came with her mother. He reached forward and gravely handed her the catalogue from the sale. It was a twelve-page booklet printed on cream-coloured paper. On the flyleaf was the engraving of the strange shrimp-like creature she had once found on the tide flats below town. There was a list of every item, with flattering descriptions. Colonel Birch told her she might keep this catalogue, that he had brought this copy for her. He directed her to read the text at the front of it and she sat on the settle and read out:

A small but very fine collection of organised fossils, from the Blue Lias Formation, At Lyme and Charmouth, in Dorsetshire, consisting principally of Bones, Illustrating the Osteology of the Ichthio-saurus, or Proteo-saurus, and of specimens of the Zoophyte, called Pentacrinite, the genuine property of Colonel Birch, Collected at considerable expense.

She read the rules for the sale and the list of items right through while Colonel Birch dozed. Then tea was brought in and, while they drank it, he told her the story of the auction from beginning to end. Buyers had come from as far away as Paris and Vienna. The sale had been dominated by a man in a velvet jacket, who bought the Ichthyosaurus head and numerous other pieces, who bid by touching his index finger to his left nostril, a finger with a long nail sharpened like a file. A stranger to the others in the room – but he had money behind him. He was certainly the agent for someone of consequence. For the Ichthyosaurus skull alone, he paid one hundred guineas! Colonel Birch conspired to be in his path in the foyer afterwards and boldly inquired whom the man represented. *Léopold Chrétien Frédéric Dagobert*, the man said in the outlandish way that Frenchmen speak. Colonel Birch looked at Mary triumphantly and she stared back. "Cu-vi-er," he bleated, and she felt a thrill go through her to think that the great Monsieur Cuvier would be studying her collection. And a sadness that her collection was all disbursed, sent out across many lands, those creatures that had all died here at Lyme Regis.

Then Colonel Birch made a ceremony of handing her the pouch. He seemed to be searching for words that would make an event of it, but finally settled for the prosaic. "With best wishes for the health and prosperity of the Annings," he said. "From their humble friend and servant Colonel Thomas Birch, S.S." He held her eye. "A sinner saved."

Some of the money was paper, and then there was a sack of gold sovereigns. "They must pay in guineas at such a sale," Colonel Birch explained, "and the auctioneer changes the coin to sovereigns or pound notes, whatever he has to hand, and keeps the extra shilling for his fee." The sovereigns had a head of the king on one side, dead now in the material sense of the word, and on the other, Saint George slaying the dragon – a dragon with pleated wings that folded like a parasol, and a muzzle and paws like a dog.

"Go ahead, my dear, reckon it up," he said. "It is all there, every pence, less your last quarter's rent." And though it seemed rude to do so, she did, for she was dying to know the sum and he seemed to want the pleasure of watching her look through the money. She sorted the coins and bills by kind and added them up, her heart pounding. Even without the last quarter's rent, it came to almost four hundred pounds.

They took their supper in the dining room, served by a silent, flat-faced girl. They ate a whole pike with a pudding in its belly, and venison pasties. It was a supper fit for a king. The sweet-meats were served in a porcelain dish with three sections like three seashells and a fish tail in the centre for a handle. How Lizzie would adore it! Back in the drawing room, they drank Madeira from the vessel with the duck swimming in the stream. With her glass in her hand, Mary roamed the drawing room. She stood by the fire, and it warmed her stomach and thighs and cast an orange light on her apron. She had not been warm that winter. It was such a fire as they would never have at home, even now, with hundreds of pounds. In Colonel Birch's house, it was possible to believe that the sea did not exist, and Black Ven. She saw herself in a house such as this, with a lace cap on her head. Everything in the room was beautified by the firelight. She knew her own beauty, just at that moment. She saw it without a looking glass, without Henry's glowing eyes on her, the firelight gleaming off her dark hair, her eyes that gathered up all the light in the room.

On a table at Mary's end of the settle was an ornament of the languid body of Jesus, laid out dead, his mother leaning weeping over him and two plump angels floating at her shoulders, one of them holding up its hand as though to say, *Do not come near.* And she had to think of Lizzie, who would never see this room filled with tender light. Sadness for Lizzie welled up, tears stung her eyes — tears for herself too. She tried to breathe steadily, in through her nostrils. She was like the flowers in the tidal pools that moved their fringes at unseen currents, curling up at the slightest touch.

Colonel Birch sat with one foot on a stool, his head tipped back against the cushions. There would be no more lewd demonstrations, he would do nothing to hold her. The fine gentlemen had overpaid for the fossils – fair market value did not always rule. She had the money bag tied to her waist and she was free to go. But the drink that had been travelling a journey from her throat to her stomach rose and warmed her mind at just that moment, and so she went and sat on the hassock beside his chair, holding her glass of Madeira.

"Why did you collect the old bones, sir?" she asked.

He smiled, showing his sturdy young teeth. His moustache did not move when he smiled. It betrayed his inner expression, which was sadness, like hers. "It's the mystery, I reckon," he said. "Something lost, turned to stone."

"What happened to all these creatures, that we never see their type no more?"

"Mayhap they all died," he said. "Mayhap they became something else."

"That is what I wish to know," she said. "Can a creature be changed into something else?"

She waited a long time for his answer, then she saw that he was asleep, his head tipped to the side and his mouth loosely open. His chest rose and fell with his breath. The firelight glowed on his cheeks, on his flesh, the something on his skull that was other than bone and would not endure. A shutter banged and Colonel Birch started. "The latch wants fixing," she said. His eyelids slid down again. She reached a hand over and touched her fingers lightly to his temple. "The latch," she said again. "It is the sort of thing that

I would take in hand." He peered at her, awake now. She saw in his pale eyes that he understood – he did not assume she was offering to join his employ as a housemaid.

His hand, dangling off the arm of the chair, reached blindly for her leg and found it, pressed the calf of her leg through her skirt. "It could never be, my dear," he said. His voice was kind. "For all my fondness – and I am very fond of you – there are proprieties." He sat and looked at the fire and then his hand dropped and he fell back into his doze.

She turned away from him and got up. She went back to the fireplace and leaned her head against the mantel. There were proprieties to her heart, her heart had proprieties, and she would have flouted them. For the fire, just for that, to be warm every night.

Book III

Book III

July 9, Paris
We are installed on rue de la Paix in lodgings that are anything
but peaceful, but were recommended by Professor Buckland.
While this is not the hotel preferred by my mother-in-law, it is
very near the Opera, which pleases just as much. All signs of
the revolution, all Napoleonic insignia, have been removed. It is
Royale-this and Royale-that, everywhere. Yesterday, eager for
exercise and missing the shores and lanes of Dorsetshire, I
walked as far as the Jardin du Roi, the vast grounds of which are
open to the public. I wandered at length through the gardens,
foreign trees and bushes sheltering foreign beasts, and listened
to the peacocks screaming. Before leaving, I delivered my letter
of introduction from Doctor Leach to a Monsieur Royer, who
seemed suitably impressed by the seal of the curator of the
British Museum, and indicated to me that an invitation from
M. Cuvier would be forthcoming. He encouraged me to visit the
exhibition halls of the museum as an ordinary sightseer, but I
believe I will rest on my privilege and wait for a tour by the
great man himself.

As for the city, which I explore daily (most often alone, as L. continues unwell), I have never seen a patch of ground where the impulses of nature have been so utterly stifled – whether by the outright razing of trees, or by tortured topiary which allows to no humble shrub the exercise of its own will, or by gardens laid out as an operation in geometry, grass replaced entirely by shingle. One cannot but think of the verdant tumble of foliage in the Undercliff. Here nature asserts itself only in the unpaved streets, when rain transforms the thoroughfare into a muddy channel.

July 22

L. is much improved, and has begun to take an interest in Mrs. Auriol's tireless efforts to locate a portraitist of social note who can do justice to her daughter's beauty, as my own portrait executed in London some years ago demonstrably failed to do. This afternoon we interviewed a candidate for the commission, distinguished by his tobacco-stained teeth and fingers and the splatters of paint artfully applied to his frock. Mrs. Auriol and my wife were entranced by the fellow and by his light-filled studio. I was obliged to point out upon leaving that a serious portraitist selects a studio with windows to the north, so as to ensure an unvarying light on his subject. Undeterred, Mrs. Auriol has managed to secure an invitation to a salon that Jacques-Louis David himself is rumoured to patronize, somewhere in the faubourg Saint-Germain. I asked how the fee to such a distinguished artist was to be paid, but in my mother-in-law's manner I detected the private conviction that M. David will insist on performing this commission gratis out of his appreciation for so extraordinary a subject.

We passed a pleasant afternoon strolling the banks of the Seine. L. has discovered pineapples and white-heart cherries and will be loath to depart for regions where they are not so readily available. She has seen a physician and her pregnancy is confirmed – an unanticipated consideration when I arranged the itinerary. So we are to be parents in the new year, with all that that entails. I am grateful for Letitia's accommodating spirit and willingness to continue the journey. I am resolved to attempt Mont Blanc before winter sets in. Our plan is to leave Paris as soon as my visit to Cuvier is accomplished.

Perforce we have visited Notre-Dame and perforce we have been impressed – as to its size. The superstition that threatens religion in England has entirely polluted the papist church and, in the palpable form of incense, chokes one upon entry. Through the vast edifice roam black-clad priests swinging censers, and across the uneven stones, supplicants inch on crippled knees towards a crypt where lie the mouldering relics of saints (a toenail or the mummified tip of some medieval wretch's nose).

July 18
Today at the Louvre I saw a recent acquisition, *Portrait d'une femme noire* by Marie-Guillemine Benoist, one of the great David's students. It represents a Negro servant against a backdrop bare of furnishings. I am told that it excited a great deal of talk in the cafés and salons – by the presentation of a Negress as the central subject of a portrait, and by the fact that she was painted by a woman (indeed, the white hand of the painter, while invisible, seems to attract more attention than the subject of the painting itself). The woman portrayed in the painting is unnamed. She wears the white turban I know from childhood and the painter has arranged a snowy cloth around her torso in the neo-classical style. Her breasts are revealed and unadorned and her strong shoulders bear their weight with inexpressible grace. Is the intention political, a brave

declaration of liberty? Or is it rather to allow viewers to glory in
the beauty of her dark skin and the golden light where the sun
rests on it?

What a strange melancholy has settled over me in this city
that I so long desired to visit, and which, in all particulars of
architecture and delectable food and amusement on the streets,
exceeds expectations. Perversely, I awaken in the mornings
longing for the rudimentary satisfactions of work under the open
sky. I spend my days with the sensation of looking through a pane
of glass at the passing pageant of the world.

July 21

M. Jacques-Louis David did not appear at the salon in
Saint-Germain; I was told variously that he has died and that
he is living in splendid health in Brussels. It was a singular
evening nonetheless. In the French fashion, the withdrawal of
the ladies signalled the withdrawal of a chamber pot from a
drawer for the relief of the gentlemen, and immediately after
availing myself of it, I was presented by our over-eager host to
an amiable gentleman identified as Étienne Geoffroy Saint-Hilaire.
In such a discomfiting position, with my hands on my flies, I met
the natural historian who accompanied Napoleon into Egypt and
carried back specimens from the ancient tombs for Cuvier's
examination. He is a genial, round-faced man with a delicately
formed mouth and a good command of English, and in that
language he inquired as to my impressions of Paris. In short order
we had moved through the revolution (of which he had high
hopes until sickened by the blood lust), the Emperor's wars, and
the restoration of the monarchy. Through all of this, both he
and Cuvier managed to keep their posts at the Jardin du Roi,
thanks to a genius for adaptation, and now have every expectation
of dying peacefully in their beds.

I stuck close to his side until I could reveal to him my association with William Buckland, whom I was sure he would know, and when I did, he laughed contemptuously, inquiring as to the state of my colleague's *digestion*. He had heard of Buckland's quest to eat his way through the animal kingdom, and the story has become so frightfully distorted that he believes Buckland to have resorted to cannibalism. I was appalled to think that the English are so demonized in this country that a man of Geoffroy's intelligence could fall prey to such a tale. Another consequence of the protracted war we have endured.

Before the evening was over, we fell into a discussion of such ideas as could never be broached in an English drawing room. I learned then that, though he and Cuvier remain on congenial terms, there is a fundamental divide in their philosophies. While Cuvier sees each biological species as having its separate logic and integrity, Geoffroy believes that all vertebrates are manifestations of a single archetype. He suggests that the Creator had one divine anatomical plan which, through the ages of time, has manifested itself in diverse forms. In this, he approaches the thinking of Jean Baptiste Lamarck, the man Buckland so disparages as "the professor of insects and worms," and for whom Geoffroy has the greatest respect.

And so I learned that I have cavalierly dismissed scholars regarded on this side of the Channel as titans of science, and that I have done so on the word of one dogmatic Oxford don. Here on the banks of the Seine, a whole different conversation is being enjoyed. Geoffroy has given himself licence to set aside divine revelation and look openly at the phenomena before him. He alludes to a created prototype, but the process of biological development that follows is reckless and chaotic (*unsupervised*, one might say), so as to have nothing of the divine in it. While we perched on *ancien régime* chairs and sipped cognac, Geoffroy spoke of the transmutation of forms with no consciousness of blasphemy, not even looking around to see who might be overhearing!

I hardly knew what to say. I have no facility to grasp ideas so novel and shocking. It is only now that I can begin to identify the questions that I should have put to him. Geoffroy has published few works himself, but recommended to me *Philosophie zoologique* by Lamarck. I am resolved to read this text and to propose a debate at the Geological Society on the notion of transmutation. Is it not *highly relevant* to our study of the giant reptiles so mysteriously vanished from the Dorsetshire shore? Does it not propose a solution we have been unwilling to countenance, that these creatures have not disappeared, but have changed in succeeding generations? How I long for this sort of scientific freedom – both to make observations from nature that have no basis in doctrine and to disagree with one's brothers. For even with Lamarck, Geoffroy has grave differences. And yet he outlined Lamarck's theories with the greatest concern for accuracy, explaining Lamarck's notion of slow change that comes through biological traits being acquired as the need arises, or falling into disuse and so disappearing (and leaving their traces only in vestigial organs, such as the shrunken and useless eyes of a mole that lives entirely in the dark). For his part, Geoffroy Saint-Hilaire holds to a different mechanism of change, asserting that species are transformed in bursts as a result of accidents of conception and incubation. As we drank coffee, this gentleman confessed his passion for fetal malformations, which in his view pull back the veil of nature to reveal valuable biological secrets.

I left the salon in a stupor that L. attributed to the drink. My conversation with Geoffroy was not an exchange of ideas: I could contribute nothing but a keen will to understand. This I frankly confessed to him, and he seemed to like me the more for my

frankness. We parted with such genuine sympathy that I have
no doubt now of being invited to Cuvier's salon, where God
willing I shall profit from further conversation with this
community of savants. At moments, I feel an undying gratitude
to Mrs. Auriol for contriving to take me to Saint-Germain,
and at other moments, I am so uneasy as to wish these pathways
of thought had never been opened to me.

August 14

We have our portrait at last. It was executed by one Jean-Marie
Poliquin, not David but a painter of some note in the city, who
won L. over in his first breath with the ultimate compliment one
can pay an Englishwoman in Paris: "*On ne devinerait jamais que
vous êtes anglaise.*" He has painted L. as an ideal primitive. She leans
on a mule and from one hand dangles a dipper for skimming milk.
Her form is as he imagined it to be before her pregnancy – I think
he intends a virginal effect. It is not entirely a successful portrait:
he has given a more discerning eye to the mule than to my wife,
and in the finely wrought hands (smooth and clean and absent of
calluses) lies, in my mind, a repudiation of the central conceit
of the painting. How much more logical to go directly for a
subject to the milkmaid on the Gosling Bridge!

In a tiny *librairie* on rue Descartes, I purchased a copy of
Philosophie zoologique. It is Lamarck, apparently, whom we can
thank for the very term *invertebrate*. He began his studies by
observing the molluscs of the Paris basin, and noting the small
changes that occurred in them through subsequent strata. He takes
as a matter of course that the strata of this basin were laid down
over a vast history, and that by studying them systematically he
can read the story of biological transmutations through time. As
an observant collector could at Lyme Regis, recording ammonite
finds on a vertical chart of the cliffs. But all these years, we clever

gentlemen of science have gazed at the strata of the blue lias, blinded by an orthodoxy that would not let us read what we saw.

August 21
Cuvier's salon.

That's all he can write. Two maids are chattering in the corridor, and he sits motionless. He's just read the entire volume through from the beginning. A journal penned by a youth intoxicated by his own idealism, ready to throw over the scholarship of his forefathers, carefully accrued through many generations, ready to leap into an abyss. And so eager to sneer at his wife for her pretensions! And yet behold the young dandy himself the night before, swaying beside a potted palm in a reception hall at the Muséum national d'histoire naturelle, a glass of burgundy in his hand (a glass he never once removed from his lips without its being immediately refilled), leaning familiarly towards the great anatomist Georges Cuvier, murmuring in classroom French, "You are familiar with English compound cookery?" Cuvier cast him a look of bemusement and contempt, but still he had to elaborate. "It is performed between the jaws of the eater," he had to add, "who spears a potato and a cabbage leaf with the same fork."

He leans his head against the cushions. He's still wearing the linen shirt of the night before – he smells tobacco and sweat, and something sickening exuding from his pores. He sent Tom out to the chemist's, which prevents him bathing. The fire has gone out, the sitting room is cold, and he has rung the bell repeatedly. A taste lingers, the taste of a certain dish from the night before, which he tried unsuccessfully to throw up into the Seine on the way home. *Lark*, someone told him, lark in a most peculiar sauce. And now, what to write as his valediction to Paris? His vertigo rises. Very well, he'll limit himself to the subject of William Buckland. He'll write just that one moment in the reception hall: when Georges Cuvier swung his shaggy red curls in Henry's direction (the head of an old-world bison) and said, "Tell me. Has your friend Buckland yet published an account of the fossils found in the Stonesfield quarries?" It was the massive thigh bone in the museum at Oxford that he meant, but other fossils as well. Apparently, Cuvier examined them in 1818 when he visited England – a piece of lower jaw with teeth, some vertebrae, fragments of pelvis, scapula, and hind limbs. Buckland had all of them in his possession. "They are, monsieur, the remains of a gargantuan land reptile, a whole new order of beast with no extant cousins."

"Did you tell Buckland your opinion?"

"Of course. He concurred with me entirely. But I knew he would not publish! He will not dare to jeopardize his chair at Oxford with a finding so contrary to religion."

Henry sits listening to shouts on the street below. He wants to be out of Paris. When they reach the outskirts tomorrow, he'll stop the carriage and make a ceremony of shaking the dust from his feet. For now, he'll write nothing but a record of bare fact, as prudent journalists do. He sits back down at the desk and dips his pen.

August 21
Cuvier's salon. I was introduced to the celebrated M. Cuvier who invited me to dine with him and ordered his galleries of comparative anatomy to be open – a collection of human skulls – gradual approach to the monkey through the Hottentot.

He slides a blotter over his journal and goes back to the divan, where he lies down, lowering himself by degrees to prevent the room revolving. There's a flurry on the landing outside the sitting room and Letitia comes in, followed by her mother and the maids. He hears them sorting out parcels. Letitia pauses by the divan. Henry lies still until she moves away. "It's a lovely lace, *maman*," she says, "but it was made in Nottinghamshire. You could have bought it at home for half the price." Some minutes later, she's standing over him again. "Henry," she says. "Where is your cloak? Where is your hat? Mercer wants them to clean for the journey."

"They're gone," Henry says without opening his eyes.

She makes an exasperated sound. "Get up!"

"I am desperately unwell, Letitia. Kindly leave me in peace."

"How much wine did you drink last night?" She stands waiting for an answer. When none comes, she crosses the room to the landing. At the door, she stops. "*Maman* and I are going to the café. Then we're walking up rue Violette to try to find a necklace like Mme Bournier's."

The door closes. On the landing, she delivers herself of a disgusted comment he can't make out and her mother murmurs a reply.

It was a long way home in the dark, along the river for an hour or more and then past the Louvre and through the first arrondissement, still shaken from stumbling through the Great Hall in the dark, moving in and out of a wineish giddiness, the cold gradually penetrating his senses, rain soaking through his coat, the realization coming to him that his cape and hat and gloves lay in an anteroom back at the Muséum. *You are starving with cold*, Mary said, tenderly.

He had parted abruptly from the company during the tour, in a gallery at the centre of a maze of corridors. They were sixteen: the geologist Brongniart, the amiable Geoffroy Saint-Hilaire (with whom Henry never managed to speak), Georges Cuvier's long-clawed brother Frédéric, prancing in burgundy velvet, and a delegation of savants from Vienna, dressed as though to evoke necromancers. But no Jean Baptiste Lamarck — an Austrian murmured of a recent rift between Cuvier and Lamarck. As they entered the gallery, servants scurried around lighting sconces. "This collection is as yet inferior to certain collections of our German friends," intoned Cuvier, "but serves to illustrate the same point." The light came up to reveal a row of human skulls with tickets. The first was labelled EUROPÉEN, the second ASIATIQUE. Someone asked how brain capacity can best be measured. Mustard seed, Georges Cuvier said, and the party laughed.

Henry stared at the great curator's own massive skull. There is not mustard enough in France, he thought. Then he turned back to the display and his eyes fell on the last skull in the row. It was the low-browed skull of an ape. They're trying to provoke, Henry thought. Well, so could he. Cuvier-the-lesser was at his elbow. "So, man is of the same order as ape, is he?" Henry said.

Frédéric smirked. "A modest illustration of the Great Chain of Being, nothing more," he said. But Henry saw something crafty in Frédéric's face, and he pressed the point.

"Your discussions regarding the transmutation of forms — do they extend to man?" he asked.

Frédéric recoiled. "Transmutation of forms? There is no such subject of discussion at the Jardin," he said. He bowed and turned to another guest.

The great bison stood by a display case in his ornate brocade coat, holding court among the Austrians. Henry moved away from them, down the row of skulls. Under the second-to-last was fixed a ticket that said HOTTENTOTE. A queer sensation ran along Henry's spine. There were four large engravings pinned to the wall opposite the display cases. Three were of apes and the fourth was a human female, certainly the woman he had seen as a youth in Piccadilly. She was portrayed naked with nothing to provide her with a modicum of modesty – not the apron, not the shell necklace. His eyes were drawn to the large areolas of her breasts. Henry walked towards the etching and stood before it. The woman stood facing the illustrator, her arms at her sides. The portrait was almost life-sized; viewer and subject were at eye level. Her eyes did not bear the anger he had seen in Piccadilly. Rather, he was struck by the comeliness of her face and by her look of sad appeal.

And then the group was moving to the next hall, Cuvier-the-lesser ushering them through double doors, and Henry was across the room in three paces and had his hand clamped to the man's arm. Frédéric turned with an amused smile on his tapered face.

"Who is the woman pictured here?"

"*La Vénus hottentote*. Surely you know of her."

"But what is her name?"

"Saartjie Baartman, I believe."

"That's a Dutch name."

Frédéric offered an elaborate shrug.

"And this is her skull?"

"It is." A little bow.

"How –?"

"We examined her here in 1815. She was being displayed by an animal trainer in rue St-Honoré. She was a dipsomaniac with a particular taste for gin, or so they said."

"Was it in this chamber that she was examined?"

"No. It was in the Pavilion, where there is room for the illustrators to set up their easels. We paid her trainer a pretty penny for three days. They promised us her full co-operation, but she refused our every question. She merely babbled in some barbaric tongue and recited bits of verse in Dutch. She would not cease from coughing."

"Was she naked throughout?"

"It was a scientific examination."

"Did you not seek a doctor for her?"

Frédéric made an amused snort. "She took care of herself, that one. M. de Blainville offered her a gold napoleon if she would show her privates, but she defied him." He planted a confiding hand on Henry's arm and lowered his voice. "We had to wait until she died."

Henry was filled with loathing of himself and of this man. He removed the hand. "There is nothing of science in this – it is prurience of a most disgusting sort!"

"*Cher ami*, you do not appreciate the science of it. You may wish to avail yourself of the entire display –" And he gestured to the cases at the centre of the room. Henry turned his head and saw in a glass case the fleshy petals of an elaborate tropical flower. Then understanding burned through him and he turned fiercely back on Frédéric. Frédéric met him with his guttersnipe eyes. "*Eh, bien*," he shrugged, and went out through the double doors.

Henry turned and stumbled back the way they had come. Ahead of him, two servants moved down the corridor, extinguishing the lights. He put his hand out to the wall of the dim corridor to steady himself. And then the servants had vanished and he was alone, almost running, trying to retrace their way, although in fact he had no memory of leaving the dining room. He found himself in a great hall lined with animal skeletons. They loomed on either side, facing inwards as though to charge, gleaming from the light of the Paris night sky let in through high windows. He scurried along, keeping to the centre of the aisle, as a child who was afraid of shadows might. At the end, he spied a small passage, and threw himself down it, and that was worse, it narrowed as though leading to a crypt. He leapt and shrieked as a door opened – it was a watchman with a massive key ring, letting in cold night air. At Henry's insistence, the man let him out, and Henry stumbled into the night and wandered a long time in the maze of the garden, almost weeping with frustration, before he found an unlocked gate to the street.

It was freezing cold and gently raining. The street was still full of carriages. The bell at Notre-Dame rang midnight as he passed. Then he was at Pont Neuf, standing before a massive statue, the new king on horseback. He leaned over the balustrade, peering down at the black water smeared with the yellow reflections of torches through the rain. Pedestrians crossed continually beside him, brushing against him. A group of English in their long cloaks, silent. A lone gentleman, his walking stick tapping on the pavement. He thought he might be sick, he longed to be sick, but not here; he wanted to get down to the water's edge. There was a wide stone balustrade built along the bank especially to prevent him, and a sharp ridge laid along the top of the balustrade for the intimate punishment of the man who tried to go over it one leg at a time. And then, somehow, he was over it and lurching down the bank. There at the water's edge was the prone body of Sophie, lying on her front, her face turned to the side. She had been lying there all night. Her body was fringed with land crabs, crabs like ivory tea saucers climbing clumsily over each other in an effort to get at her. His mother sat sipping punch. *Poison*, she said. *She would have picked it in the jungle. Something only the Creoles know of.* He looked for his father, but his father was gone. It was Peter, the Igbo houseboy, who took his hand and led him stumbling back up to the bridge and across to the other side.

◄[T W E N T Y - E I G H T]►

He was gone; that dangerous season of her life was over and done with. But the townsfolk never forgot. Walking up Broad Street on a windy April day, Mary encountered Mrs. Stock, the brim of her bonnet fouled from the blacking she smeared on her whitening curls. Mary refused to lower her gaze, and Mrs. Stock muttered something and stepped back elaborately to avoid passing too close.

Mary was on her way to take tea with Miss Philpot. She was not seated five minutes in the back parlour of Morley Cottage before the reason for the invitation was carried triumphantly out, in the form of a book in snowy covers: *Outlines of the Geology of England and Wales* by the Reverend William Conybeare. A *magnificent* accomplishment in geology, Elizabeth Philpot said, all tremulous with excitement. It listed every fossil ever found in England, along with the names of the gentlemen credited with the finds. So William Buckland was in the book many times over, and Henry De la Beche, Esq., and Colonel Birch, and Squire Henry Hoste Henley (for the Ichthyosaurus Joseph had found and Mary had excavated when she was twelve), and of course the good Reverend himself (for an *Ichthyosaurus communis* Mary had found and Henry had sold to Conybeare on her behalf).

All this was the modest preamble to the centrepiece of the book: the name *Miss Elizabeth Philpot.* Elizabeth flushed as she flipped to this page and ran her finger down the line to her own lady's name, there among all the gentlemen's! Her citation was for a *gryphaea* she had found and collected herself. (But *I* identified it! Mary might have blurted. *I* showed you how to clean it.) Reverend Conybeare had sent Miss Philpot a copy of the book with his compliments. She wanted to spend a few more days studying it, but Mary was welcome to borrow it after that.

"I have scant leisure for reading these days," was all Mary said, stiffly.

When she stepped out on Silver Street, she found that the wind was worse and there was a hum in the air that accorded very well with her temper. The Cobb was crowded with ships seeking shelter. While she'd been sitting in the back parlour of Morley Cottage, the clouds had built into a ledge looming over the sea, navy blue in colour. By the time she was halfway down Broad Street, wind had drawn that ledge into a gargantuan sharp-prowed schooner that was carrying a gale swiftly across the Channel towards them.

The river was swollen from spring rains. "The workshop will flood, certain-sure," she said to Molly. She made four or five trips from the workshop, carrying up the tools and the small and fragile specimens and stowing them in the kitchen. Lizzie was slumbering on the cot. Her face was puffy and her colour was very poor. "Sit up, lazy," Mary said. "You need to wake up before bedtime." She took a cup of broth from the pot and sat on the cot beside Lizzie. Lizzie half opened her eyes.

"*Flood*," she said. "I heard you." Her breath was so short that every phrase was an accusation. Mary helped her raise her head to sip from the cup. Lizzie was parched, always, but the broth she drank did not come out as piss. It pooled in her legs, as Henry's doctor had predicted. If they kept giving her drink, they would hasten her death, the doctor'd said, and Mary had countered, "Without drink, she will die in misery," and he hadn't had an answer to that.

When the broth was mostly gone, Mary picked Lizzie up and carried her upstairs. Settling Lizzie into bed, she avoided looking at her legs, swollen like the legs of a fat old woman. "What story do you want?" she asked, and Lizzie whispered, "The Flood."

Mary went to the window that looked towards France. The waves were immense – a vertical boulder of water lifted as high as the window and fell back. She stood by the shelf and lit candles, a row of three, and took down Mr. Buckland's bible. It opened naturally to Genesis, and she turned the pages and ran her eyes over the story of God falling into a temper with man, and then deciding to rescue Noah. With her free hand on Lizzie's hand on the coverlet, she began to read, lowering her voice below the fretting of the wind.

> Make thee an ark of gopher wood; rooms shalt thou make in the ark, and shalt pitch it within and without with pitch. And this is the fashion which thou shalt make it of: The length of the ark shall be three hundred cubits, the breadth of it fifty cubits, and the height of it thirty cubits. A window shalt thou make to the ark, and in a cubit shalt thou finish it above; and the door of the ark shalt thou set in the side thereof; with lower, second, and third stories shalt thou make it.

Lizzie's eyes had already closed and her chin had sunk down on her chest. Mary paused in her reading. When Lizzie didn't stir, she got up and put the bible back on the shelf. Some nights, she kept reading after Lizzie drifted off – might the words not keep Lizzie company in her dreams? But tonight her feelings were too roiled up to endure it. Wind edged its way through the cracks around the window and prodded at the candles. She took up the tallest candle and lit three more from it, dripping a bit of wax on the shelf to hold each one. Molly came up the steps just then. "She's seen enough of darkness," Mary said, to forestall her mother chiding her with waste, and her wrath parted a little and let gratitude waft in, for the four hundred pounds the learned men had given her that bought beeswax candles and coal and marrow bones to make broth for Lizzie.

They took their places on either side of Lizzie, with their backs against the corner posts of the bed. For a while, Lizzie turned her face from one side to the other, as though the guttering bright candlelight was bothering her. She was panting strangely. But in a few minutes, peace came over her, and Mary passed the second pillow to her mother and put the bolster behind her own back. They did not bother with their nightdresses – there would be no sleeping for either of them. Water had begun to boom against the seawall, as loud as a cannon blast. Joseph would be anxious for them. If the Lyme flooded its banks, he would come and take them up to Church Street. Lizzie had fallen into a deep sleep. Even after the bell in the square set to wild clanging and the timbers of the house began to groan, she did not stir. Molly sat with her shawl wrapped around her and did not stir either. This was the way she always sat in the evening, motionless, like a turtle, to save her force.

Mary leaned back and closed her eyes. She should have agreed to borrow the book. She could have counted the number of times the name *Mary Anning* was blotted from it. *I have scant leisure for reading*, she'd said. Not another soul on Bridge Street would express itself in those words. She had gentled her speech to the point that the townspeople mocked her – and to what purpose? She was like the Ichthyosaurus: she was neither fish nor fowl.

There was a crash somewhere below. Mary tried to think what could have fallen. Oh, well. There were no treasures in this household, no useless china vases. It was a new sensation, being so vexed with Miss Philpot. *I will avoid her from this day on,* she thought. From now on, she would sell everything she found as curios. She would promote the use of rare vertebrae as candle-holders. She'd learn French and sell to the French, who had no concept of the value of an English coin. In any case, there would be no more sales to the learned gentlemen. The next astonishing skeleton she found, she would hide in the workshop until she could publish her own text. She had a gift for this work that could not be learned. It was a kinship with the bones you needed, a reptilian eye, to see what had never been seen or even imagined. *That* the scientific gentlemen would never have!

Something wooden ripped below them. Should they try to leave? She looked at her mother, but Molly gave no sign that she had heard. Mary pictured them staggering up the hill to Joseph's with Lizzie in her arms and all the floodgates of heaven open above them and bricks tumbling from the chimneys. They'd left it too late. If Joseph had had any thoughts of coming for them, he'd left it too late as well. She put her hand on Lizzie's cool forehead. "Here we are, Lizzie," she said. "Safe and dry in the ark." She sat and watched the candles unevenly burning, and when the first guttered out, she got up and lit a new one in its place, and wondered how the Bennetts were faring next door, huddling there in their grief, for it was just last week that their William was transported to Botany Bay for snaring a pheasant on Squire Henley's land, and they would never see him no more in their lives.

The candles bowed and rose in the draft. *I will blot out man whom I have created from the face of the land,* God said. She saw the hoarding, thieving gentlemen bobbing in the black swell, clutching desperately at their top hats as buoys. Reverend Conybeare, with his long, sneering nose and knowing eye – it was Conybeare's sworn purpose to exclude her. He had organized *Outlines of Geology* by buyers, not by finders, to snatch all the glory for himself and his friends. Let him clutch his *Ichthyosaurus communis* to him – it would only sink him! And as for Henry De la Beche– But she could not think of Henry. She got up instead to light another candle.

Her mother rose as well, to attend to Lizzie. Mary stood by the shelf, pressing the new candle into soft wax, and when she turned, she saw that Molly had fallen to her knees by the bed with her ear to Lizzie's face. A black shadow dramatized her movements – it seemed she was demonstrating a procedure in the care of the gravely ill. She lifted herself heavily up, her face stricken, and said something that Mary could not hear for the gale, and then she bent and passed her hand over Lizzie's eyes as though to close them. Do not mock us, Mother, Mary thought, before understanding moved hideously through her. She leapt to the bed and snatched Lizzie up by the shoulders. Lizzie's head fell lifelessly back, and then Molly was there and took the child from Mary and laid her tenderly down, smoothing her hair, touching her cheek. "Let Jesus carry her now in His bosom, the poor lamb," Molly said in Mary's ear. She made to lay a kiss on Mary's cheek, but Mary flung herself away with a cry.

Oh – that she could snatch back the last hour! In one of its moments, while she boiled and ranted, Lizzie's spirit had slipped from the room. But she had sensed nothing – those vicious gentlemen had stolen from her the sacred hour of her sister's passing. Or *she* had thrown it away. She had let Lizzie fall. She had been caught up in drowning her enemies, and it was Lizzie who had slipped beneath the waves. Mary let the candles gutter out, and when the last was gone, she saw that her mother had fallen asleep, but she could not bring herself to take her place on the bed. Finally, she slid to the floor and laid her head against the bed, reaching a hand towards where Lizzie's lay. She did not sleep but wept, pressing her face into the coverlet. She wept and wept, and when her tears were gone, she stayed on the floor in the posture of exhausted prayer, listening to the water thrashing like a beast below, and thought that it was right that the sea should convulse so for the loss of this child.

It was full light of a grey day when Mary woke in a strange, soft bed with a curtain around it. At her waking, a new weight in her chest reminded her that Lizzie was gone. This day has come, she said to herself, as we knew it must, and we can take up the burden of our grieving. The timbers of the house she was in groaned, but they were up on the high street and the roaring of the sea was low and distant.

Her mother slept beside her under a white coverlet. "It is a great charity she shows us," she'd said in the early morning hours, as Mary held her by the elbows and helped her lower herself onto the night bucket. "A great charity, and her with that goitre." It was Mrs. Jefferd she meant.

"It is not a charity," said Mary. "They will send us a bill and we will pay it."

Henry Jefferd did not have her father's skill with a dovetail join, but he was the only undertaker now in Lyme, and a kindly man. When Mary had pounded on his door at first light, he'd said they must bring Lizzie to be laid out there, for the Lyme would surely flood. His wife saw Mary drenched in the kitchen and knew without having to be told, and she said they must all come, there was a bed to spare.

Mary's heart had pounded with an unreasoned hope when she led Henry Jefferd into the bedchamber of their house, but in the grey light leaking around the shutter, she saw that Lizzie's face had transformed through the last hour into something no longer human. Mr. Jefferd had brought a canvas with him. Inside was a wool blanket proofed with lanolin. He laid the blanket on the bed and lifted the body onto it, tucking the blanket tightly up over the face, and then wrapped the whole thing into the canvas. He lifted this bundle into his arms with the gentleness of a father, and Mary closed up the house and she and her mother followed Jefferd up the rain-dashed street, with the wind pushing at their backs like a giant hand. At his house, he went straight through to the laying-out room and Harriet Jefferd showed them to their bed. "Hand your skirts out to me, my dears, and I will dry them by the fire," she said. "And we will think nothing amiss if you lie abed late after all your troubles."

The Jefferds' kitchen window afforded a view of the eastern shore. The veil of rain had thinned and Mary glimpsed the sea piled in untidy heaps below. The wind seemed shriller this morning, and now it raked on Mary's nerves.

Harriet Jefferd turned from the fire and greeted Mary and offered her a cup of tea, and for the first time, Mary saw the goitre poking from the side of her neck. And there by the mantel was another visitor, Mr. Gleed, steam rising from his coat in the warmth of the coal fire. Mary sat down and he inclined his head towards her. "Miss Anning," he said. "My sympathies at this dark hour." When Mary thanked him, he reached out and touched her on the shoulder. "Hoping to serve you in some small way, I have carried the sad news to your brother." He cupped his hands as if to show Mary how this was accomplished. "He will come the instant the storm allows. Your sister-in-law is in a very delicate state."

"Indeed," Mary said, and after a long pause, she thought to thank him again. It was not a small thing Mr. Gleed had done, braving Church Street hill in this gale.

Mrs. Jefferd sat herself down in the inglenook and gave Mary a soft look.

"Your family has been sorely tried," Mr. Gleed said, intruding his face into Mary's thoughts. She noticed that he had a plate of bread and a cup of tea on the mantelpiece.

"I must agree," Mary said. "Mr. Gleed, do sit down," she added, although it was not her place.

"Can't sit, poor chap," murmured Mrs. Jefferd in Mary's direction. "It's his ulsters." She gestured towards her own hindquarters.

He took a swallow of his tea. "The Scriptures tell us of Job, who was also sorely tried. And in the midst of his great suffering, counsellors came and tempted him to curse God and die."

Mary sipped on her tea. She wished for a bit of sugar. And also for a bit of silence. Lizzie will stay with us for just a while longer, she thought: a sense of her, of her hot breath and her husky, petulant voice. While a sense of Lizzie lingered, she longed to be left in peace to attend to her. And then Mr. Gleed was back at the table, like a server offering her the jug of milk. "Our thoughts can be our counsellors," he said.

"They can, indeed," said Mary.

"Many do not grasp this. They think of counsellors as aged men in robes. But we are all counselled by our thoughts. I hope your thoughts do not tempt you as Job was tempted."

"No," said Mary, finally provoked to talk. "Although I ask myself, Mr. Gleed, I do ask myself why God, having performed his experiment of mortal tortures on Job, feels the need to visit it again upon the Annings."

Mrs. Jefferd pulled her breath sharply in, but Mary did not relent. She stared Mr. Gleed into silence. She did not want to be in a temper again on this day, but she was in a temper, and would be in one until she had the quiet of her own thoughts.

The flood waters retreated the day of Lizzie's funeral, and after the burial, Mary and her mother moved back home. In the end, only the workshop had flooded, to a depth of Mary's waist, as you could see by a line of soil on the wall. The quantity of seaweed and clay that had washed in testified to what a loose sieve their little house was. Through the silt poked the larger fossils she had left on the floor – a hip bone from an unidentified beast, and a femur, and a large piece of jaw.

She was three days washing out the workshop and cleaning up her collection. It was like excavating these beasts a second time, and it was work she was glad of. This is what I do, she thought: I am a fossilist. She thought of Conybeare's book and her notion that her name had been blotted from it, a notion she saw now as absurd. The names of the high-born would never be recorded in a book side by side with the low: such an association would debase them. Her impulse to think beyond her station was like a flagrant vine that needed constant pruning. Reverend Conybeare did not need to make an effort to exclude her – the order of things accomplished that task for him. Noah led the animals both clean and unclean onto the ark, but the high-born did not consider her and such like her.

When she was too tired to work, she went down to the shore. Scavengers had cleaned up, dragging home driftwood and bottles and barrels and all the other treasures a gale will steal from one shore-dweller and bestow on another, but worn pillows of foam still bobbed in inlets, and huge new excavations marked the face of the cliffs. She sat herself down on the shingle. Everything was in motion: the springy waves, and little boats bobbing, the colours throbbing against her eyes, the stirred-up sea full of its secret life. Creatures crawling in dreamlike existence along the bottom.

She'd made a choice, that her sister would die by drowning and not by parching. But she would die all the same – that part was outside Mary's powers. How keenly Lizzie had tried, with her clever little airs, to grow into a young woman in their narrow house. The poor love life as passionately as the rich do. Perhaps more, for the effort it takes to cling to it. In spite of Mr. Gleed's influence, Lizzie did not desire to go to the next world. Mary leaned forward then, burying her face in her old plaid skirt, and wept for relief that death had donned the guise of sleep in coming for Lizzie.

The day Mary finished scrubbing out the workshop, Miss Philpot sent to ask her round for tea. Mary could not summon up the energy to refuse. On the table was a beautiful vase of white peonies.

"This is for you, as a remembrance," Miss Philpot said. She handed Mary a white card on which she had written a verse:

In all my troubles, Thou art nigh,
Thou sympathizing Friend!
Thou sees my pain, and from on high,
Dost consolation send.

With the card was a picture of a young girl with a mass of wisteria behind her. Weeks ago, they had looked through a folio of engravings and Mary had commented on the marvellous resemblance this one bore to Lizzie. Mary was touched by Miss Philpot's kindness in giving her this portrait, although she did not see Lizzie so vividly in it now. This child had a narrower face and was inordinately decked out in ribbons. With time, she thought sadly, Lizzie's aspect will vanish from my mind and the girl with the ribbons will take her place.

Miss Philpot was soft in her manner and solicitous about the condition of the workshop and Molly's health and spirits. Mary found she could not hold on to her resentment. They were two solitary women together, whatever others might see. But she sensed a new sadness in Elizabeth Philpot, sadness and nervousness. While they chatted, Elizabeth broke a peony from its stem and methodically ripped it apart with her bony fingers, laying the frail bits of bruised petal along the tablecloth in order of size. The maid came in and set a tea of biscuits and fresh cream on the table, ignoring the disassembled peony. When she was gone, the startling news finally came out.

Mr. Buckland was to be married! He had written to announce his engagement, but had been uncharacteristically vague about the manner of his meeting the young lady. It was Charlotte Murchison who told Miss Philpot the real circumstances.

Two months ago, Mr. Buckland had boarded a public coach in Oxford in which a single other passenger, an unchaperoned lady, sat reading. Mr. Buckland intended to profit from the journey by reading himself, and he withdrew from his portmanteau the volume he was carrying – *Recherches sur les ossemens fossiles,* the newest study by Georges Cuvier – hoping, no doubt, to impress the lady by his erudition in reading such a volume *en français.* And then he heard the lady laugh and looked up to discover that she was holding the identical volume! Not only that – this lady had been sent a complimentary copy, for she was a skilled artist and had supplied some of the illustrations in the book. And so, without a proper introduction, they fell into conversation. The upshot of it was that they were to be married in July! She was a Mary as well, Mary Moreland.

It seemed the fiancée was much younger than Mr. Buckland. "About your age, Mary," Miss Philpot said in a voice that was quite bitter. Her face twisted into a sardonic smile. "What do you think is behind it?" she asked, with a visible effort to lighten her tone. "Love for the lady or the prospect of a new illustrator, now that Mr. De la Beche has gone to France?"

Mary had heard others mock Mr. Buckland, but never Miss Philpot. "It's the satisfaction of stealing her from Cuvier," she said, noting the vain little touches in Miss Philpot's dress, the puff sleeves so ill-suited to her frame. She drank her last swallow of tea and thought, How very much I do not see. It had never once occurred to her that Elizabeth Philpot might have any desires at all. She looked thoughtfully at her friend's face, made all of straight lines and flat planes. The pockmarks had faded in the years of their acquaintance, but there was nothing lovely in the face save its humour and intelligence. And today the humour was soured and Miss Philpot's shoulders were held rigid with the knowledge that she had betrayed herself. So Mary turned the talk to her work, and they sat in the parlour and talked about sea creatures until the light began to dim.

"We will ask Mr. De la Beche," Miss Philpot said about some point or other. "Mr. and Mrs. De la Beche will be returning over the summer, I expect. I always thought his manners rather French, and they will be more so now."

"Do you hear from him?"

The maid came in just then to light the lamps, and Miss Philpot sprang up to draw the curtains. "Oh," she cried. "Mary, I am a donkey! There is wonderful news from Mr. De la Beche. I heard days ago from Mrs. Aveline, but we were so occupied with the *Outlines of Geology* that it slipped my mind. Henry is a father! They have a little girl. She came earlier than expected, while they were in Grenoble. It was the infant's act of mercy to her mother, arriving early, for poor young Mrs. De la Beche found her confinement very difficult. They have named her Elizabeth, after Mr. De la Beche's mother, but Mrs. Aveline says I may take it also as a compliment to myself." To make up for her oversight in not immediately sharing this news, Miss Philpot got her book out of a drawer, a commonplace book, she called it, where she wrote her thoughts and such thoughts of others as merited recording, and she looked through the pages to find the exact date of the baby's birth.

Of the months that followed Lizzie's death, certain moments lay complete within Mary like fossils in the lias: Annie Bennett and her two black-eyed children strolling along the path to Pinney Meadow, Annie lifting the little girl to tickle her face against the fleabane growing on the wall. Will Darby and his bride walking up to the church and the rain starting to fall, and the groom taking off his hat and solemnly holding it out over his bride's veiled head. And Molly – she would always remember Molly coming across Lizzie's comb behind the cupboard, sitting down on the bench, holding the comb in her two knobby hands. "*Nay*, I say, as stern as can be, *I'm not a-plaiting it again*, and then I come in and she has it all undone, the imp, so I have to set about a-plaiting if I wish to or no."

Time did not stop, it kept going forward, and Mary stood still and watched it on its way. There was the rhythm of the seasons and of the tide, momentary change with the promise of sameness in it. Everyone around her was part of it; they flowed by her in a stream. But Mary Anning was not – she had been formed of lightning, she was neither fish nor fowl. When the high-born got off the coach, she met their eyes with such boldness that they turned away alarmed. "A cat may look at the queen," she called once, and laughed when the lady's husband came back to the table and threatened to get the magistrate.

Pride and fury drove her every moment of the day. She walked with Richard Anning's quick step and the insolent set of his jaw. Time was not standing still, it was speeding up, and it had her in its clutches as well, and was carrying her towards a fate she did not choose to meet. If I am to be an old maid, Mary said fiercely to herself, I will be an old maid such as Lyme Regis has never seen. *Mary Anning*: an unknown species, her tendencies unpredictable. None of the doctrines of the high-born explained her – she did not exist in their taxonomy. Why had she so hungered to be one of them? Thwarted, that hunger would turn her into a certain kind of monstrosity; fulfilled, it would turn her into another. One day, she was sifting through a tray of shells for a child in the shop, and she saw herself as if caught in a shaft of light, sturdy, plainly dressed, efficient, sharp-tongued, smelling of starch and sea salt and the salt of her own sweat, and she knew that that particular ambition had withered. Other hungers would take its place, for people are always hungry. She straightened up and brushed her hand over her skirt, and felt one of those hungers, a fierce curiosity to see what she would make of herself.

The Grove on Pound Street was to let. They were in Stras-bourg when his mother wrote to tell him. "It will serve for a start," she wrote, but the day he returns to Lyme Regis and walks through one finely proportioned room after another, he decides he must live in this house for the rest of his life. Open beams frankly show its structure. The upstairs windows offer a view of the sea over rooftops, although not of the shore. He chooses a back room on the ground floor for his study, for the broad windows that open to an ash grove on the west and to an artless garden of fern and periwinkle on the north. The drawing room is painted a blue unknown to the sky (a deriv-ative of copper, it must be), but that is easily changed.

The property is to let furnished, by a Mr. Linnison. Letitia is appalled by the serviceable mahogany dining room table and he agrees to replace it when he is able. An Axminster rug they select together is laid in the drawing room. Milkmaid Letitia gazes pensively from a Chippendale frame in the hall. In the entry leans a massive polished ammonite, abandoned by the previous tenant. "Couldn't lift it to take it away," explains Mr. Linnison, demonstrating. "And nor more can I." Though, somehow, it was transported all the way from the west end of Monmouth Beach.

The Bucklands are invited to dinner and arrive while Letitia is still dressing. "Here's a beauty," says Buckland. It's the ammonite he means; he crouches to examine it, abandoning his wife. Henry looks at her curiously – a small, awkward collection of parts (both bony and curvaceous) dressed in pale green chambray. From upstairs floats the chiding voice of Sally, the nursery maid, and an indignant response from the baby. Buckland gets to his feet and surrenders his hat, revealing a pate newly hairless, except for its victorious forelock. "*Paracoroniceras lyra,*" he says to his wife.

In the drawing room, Henry raises a glass to his guests. "I wish you the joy of each other," he says, thinking it a wish likely to be fulfilled. Fate has granted the professor a rare gift, it seems, a clever woman equipped by her own peculiarities to tolerate his. She moves like the geckos of Henry's childhood, standing frozen by the window one minute, and the next, materializing with chin held high on the edge of a chair across the room. Buckland himself has strolled over to the cuckoo clock they carried home from Switzerland, and is manipulating its chains so that the tiny bird within pops in and out in a frenzy.

Letitia trips through the door and across the carpet, dressed in a delicate gown that recalls the muslin of her girlhood. She curtsies to both guests. "The bow is bent, the arrow flies, the winged shaft of fate," she murmurs mischievously as Buckland kisses her hand: it's the start of a charming performance she can sustain for about ten minutes. But the sight of Mrs. Buckland in her lettuce-coloured ensemble breaks Letitia's rhythm. She allows a fatal pause, and then Buckland is in, snatching them away from romance and into his recent escapades in the ochre caves of Wales. Only the maid announcing dinner can pry them all from the ochre caves of Wales.

Over the soup, Letitia finds an opportunity to turn the lovers back to the circumstances of their first meeting. Indeed, they are eager to tell: the damaged wheel at Oxfordshire (what he said, what she said, what the coachman said), the bread and cheese and figs she carried, the clasp knife he was able to provide. *Recherches sur les ossemens fossiles* serving as a table. It's the sort of joint entertainment Henry has often seen newly paired couples attempt. That impromptu picnic in the coach was a scant four months ago. Now Mrs. Buckland is occupied in furnishing their new home. Buckland has made a tabletop for the hall table, a mosaic of sectioned coprolites that his wife calls *fossil rejectamenta*.

Henry looks across at Letitia, but mercifully, she's wearing the mother-of-pearl earrings she bought in Paris. "We may soon relocate to Jamaica," he says by way of accounting for their status as renters. "The situation there has worsened in a way that no one anticipated. As an absentee planter, I consider the blame for this to be mine, at least in part." Letitia sits with her eyes fixed to the tablecloth. Mrs. Buckland has straightened her spine. On her face dances the desire for a debate on the morality of her host's sources of income. "In any case," Henry says, deciding not to provoke everyone further for the moment, "the last year has been full of event for all of us." The baby emits a corroborating cry from the room above.

The fish is brought in, a mackerel dressed with parsley. As Daisy serves it, Henry's eyes are caught by the iridescent green jewel at Mrs. Buckland's throat: it's a hummingbird's tiny head. He feels misery rising like a gas from his diaphragm, his buoyancy draining away. He resolutely turns towards Mrs. Buckland and offers her a smile.

"I have been thinking a great deal about *time* in these weeks since our return," he says. "Not just about the profound effect on our destinies of certain single moments, but how elastic time is.

Some days you are to bed before you properly know that you have risen. Other days seem an eternity as they transpire."

"Indeed," says Buckland intently. "And if I may be excused for turning to natural philosophy over dinner, in this very phenomenon may lie the solution to the scientific problem that has vexed us for years. Perhaps our interpretation of the *day* and the *week* in the Genesis account has been all too literal from the beginning. Scripture itself tells us that a day with the Lord is as a thousand years, and a thousand years as one day."

Mrs. Buckland makes a sly movement with her fingers. "You assert that the sun rose and set over two million times during the week of Creation?" she said.

"Not necessarily, my dear," says Buckland. "It's always possible the earth rotated more slowly that week. A prudent measure, from a mechanical point of view, for so new and complex a system. And given the molten nature of the primary rock, a cooling period would have been necessary. Newton himself allows the possibility."

Everyone is momentarily silent, contemplating the notion of the sun taking a millennium to crawl across the heavens. Henry peels back the black skin on his piece of mackerel. And then Mrs. Buckland abandons Newton and the sun. She moves back to Oxford, to a story of her husband's folly, eagerly describing the bear Buckland has procured for himself. A tame bear, it wears an academic gown and cap. It is introduced to the Oxford dons at garden parties as Tiglath Pileser. She named it herself – William told her she might. The mutton is carried in and Henry must carve, a task he sets about silently. Letitia is trying hard to catch Henry's eye, but he resists her.

With the last spoonful of pudding, Letitia turns to Mrs. Buckland and suggests that they imitate ladies on the Continent and join the gentlemen after dinner. Henry recalls no such custom, but he makes his way around the table and offers Letitia his arm, almost withdrawing it at the savage look she gives him.

"Will you be attending at the annual meeting of the Geological Society?" Buckland asks when they're settled in the drawing room.

"I intend so."

"You're going to London?" says Letitia with sudden interest, but Buckland is speaking over her, asking Henry about the Jardin. Which of Cuvier's savants did Henry meet? Henry goes through the list. Buckland remarks on how they managed to keep their posts through so many political transformations.

"Indeed, it shows an admirable talent for dissembling," says Henry. "You and I would not so reshape our science to suit our masters." Buckland's eyes are fixed on the fire; he declines to take the bait.

"Lamarck was not present?"

"No, and I was especially sorry not to have the opportunity to meet him. While in Paris, I read his recent paper with great interest. He begins by studying invertebrates – molluscs in the Paris basin – and finds slow changes that seem to act as an index to the age of the rocks. It would appear to be a useful method in identifying strata where there's been a disturbance in the earth. I have been wondering whether we could work with Mary Anning to use the ammonites in the same way."

"Mary Anning may not condescend to work with my husband," says Mrs. Buckland, putting up her chin. "She recently expressed scorn for his knowledge of the lias fossils. Mrs. Murchison reported this to me."

"She has taken to wearing a gentleman's top hat," says Letitia suddenly. "I saw her yesterday, climbing up from the shore. Is she deliberately ridiculing her betters?"

"She's simply being practical," says Henry.

"What is practical about a top hat?" cries Mrs. Buckland. "They were designed solely and purposefully for ostentation, to add inches to a gentleman's height."

"On the contrary," says Henry. "Such a hat will provide Miss Anning protection from falling rocks. A modicum of protection, at least."

"She *parades* her lack of femininity," says Letitia. "What can be her motive? It must provoke disgust even in men of her own class."

"It is not the top hat that accounts for our discomfort with Mary Anning," says Henry. "It is Mary Anning's superior knowledge in all subjects related to her field. It is her refusal to pander to male vanity and pretend that the gentlemen with whom she discourses have come to this knowledge before her. That is the true challenge Mary Anning presents to men of every class."

In the satisfying silence that follows this little speech, he gets up and crosses to the window. He opens the casement with the thought that, when the tide is in, as it will be now, its roar might be heard as high as Pound Street. The only sound that floats in is the cooing of doves in the ash grove. He has spoken to Mary only once since his return. She was with Miss Philpot, down at the jetty taking up sea water in buckets to clean their fossils. Behind them, patient horses dragged their caravans into the waves. She was still in mourning. Her face was a bit thinner, but the black bonnet imparted a new elegance to her appearance. He offered his condolences, and she thanked him and met his eyes calmly. He stood there, bereft of words, and gems of sunlight scattered off the flailing forms of supplicants lowering themselves into the water.

"I ran into Colonel Birch last night," Henry says finally. "He tells me that Mary Anning has secured a London agent."

"And who would that be?"

"George Sowerby."

Buckland recoils sharply in his chair. "Related to the botanical artist?"

"Eldest son of. A most esteemed and well-connected fellow. It is excellent news for Miss Anning."

Buckland raises his eyebrows and presses his lips together in a sour approximation of gladness for Mary.

"On another subject, Mr. Buckland," Henry says. "A disturbing rumour concerning yourself has made its way across the Channel. The French are greatly agitated by a report that you participated in the desecration of the remains of their greatest monarch. I stoutly denied it on your behalf."

Buckland emits a high-pitched whinny of a laugh, and Henry sees that he is guilty. So does Mrs. Buckland: a little frown appears on her forehead.

"I see," Henry says. "And how ever did Lord Harcourt gain possession of the heart of Louis XIV?"

Buckland gets up and crosses to the hearth, so that they are both standing. He reaches for the poker and begins to rearrange the coals with every appearance of nonchalance, but a sudden flush has risen in his cheek. "The royal tomb was ransacked during the revolution. I believe this particular relic changed hands several times in the intervening years. Someone approached Harcourt about it at Versailles, just sidled up to him in the garden. I suppose he'd been noticed in Paris buying all manner of nonsense. He has quite an amusing collection of esoterica."

"So he was displaying it at Nuneham?"

"In a silver casket."

"And when he showed it to you, you snatched it up and ate it?"

Buckland props the poker back at the hearth. He shrugs and slouches to his chair, never once raising his eyes to meet the three pairs of eyes fixed on him. "And a nasty morsel it was! I later learned that it was *gangrene* that dispatched the Sun King! Nothing I've eaten revolted my digestion more—except possibly the hyena. But it was worth it to see the expression on Harcourt's face. He'd paid a fortune for that putrid lump. A king's ransom, dare I say, ha?"

"So I see I needlessly tarnished my reputation in defending yours." Henry is still standing at the window. "I was also questioned as to why you've not announced the discovery of a massive land reptile found at Stonesfield."

"Everything in good time." Buckland sprawls in his chair with legs outstretched. His lips are pulled tight across his teeth: this is rage disguised as geniality. "Tell me, Henry. How was your assault on Mont Blanc?"

"It failed. No doubt you've heard."

"Doubtless there will be other opportunities." He begins to kick the hob with a boot. "If I may say, Henry, about your notion of organizing the fossils by the light of the strata, or the strata by the light of the fossils—it is manifestly a fool's enterprise. Which is to be taken as absolute index?" He continues to beat out a rhythm on the hob. "In any case, I quarrel with the direction such studies tend, the pernicious theory behind it, which is one of gradual change. I quarrel with finding man a crocodile improved." He reaches a hand towards his wife's chair and turns an affectionate eye towards her, as though in her upright, dumbfounded form is proof positive. "I fear there is a draft from that window. Are you warm enough, my dear?"

⊰❪ T H I R T Y ❫⊱

ary had a new companion and she stopped in at the quarry to show him off.

"Mr. Bennett gave him to me. He belonged to their William."

"No dogs where William's gone, poor perisher," someone said. The quarrymen leaned on their picks among the broken stone, their faces masks of dust.

"What be 'er name?" Simon Larch asked.

"*Tray*, Bennett called him."

"Where's the sense in that?"

"Do you expect sense from a Bennett?"

Mary was ready to leave, but the dog had vanished. She whistled and he came bounding out – he'd been investigating one of the tunnels. "You'll be flattened when these cliffs collapse," she scolded him. "And they will, you know," she said to the men. "Why does Phelps have you digging so deep?"

"Do you expect sense from Old Phelps?" Simon said.

That was true enough. Just the morning before, Mary had been looking out the window at the rain and had seen Phelps's opulent new four-in-hand driven into the square. Heedless of getting wet, she'd run out and tapped on the window where the owner of the lime quarry sat, and the liveried groom had come round and opened the door. "You are destroying Church Cliffs," Mary had cried. "They will never sustain such undermining with all this rain."

In spite of the rain, Mr. Phelps had paid her the respect of putting his head out of the carriage door. "What do you suggest I do?" he said helplessly, charmingly. "There is a prodigious hunger for Dorsetshire lime in Paris and London – they can't get enough of it. I had three more orders today."

"Set gunpowder under the cliffs!" Mary shouted in rage as he drove away. "Blast them down and be done with it!"

She said goodbye to the quarrymen and walked up towards Black Ven. Tray followed at her heels as though he'd belonged to her forever. She had three skirts on her for warmth and her varnished stovepipe hat on her head. Summer was gone. Others had been lucky in collecting that summer, although not Mary. Reverend William Conybeare had been fossiling on this shore and had found a skull he was convinced belonged to the flat vertebrae that intrigued them all. It was narrow, like a turtle's, and its big teeth were set in separate sockets. On the strength of it, he'd coined a name for the creature: *Plesiosaurus*. Mary did not see him or the skull – she heard all this from Miss Philpot – but she understood in a flash. Conybeare was trying to assert his right to a new order of animal before anyone else found a full specimen.

And one day, Mr. Gleed had approached her on Black Ven, all sweaty and agitated, and led her reverently over to something he'd found in the cliff. It looked like the headless remains of an Ichthyosaurus and she told him so, although she couldn't identify the species without the skull. By his crafty expression, she saw that he didn't credit it. The next Sabbath, she stepped into the vestibule of the Independent Chapel and there were some ribs and a few broken vertebrae displayed on a table, with a notice affixed to the wall behind them:

ADAM — 123 FEET

EVE — 118 FEET

THERE WERE GIANTS IN THE EARTH IN THOSE DAYS, GENESIS 6:6.

Now Mary had the shore to herself, and she was glad of it. A week ago, a fog had rolled in, so dense that the townsfolk avoided going out, afraid of disappearing into it altogether. But fog was Mary's ally; it focused all her senses on a little pod of shore. In that pod, she bent to scour the cliff face, cocking her ear for her invisible partners, for the gulls screaming advice and warning, and her father just a few feet ahead, his boot crunching on the shingle. Today, she said to herself. Today the cotton veil would lift its hem and she'd see bones in the rock.

And not ten minutes after starting out, she was proved right. But it was a saucer-eye she saw and a row of familiar grinning teeth set in a trench, high above the tide line. Not the new dragon they were all racing to find, but the uncanny head of a massive Ichthyosaurus.

It turned out to be an *Ichthyosaurus platyodon*, with eight perfect ammonites fused in careless adornment at its neck. Thirty-five feet long – there was much amazement in the town at the size of it. Mary hired Henry Marsden, the chemist's son, to help her. He was a twelve-year-old with a child's ways about him, pulling his hands up into his sleeves in idle moments and flapping them like wings or fins. But he knew how to be quiet and look, and within an hour, he'd learned to tell fossilized bone from rock. They had a month of companionable work, chipping off the overburden of slate.

Then Mary found a five-foot *Ichthyosaurus vulgaris*. This one was so perfectly preserved that between its ribs lay embossed stone that she recognized as bits of skin. A few yards away, she found another. It was an excess of riches. This is what comes when your eye is single, she told herself. Joseph came by in the evening and helped her build frames. She'd been mounting her specimens in hot wax and sand, but no more: a wagon rolled up and a tranter unloaded plaster of Paris in leaden sacks. "A waste of good money, that," Joseph complained, and Mary laughed. She strode beside the cart that carried the frames to the Cobb, parrying jests with the tranter, and then watched the dockers sag under the weight as they carried the bones down into the ship – ancient bones taking to the sea, sailing east up the coast to Southend-on-Sea, and then up a wide river to London, where Mary had never been, but where she might one day go.

Henry De la Beche, Esquire, was back in town from his grand tour, not so prone to smiling and laughing or even to talking as he once was. He and Mary had encountered each other in the lower town when he was first back. She was with Miss Philpot. He had offered his condolences regarding Lizzie and she had replied with the civility that her pride required of her. He did not work the shore now – it seemed he was often off geologizing in other parts. Twice she'd seen him driving his barouche alone up Church Street towards the Charmouth Road, his valise in the back, but she never saw him return.

Then one day, when she was waiting in Cockmoile Square, he materialized in front of the table. She got quickly to her feet. She had no idea how he had crossed the square. He greeted her and bent to greet her dog. "I have something for you, Miss Anning," he said, straightening up. He held a small paper package out to her, and she took it and unwrapped it to find a pocket watch worked in gold. "I bought it in Switzerland, in a shop with clocks ticking on every wall. You should carry a timepiece when you work the shore, you know. One day, it might save your life."

She thrust the package back at him. "Timepieces are for them that can't read the sun and the tides. I have no interest in frippery."

He was not deterred. "Take it, Mary," he said gently. "Let me give you that." Across the square, puddles of water gleamed in the sun. His hand was on the table now, an inch from hers.

She pulled her hand back. "I'll keep it against a dark day," she said. "It will be easier to hock than the furniture."

That afternoon, she felt queer and was disinclined to go to the shore. She climbed the stairs and lay down for a minute, and then she got up and pulled a box out from under the bed. It was the repository of useless things she could not throw out – short bits of string and the shards of a broken saucer, a comb with missing teeth. She dropped the timepiece into it and then sat on the bed for a moment more, wondering why this fine gentleman, who had everything in the world he wanted, should not leave a poor spinster in peace. Then she went down to the workshop. She would work on her study of the belemnite fossils. Buckland had no idea what the belemnite was, but Mary did, and she would prove it.

A week before, she had dissected a cuttlefish a fisherman sold her, to study its correspondences with the belemnite. She had not been able to separate out the ink bag, and ink had seeped from the flaccid mass of the cuttlefish at every touch – just here on the table were its stains. She ran her finger over them. A pity to have stained this table where her father had made his cabinets, the table where the head of the Ichthyosaurus lay all one winter when she was just a girl. A vexing current of feeling swelled in her chest at the thought of herself back then, how simple and resolute a girl she had been. And then absurd tears stung her eyes. This was his effect on her, Sir Foppling Fossil, and she hated him for it. He had made her cry more than once in the Undercliff, turning her into herself, drawing up her sad stories. That morning at the table he'd taken her off guard – she would need to arm herself against surprises.

And so, waking up in the mornings, she set about judging whether he was in town just then, based on the light and the air. He was certainly home, she decided one morning in late September. But Miss Philpot came by towards noon and she learned that Mr. De la Beche was gone away again, he was in Cornwall, so her science of divining his whereabouts was in its infancy.

A week later, she was at the window and saw him riding up Broad Street, and longing twisted inside her at the sight of him, so *familiar* in his top hat and blue jacket. All his lively way of being in the world apparent in the way he sat his horse. And then she found herself practising jommetry, sending her will out to turn him around and bring him down to the square. Not *Mary's* will – Mary Anning wanted none of it. It was the will of the wayward girl who (without sharing her intentions with Mary) had contrived to be alone with him on the shore, and had showed him the path to climb up to the Undercliff, and lingered with him in the forest. It was that foolish girl returned to bewitch her. So Mary gathered up her tools and took herself out to Monmouth Beach to replenish her store of ammonites. And wandering along Monmouth Beach with her wedge hammer in hand, she found herself in a waking dream where she was on a ship, making for a strange northern shore of red cliffs. A shore he had spoken of one day, a world like theirs but wondrous different, where everything was created anew before your eyes. They were standing on the deck, she and Henry, the two of them dressed in warm cloaks, his arm around her shoulder – and the inexpressible joy and comfort of it made her lean against the cliff and bow her head and choke out tears onto the shingle. It was not Hope, her old enemy, tormenting her in this fashion – Hope was well and truly dead. It was something else, a species of insanity. So prudent, so hard-headed she had been all these many months. But she had let her *anger* go dormant, she had left a chink in her armour, and this insanity had slipped in.

But still she sent her will out, and on the third day, he walked up from Marine Parade and stopped by the table, and the demented creature who had taken possession of Mary regarded this as a potent sign.

"You're not in Cornwall," she said.

"I'm back just briefly. I'm leaving for London tomorrow." Just now he was on his way to the tailor's, where he was having his jackets made over as a means of economizing.

Two French schooners lay at anchor at the Cobb that day, and a party of French tourists strolled about the square. "We always feared being invaded by the French," Mary said. "And now we have been."

Henry looked at her soberly and did not reply. He was a stone thinner, she reckoned, than when he went to France. She turned on him the eyes she turned on rocks, and saw through his ribs to his heart, where sadness lay, and self-pity perhaps, but no love for his wife.

"Wait just a minute." She ran down into the workshop and fetched up the bottle of sepia. "You're using up old things out of thrift," she said. "It's eons old, this ink, and it cost nothing but a little labour." Hours and hours of labour, in fact. This was the fruit of her study of the belemnite – proof positive that the belemnite was like a cuttlefish, made ink. She had reconstituted it from bits of black she'd chipped from the fossils.

He took the bottle, tilting it to admire the ink inside – he seemed quite overcome by this gift. When he was gone, Mary went upstairs to the bedroom and picked the watch out of the box under the bed. It was the size and shape and weight of the best of the pyrite ammonites. It was a buttery gold, softer than the fossils. No one in the square had been watching to interpret this gift as the world would interpret it, there was only Mary to decide what it meant. The watch had a satisfying weight to it, and she found a length of ribbon and hung it around her neck, tucking it away under her waistcoat.

That afternoon, it rained again. Instead of working on her fossils, Mary sat sewing in the kitchen. It was her faded plaid skirt she sewed, refurbishing it, a job she'd had in mind for some time. A simple matter of picking out the stitches that held the skirt to its waistband and refolding the pleats so that the brighter strips that had never seen the sun were now to the outside. She sat and stitched the waistband back on, feeling the watch nestled between her breasts. She had told him things she had spoken of to no one else in her whole life. And he had listened with sympathy – it seemed a sort of miracle when she recalled it now. Then Miss Whyte traipsed into the square like a wicked fairy. After that, Mary had seen nothing but deception and lust – her fury had coloured everything that came before. But in truth, Mary thought as she stitched, his every gesture towards her spoke of kind regard. Kind regard? Her heart began to pound and she had to sit still until her hand steadied. Oh, not *kindness* – she could not let herself put a name to it.

In the evening the rain cleared, and at first light she walked out and sat on a rock at Black Ven to eat her dewbit, looking across the narrow foreshore. Tray sat alertly at her feet. The sea was the very silver of the back of a fish, and Mary felt a peace and happiness she had not felt for many months.

This was the rock where she'd sat with him once long ago, when he had come back from his many journeys a grown man and a stranger to her. They had eaten boiled eggs together, and he'd told her his notion of marriage, which had struck her as marvellous strange – but mayhap, she thought now, explained a great deal. She would have to think back over all their times together, to understand the true meaning of it. The stories of his childhood, which seemed in the nature of a confidence. It was a gift of himself: he had chosen her to talk to above all others. And in her rage, she had regarded his attentions in the sordid way the world would regard them. The world had denied her so much, and it seemed she had joined forces with it.

She finished her bread and sat still on the rock, lost in contemplation, watching with half a mind the waves steal up the sand, and after a time she realized that her eye was snagged on a shape near the water's edge. Something was buried in the clay. It looked like a hand, the long-fingered hand of a sorcerer. She snatched up her tools and walked over to it, crouching. It *was* a hand, though it had an inordinate number of finger bones. The clay came away easily. The hand led to a long bone, which led to another – arm and shoulder bones, she reckoned. She followed this up – and then her trowel exposed a chain of narrow vertebrae, and she felt the back of her neck tingle.

She put the tip of her trowel under one of the vertebrae, prying it out. It broke. The fossil was in a soft marl plateau, exposed overnight by the tide. The marl was not just shrouding the bones from discovery – it was holding them together. But she could see that the vertebra was not indented like an Ichthyosaurus vertebra. It was almost flat, like a shark's. But it was not a shark's – it was five times thicker. She sat back on her heels, breathing hard.

The tide was rising. She pulled her watch out of her waistcoat – she had an hour before the fossil would be under water again. It would take her half of that hour to walk to town for help, and the other half to return. She fell to her knees and set frantically to work. Within twenty minutes she'd exposed a great snake – but halfway down, it sprouted a body with an undercarriage, like a turtle's, and from that undercarriage hung amazing flippers that seemed to be made of fingers, although there were more joints than any earthly finger had. Turning back in the direction where the head should be, she followed the spine up until it petered out to nothing. There was no head.

By the time she'd uncovered the entire fossil, the tide was licking at its tail. She divided the skeleton into sections and pulled sacking out of her basket. She shovelled the sections one by one into separate sacks, running up high to the cliff line to stash each one, the dog barking at her heels in excitement. It was a sin to treat this rare find in this fashion, but by the time the tide rolled out again, it would be worried into dust by the waves.

The minute Mary was back in the workshop with the sacks, she sat down and made a sketch of the bizarre skeleton. People who had not seen this creature lying in its grave would never credit it. The next morning, she set to work rebuilding it on the workshop table, the sketch tacked to the wall. With careful handling, most of the bones held together, but some disintegrated like wet chalk or burnt-out log ends as she touched them. She would reconstruct them as she set the specimen in plaster. For now the roughly reassembled neck lay on the work table, across the blotches of cuttlefish ink. Misshapen continents on a fantastic map, those stains looked now, as if to illustrate the origins of the fossil. Such a pity Henry was not in town to see!

Mary worked all day, deeply absorbed in the job and in her thoughts. It was close to suppertime before she pried herself off the stool. Stepping outside, she could hardly believe how low the sun was over the Cobb. She took a bowl of soup with her mother and then lit candles at intervals along the work table. By their light, she began to fit together the elaborate flippers, making educated guesses as to the place of each crumbling shard. There were *ten* flanges to the longest of them. This beast fit nowhere in the world. She'd been in a dreamlike state when she spied it – she'd never have noticed it when her eye was single.

And this combination of shoulder and arm and flipper – it was brutal and graceless, she could think of no parallel. Science would have a job wrestling with its oddities. Buckland and Conybeare would never fit it into their fairy stories. *We are all wrong*, she said to Henry, to the thin and sober Henry who had come back from France. *I know we are*, he said. Then he was vivid in her mind, his face lit up with eagerness, as it had been when they met at the cliff edge just before his wedding. Their *work* he had talked about, the work they might do together. And what extraordinary qualifications for this job the two of them had together!

By the middle of the night, she was working half asleep. A pain was shooting up from her hip, and her elbow hurt like the dickens. Only one candle burned. There was just the tail left to rebuild. She shifted her own bones on the stool, and jumped at the sight of a white human face watching her from the black glass of the window. She bent over the puzzle of the bones again, over the mucky remains of this fantastic creature that had lashed its tail and writhed itself down into the fearsome deep, where man could not go, where human curiosity and the light of the sun would never penetrate. The sea had made this creature for its own purposes, which are unknown. It is all blind locomotion and no direction, she thought, gazing at the long, headless neck, it is life to no purpose except as life, and then she laid her head down on the table among the ancient crumbling bones and sank into sleep.

That afternoon, she met Colonel Birch on the street. He laboured goutily down the workshop steps to see. "A snake that swallowed a turtle!" he cried. Eighteen shillings her father had been paid for a similar backbone, or so she seemed to recall. Now Birch offered her sixty pounds – that was the difference between a curiosity and a scientific specimen! They agreed that she'd build a frame and set the bones in plaster.

When he was gone, she wrote to Sowerby to ask for clearance to sell it herself, and walked up to the Three Cups to post her letter. Annie and her husband were in the public house and she sat and took a cup with them. When she stepped out of the door, there was one of those extravagant sunsets, the old sun falling into the sea behind the Cobb, everything orange, and Henry was far away in London, and she could not breathe for the dangerous beauty of it. Walking by the smithy's, she got a powerful whiff of the pig penned there. She stood a long time by its pen, marvelling that, in this world, a pig should look so and smell so. Her dog came up to meet her, wiggling with joy, and she bent to scratch his compact, perfect head. Then she walked down to the shore and leaned on the seawall. Every bird in the harbour was wheeling in the crimson sky in celebration of the night, and Mary was near to fainting with fatigue and cider and delirious love for the world.

When at last she went into the house, Molly was down in the workshop. She was standing by the table, rubbing her arms in vexation at the sight of the fossil.

"It's a true dragon, that one," Mary said.

"It's an ugly devil, I know that," said Molly. "Do the bigwigs have a name for it?"

Oh – and Mary thought of her letter to Sowerby. She'd called the specimen a Plesiosaurus – truly, she was a stunpoll! "They may trot out whatever names they please," she said hotly. "It'll be Mary Anning who names this one."

"You'd need Greek for that, my girl."

"I'll need Latin," said Mary. "Mr. De la Beche has Latin."

From the sunshine of Lyme Regis to the smoke and fog of London. Driving in slowly to spare the horses after two long days on the road, watching the towns thicken into a single metropolis, the earth vanish beneath granite and cobbles, the trees disappear. How human to contrive such a home, he thinks, how *not* like the beasts (for everything in his mind now is a sorting of evidence). What a contorted, misguided imitation of the creative function, this London grotesquely bloated from the Regency, grandiose empty domes and plaster statues lining the streets, this lurid artificial light, this incessant reaching up and out. And it comes to him to wonder how far it will go, and what will be the end of it.

He should stay with Clement for the economy of it, but he puts up at the White Horse Cellar Inn. When he comes out on the street, there, for his sins, is Edmund Sutton in beaver hat and trim grey coat. Sutton presses him to sup at a club, and Henry is obliged to go. It is his duty to who he is, to break bread with Edmund Sutton; it is a wilful pressing of his open palm into the burning coals of his dilemma.

Not that Sutton seems at all touched by the questions that rack Henry. He is bland and genial. He complains mildly that his cigar is stale, and presses upon the waiter his disappointment that venison is not on the menu. But over the leg of lamb, he talks of nothing but the uprising at the English colony at Demerara. A dozen planters dead, thousands of slaves from fifty plantations involved.

"How ever do they organize such a thing?" Henry asks.

"It's our own leniency, you know," Sutton says. "My overseer is always giving them leave to travel around the country to attend some burial or other. You heard what was behind it all, didn't you? The revolt? Somehow they got the notion that the king had already freed them and no one was letting on. Somehow a Parliamentary motion in Whitehall made its way out onto the cane fields in the West Indies. I ask you – how was that possible?"

"The planters will talk at table," Henry says, "and they persist in believing that the man standing behind their chair is insensate." He lines his knife and fork up on his plate and wipes his mouth. Perhaps, he thinks, I'll be relieved of the need to act. Perhaps the burden of action will be taken up by people more desperate than I.

The meeting at the Geological Society is set for four o'clock the next day. In the morning, Henry walks through the West End, pressing through crowds filling the streets like a cattle drive. A daylight moon, incongruous, white, floats behind the screen of smoke from a hundred thousand hearths. There on Piccadilly is the Egyptian Hall, the white marble statues of Isis and Osiris that serve as its pillars, carbon-streaked. The auction sale Mary mentioned was held there. From there, Birch's collection (*my* collection, she called it) was disbursed across England and even to France. He pauses at the door but drifts on. And farther up Piccadilly, near the Circus, was the exhibition hall that he'd entered with his uncle all those years ago. The buildings are renovated in this quarter, all put to more respectable uses, and he walks straight along and does not try to puzzle out which door it was.

On Bedford Street in Covent Garden, he presents himself at the offices of the Geological Society. William Babington, the Society's president, happens to be on the premises dealing with correspondence, and receives him warmly. A small, neat man with an expressive, mobile face, a medical man with a passion for mineralogy.

"I won't take up your time," says Henry. "I just want to inquire whether there's room on today's agenda for a further item."

"There is indeed." Babington opens a drawer in the desk and pulls a page out. An iron pen such as Henry has never seen before lies among the samples scattered on the desk, and he takes it up.

"I wish to report on certain ideas I encountered in Paris recently, and canvass the members for their reaction. Begin a debate, I suppose."

"On what subject?" Babington asks, nudging the hinged lid of his inkwell up and dipping the pen.

"On the subject of transmutation, as proposed by Lamarck and Geoffroy Saint-Hilaire and others." He manages to keep his voice even.

Babington's expression changes. He puts the pen down. "Have you a written submission?" When Henry replies in the negative, Babington outlines the policy for agenda items: a written paper, with the signatures of two peers. "I'm sorry. It's a recent policy. I should have mentioned at the outset."

Conybeare is not in attendance and Henry keeps his distance from Buckland. He spies an empty seat by Gideon Mantell, another physician and a most passionate collector. Mantell is somewhat shunned in this company – his over-brushed suit and cadaverous eyes and his general air of reproach and defeat always call up the confinement bed and beakers of leeches, an association Babington somehow manages to escape. In the last year especially, Mantell has become something of a joke for his obsession with certain huge bones and teeth he's been finding at a quarry in Cuckfield. Having subjected them to Cuvier's principles of proportion, he insists they are the remains of an unknown land creature sixty feet long. He nods gravely as Henry sits down. Together they watch Professor Buckland glad-hand his way around the room, his prominent eyes red-rimmed, his gestures comedic. Henry feels the tug of an old affection. Buckland will be occupied in turning his new notion about time into a theory. Apparently, the laws of nature pertain when convenient to our theories, but not otherwise. He will certainly be attacked for it, from both sides, poor fellow – when all he wants is to be admired. But he never bragged about eating the heart of Louis XIV. Maybe he's starting to be frightened by his own compulsions.

Henry leans towards Mantell. "Have you thought of announcing your recent finds? Have you ever discussed this with Buckland?"

"Indeed I have. But Buckland advised me to wait." He makes a little moue. "How can one ignore a caution from such a quarter?"

"Perhaps he's collecting his own evidence to publish in advance of you?" Henry says. He can see Mantell turning this over in his mind as the meeting is called to order.

The meeting is brief and concerned mainly with the orientation of new shafts for a tin mine in Cornwall. In the election of officers, Buckland is duly named president. Afterwards, there's a general movement to a club. Henry slips out and walks back through the West End and into Green Park, where the noise of the city fades. A nurse with a little boy hanging on to each hand walks a path towards him and he looks eagerly at her face. He's in one of those moods where everyone he encounters looks uncannily familiar. He finds a bench to sit on and is overtaken by the anxiety he's been avoiding since he drove away from Lyme.

Letitia's keenness when he first mentioned this trip: it was not a desire to go to London herself, but a desire for her husband's absence. And he is so often absent. A suspicion he thought he had mastered flared up at the sight of her face in that moment, and has since grown. He has no material proof. But it is a fact, daily he is faced with it, that she is fed by an emotional current that has nothing to do with him. He gets up and begins to walk quickly towards Pall Mall, trying to shake off his panic. When she told him she was pregnant, back in Paris, he fixed in his mind the occasion of conception. Just after they left Lyme – he could recall the inn, the disagreeable, distracting smell of the bed linens. But during the whole Mediterranean leg of their tour, he was consumed with anxiety. It began in the southeast corner of France and deepened as they passed into Italy. It became an insane preoccupation. He was not well, he was never well after that night in the Muséum, and his suspicion seemed of a one with the filth and the garlic-reeking food, the gabbling, rude press in the streets, the black-clad quarrelling widows (so resembling his arachnoid mother-in-law), the winking, leering gigolos, the yellow sun, and the smell of sex hanging in everything. Letitia was miserably pregnant by then, and one day, helping her step heavily down from the carriage, it struck him that her pregnancy was the material proof he lacked. She had come straight to him from London because she needed to be married. His mother (it was suddenly clear to him) was complicit in the deception. He can compute a gestation period, and their baby's appears to have been seven months. It's a law of nature, the human gestation period, but somehow his first glimpse of Bessie's puckered red face in the folded opening of a white shawl swept suspicion from his mind. And now it's back.

He's previously set up a two-day meeting regarding a geological survey of Devon. A lucrative contract – he can't afford to jeopardize it. He reads through most of the night to keep Letitia from his thoughts, but by morning, his anxiety is so consuming that he writes to say that a family emergency recalls him to Dorsetshire. Tom had set his heart on two days at Barnaby Fair and he snaps the reins sulkily all the way out the Clapham Road. Indeed, the whole trip was an utter waste of time and energy, typical, Henry thinks, of how he's managing his affairs.

Outside the city Henry falls asleep, and sleeps until they stop at Chertsey. He wakes in an easier frame of mind. Grateful to the cautious Babington, relieved not to have opened that most fraught subject of debate. There was a day when he saw science as the most manifest expression of reason. But really, it's a cauldron of bubbling lava; without warning, it will spill over and destroy them all. He, certainly, doesn't have the stomach for it. He's a thinker no longer, but a meticulous clerk, his intellect reduced to *sorting*, compulsively sorting everything he sees. He'll make a detailed set of charts of the Lyme Regis coast, that's what he'll give himself to, using colour to indicate the type and age of rocks. The thought of it is deeply comforting, a return to an old passion. In the front cover of his notebook is a list of the strata. He takes a pencil out of his bag. As they drive, he begins to make a list of corresponding pigments. He'll hire a boat and do a small-scale schema first. Ink in the general outlines and the major strata, and then begin with the pigments. It will be an immaculate, detailed chart, devoid of explanation. Asking nature to explain itself is pointless. Ask nature a question and it replies with a bank of navy clouds or the red dots in a frond of seaweed, it explains mystery with mystery. He will not ask; he will observe and chart. Others can theorize, those equipped by temperament or circumstances to afford that luxury.

They stop at an inn at Overton for their dinner and rest the horses until mid-afternoon. Back in the barouche, he falls into a reverie of Lyme. He's walking slowly up to the jetty, carrying a mackerel wrapped in a paper. The tide is high; Mary won't be collecting until almost noon. She'll be working at home, rinsing and sectioning and polishing fossils. As he reaches the outlet of the Lyme, she crosses the shore from the back of her house and bends to fill a bucket at the water's edge. He knows her: his knowledge of her life is the deepest comfort of his.

He drives all morning of the second day through rain. After Salisbury he gives the reins to Thomas and dozes with his chin in his chest. All through Wiltshire, he has the sensation that the coach is fixed and the rising landscape of the Southwest is being pulled towards him. In and out of sleep, he develops the happy conviction that his mother-in-law is in Lyme: she will be supervising. But of course, Mrs. Auriol is in Bristol, he realizes when he pulls himself awake. Letitia is alone with the servants. They stop at Sherborne and he takes the reins again.

It's early afternoon of the third day when they roll into town, a Lyme scrubbed clean and heartbreakingly beautiful in the sun. He pulls up at the stable and Tom gets down to open the doors. A tall black gelding with severely docked tail and military caparison stands in the first stall of the stable. A single, material horse. "Coldstream Guards, sir," says Tom.

A plumed hat rests on the stand just inside the door. Daisy hurries down the hall to meet him, to take his hat, her smile frightened. In the slice of drawing room framed by the door, Letitia is reclined on the settee, caught just in the moment of sitting up and swinging her feet to the floor. "Mrs. De la Beche be in the drawing room, zir," Daisy says, "with Colonel Wyndham."

Henry Wyndham! He has his back to the door – he's sitting on a chair drawn up to the settee. He and Letitia both jump to their feet as Henry enters. Letitia is bright-eyed and smiling, intensely present, visibly arranging her thoughts. Wyndham is still taller than Henry. Stouter now, his bland, handsome face a little haggard, sandy hair beginning to retreat from his forehead, but Henry would have known him immediately. His eyes glaze with what can only be fear. Or shame. He begins to talk in an excessively amiable manner. He was staying with friends in Exeter and heard that his old comrade lived in Lyme Regis. He thought to renew an old acquaintance, and to meet De la Beche's wife.

Henry crosses the carpet and shakes his hand. "But you and Letitia *are* acquainted. It was at Ascot that you met, wasn't it?"

"Indeed, as I discovered this afternoon," says Wyndham. Henry is surprised at how inept he is, how ill-equipped for the perfidious enterprise he's launched himself into. He was always inept, but one might have expected ten years as a military officer to have sharpened him. Henry feels his own energy concentrate, as it always did in Wyndham's presence at Marlow, feels himself grow darker, quicker, more audacious and sardonic. He sits down beside Letitia. Clumsily, Wyndham pulls his chair a few feet away from the settee before sitting.

"You discovered?" Henry says, preternaturally calm. "I understood you to have unearthed Letitia's connection to myself on the occasion of your meeting two or three years ago. But never mind. It's remarkable that our paths have not crossed in some drawing room or other in all this decade since I was removed from Marlow. However, my travels have been prescribed by my profession and have taken me in directions very different from yours, I dare say."

For the first time in many months, he is exuberantly alive. He has all of his faculties after all; it is tremendously reassuring. He stretches one arm along the back of the settee, looking at the two with gratitude. Now it's Wyndham's turn to speak, but apparently he can't manage it. "This is really a very pleasant room," says Henry, providing the requisite line. "I'm always glad to return to it after a day in the field."

"You work as an engineer?" Wyndham says finally, shifting in his chair.

"As a geologist. It's a profession that suits me better than I could have imagined. I would have made a poor soldier indeed. And you command a battalion of the Coldstream Guards. Butler told me. I encountered him some time ago in London. Tell me what action you've seen. I believe Letitia mentioned Waterloo?" It's a delightful scene and he wishes it to go on forever.

"We were part of the brave assault on the fortress of Bergen op Zoom in '13. Then we garrisoned in Belgium, and were still there when Napoleon escaped Elba. And so we fought in Waterloo. We held the fortification at Hougoumont, the right flank. I was grievously injured, but my valiant men were able to hold." He has an imprecise articulation that Henry recalls from boyhood – almost a lisp.

"As Napoleon said, long wars make good soldiers. What was the fortification like at Hougoumont? I have heard much of that battle, but I've never been able to envision the site."

Letitia is silent. Her face is pink and her lips pinched together in an uncharacteristic expression. Doubtless she is trying not to cry.

"They call it a *château*," says Wyndham heavily. "But it was just a farmhouse and outbuildings, with a wall around."

"And the French broke through the wall with axes?"

"They had axes, but no call to use them. I regret to say the gate was left open. We were setting up, bringing supplies in. We thought the French miles away. Of a sudden, they burst from the wood nearby and were inside, and we must struggle to close the gate and get the bar across before the fortification was entirely lost."

"Didn't Wellington himself acknowledge that Waterloo turned on the closing of that gate?"

"I believe he did."

"I remember your father from Marlow days. He must be tremendously proud of your military honours. Or – is he still alive?"

"He is." Wyndham inclines his head politely.

There is a dreadful silence.

"You will dine with us?" Henry asks. "Letitia, have a word with the cook."

"No, no. Thank you," says Wyndham. "Very kind, I'm sure, but I'm expected in Exeter."

"What a pity. It would have been amusing to reminisce about our youthful follies. Well, in that case, let me have your mount brought round." He rings for Daisy. They fall back into silence. The Swiss clock ticks in the adamant manner it assumes when you are alone in a room. This must indeed be a wrenching separation for Letitia, for both of them – if regret and pain can make themselves felt through all the other sensations of the moment. Henry watches her, wondering if she will risk a glance at Wyndham, but she does not. She sits with hands clasped, her eyes on the lozenge border of the rug. She's wearing a rose-coloured gown that particularly suits her (as he has often told her, his favourite among her dresses), and it seems the worst of it, that she donned this gown that morning. He suddenly loses his stomach for the scene. The walls of this room are intolerable: it is the blue of insanity. Then Daisy is at the door and he refuses to look up, and so Letitia is obliged to ask to have Colonel Wyndham's horse brought round.

The silence resumes. Finally, Letitia rallies herself to speak again. "Bessie has been a little madame since you went away."

"I'll go upstairs and see her. Excuse me."

He gets to his feet and walks across the room. Up in the nursery, Bessie lies with flushed cheek against the flannel sheeting, deeply asleep. Daisy appears at the nursery door. "Where is Sally?" he asks.

"Her mother be taken ill, zir, and Mrs. De la Beche give Sally leave to see to her. I been seeing to Bessie these three days."

A bright object the shape of a root vegetable lies on the mattress. It's a wooden top, painted blue. He picks it up and thumbs the sharp point at its base. "This is not a toy for such a small child. She will injure herself with it."

Daisy takes it from him. "Oh, I know, zir. But she would not give it up. There was such fits of crying as you wouldn't credit. She must sleep with it these three nights."

"Where did she get it?"

"Colonel Wyndham brung it, zir," says Daisy, meeting his eyes steadily. "As I said, zir, she has not once let it go in all this time."

Wyndham has parted from Letitia. He is moving down the hall to the front door as Henry comes down the stairs. "I hope you were not about to leave without a farewell?" says Henry, taking his arm.

Daisy has left the main doors wide open. They walk past the portrait of Letitia, towards the sunlit green square at the end of the hall. "Tell me – do you have a wife of your own?"

Wyndham is breathing audibly; he will not dare to resist. "We've been estranged some years. The military life and family life are difficult to reconcile." He delivers this last line as though it's a profound and original thought.

They stand at the open doorway by the massive ammonite, waiting for his horse. Henry has picked up Wyndham's hat, and he hands it to him. The grove around the house is tremulous and green, glistening loyally with sun.

"At Hougoumont," Henry says, "by the time you were able to close the gate, how many enemy soldiers had penetrated the *château*?"

"There were thirty forced their way in."

"And you had to kill them all in close quarters?"

"We must needs fight them in a courtyard no bigger than your parlour." He holds the plumed hat to his chest.

"What is it like, hand-to-hand combat with a French soldier?"

Wyndham has flushed. Henry can see perspiration gleaming on his temples. "It was not the sort of fighting we were trained for at Marlow. I was always an artilleryman."

"Indeed," says Henry. "But tell me what actually transpired." Tom comes up the shingle drive leading Wyndham's horse, but Henry puts a hand on Wyndham's arm to detain him. "How does one fight at such close quarters, and unprepared? Did you have your muskets about you?"

Wyndham shakes his head. "They would have been useless in any case, or certainly after one shot. It was a schoolboy brawl to the death." He puts his hat on. He will not meet Henry's eye. "To this day, I am sick to my stomach to hear a man scream, or to hear Frenchies shouting their oaths. I have been left with a horror of a closed door." On his face is the misery of having given up something he did not wish to disclose.

"Letitia alluded to something of the sort several years ago,"

Henry says. He moves into the entrance. "I'd like to understand such an injury. Such a pronounced wound to the spirit. A wound that is not physical." The horse tosses its head impatiently and again Wyndham makes to leave, but Henry blocks his way. "How, physically, does one kill a man with bare hands?"

There is another anguished pause. Henry is filled with pity for Wyndham, and disgust, that even now the man cannot withstand him. "There was strangulation," Wyndham says finally in his halting way. "Cracking heads on the paving stones. That sort of thing. Those that had daggers used them."

"And I suppose the French had the axes you spoke of," Henry says.

They do not take a formal leave of each other. Colonel Wyndham has a slight limp, Henry notes as he makes his way to his horse, the physical souvenir of an injury sustained in a battle that he won.

Letitia has not moved when he returns to the drawing room. He stands in the doorway and looks at her. "You are elaborately bedecked, Letitia, for a chance social call."

She looks at him defiantly. "Is a gentlewoman, the instant she crosses the threshold of marriage, to abandon all the delicacies and decencies by which she attracted her husband?"

"Do we consider lace and corsets a particular of *decency*?"

She doesn't answer. From the kitchen comes the sound of dinner preparation. "Come upstairs with me," he says. He goes quickly up the stairs and into her room, and she follows. He reaches around her and closes the door. The bed is made and the room is tidy. On her dressing table is her little clock and the clay curlers, lined up on their warming tray. The remains of a fire burn in the hearth; she often occupies herself in her room past midday. There is her pitcher and basin, a few inches of cloudy water in the basin. The first time he undressed her, when the meagre muslin gown was still in vogue, he discovered her trick of wetting her petticoat before she donned it so that it would cling to her. Removing it was like peeling back a skin.

He stands at the side of her bed. "This door, at least, he is prepared to close?"

She is very frightened. When they argue, he often feels he's exploiting an advantage with words, as low as a man's use of strength to lay a woman back on a mattress. He's surprised by how gentle his voice is now. "You have deceived me, Letitia, in a most egregious way." If she were clever in the way that he is clever, she would not deny the affair, but she would protest this charge. *There was no deceit*, she would say. *Five minutes after I first laid eyes on you, I followed you into the woods alone.*

But she is not clever in that way. In a high and shaking voice, she professes indignation at his lack of trust. She professes her right to innocent companionship when her husband is so often away. Gathering confidence, she asks herself whether she can live with a husband who so impugns her honour, who so neglects her, who treats her with such cruelty. By then she is crying – it is the piteous image of her own plight that finally releases her tears. His composure, the pride and indifference that served him so well this last hour, crumbles. He snatches up his last resort, his mother's customary last resort, and threatens her with Jamaica.

Later he sits alone in his study, watching the light gradually withdraw from the ash grove outside the window. Within his chest cavity, a relentless thrumming is causing him pain. There was one insane moment in her bedroom when he contemplated undressing her, saw himself undoing the laces of her corset, laying her back on the bed, running his hands up her thighs, exposing the warm, wet place within her skirts, an entry prepared by his rival.

As a sort of experiment, he would do it (with his eyes on her face the whole time): to see how far she would go in her duplicity, how far she would suffer him to go. A hideous, lost opportunity to know himself, to see whether and in what fashion his body would respond, to learn what it is that his manhood comprises.

He opened the door to this, to all of it, he thinks heavily, although he lacks the energy to trace that thought to its source. He did not speak of the baby to Letitia – he can't give Wyndham that. They *will* go to Jamaica. Mentally, he casts his family into his long-ago childhood: Little Bessie plays on the wide, airy veranda of Halse Hall, reaches her plump arms up to her coloured nanny, is carried down a wickered path, lying in pseudo-sleep with her eyes open against her nanny's bosom. Letitia clutches the hull of an upside-down lifeboat, tossed by indifferent turquoise waves, while he lies alone in a tropical inn, floating on fever under a mosquito net, eyes half open to a dirty room he's never seen before.

"You are a child," Mary said to him once. Somewhere on the Continent, in one of the reeking cathedrals, he saw in an illuminated bible the depiction of a dying man. A hanged man – Judas Iscariot, it must have been. The Devil hovering over him on black wings, pulling the poor wretch's soul out from between his ribs, his soul in the shape of a sturdy little boy.

⚬[T H I R T Y - T W O]⚬

O n the second day of October, when a gleam in the clouds over the Channel told her Henry was at home, she went to his door, walking across the shingle drive in her renovated plaid skirt. For all it was past Michaelmas, the air was warm and close, like an August day, and the notion of inviting him up to the Undercliff had raised its head like a bright-eyed fox looking over a mound. In the library, she told him about her strange find, and they talked about the fact that mammals have always the same number of vertebrae, even in the case of the camelopard with its long neck, while in birds and reptiles, the number of vertebrae varies. Their conversation (which began in the library but took them to the western shore and continued in the Undercliff) distracted them from making even a pretence of collecting. But she came away from it sure that he would help her, and at the stationer's on Broad Street, she paid seven shillings for a leather-bound book with blank pages in which they would draft a text about the new fossil. After that, she felt more driven than ever to find a full specimen. As winter set firmly in, she spent all her time in the area of Black Ven, where, if one serpentine reptile had died and been preserved, surely others had as well.

Meanwhile, Reverend Conybeare visited Colonel Birch in Charmouth, with the express purpose of studying the new find. She did not see him, but Colonel Birch told her. She had not seen him for years, in fact. If Henry had been there, she would have asked him why his friend had such a consuming interest in this fossil. But Henry had gone away again. She'd been standing on Church Cliffs and seen him leave with his groom driving him. Well, there was enough in their last conversation to sustain her for the entire winter, if need be.

In December, Mary found it. It was evening, and so cold that she had no fingers at all as far as she could tell. She had been about to turn back home when she spied the characteristic rounded surface and defining edge of a vertebra. On closer examination, six or eight smooth discs peeped out. The matrix was shale and limestone. It would be hard to excavate, but the fossil would be more enduring.

"Stay," she said to her dog, and he crouched conscientiously, guarding the fossil. In the town she recruited Henry Marsden, her brother Joseph, and then Simon Larch and George West, whom she encountered as they left the quarry. They all ran home to fetch lanterns. At Black Ven, Tray was still guarding the fossil, although he had edged a foot or two backwards to avoid the rising water.

"About here?" said Joseph, setting his stone chisel a foot beyond the bones.

"Use your wits!" Mary cried. She forced them to cut a slab that allowed for three feet at either end. The vertebrae were three inches across; you had to assume a body length of five feet for every inch of diameter to a vertebra. All the time they dug that huge trench, they were cursing her under their breath. But they did it. They worked through a freezing night in sea spray to chip out a pedestal under the fossil, and then, in early light, they recruited a gang of helpers and broke it off and carried it up to the workshop in its matrix.

This creature was nine feet long – so her calculations had been about right. And it was intact, and solid. In the workshop, she chipped open the neck first, thirty-five vertebrae, and discovered a narrow old boot stuck to the top of the spine – the head, not much wider than the vertebrae. An almost brainless reptile, breathtakingly disproportionate. Conybeare's name for it meant "almost a lizard" – or so Miss Philpot said. It was utterly meaningless. She would find a better.

She would let Henry know by post. She could walk up to Aveline House or to the Grove and ask his whereabouts, but something in her revolted at the thought of approaching Mrs. Aveline or Letitia. She would write to Buckland. He had not been working that fall – a fragment of rock had lodged in his eye when he was wielding his hammer, and he'd had several surgeries. To inform Buckland was to inform everyone of his acquaintance. She would send a drawing. It was a careful drawing, but a graceless one – a cry for help, to show such a drawing to Henry De la Beche. She sent it and within a week, her reply drove into the square in the form of a robed professor sporting a black patch over one eye, and Mary felt a stab of disappointment at the sight of him.

He could hardly stop to greet her, so eager was he to see the specimen. "Holy Methuselah!" he cried when he reached the bottom step and clapped his one available eye upon it. "No wonder we've never found a head. You need a jeweller's loupe to see it!"

"The body is five feet across, counting the flippers, and the head is four inches wide," said Mary proudly, as though the extremity of the creature were entirely to her credit. "But the head is perfect and complete. And note – the teeth are not in grooves, like the Ichthyosaurus. It has the teeth of a crocodile."

"Glorious!" exclaimed Buckland, pacing around it. "It deserves to be cast in gold and circulated over the universe."

By wonderful chance, Reverend Conybeare had been in Oxford when the news came; he was there to deliver a guest sermon. "I found him in his lodgings surrounded by his women: the wife, the daughters, the unavoidable spinster relation. His sermon was on the morrow, and he was just in the midst of writing it. The news threw him into such a frenzy that he was unable to finish. My eye fell on the spinster sister-in-law, a barnacle, dare I say it, upon the household since the day Conybeare married. *There's a task for her*, says I. So he sets her to work on the sermon, chuffed that for once she's earning her supper, and we gallop off to the printers to have plates made of the drawing. Then we settle ourselves down with a celebratory bottle of port."

"I'm sorry you're printing the crude drawing I sent you," said Mary. "I intend to ask Mr. De la Beche to make a formal illustration. Have you seen him?"

"The Bristol Society is meeting tonight," said Buckland. "Conybeare is hastening down so as to make an announcement. Difficult to discuss the find without an illustration."

She asked him again about Henry. He shook the question off with annoyance. "How would I know where he is? Am I the fellow's keeper?"

She had been standing on Church Cliffs the morning Henry left, and she had noted the number of valises and cases in the barouche. She could have watched him all the way up the road, but she'd turned away. It was ill luck: you would never see someone again if you watched them out of sight. "Whist," she'd called to her dog, to move him down the path and prevent him looking as well. She'd been surprised that Henry had not come by the table to say goodbye. He communicates through silence now, she'd told herself. Well, silence I have in abundance.

She cleaned the creature with the greatest care, and set it in a frame for transport. It was a massive frame, six feet wide and ten feet long. Whether or not she wanted to sell this specimen, she would have to. Prices were depressed at that moment, but it would still bring a hundred pounds. It might be a decade before she earned more than shillings again. But she could delay the sale until they classified the creature and made a formal announcement. She imagined Henry, trimming his side-whiskers and donning one of his wonderful coats and carrying the paper in to the Geological Society, a paper with both their names on the front.

Except that Henry remained stubbornly away. At night, when it was so dark you could not tell the sea from the sky, she climbed the hill and stood looking out over the town, flittermice swooping and darting around her. The moon rose while she stood there shivering, the slate roofs of the houses across the valley showing up as separate patches of pale grey. She counted out the houses until she'd picked out the roof of the Grove, and then she went again over every detail of the day she'd gone into the library of that house, a story that seemed, these days, to have a different meaning every time she told it to herself.

On that October day of summer haze, she had knocked boldly on the front door of the Grove. "Your card, miss?" said Tom, Henry's lanky young groom. Then he laughed and held out a hand for Mary's top hat. He went up the hall and Mary waited beside the huge *ammonite coroniceras* that she herself, with Joseph's help, had hauled up from the western point on a carrying board. The timepiece was turned on its side and digging into her breast, and she nudged it flat inside her waistcoat. In a minute, Tom was back, inviting Mary into the library. Henry was standing by the desk. He crossed the room to greet her, a look on his face that suggested he had brought her up the hill by his own practice of jommetry. He did not contrive a pause that would ask her to explain her purpose, but led her to a chair and began with the courtesies the high-born employ in a social call. He asked if she would mind sitting where they were, as he found the drawing room unpleasant, and then he called a maid to bring sherry in. He was pale and his sidewhiskers stood in the shadow of unshaved beard. He said that his wife was in London and had taken two of the servants, and that he himself was busy with plantation affairs. He'd had to let his overseer go but had managed to hire a new one in Kingston. Not an experienced man, but one who seemed in his correspondence to have a progressive attitude. "I was relieved," he said, "to find a fellow who will try by whatever means to ameliorate the conditions of the poor creatures we employ."

But the new overseer spent his days writing plaintive letters to England, seeking advice regarding the most routine of matters. "What am I to do with this?" Henry said humorously, waving a letter before her. "It was posted in June and arrived yesterday. It will be the new year before my reply reaches Jamaica. By then, he will have found his own method of dealing with the thieving of the bookkeeper's boots." This was his usual jocular way of talking, but his eyes had smudges of sleeplessness under them. It was a wonderful room, rock samples scattered on the shelves, and row upon row of books, a room filled with the cooing of doves and with air from all its windows open, and he sat alone in it, misery and sadness exuding from him. *Creatures we employ*, he said. *Slaves* he did not say. She pitied him terribly. How could your eye be single in such a world as his? The sherry itself had a cloying, too-smooth taste, the taste of artifice.

But for all that, a glass of sherry in the hand cries out to be drunk, and she drank it down at once and told him about her headless, crumbling find, recently sold to Colonel Birch. He looked up in quick interest and said they must go out and look for the head. "There is no point," Mary said. "The whole muddy ledge was taken away by the tide. But you must visit Colonel Birch one day to see the rest of it. I was astonished by the neck. Longer than a swan's, proportionately."

Both of them turned to look at a framed picture hanging on the wall, a study of a bird and its skeleton. She got up and went over to it, and so did he. They stood and counted the neck vertebrae of the little sparrow he had painted. Nine.

"Do you still have the skeletons?" she asked.

"No. They were thrown out during one of my absences. This is the only picture I have. The dunnock. A canny bird, or at least the female is. She will court a second male and mate with him. It's a clever strategy to get both males to feed the chicks."

What a bitter edge there was to his voice. "Do you still paint?" Mary asked, feeling regret that no pictures done in ancient sepia adorned his walls.

"No. I must needs earn my keep now," he said, turning towards her a look such as she had never seen from him. They were standing very close together. And then he put his hand lightly on her waist. A downdacious gesture, except that the air between them was already holding them as close as an embrace.

There was no sound from the servants. A man can do as he likes in his own house, thought Mary. But then a child squealed above them and something fell in a series of thumps down the stairs, and there was muffled laughter and more squeals.

"Mary, have you time to go to the shore?" he asked.

"Yes," she said, her heart beginning to bang in her ears.

They took up their hats and walked out onto the drive. When any two souls walk together, there is one who signals the way they will walk, and it was Mary who turned ever so subtly at the corner, Mary's foot that fell in an angle that implied *west*, towards the Undercliff. A private word, that's all I want, she was saying to herself. When the road branched down, they took it and walked out on Monmouth Beach under the hazy sky. She went swiftly ahead, as she always did, to show the best way across the Devil's treacherous stones. Finally they were on the smooth ammonite pavement at the end of Monmouth Beach, and then they were around the point and could see Pinhay Bay, the white surf and the fog that veiled the wandering shore beyond it, one tier laid on another, and gulls soaring and dipping, vanishing into it on their snowy wings. She stopped and waited for Henry. He stumbled just as he came up to her. She put out a hand and he clung to her.

"I don't know how to look at it," he said, as though she had commented on the beauty of the scene. "I see God withdrawn from it all."

"Well," said Mary, looking closely into his eyes, with their irises of brown and green. "Well, it is no less the miracle for that."

They moved up the foreshore towards the cliff face and she let his arm go and began to climb. It had been two years and the path at the top was entirely laced over with vines: it opened like a throat. They scrambled into it, and then the ground levelled off and Mary looked back and saw the sea below them through the trees, and then the torn thatch of Digby's hut where a bird had made an untidy nest.

When they came to the clearing, she did not sit down – she turned to face him. He took off his hat and held it in his hands. "I always thought of this as Eden," he said. "The question was – who was I? Adam or the serpent?" There was the old cleverness in his words and on his face, and she could not bear it.

"You have changed," she said. "What changed you?"

"Oh, Mary," he said. He dropped his hat and turned slightly away from her. "Oh, Mary, my dear —"

She would not let him turn away. She reached out and drew him to her, pressing her body against his, and gave him such a kiss as she had wanted to give him for many a month. She stepped back then and began to undo his cravat, unwinding it from around his neck, and with his white cravat dangling from one hand, she turned and waded through the bracken to the roots standing up at the end of the fallen tree in a frazzled mass. For a minute she thought he was not following, but then he stepped around the roots and she drew him into the den, this den that, all the months they'd come to the clearing and all the months since, had been furnishing itself with a carpet of moss and bracken. He made to ease her down to the moss, but she stumbled back a step and began to unbutton his waistcoat. When it was off, he reached up himself and pulled his shirt over his head, and she ran her hands around him and felt the separate vertebrae that stitched his backbone. She felt his sadness leave him then, she felt life surge back into him, and she gladly met it. Then they were on the moss, he was helping her with her skirt, he was pushing her stocking down, stroking the soft skin at the top of it. This was a hunger, she saw, that grew by being fed. "Mary, I will hurt you," he said, trying to slow her, but she would not wait. There was a knife pain to it, but a pain so silvered by desire that she tilted her hips into the plush of the moss for more of it, until the pain was all suffused with something else and finally with white light trembling in a sheet.

It was all so quickly done, but afterwards they lay in its glow. A wonder to see him, a beast among the autumn green. With his skinny flanks, and the slight beginning of a belly (he was not so thin with his clothes off), and the line that ran from his muscled chest to his navel. She kissed that line and ran a hand along the cage of his ribs. In the forest light, their skin had a greenish tinge, the skin of things that grow in secret. They lay and talked in low voices, and she told him everything – Lizzie's sad dying and the *Outlines of Geology* and her intention to take charge of a new find – and all the while, her body lay warmly the length of his, and his arms were around her as if it was a treasure he held. He picked up one of her hands then and kissed it. "Oh, my geological maiden," he said.

"Even old Cuvier will marvel," Mary said stoutly.

"I went to his salon in Paris, you know."

"I thought you must have. What did you see there?"

"I saw a pseudo-science that issues from the foul imagination of man. I saw the end of all our theories. I saw myself." Mary raised herself up on her elbows in shock, but his face was bland, as though he had said nothing of significance. He laid her back down and smiled, leaning over her, folding her heavy braid in his hand to admire it. Tenderly, he traced the red mark on her neck made by the ribbon that carried her timepiece. "Your watch is too heavy to be worn this way," he said.

"I need to sew a pocket into my skirt."

"They sell ladies' watches to be pinned to a dress by a brooch. That's what you should have had."

It was in that moment that melancholy rose up between them. He bent and kissed her, and it may have been that he felt the gooseflesh that had come out on her, for he sat up and reached for his shirt and pulled it on. It was chilly after all. When he drew his trousers towards him, his talisman fell out of the pocket. She picked it up. "I was a child when I sold this to your mother. All these years, it's protected you. We used to sell them as a charm against blindness."

"You shouldn't have advertised blindness, Mary," he said. "It's never helped me with that." Then he was kneeling beside her with his face in her hair, and he said something she did not care to hear, words she let fall into the bracken.

"Go back first," she whispered. She lay still with her eyes open. All she could see was his legs and feet as he moved about dressing himself. She was overcome with languor. She did not lift her head to take in the rest of him, and then he moved out of her line of vision and she knew he was gone down the path. Still she lay, with her skirt pulled loosely over her. She had seldom lain on the ground. In spite of the damp, she felt like a child held by a firm, kind bed, and thought that it would be fine, after she died, to be buried so, with the weight of the earth piled upon her.

·◄[T H I R T Y - T H R E E]►·

In that overwrought winter, while the dragon with the shrunken head slept in the workshop and Mary waited for Henry to drive back into town, another terrible gale blew up. It was spring tide, and it rose three hours before it was due; no one had ever seen the water so high. Joseph stopped to ask them up to his house on Church Street, and they slept the night in the attic there, although the Lyme was low and the houses on Bridge Street were unlikely to flood. But it was a disastrous gale – beyond any in the memory of the townspeople, for the Cobb was breached in the night, and all the ships sheltering in it were washed away, and two men in the revenue tender drowned. And then the sea was unfettered and the towering waves were free to smash the town. Two houses at Cobb Hamlet were destroyed, and part of the Folly Public House. In the morning, Mary stood up on the edge of the western cliff and looked down at a marvel: the Cobb that had lain for hundreds of years holding its brood of boats in its long arm, saying to the sea *Thus far and no farther,* broken open now to a width of thirty feet, and huge breakers smashing against Marine Parade. No ships would enter the harbour that winter; indeed, there was no longer a harbour to enter. It would be a winter without coal.

The Annings had money and had thought that for once they were well provisioned. There was a brown hen underfoot and two hams hanging in the inglenook, a basket each of russets and swedes in the corner, and, in the dark space under the bed, sacks of dried beans and peas, sorted this year by Molly. But apparently there was a decree that they should continue to suffer. Not that the Annings, or even the town of Lyme, had been singled out for hardship and privation. All of England was seized with a shocking cold. One frosty morning when the Carlisle coach rolled into London, two poor women sitting outside were frozen into blocks. So people said. Later versions of the story reported that one of the women was with child. People relished such extremes, the thought of a perfect frozen bud curled inside its lifeless mother.

Mary strewed the floors of the house and the workshop with rushes as in the old days to keep their feet up out of the cold, and she bought sheepskin to stuff into their boots, recalling the days when she'd had to beg straw for that purpose. If it continued so very cold, grey geese would come to the sea in a V just after Christmas, and the men would go shooting, and there would be after-Christmas geese for the whole town for a song. This had happened before – the old people talked of it. So desperate a winter was bound to bring bounty with it, she told herself.

The news of her find was spreading fast – jackdaws carried it over the entire country. Sowerby heard without her informing him. He wrote to say that he had an eager buyer for the plesiosaur (he called it a plesiosaur, as it seemed everyone did), one Richard Temple-Nugent-Brydges-Chandon-Grenville, Duke of Buckingham and Duke of Chandon. Mary had never heard of such a man. What did a gentleman so over-endowed with names and titles need with her new dragon?

Then he wrote again, this time to say that Reverend Conybeare had arranged to present the plesiosaur at the Geological Society in February. William Conybeare, who had never clapped eyes on it! He was basing his talk on Mary's drawing. He had decided on a species for the creature: *Plesiosaurus conybeari*. The fossil would be delivered to Bedford Street for display at the Geological Society upon its arrival in London – Conybeare had made arrangements with the Duke of Buckingham. These three men, Sowerby, Conybeare, and the Duke, had among them what Sowerby called "a gentlemen's agreement." All that remained was for the money to change hands, upon receipt of Miss Anning's authorization. Impatience disguised as patient condescension underlay every sentence of Sowerby's letter, as though he had taken up the mantle of teaching Mary how to comport herself.

Three days later came a letter from Buckland. He had taken it upon himself to inform Georges Cuvier of the staggering find. He had sent Cuvier a copy of the drawing. In a prompt reply, M. Cuvier informed Buckland that the creature was almost certainly a forgery, a snake's head and neck clumsily stuck onto an Ichthyosaurus body. There was, indeed, a crack in the vertebrae where the neck met the body. Mary had been meticulous in documenting that crack, and he made much of it. This biological absurdity violated all laws of proportion, and M. Cuvier saw its circulation by the English as an insult to his life's work. What was Buckland's tone in telling her? There was no tone at all – it was most strange. But Mary knew that Buckland did not understand the concept of discretion. It was only a matter of time before the townspeople would be feasting on the story. Where was Henry De la Beche, who would have been her champion?

Another letter came from Sowerby. He had encountered Buckland at the University Club on Suffolk Street. Tactfully, Sowerby wrote, "I understand that this latest find has failed to win the approbation of the French." Sir Richard Temple-Nugent-Brydges-Chandon-Grenville was tied up in assizes at the moment. The instant he stepped foot in Covent Garden, he would be besieged with the news. It was imperative that Mary authorize the sale before that happened. George Sowerby did not charge Mary with duplicity; he merely urged her to act. If I am forever discredited, Mary thought, he will have this last commission.

Beside the cauliflower cart in the market, Mary encountered Miss Philpot. "Regarding this new find," Miss Philpot said, putting her gloved hand on Mary's arm. "The forger showed a singular stupidity, wouldn't you say, in drawing a line to indicate where the sham head was attached?"

"Is it Reverend Conybeare's plesiosaur you refer to?" asked Mary.

Elizabeth Philpot laughed and invited Mary for tea. The minute they were seated in the back parlour, she began to talk freely about an unexpected visit she'd had that morning from Mrs. Aveline, who had been in a state of great distress. Henry was gone away and had informed no one as to his whereabouts. And then Mrs. Aveline confided what was at the heart of it. It seemed that Mr. and Mrs. De la Beche were contemplating separating. Henry had made outrageous accusations against his wife, and she could no longer honourably live with him. At first, Mrs. Aveline had tried to take her son's part, but this was becoming difficult. He had always shown a shocking disregard for the proprieties, she was now prepared to admit it. "Although," Miss Philpot added, "he's always been a particular favourite of mine."

Mary drank her tea. Nothing had changed in this room since she came with her father to deliver the collecting cupboard. All

its homey, comfortable objects spoke of kindness and discern-
ment: the beast-footed side table and the striped tan and blue
paper on the wall, the curtains held back with a braided gold sash,
the books with their worn leather covers, the collecting cupboards
and specimens still on every surface. Tears burned behind her
eyes, from the love she felt for this room. "I used to come to your
kitchen for salve," she said after a minute. "Do you remember?"

"I do," said Miss Philpot. "You could make your own, you
know. It is tobacco juice and lanolin and myrrh in equal parts,
and my sisters would have my hide for telling you."

In her conversation with Henry as they lay in the Undercliff,
there had been a similar ease, a sense almost of domestic comfort.
She had felt no shame. Some few hours Mary Anning and Henry
De la Beche were on this earth – was it not fitting that they
should spend one of them thus? But in the quiet of Miss Philpot's
parlour, Mary found the courage to think about the moment
when she had told him of her plan to write a paper about the new
reptile, when she had asked him if he would do the illustration
and present the paper to the Geological Society on her behalf.
She could not recall him putting his agreement into words, only
the way he had picked up her hand and kissed it, which had
seemed a seal on their contract. "My geological maiden," he
had murmured, words Buckland had used when she was a girl.

Miss Philpot set her cup down. "Mary, it occurs to me that
you may know where Mr. De la Beche might be."

"No," Mary said, looking steadily at Miss Philpot. "I have no
idea at all."

After Mary left, she walked up Church Cliffs, across the path
over the graveyard and down to the sea, where she found herself
studying the horizon as though he had left by ship and would
return the same way. It was a habit to think of him in France.
She began to walk east. The tide was low. Ahead of her,

oystercatchers sank crimson bills into the soft sand. The littoral zone, Henry called the foreshore, where twice daily the sea and land passed the same bit of shore back and forth between them. Mary bent and picked up a bit of bladderwrack, popping one of its leather bladders between her fingers, feeling warmed sea water run out. Here the sea bottom lay exposed and shining in the sun, sea anemones and dulse and maidenhair weed dried and lifted by the wind. Sea water was their element and their sustenance, and daily they felt it withdraw, felt themselves abandoned to an alien environment. But perhaps she was wrong in her understanding – how could you tell which world they considered their true element? Perhaps they were dual in nature, and counted on the rhythms of the tide to take them from one world of need to the other, and twice daily the tide obliged.

But that night, something began to clutch at her guts, a realization so cruel that she must hold herself above it, she could not allow herself tears. She paced back and forth in the workshop and finally sat down and wrote to George Sowerby. She wrote in a bold hand, in letters almost an inch high. *The Cobb has been breached. I must needs ship the specimen from Weymouth. I will look for payment by return post. I will not let this fossil go for less than £125 – whatever your gentlemen's agreement.*

The meeting at the Geological Society was held on February 23. Mary wrote a detailed account of it in her mind. One day soon, she would take up pen and ink. When she did, she would preface her account with a disclaimer:

> The Author, being prohibited from attendance at the Society, here confesses the uncertain source of her intelligence: Roderick Impey Murchison, Esq., who carried an account of the evening to his wife Mrs. Charlotte Murchison, who took the story round to

Miss Elizabeth Philpot, who recounted such as she recalled of it to Miss Mary Anning, who recorded it here as she saw fit. Which Record is therefore subject to the Deformities of all Accounts set down independent of the principal Actors.

In fact, the fateful meeting had been intended for February 9 but was two weeks delayed, because the ship that bore the plesiosaur from Weymouth had to be dry-docked at the Thames estuary for a repair to its hull. Reverend Conybeare went down to the London docks daily to await its arrival, out of fear that Sir Everard Home might intercept it before he did. When the ship finally arrived, the specimen in question was transported to the Geological Society rooms in Covent Garden, where eight stout youths attempted to carry it to the meeting chambers on the first floor. But it was a very wide frame that the finder had built and the exhibit got firmly stuck in the entry, so that the scientific gentlemen arriving for the meeting had to jockey for position on the stairs, where they examined it by candlelight. Reverend Conybeare hovered above it in an ecstasy of ambivalence, desperate to seize whatever glory attended the find, anxious to avoid disgrace should the creature turn out to be fraudulent. Finally he settled on pointing out a mistake in the presentation (the radius and ulna had been carelessly transposed, he said), forced to acknowledge at last another hand in the fossil's preparation. But the consensus was clear, and there were no less experts than Charles Lyell and William Buckland and George Sowerby in attendance: every part of *Plesiosaurus conybeari* conformed to the scattered pieces they had been finding for years.

After they had looked their fill, the scientific gentlemen were summoned to the meeting proper in the room above, which they had to access by the foul and treacherous servants' entry at the back of the building. In the upper room, Reverend William

Conybeare entertained further questions. Then the attention of the company was seized by the Society's new president, the illustrious undergroundologist William Buckland, who rose to make a sensational announcement: the discovery of the first ancient land reptile. Old bones long considered to be those of elephants brought over by the Romans were in fact, when seen in connection with recent finds, the remains of a massive meat-eating land reptile that he had named *Megalosaurus buckland*. This identification had been validated by Georges Cuvier himself, and indeed was confirmation of recent Biblical scholarship, which indicated the creation of earlier worlds before the present one, worlds alluded to in the phrase "without form and void" in Genesis 1:2.

Buckland's presentation was followed by the eager leaping up of one Doctor Gideon Mantell, who had waited four years to announce indisputable evidence of a massive land reptile found in the Cuckfield quarry, but whose findings, alas, were not recorded in the formal Proceedings of the Society on a point of order, as he had not arranged to be on the agenda.

A seasonable day in late winter, near noon. A heavily laden carriage was stalled on a steep road in Oxford-shire. Shotover Hill had thwarted the horses, two poorly matched pairs of blacks. They tottered with swaying heads, help-less against the whip, their heaving sides brindled with lather. The gentleman inside the carriage tapped sharply on the window. "Oy!" the coachman shouted to a lad standing by the road, and the lad looked up eagerly and deftly caught the coin the coachman tossed him. He yanked open a gate and a black and white blur exploded from the yard, a baying pack of furious Dalmatians. The blinkered horses rose in terror in their traces, and in the ter-rible din that ensued, the carriage crowned the hill.

Sacks of rocks and crates of books crammed the carriage, gear the gentleman within insisted he needed and never looked at or unloaded from one trip to the next. His wife sat with her maid on the back-facing seat. A jewelled watch was pinned to the front of her coat and she tipped it up to check the time. They'd been on the road before dawn both today and yesterday. William couldn't sleep, so why not? Mrs. Buckland turned her intent face to her husband. They'd met in a coach, hadn't they (the figs, the clasp knife), and they'd recently been much feted in London for the *Megalosaurus buckland*. But her expression was not tender. That last afternoon in London, they'd toured St. Paul's and watched amused when an old woman bent to kiss a stain on a limestone set. "Papist," someone in their distinguished company murmured. "She believes it to be the blood of a saint, poor thing," and then Mrs. Buckland heard her husband's knees creak and *he* was prostrate in the aisle, putting out his tongue. "Bat's urine!" he declared as he scrambled to his feet. She sat very still, the former Mary Moreland, sat and watched her husband with her clever eyes.

What remained of William Buckland's hair was grey, and a bit of a belly was forming under his waistcoat: he'd be forty in three weeks' time. The eye patch was gone. The excellent surgeon had pronounced him fully healed, not a hint of scarring on his pupil. His eyes were turned to the window – he was intent on the peerless landscape jostling past, feeling his customary vexation with God regarding the Land in faraway parts designated Holy (that barren, salty, prickly, stony flood plain, a realm that attracted infidels and was suitable only for infidels!). But as he gazed at the meadows of Oxfordshire with both eyes, he observed a flatness, as when he'd worn the eye patch: a loss of colour or dimension or vitality. If he covered his bad eye and looked through his good, the absence was just as pronounced. He gazed on the green and pleasant meadow, a landscape familiar and diminished, and grief pressed on him, a wordless grief. "Will cook have dinner when we arrive?" he said to his wife, but she pressed her lips together and looked away.

Almost noon, but down in London, Reverend William Conybeare was just then being shaved in his rooms at the Salopian Coffee House. Conybeare's face had been pressed into hot towels, and now he was perched beside a dirty east window for what light it afforded, being deftly scraped with a perfectly whetted blade wielded by his man Anthony, a consummate craftsman of the gentleman's whisker. Conybeare had full confidence in Anthony. He closed his eyes and his thoughts slid swiftly back to the Geological Society meeting the week before, to the splendid moment when Charles Lyell approached him and warmly congratulated him. "It heralds a new age in science," Lyell said, "when one can predict a species never seen before, and have his predictions borne out." While Anthony carved delicately around the sidewhiskers, Conybeare squeezed his folded arms and wished he'd asserted the authenticity of *Plesiosaurus conybeari* with more authority from the outset. But it was hard to know what that grotesque female might have been up to. When he'd first heard Cuvier's accusation, he'd felt a frisson of horrified conviction: he had been right about Mary Anning all along! And what a fiendish plot it would have been, too, what a clever scheme to undo them all – although, in the event, it was clear he'd overestimated her.

It would be Friday night now before he rolled into the rectory – he'd be hard pressed to cobble together a sermon for Sunday. He should have been working on it that morning. Maybe he could use a text connected to his monster, something from Genesis. When he and De la Beche found the first chain of narrow vertebrae a few years back, Buckland had insisted it was the serpent that tempted Adam and Eve in the Garden. Then, of course, it was discovered to have *flippers*. But when you thought about it, the tempter in Genesis had some sort of limbs the week of Creation; it was only after the Fall that God cursed it, and put it to crawling on its belly. Which would mean this fossil was from *before* the Fall, not from the Flood – a possibility that suddenly taxed and tired Conybeare's brain. He couldn't summon the will to pursue it.

"Basin, sir," Anthony said, and Conybeare lowered his face into warm water and endeavoured not to breathe. It was hard to grasp God's intention in creating the grotesque, to understand how such creatures served His purposes (but consider the *octopus*, as hideous as the underside of a tongue, endlessly shape-changing and writhing its numberless legs with their repulsive suckers; consider the brood of children born in his village with no colour in either their skin or their eyes or their hair, so that they looked like grubs or disembodied souls), and he raised his face and buried it in the towel his man was holding, and regret stirred: that such an unlovely creature should forever bear the name *Conybeare*.

In the counties of the Southwest, it was one of those days when breezes chased clouds across the sun, laying bands of light and shadow over the land and the sea. A Wednesday, and proceeding in the small coastal town of Lyme Regis as many Wednesdays do. Squire Henley was supervising the dredging of his trout pond. Joseph Anning was down at the knacker's, trying to negotiate a better price on the bundles of horsehair he needed for stuffing. Mr. Phelps was at the edge of the quarry with a set of rolled drawings under his arm. They illustrated his plan for laying iron tracks under the cliffs, so the lime could be hauled out more effi-ciently in donkey carts. Not a small investment! And his foreman (an infuriating hireling, stuck in the last century, devoid of busi-ness sense) had balked at the notion, and dragged Phelps out to see for himself the fragility of Church Cliffs. And so there he was at the quarry, his Wellington hat massive against the sky, glaring at his foreman, and then the bold curi-woman with the top hat came walking up from the eastern shore, and she did not scruple to stick her nose into his business. He could stomach no more of it, and he turned back to his horse and swung up into the saddle (for his girth, he was still a man of vigour, and if the cliffs collapsed, he had already made his fortune). He wheeled the horse around and called over his shoulder in a hearty voice, "God bless us! What a world is here, It ne're can last another year!" and set his mare to trotting heavily up the foreshore, leaving them to stand and stare.

Meanwhile, at the top of the town, at picturesque Morley Cottage, the three Misses Philpot sat in the morning room arguing companionably about their garden. They meant to redesign the east-facing beds that spring, and three schemes had been put forward. Elizabeth had pulled out a drawer with the packets of seeds they harvested last summer. She'd opened the papers and was pouring seeds into saucers to count them in defence of her scheme. Poppy seeds (impossible to count, in any case) were stuck like sand under her fingernails. "There's enough here to feed every sparrow in Dorset," she said. "There's more than enough."

In a big square house halfway down the hill, Mrs. Aveline sat by the fire with her hands in her lap. Her husband was reading from a poem called "The Castaway." Mrs. Aveline's hair was pinned loosely up around her face and tumbling into curls at her neck, her morning compromise between readiness and deshabille. She tried her best to listen, but the melancholy verse had turned her mind to her mysteriously vanished son, her so terribly altered boy. What a perfect companion he'd been when he was small, willing and interested in everything, trying hard not to chaff on her nerves. But all those years of his growing up, it seemed he was occupied in transforming himself into something she did not understand, a man intent on having a difficult life. Her husband's voice penetrated her thoughts (it was that mournful emphasis on each line end that wormed its way in) and she leaned forward with an expression of wifely interest, just in time to take in the last three lines:

We perished, each alone:
But I beneath a rougher sea,
And whelmed in deeper gulfs than he.

"And so the castaway perished?" she asked into the silence.

"He did, my dear," said Mr. Aveline, straightening his leather bookmark and putting the book on the table.

"And the poet as well?"

"In a manner of speaking."

"What were the gulfs that overwhelmed him?"

"Melancholia, my dear."

"I thought as much," she said, and put her hand to the hair at the nape of her neck.

Down in the lower town, the dissenting pastor John Gleed was crossing Cockmoile Square on a pastoral call. His gait was the gait of a tired man. He was just back, as it happened, from a synod of Congregationalist elders and sermonizers at Bridport, where he'd found himself a person of some interest because of his knowledge of the Lyme Regis fossils. But the talk was not of Adam and Eve, nor even of Noah — no, the *end* of time was the topic. It was all Apocalypse now, brimstone falling and the Lord visiting His wrath upon the earth, the dragons in the cliffs waking to join their evil maker in a final battle. And so Pastor John Gleed, hurtled overnight from the Old Testament to the New, had ridden back from Bridport in a dogcart with his peace of mind gone, along with his means of earning extra income.

As he crossed the square, Mary Anning came up Bridge Street from her morning foraging on the shore. He turned his eyes towards her, eyes that burned with a knowledge of the true meaning of dragons, said her name, and bowed. She noted that he had a bible in the crook of his arm and that his collecting bag was nowhere about him. Watching him walk up the street, she tried to understand his demeanour. Maybe he'd just heard the news, that the plesiosaur was genuine after all. Maybe he'd learned that in a titanic battle of scientific credibility, Mary Anning had bested the great Georges Cuvier, that Mary Anning was not a cheat. Or so the bigwigs had decided. And maybe Mr. Gleed had heard.

Mary turned towards her door, but before she could open it, a fashionable and beautifully maintained brougham, a brougham with familiar arms on the door, rolled along Bridge Street and turned up Church Street. A carriage unseen in this town for several months. Mary stopped on the doorstone. The liveried coachman – Tom – sat alone on the box, and within was just one slender figure in a bonnet. No cases or valises were strapped to the carriage – this had every appearance of a social call. Perhaps to the Murchisons'. Mrs. De la Beche liked to visit Mrs. Murchison. But when had they come back to town? It must have been last night, after dark.

Mary stepped into the house to deposit her basket. She moved a damp flannel over her face and smoothed her hair. "I've bought a bit of hard cheese," she said to her mother. "We can have it for our dinner. If I'm late coming back, go ahead and eat it." "It's a vinny cheese I asked for," Molly said, but Mary did not stay to debate it. She put on a clean bonnet and shut the dog in the house. Then she climbed up past the shops on Broad Street, turning left onto Pound, and walked to the Grove. She knew where he would be – he would be sat at his desk in the study with windows looking out to the ash grove, his head bent over the papers. She turned into the drive and crossed the shingle that had been carried up from the shore, walked on legs that had lain entwined with his in the bracken, walked up between the stands of ash with their bare branches, ivy cloaking their trunks, life to no purpose except as life.

When the squat girl Daisy came to the door, she did not invite Mary into the hall. "Oh, no, miss," she said. "We've just got word. He is gone to Jamaica. This two, three month he were gone, and no one knew. Not even the missus – fancy that! *Jamaica*. But now they know, and they've given up the house. Mrs. De la Beche come in last night and she's after leaving at the morrow, for London. I must just help with the packing up. I must just do the cleaning." And she allowed herself a little display of temper, kicking her foot at the door frame. "I'm good enough for that, mind, the packing up and the mucking out! She's after getting herself a fine new lady's maid in London."

Mary said goodbye and walked back across the shingle of the drive. There was a roaring in her ears – she strayed off the roadway more than once and stumbled, her boots catching in the weeds. At Pinhay Meadow, she stood looking across at Church Cliffs, at the graceful slopes minutely composed of the plants and animals that had lived and died there through thousands of years. In that moment, she seemed to hear the rumble of falling rock, seemed to see the layered cliffs shudder and hang in the air, then drop to the shore. Standing in sunlight at the edge of the meadow, Mary saw it all gone. Her father's thin bones and the crumbling skeletons of dragons, the secret paths of mouse and vole and sharp-faced fox, the stands of coltsfoot and iris. All of it a raw unsightly mass of earth and broken stone clogging the shore. Oh, how much quicker it was to tear things down than to build them up!

She turned back towards town with the conviction that a square of hard cheese would not suffice. On her way down, she stopped at the butcher's and bought a half pound of bacon. She fried up all eight ounces of it and they ate it with bread, and she saved a last piece for Tray, who swallowed his whole. Then she sat in the square and waited for the coach, running her thumb over a callus on her palm that was causing her pain along its edge, thinking all the while of Conybeare's nameless sister-in-law, who'd sprung into Mary's imagination the morning Buckland talked about her. She saw the sister-in-law settle herself at a desk in the corner of an elegant parlour: a tall woman dressed in blue, eagerly taking up the chance to put words into the mouth of the distinguished Reverend. And then Mary followed them all to the church in the morning, and saw Conybeare standing in his robes at the pulpit, his brain soggy from the revelries of the night before, reading along with his fine, meticulous elocution (the text travelling straight from his eyes to his mouth without troubling to go through his brain), and suddenly hearing his own voice and looking up from the page in consternation, spying his sister-in-law's impish face in the congregation below. But what was it the sister-in-law wrote in that sermon? Mary would think about this until she knew; that's how she would occupy herself through the rainy days of spring.

Trade was reasonable that day: she sold five small curios for a total of one shilling tuppence. When she came in afterwards, the fry pan still sat on its trivet, white fat congealed. It was growing dark, so she carried the pan down to the workshop and touched a taper to it, and it flared up and filled the room with a lurid light, adding the fleshy smell of cooked fat to the earthy air of the workshop. *Jamaica.* Daisy, who'd never lost a bit of her Dorsetshire speech, bore that word on her lips like a strange form of insect had landed there.

Mary sat down in her writing corner and took up the book she'd bought at the stationer's in the fall. The fine pen-and-wash map Henry De la Beche had made for her still hung on the wall over her head, each of the new finds marked on it in her own hand. Beside her lay a wonderful ammonite sliced open to show the crystals growing within. The ammonites did not grow in the rocks, as she'd thought when she was a girl, but crystals grew within the ammonites. She'd made this observation to Buckland once, and he'd disputed it. He'd said the crystals must have been formed by God at Creation, because the filthy earth could not produce such pellucid matter. They gave all the goodness to God, these fine men, and none to the earth.

Mary ran her hand over the leather cover of the unmarked book. She took out a bottle of sepia bought at the stationers, the only sepia she had at the moment, and she picked up the crow's quill she'd found on the road to the mill. She spent a long time preparing her pen to perfection, and then she opened the book to its first snowy page.

She would never publish a scientific text and sell subscriptions to it. It was an alien language the high-born spoke, in which there were different terms, even, for something as simple as *goodbye*. *Forgive me* was one of those terms, when whispered after the act of love. They'd had no common ground to stand on to learn each other's language, she and Henry De la Beche. She had thought science was a common ground, but it was not. Even if she managed to write a scientific text in words that did not offend, her mere name on the frontispiece would. She had been drawn into believing that a massive new continent was about to heave into sight on the horizon, that this last autumn was the beginning of something. It seemed a kind of madness had seized her, a reptilian logic.

COMMONPLACE BOOK, she wrote. She turned the page and paused in the dying orange light, wondering what to put next. Then she fetched down the text about the fossils that she'd written as a girl and began to copy it in, adding such new thoughts as came to her.

Mayhap the Bones were never living Creatures at all, but Monuments carved by the Hand of God as two Eagles be carved in Stone on the steps of the Great House by a Sculptor come from Bristol. Or adornment laid into the rock as a tree trunk has circles in it, for the rock was formed by the same Hand that formed all Living Things and with the same Fancies of adornment.

Or Patterns drawn by Lightning. Or Ornaments formed by Crystals, as Frost is formed, or Salt. Or borne of Eggs washed into Rock, a coupling between Fish and Rock. Or Fossils that grew within the Earth due to the fertile powers of the Earth itself.

Mayhap they were Dragons made by the Devil to tempt the weak away from Religion and to mar the Creator's Handiwork – Which Dragons lived on the Earth until overcome with Shame they burrowed into Rock and turned to Rock. Or swam in the Sea until the Waves turned to Shale and held them.

Mayhap they were Beasts too immense for Noah to house on the Ark, which therefore perished in the Great Flood. Or Beasts which he judged could swim, and could not, and so drowned – Whose bodies Our Lord turned afterward to Stone as a testimony to the Great Flood and a Warning to us all.

Mayhap they were Beasts that roamed the land and sea, nor God nor Man yet thought of – And, the Earth changing, perished.

These things have I not shewed unto all men, but unto thee and a few like thee. (2 Esdras 8:62)

Mary Anning, Lyme Regis
In the year of Our Lord 1824

In 1831, a frank and lively young woman named Anna Maria
Pinney came to stay in Lyme Regis. She was seventeen, the
daughter of prominent Bristol planters, and a keen observer and
writer. Her journal is one of our richest sources of information
about Mary Anning. "She glories in being afraid of no one and
in saying everything she pleases," wrote a fascinated Anna Maria
soon after she met Mary.

In January 1832, Mary apparently confided in Anna Maria
that she had been in love with a person of a higher social class
and that, eight years before (i.e., in 1824), she had seen her hopes
cruelly dashed. I say "apparently," because Pinney, although
astonished and even titillated by this confidence, was moved by
its details to an uncharacteristic discretion.

> Her wonderful history (which I cannot consider myself at liberty
> even to write) interested me, because I understood, I felt the
> power of the [e]motions by which she was actuated . . . during
> that time, the bodily anguish was small compared with what must
> have been suffered by a proud mind, who had hoped from

childhood to see herself removed from her low station in life, and suddenly saw these hopes blasted by Satanic treachery.

Having suffered "as much as mortal can endure for years," Mary Anning claimed to be thankful that the affair (if an affair it was) had ended: "Had it not been so," Pinney quotes her as saying, "I would have lost what little religion I now have."

> She is not quarrelling with what she cannot obtain, the season of worldly happiness once would have returned again, and I believe would even do so now, but she is wise. Her wildness of manner and late horror of everything in the world is taken for madness by those who do not understand the agony of blasted hopes.

Well, what are we to make of this? Anning scholars, perhaps reluctant to see romantic speculation overshadow Anning's long-delayed scientific reputation, have tended to dismiss these entries as the fantasy of an over-excitable teenager. Mary's distress was caused by her brother Joseph's marriage, they suggest. Or by the thwarted hope that Miss Philpot would elevate her socially – a more plausible theory, although it does not quite account for Anna Maria Pinney's excitement. In fact, I find it impossible to read these journal entries as anything other than a veiled account of a romantic attachment; one that, after the initial crushing disappointment, continued to tempt Mary with the prospect of illicit love. And so I think we must put our minds to the question of who, among Mary's acquaintances through those years, might have raised her hopes and caused her so much pain and confusion.

I think we can dismiss William Conybeare. He was adamantly blind to Mary's work, and in a rare mention of Anning in a letter, he gets her name wrong. What about Thomas Birch? He was more than twice Mary's age, but he was amazingly generous to the Annings, and a letter of the period mentions salacious rumours linking Colonel Birch and Mary. Then there is William Buckland, with whom Mary worked closely for decades. If Mary Anning had set her hopes on Buckland, his 1824 marriage to Mary Moreland might indeed have been felt as a "Satanic betrayal." So I think that both Birch and Buckland must be considered candidates, although Buckland's piety makes him less likely to have embarked on a "season of worldly happiness" with Mary.

As for Henry De la Beche, he seems a man inclined by temperament to chafe against social constraints. He was indeed expelled from Marlow for insubordination, and his drawings and journals are satiric and irreverent. And he was a true friend to Mary Anning for many decades. When Cuvier questioned Mary Anning's integrity regarding the plesiosaur, De la Beche wrote from Jamaica in her defence. In 1830, his drawing *Duria antiquior* (a detail of which forms the cover of *Curiosity*) was printed and sold as a benefit for the Annings. At Mary's death in 1847, it was Henry De la Beche who delivered a eulogy at the Geological Society, the only time Mary Anning's name finds its way into the Society's proceedings. De la Beche's separation from his wife and his departure for Jamaica occurred the same year as the Buckland marriage, 1824.

Aside from the appeal of these facts, I was irresistibly drawn to Henry De la Beche as a fictional subject, and I wrote *Curiosity* not as a historical argument regarding his relationship with Mary Anning, but as an attempt to imagine what such a romance, so impossible and so full of possibility, would have meant to both of them. The progressive attitudes De la Beche expresses in his journals were terribly at odds with the reality of his life: he was a slave owner at a time when the conscience of England had awakened to the atrocity of slavery. All the individuals working with the fossils at Lyme Regis were confronted with the need to profoundly revise their view of the world and their place within it, but the challenges for Henry De la Beche were more personal and profound.

Curiosity is broadly (and usually factually) consistent with the historic record, although I have invented freely where no record exists. Almost all the characters, including such minor figures as Mrs. Stock and James Wheaton, are based on real individuals. As for chronology, time in *Curiosity* has had to conform occasionally to the higher purposes of the story, as it did for William Buckland's God.

What happened to these people? Henry De la Beche's 1824 journey to Jamaica did not make an emancipationist of him; instead, he used the occasion to write a book urging the humane treatment of slaves. When he returned to England, he resumed work as a geologist, and in 1842, he was knighted for his contribution to the science. Henry and Letitia divorced in 1826. Sir Henry De la Beche did not remarry and died in London in 1855.

The Megalosaurus announced by William Buckland at the famous meeting of February 1824 was the first primeval creature to be given the name *dinosaur*. William Buckland outlived both Mary and Henry. He died of dementia in 1856; an autopsy revealed a long-time tubercular inflammation of the brain.

The Khoisan woman known as Saartjie Baartman was exhibited in London from 1810 to 1814. Henry De la Beche's visit to this exhibit is fiction, but his Paris journal reports a tour of the Cuvier salon where her body was displayed. Her remains circulated amongst Paris museums until 1974. After negotiations by the Griqua National Council and the South African government, they were returned to Africa in 2002. She was buried in her hometown in the Eastern Cape.

Mary Anning continued to collect, locating the first British pterodactyl in 1828. She never married and struggled intermittently to put bread on the table. She died of breast cancer at forty-seven and shares a gravestone with her brother Joseph in the churchyard in Lyme Regis. Many of her finds can be viewed in the Natural History Museum, London, credited to the gentlemen who acquired them from her. The efforts to establish Mary Anning's scientific credentials did not begin until the 1930s, but Mary Anning was never really lost to local lore – the well-known tongue twister "She sells seashells by the seashore" is almost certainly about her.

⊷❧ A C K N O W L E D G E M E N T S ❧⊶

All Biblical quotations in *Curiosity* are from the King James Version. The lines from William Cowper's "The Castaway" are from *The New Oxford Book of English Verse* (Helen Gardiner, ed., Oxford University Press, 1972). Richard Anning's hymn is based on Psalm 50 and is credited to E.J. Coale.

Thank you to the National Museum of Wales for permission to reproduce a detail of Henry De la Beche's *Duria antiquior* as the cover image. De la Beche was an avid journalist, and his beautifully illustrated notebooks can be found at the National Museum of Wales. The journal entries ascribed to him in *Curiosity* are almost entirely invented. They allude to his actual journal only in the references to the Catholic Church and to Italy, and reproduce it only in one entry, which I take verbatim from his Paris journal: De la Beche's cryptic account of his visit to the Cuvier salon.

Among the many print and Internet sources I consulted in writing *Curiosity*, I would especially like to acknowledge *The History and Antiquities of the Borough of Lyme Regis and Charmouth* by Mary Anning's contemporary George Roberts (first published in 1834 and reissued in 1996 through the Lyme Regis

Museum); Christopher McGowan's *The Dragon Seekers*
(Perseus Publishing, 2001); on Saartjie Baartman, the writings
of Yvette Abrahams; *The Prince of Pleasure* by J.B. Priestley,
a delightful account of Regency England (to which I owe
Uncle Clement's story of the locks of hair); *The Dinosaur
Hunters* by Deborah Cadbury (Fourth Estate, 2001); *The
Meaning of Fossils* by Martin Rudwick (University of Chicago
Press, 1972); and Hugh Torrens's definitive summary of schol-
arship on Mary Anning: "Mary Anning (1799–1847) of Lyme:
The Greatest Fossilist the World Ever Knew" (*British Journal
for the History of Science*, 28). Shirley Brown's show Vestiges
(Winnipeg Art Gallery, 2005) was a revelation regarding the
aesthetics of bird skeletons.

It was a great pleasure to conduct research at the British
Library and at the Natural History Museum, London, where
many of the fossils and documents that figure in *Curiosity* are
preserved. Anyone researching the life and accomplishments
of Mary Anning owes a fundamental debt to the work of
W.D. Lang, whose assiduous efforts rescued many papers from
oblivion, and whose own studies of Anning's contribution to
British paleontology are available through the Proceedings of
the Dorset Natural History and Archeological Society. For information about Dorset in the early nineteenth century, I'm
indebted to the writings of Jo Draper and to the novelist John
Fowles, who was curator of the Lyme Regis Museum from 1979
to 1988, and whose passion for the area produced detailed articles and monographs.

A warm thank you to Tom Sharpe, Curator (Paleontology
and Archives), National Museum of Wales, Cardiff, for his generous help and insightful observations about Henry De la
Beche. Thanks to the Canadian Fossil Discovery Centre for a
fascinating Plesiosaurus dig in an escarpment in southern

Manitoba, and especially to my informative guide Evan Nordquist. Thanks to Dr. Gordon McOuat, Director, History of Science and Technology Program, University of King's College, and to Dr. Jenny Cripps, Collections Curator at the Dorset County Museum, Dorchester. Thank you to everyone at the wonderful Lyme Regis Museum: Mary Godwin, Curator; Paddy Howe for fossiling excursions; and the museum's team of volunteer researchers. Thank you as well to Bonnie Bodnar in Interlibrary Loan at the Winnipeg Public Library.

I'm grateful to the Canada Council for the Arts, the Manitoba Arts Council, and the Winnipeg Arts Council for grants that made the research and writing of this book possible. My appreciation also to the Banff Centre for the Arts, where a section of this novel was written at the 2007 Writers Studio, and to Riding Mountain National Park and the Manitoba Arts Council for a stay at the Deep Bay Artists' Residency.

Thanks to readers who offered feedback on portions of the manuscript at an early stage: Susan Rempel Letkemann, Michael Helm, Edna Alford, and Martha Magor. For a wonderfully insightful reading, I am indebted to Greg Hollingshead.

My deep appreciation to my editor, Lara Hinchberger, for her fine judgment, vision, and confidence. Many thanks to my agent, Anne McDermid, who has been unfailingly enthusiastic about this project since I shared the idea with her almost a decade ago. Thank you to Zoë Waldie at Rogers, Coleridge & White in London, for forthright advice.

I'm so grateful to my friends and family for their interest and encouragement and for companionship on trips to Lyme Regis. My appreciation and love to my daughter Caitlin. To Bill, thank you for the gift of a pyrite ammonite and for everything else.

© Sam Boardman

Joan Thomas's 2008 novel *Reading by Lightning* won the
Commonwealth Prize for Best First Book (Canada and the
Caribbean) and the Amazon.ca First Novel Award. Joan
has been a contributing reviewer and book columnist for the
Globe and Mail. She lives in Winnipeg. Visit her website at
www.joanthomas.ca.